SAD'S PLACE

Martin Price

Sad's Place

This is a work of fiction. Names, characters, places, incidents and events are all from the author's mind. Any resemblance to persons either living or dead is purely coincidental.

Sad's Place

For Katie. Luvya Getcha, always.

Sad's Place

"Sometimes bad is too evil to beat, and good is too perfect to save"

Cale Redstone

Sad's Place

Chapter 1: The Mallet

A stack of timber fell on Cale Redstone's father, and there he lay, his legs broken, his hips shattered.

What did Cale do? He put a pillowcase over his father's head and killed him.

With a mallet.

'For Tommy,' he said. Then he dropped the mallet and set about removing the timber. By nine o' clock and with the sun a positive, burning plate in the sky, not just a sketchy floating object jostling for room with the clouds, Cale had cleared away the timber. Had in fact stacked it, and neatly, around the back of his father's workshop.

Several lengths were splashed with blood. After grabbing a bowl of hot water out of the house, along with a stiff scrubbing brush, Cale did his best to clean the blood off. But it was like dye and left a murky, stubborn stain that could be taken as anything from boot polish to creosote. It would have to do, though. Yes, it would have to do.

He went back into the house, changed the bowl for a deep, metal bucket that was under the kitchen sink, behind a pleated swish of brightly-patterned curtain. Like the bowl, he filled it with hot water and went back outside to clean the blood from the grass. He threw several bucketfuls on the grass, until finally it was gone. Then he moved onto his father's body, which he had dragged, by the arms, around the back of the workshop on an old tarpaulin.

From his father's chest down, Cale saw a body that looked as if it had been fed, feet first, into a mangle. His boots had split open, and his feet poked out like limp tongues. His ankles hadn't snapped, or even popped. *Exploded* was the word that came to Cale's mind. As for

1

his father's legs. It seemed he had no legs, not anymore, just two denim tubes that looked filled with barbed-wire and broken glass. The fly of his father's jeans had burst open, and now it grinned with little brass teeth.   Under the bloody tails of his shirt, and the torn buttonholes, his father's hips lay open like a looted carpetbag.

And finally his hands.   Those prize possessions of his were scratched, broken, and bloody.   More to the point, they could no longer be offered up to little Tommy as a choice of fate. *Which one do you want, Tommy? Hospital or Death? What's up, the question too difficult?*

Not long before he died, Ewan Redstone had said to Cale: *It's going to take a while for me to get back on my feet again.* But looking at the horribly mangled man who had spoken those words, it was hard to believe that ever would have happened, not even with the aid of crutches. Cale's father looked like an animal which had been run down in the road. An animal some motorist might drag into the woods, out the way of the traffic, and then leave there for the rats and flies to pick over. But of course Cale Redstone couldn't do that.

He needed to bury his father...

Somewhere.

He rummaged around in his father's pockets. Found a penknife, the one he sharpened his joiner's pencils with. Found his father's wallet, too, and a large bunch of keys on a brown leather fob. That was all.

Cale stuffed the wallet into his own back pocket. The knife went into his front pocket. He then began to sort through the keys, ticking each one off when he knew which key fitted which lock. Here was the front door key, tick. The back door key, tick. The workshop key, tick. The storeroom key, tick. The key to his father's toolbox, tick. The key to his father's truck, tick. The key to the front gate, tick. The key to his father's writing desk, tick.

Eight keys, all accounted for.

Except for the ninth, which was an old-fashioned, rust-speckled piece of metal with a large, toothy end. Which lock did this fit?

Cale gazed across the back lawn, and there, at the side of the house, was the little stone building with its blue, paint-peeled door.

Sad's Place.

He couldn't recall the name of the previous owners of the house, not with any conviction, anyhow. He thought it may have been Blunt or Hunt or even Dunn. It had been some name with a U in it, anyway. Those people had had a daughter. At the time Cale had been four, an age when a young girl's face, no matter how pretty, would not have meant that much to him. Older and he'd have appreciated it. Might even have drooled over it. But mostly he remembered her because, beneath her looks, he had sensed a terrible feeling of loss, although despite that loss, she had still been more *there* than everyone else out on the back lawn that day. There had been Cale's mother and father, who'd been the potential buyers, and the Blunts, the Hunts, the Dunns - whatever their name had been - the potential sellers. All of them grownups no more there than shadows. Apart from the girl. The striking girl. The one who'd floated in a gauzy dress the colour of a boiling sun, whose hair had been as black as oil, whose skin had seemed waxed, and whose dark, smoky eyes had drawn Cale in and taken him to some other place beyond all he could see, touch, and smell.

That had been a long time ago, though, some fifteen years to be precise. Back in the dark ages, almost. Some awfully pretty girl wearing a brilliant orange dress, but underneath, she'd been an empty shell whose pony had died, and soon she'd be moving home, and likely she hadn't wanted to move home.

How did Cale know her pony had died? He didn't. And the girl never told him. It was simple deduction. When Cale had been of an age when he could deduce, not just regard with a slow, casual eye - he must have been around six by then - he looked at the dull, brass letters screwed to the door of Sad's Place, and realised that originally they had not spelled SAD'S PLACE but something else. It had been SADIE'S PLACE, but either the I and the E had fallen off...or they had been taken off. And Cale believed it had been the latter, that it would have been too much of a coincidence for those two letters to just have fallen off on their own. That someone must have deliberately taken them off. The girl in the orange dress, had to be. She had likely done that to express the way she felt now that her pony was dead. No longer SADIE'S PLACE filled with Sadie herself, but SAD'S PLACE, which Sadie filled no more. SAD'S PLACE, which actually looked like this: SAD S PLACE, the two gaps occupied only by the empty screw holes and the vague impression of an I and an E.

The door was a stable door, and that should have been a dead giveaway, too. One of those doors which in actuality was two small doors, the upper one that could be opened on its own so that the horse inside could stick its head over it. But as a kid Cale hadn't taken much notice of that, either. His knowledge of doors would come later, along with his knowledge of staircases, window frames, and pretty much anything else that could be made out of wood.

He went over to Sad's Place. Wouldn't be taking bets that the key would fit, but all the same, the odds were good, he thought, considering there weren't any other doors around here unaccounted for.

And what was in Sad's Place, exactly? No pony, that's for sure. Just junk, mostly.

Or so Cale believed.

Truth to tell, he hadn't been in here since his mother had left. Back then, the door hadn't always been locked, and sometimes he and Tommy had played in there. But since their mother had left, the door had always been locked.

Cale put the key in the lock, twisted it, and with no fuss, no bother, the door became unlocked. He swung the upper door open, reached inside, unbolted the lower door and swung that open, too. Its hinges were badly rusted, as was the bolt, but with a little lifting and shoving, he was able to swing it right back against the shed's outer wall. The grass around this little building had grown to knee-height in some places, but the weight of the door simply brushed the grass aside and then flattened it.

And so it was that Cale Redstone stepped into Sad's Place.

Stepped into its terrible secret.

~

He'd been crying now for half an hour.

The sun had finally dried the dew on the grass. Not the blood, though. The blood still leaked from the smashed lower half of his father's body. Still leaked from his mouth, as well, and now the pillowcase over his father's head was a red, clinging hood which had begun to attract the flies.

The necklace was looped over the middle finger of Cale's left hand and hung all the way down to the middle of his forearm. His mother's necklace, the one she had worn almost all of the time back then. The Coca Cola necklace, Cale had dubbed it, and when Tommy had been old enough, he had called it that, too: the Coca Cola necklace. Only when Tommy said it in that gabbling, runaway voice of his, it always came out as *Mummy's Cowa Cowa neckis*. And Cale would often say, *Tick-tock, Tommy, remember the clock. It's the only way to stop your words from crashing together.* But even now, Tommy still needed to be reminded of the clock, and at an age when the concept, after all these years, should not be a concept anymore but a simple common practice.

'I might have known,' Cale said. 'I might have known he did away with her. It makes sense now. It makes all the sense in the world!'

His cheeks burned. Snot ran from his nose. His eyes were hot and sore. He regarded the necklace through a misty sheen of tears. He had dubbed it the Coca Cola necklace due to its stones - stones which to Cale, as a child, had looked the brown-red colour of Cola, but were in fact garnets. Eighteen in total, each one set in its own gold claw.

There were little chunks of rotted flesh stuck to the necklace, here and there. His mother's rotted flesh. In other places the necklace was almost black, where it had been buried under the stale, damp dirt in Sad's Place for the past five years. Cale had removed the necklace from his mother's dead body.

Had *somehow* removed it.

Her face had been worm-eaten. A worm had even been curled up in one empty eye socket. Two-thirds of her face had been chewed away, and the rest had been a baggy, slushy mess sloughed off to one side like a wrinkled stocking. And the Coca Cola necklace had twinkled there in a dust-filled bar of sunlight. Had twinkled in the filigree of rotted fibres, strings, and leathery webbing that was now his mother's throat.

That's why your mother and I argued that day, five years back, and she walked out on us, his father had said, trapped as he'd been under all those heavy timbers. *I found out, Cale. I found out that Tommy wasn't mine.*

But Cale had known that was a lie. The same as he had known, and all along, that his mother never walked out on them. Not the kind of woman to just walk out. No more than she had been the kind of woman to become pregnant with another man's child. A one-man woman, that had been Natalie Redstone. A one-man woman through thick and thin. And most of it had been thin - thin on affection, thin on compliments, thin on appreciation, thin on stability.

And thin on love.

Cale believed his mother must have known her husband might one day snap and kill her, that she wouldn't always be able to cover up his violence with makeup, or simply stay at home until the bruises had faded. At some point she must have known.

Yet she had stayed.

Why was that?

'For us,' Cale said out of a numb, dry mouth. 'For me and Tommy.' He looked down at the necklace. She had stayed because of her sons, and almost certainly she would have continued to stay, always taking the blows, always taking the abuse, at least until her sons had been old enough to look after themselves.

But in the end he had killed her, and then buried her here in Sad's

Place. His mother, not living another life in some other town, sipping tea and chatting with her new neighbours, and maybe thinking every now and then of the two sons she'd left behind in Unity Gate.

His mother, dead.

Dead now for five years.

And all the time she had been right here, hidden under the junk their father had tossed on top of her: two old paraffin heaters, paint-peeled and rusty; an assortment of busted garden tools; a ramshackle deckchair, its canvas seat torn and ragged; a not very good painting of a Collie dog sitting on a grassy hillock; a pile of magazines from the forties, damp and yellowy, and a pile of books, most of those damp and yellowy, too. Apart from a hardback copy of Of Mice and Men by John Steinbeck, which had somehow survived the damp the way that poor, hapless Lennie, the story's lead character, had not survived his old friend George's bullet in the back of the head.

Cale let the necklace fall into his palm. It curled there like the worm in his mother's left eye socket. Then he slipped it into his pocket. Later, he would clean it up until it sparkled again, as it once had on the fine, gentle slopes of his mother's throat. For now, though, there was work to do. More work. With no end to it in sight.

He went back into Sad's Place. Picked up the shovel, which he'd fetched from the workshop earlier. Without looking, he scooped up the dirt and gently dropped it back on his mother's face, until once more she was covered.

Then he sank to his knees and patted the dirt flat. Closed his eyes, clasped his hands together, and said, 'Oh Lord, at the moment I can't think of a better a place to bury my mother, so I will have to leave her here in this old stable. I'm sure you understand that, and if you don't, well, it's all I can do. I pray that no harm will come to her. I pray that you will watch over her. And...well, that's just about it, Lord. I can't think of anything else to say. Except why did you let my father kill her in the first place? Can you answer me that?' He paused. 'No, I didn't think you could. Why am I praying to you, anyway? Useless, that's what you are!'

He got back on his feet, grabbed the shovel again, and began to dig another grave, one just as shallow as his mother's. An hour later and it was done. He let the shovel fall to the ground and went back outside. Picked his way through the junk, the junk he'd dumped out here so it wouldn't get in the way.

He went over to his father's body. The flies were now feasting on the bloody pillowcase, especially at the places where the blood was at its freshest, around the nose and mouth. More flies were feasting on the blood that still leaked from his father's crushed hips, and they buzzed under and around the sodden flaps of his work shirt. There was even a large bluebottle, Cale saw, sitting in the hairy cup of his father's navel. Nice.

'No more than you deserve, though,' Cale said. His voice calm. Not a scrap of anger in it. Yet he drew back a foot and began to kick his father's head in...again...and again...and again. The flies scattered but stayed close. Cale, meanwhile, just went on kicking and kicking and kicking. His father's head flew loosely to one side. Blood squirted in an arcing, red spray. He heard his father's jaw shatter, all of it taking place, unseen, beneath the bloody clench of the pillowcase.

'Bastard,' Cale said. Still no anger, though. He simply kicked, and kept on kicking, until what lay under the pillowcase no longer looked like a head but chunks of water melon. He stopped, hunched over, hands on hips, panting hard. 'Just a shame that I've got to bury you in the same place as my mother. You don't deserve that. You don't deserve to be on the same planet as her!'

Impatient, the flies began to zoom in again, ready for another strike at the corpse. Cale crouched down and whipped the tarpaulin's flaps over his father's body. The flies dived here and there, confused. But the moment Cale began to pull his father's body along, they soon followed.

He dragged the body into Sad's Place, then into the grave. It fell in there with a heavy *boof!* The flies circled outside the stable door, thwarted. No prayers this time, though. Cale simply picked up the shovel once more and filled in the hole.

Ten minutes later and all the junk was back in the stable, this time piled on Cale's father's grave, not on his mother's. His mother's grave he reserved for something a lot less heavy and a lot more fitting: a bunch of wild flowers. These he picked from around the back of Sad's Place: Lady's tresses, buttercup, and corn cockle, mainly.

He found a piece of string hanging from the stable's low rafters and used it to tie the flowers together. Then he placed them on his mother's resting place. Her temporary resting place - he vowed one day that he would lay her to rest in the cemetery on Lavender Hill. Still, for now there was only this: under the dirt floor of a stable that was not a stable anymore.

Just Sad's Place.

He closed the door. Locked it. Went back across the yard to where the wood stack had fallen on his father. Picked up the mallet and went into the storeroom. There was a small, metal sink in here in which he washed the mallet. Then he hung it back on the rack, next to the bandsaw.

After that he locked up the workshop.

Then a car rolled up.

Not just any old car, but a police car.

It was Don Willoughby. Sergeant Don Willoughby.

He began to get out of his black and shiny Humber Sceptre.

On legs that suddenly felt incapable of receiving even the simplest of commands - like forward ho! - Cale went down the driveway like he'd been pulled out of bed and told to get walking. He went down to the gate believing he wouldn't reach it before Willoughby did, that Willoughby would walk through it before Cale could close it and throw the bolts. And once in the driveway, Sergeant Willoughby would be a hard man to discourage from coming all the way up to the house.

Don Willoughby was one of Ewan Redstone's friends. Correction, his *only* friend. Ewan Redstone had never been a popular man in Unity Gate. His heavy drinking was almost as legendary as his bad temper.

Willoughby was now coming around the front of the Sceptre. The upper half of his face was hidden under the peak of his cap, around the rim of which was a black-and-white chequered band, while pinned to that was the badge of the Hampshire Constabulary.

It glimmered there like a third eye.

A third and constantly suspicious eye.

Cale wasn't going to make it, he was sure of it. He came down the driveway, either tripping over its grassy crown, or slipping down into its deep wheel ruts, knowing he couldn't run because if he did, Willoughby would know something was wrong. So all Cale could do was walk, and even then it was not a walk, more like an idiot dance.

Oh God, if only he hadn't spent so much time having a meaningless conversation with his father (his father who would have died, anyhow, because, let's face it, a man crushed from the ribs down, his internal organs mashed to a pulp, would have died in the end, no doubt about it), then maybe all of this would have been over a while back. Straight after, Cale would have walked down the driveway, flipped the sign on the gate over from OPEN to CLOSED, shot the bolts, snapped the padlock in place, and that would have been that. Job done. But as it stood, here was Sergeant Willoughby. Here. Right here.

Like the end of the world.

'Morning, Cale,' Willoughby said, raising a finger as if he were drawing a tick in the air. Then, like a merciful surprise pulled out of a hat: 'What the heck is that? More birds' shit? God, I'll have to get those trees cut back. I will. I really will.'

All at once Willoughby came to a stop, turned on his heels, and glared down at the Sceptre's bonnet. The offending splodge of shit to which he was now paying attention - and paying his full and undivided attention - had obviously come from a bird in the trees in the police station's forecourt, and Willoughby was none too happy about it.

He leaned over, his nose almost touching the mess, as if he were smelling it. But in truth he was studying it, like a piece of evidence at a crime scene, his eyes narrowed, his chin thrust out, his hands linked behind his back. The stance of a man who has seen this kind of thing before, many, many times, but still finds it annoyingly fascinating. And filthy. Just filthy, filthy, filthy.

Finally, he took out a handkerchief into which creases had been ironed every bit as sharp as the ones in his uniform trousers. He unfolded it, crumpled it up, poked the tip of his forefinger into one corner, and then carefully began to wipe off the splat of whitish-grey muck. 'Stinking flying shit machines,' he said. 'No respect, not even for a vehicle of the law.'

While Willoughby cleaned, Cale went up to the gate, swung it quietly shut, and just as quietly he slid the bolts into place. The final touch, for the time being at least, was to slip the padlock's curved arm into the hasp and turn the sign over - which was suspended on a brass chain - from OPEN to CLOSED. 'Morning to you, Sergeant Willoughby,' Cale said after that. 'Having a spot of trouble, are you?'

'Hmmm?'

'A *spot* of trouble?'

'Oh yes, a spot of trouble. Very humorous, boy, very humorous.' Willoughby went on cleaning, and when the spot was gone, he still went on cleaning, but he used another section of the handkerchief, a cleaner section to buff the place where the crap had been.

'So what brings you here on this bright and - '

'Hold on, Cale, and I'll be with you in a moment,' Willoughby said. 'Just let me finish what I'm doing.'

Cale nodded, then settled his arms, his trembling arms, on top of the gate. He was wearing drainpipe jeans with two inches of turn-up at the bottom, and a shirt with the collar up. Not moodily, though. Cale Redstone was not the moody type, not even fake moody. Pretty much happy-go-lucky, all told. The upturned collar was simply the fashion, that's all. His hair was short and blond. A quiff was combed into it, held in place with a little hair oil. His eyes were blue. Not cold blue, and definitely not the dead grey colour of his father's eyes. Cale's eyes were a warm, friendly blue.

There was a small, hooked scar on his forehead, the result of a run-in with a length of barbed wire when he was seven and too busy laughing to notice the sledge he was riding on that winter had been heading straight for a cattle fence at the bottom of the hill. His right cheek was pockmarked, a little gift left there by the chicken pox, although these marks could only been seen in a certain light, and they were not in any way disfiguring.

'There, done,' Willoughby said. He gazed up the long, highly-polished length of the Sceptre's bonnet as if he were gauging how true a piece of wood might be. He did this in order to check that the blemish wouldn't suddenly make a return, like a damp patch on a wall. 'It can burn a mark into paintwork. Did you know that, Cale? Birds' shit can burn a mark into paintwork? Must be something in it, I suppose. Like acid.'

'Really?' Cale said. 'I didn't know that. You learn something every day, don't you?'

'You do, if you've got half a brain,' Willoughby said. He walked around to the rear of the car. Opened the boot. Holding the handkerchief between his thumb and forefinger, he dropped it in there. Closed the boot, brushed his hands together, then finally he came up to the gate. 'Well, lad, open it up. No idea why you closed it in the first place.'

'I closed it because me and my dad are not feeling too well,' Cale said. 'It might be a summer cold, or perhaps something we ate. My dad's in bed - that's how terrible he feels. So now we're closed until further notice.'

Willoughby took a step back. Looked at the sign like he'd never seen that side of it before - the side with CLOSED on it - and probably hadn't; Redstone Joinery was always open, apart from on Sundays. 'Must be bad for your father to be in bed,' he said, and that made him take another step back. 'Still, you do look a little pale, boy. Sweaty, too. And you're shaking.'

'Like I said, my dad's in bed, and probably I'll go to bed as well, once I've locked this place up.'

'Sounds like a good idea,' Willoughby said, making sure the gap between himself and Cale was a large, healthy one. 'Tell your dad I hope he gets better soon. You, too.'

'Thanks.'

'Anyhow, I just wanted to tell your dad that a few of the old people around here have been fleeced just lately. Con-men doing the rounds, you know? They pretend to be meter-readers, get into the house, then steal any valuables they can while the owner's back is turned. I hate that kind of a crime. Despicable. My mother's pretty old herself. Frail with it. If they got into her place, I'd never forgive myself.'

'Have you warned her about these men?'

'No, it's not so easy to warn old people without scaring them. You've got to tread carefully. Still, I've done a few security checks, and I fitted a strong chain to my mother's door. What I'd like is to get a panic-button installed, but as it's my mother, that might look like favouritism. Better, I think, if I just caught these people and brought them to justice.'

'So you'll be on the lookout, will you?'

'I will,' Willoughby said. 'I've decided to drive around and see if I can catch them in the act.'

Cale nodded. Strange. All of a sudden he felt like laughing. Or crying. Or just telling Willoughby to forget all about those con-men and come and see a crime that would not, if it was discovered, make the fifth page of the Upperlands Post, or the second page of the Unity Gate Gazette, but would almost certainly make the front page of the national papers. Might even be the headline on some. *BOY KILLS FATHER WITH MALLET.* Then, underneath: *Put pillowcase over his father's head so he wouldn't have to look into his eyes.*

'You really do look pale,' Willoughby said. 'Think I'd better be going.'

'Right you are,' Cale said. 'Hope you find those men.' He snapped the padlock shut and locked it. He slipped the key back in his pocket and watched Willoughby drive away. Watched the Humber

Sceptre gliding smoothly into the distance. Turned. Walked back up to the house.

He stopped. His belly rumbled. His throat burned. His eyes watered. The world began to sway. He gazed, pale-faced, at the hedge at the side of the driveway. Then he puked into it. As he did, he replayed his father's death over in his mind.

Chapter 2: Hospital or Death

From inside his father's workshop, Cale hears the stack of timber fall over and hurries outside, mostly expecting to find his father a little bit scratched, a little bit ruffled-up, but otherwise okay. And he'll be angry, of course; the one emotion you can guarantee from Ewan Redstone is anger, as predictable as rain on Sundays.

However, when Cale reaches the scene, he realises that for once his father doesn't have enough strength, or enough air in his lungs, to be angry, not with all those eight-by-twos pinning him down. He can only lie there, helpless, and save his anger for later, for when he is out of this jam and able to unleash that legendary temper of his without gasping every time he takes a breath.

Cale kneels beside his father's head, that large, rock-like head which has no business having eyes in it and hair sprouting from it and soft, pliant ears attached to it. Just a rock, that's how it always seems to Cale. A rock which has somehow grown in place of a real head.

'Help me, Son,' Ewan Redstone wheezes. He gazes up at Cale with eyes that are not exactly beseeching, but for the first time ever Cale sees real fright in them, a low-level but nonetheless perceptible fright that trims his father's small grey eyes like dark, shimmering lace. 'You need to get these timbers off me. But gently. I can't feel a thing from the waist down.'

'Okay, okay,' Cale says. 'But don't you think I should just telephone for an ambulance? The ambulance-men will know what to do without causing you any more pain.'

'No, take them off me, Cale. You can do it. Just take it nice and easy. Anyway, the ambulance will take a while to get here, and I'm in pain, Son. I'm in a lot of pain.'

'All right, I'll do it,' Cale says.

But he realises then that his father's hands, the one he calls Hospital (the left), and the one he calls Death (the right), are also trapped under the timbers. Which one do you want, Tommy? Hospital or Death? What's up, the question too difficult?

Tommy, yes, there is Tommy, too, isn't there? Little Tommy Redstone, who is Cale's younger brother by eight years. Tommy's left leg is two inches shorter than his right, and his face droops on one side due to the fact that during his birth the midwife had been a little too enthusiastic with the forceps. He also talks too fast, especially when excited, but Cale understands his brother. Never misses a word, in fact. It is mostly just a problem for those who don't know him, or who perhaps are a little hard of hearing.

Tommy is at summer school right now, a one-week affair run by the headmistress of Brougham Moor School, to which Tommy will be going, full-time, when the summer holidays are over. The headmistress, a noisy and blunt but generally kind-hearted woman named Elsa Lovell, has been running the school for several years now, mostly for the children who might find the leap from middle school to secondary school something of a daunting leap, and it is her way of hopefully turning that leap into a short, gentle skip.

It is Tommy's first day at the summer school. Cale has been looking forward to this day, too, maybe even more so than Tommy, because for five days Tommy will not be in the firing line of Hospital and Death. And Tommy is always in the firing line. Which one do you want, Tommy? Hospital or Death? What's up, the question too difficult?

In the end the boy always chooses Hospital. Who wouldn't? But Cale suspects that one day, and one day soon, their father might not even offer him that choice. He'll just select Death and beat poor Tommy until the screams stop and that drooping mouth of his ceases to draw in another breath.

It is becoming that bad, that serious, that damned fateful, like a whirlwind glimpsed on the horizon that you know, just know, will not suddenly change direction or fizzle out at the last minute, but will keep on coming, strong and lusty and full of destruction, and simply flatten or uproot everything in its path.

Cale had glimpsed that whirlwind at the start of the school holidays, and had believed, had truly believed, that by the end of those holidays that Tommy would no longer be around. That their father would finally lose patience with the sound of his built-up shoe clumping around the house and with his gabbling, runaway voice, and just erase the boy, once and for all, from the face of the planet. No more Hospital.

Just Death.

Cale stands up, feeling no pity for his father. Feeling no urgency, either, to get all those timbers off the man and free him. He hates him…although, in truth, Ewan Redstone has done very little personally to Cale to deserve this hatred. But of course he has done plenty to Cale's brother. And mostly Cale has stood by, unable to defend his brother, this despite the fact he is eighteen, well built, and it would never have been a certainty that if Cale had thrown a punch at his father, that his father would have won the resulting fight.

But throwing a punch at his own father? That has never really occurred to Cale. Sacrilege. So mostly he has turned a deaf ear and a blind eye to the beatings that Tommy takes. Those beatings that take place most times for no reason, just because Tommy is there and simply happens to be pissing his father off…and Cale has begun to hate himself for that. Has come to believe that not defending his little brother marks him out as a coward. The whirlwind had been on the horizon, looming big and dark and menacing, and now fate has stepped in and trapped it under all that timber. Fate, or God, or just plain old good luck. Which one, Cale doesn't know, but it begs a question, doesn't it?

'How did this happen, Dad? This isn't like you to be so - '

'Careless?' Ewan Redstone says. 'I must have lost all of my common-sense. I tried to wiggle one of the lower timbers out of the stack, it was just the right length, and crash, the whole lot came down on me. But let's forget about that for now, can we? Get me out from under here, boy. I'm finding it hard to breathe!'

All of a sudden Cale wonders how long it will take before his father can't breathe at all…and then dies. An hour? Two? The rest of the morning? Or will he somehow hold out into the afternoon? Maybe even into the night?

How long? Maybe not that long because there will be internal bleeding…and there is certainly external bleeding, Cale knows that much. He can see blood down there in the grass, between the timbers, like spilled paint. Ewan Redstone will die, all right. But how long will it take?

'Hurry it up!' his father urges. 'Free my hands for me at least!'

'Your hands,' Cale says, before he can stop those two little words from coming out of his mouth. They taste bitter and unusual, like a drink he has never tried before.

'What?'

'Your hands,' Cale says again. 'Finding it hard to get along without them, are you?'

'What are you talking about, Son?'

'I'm talking about how your hands are everything to you. Hospital and Death. What's up, the question too difficult?'

It takes a while for his father to understand what is happening here, which it would, wouldn't it? For here is his son, the one who is handsome and strong and able-bodied, the one who can use a lathe to turn ornate stair-rods, who can dovetail and mortise, who can build a dog-leg staircase, who can erect a complicated cut roof with gables, cropped gables, and dormers. That son. Not the small, weedy one with the gammy leg and the wonky face. This is the son Ewan Redstone is proud of, the son to whom Redstone Joinery will be passed down when he, Ewan Redstone, retires. The son he trusts also. Trusts completely.

Yet now that trust has been broken.

'Oh, I get it,' Ewan Redstone says. 'Payback time, is it?' His voice is calm enough, but underneath, Cale knows that the anger and the disbelief will be lurking there like a monster floating just below the surface of a shallow lake. 'Been storing up your hatred for all these years, have you, and now it's time to get your revenge, eh?'

'No,' Cale says. 'I don't want revenge. Just justice. For Tommy.'

'For Tommy? Why do you care about him? He's nothing but a nuisance. He's in the way. It would have been better if he'd been the one trapped under here. Then I'd have had the excuse to end his miserable life and get him out from under our feet.'

'He might be under your feet, but he's not under mine,' Cale says. 'He's my brother and I love him. I can't believe you said that, that you'd end his miserable life?'

'I can't pretend,' Ewan Redstone says. 'That boy's life is miserable, and it'll become even more miserable as he grows. Who'll employ him? He can barely string a sentence together that makes any sense. And what about marriage? Do you know of a woman who's going to fall in love with that boy? And what about children? If there's a woman out there stupid enough to open her legs for him, that is. They'll be even thicker than him.'

'That's cruel, Dad. That's just so, so cruel.'

'Maybe. But I just happen to live in the real world, not in some sweet, sugar-coated world where do-gooders believe that everyone deserves a life. They don't. Some people just don't deserve a life at all. Why? Because life is hard enough, that's why, even for the people who can walk straight, talk straight, and put a tie on without trapping their fingers in the knot. But for the Tommy's of the world? Deserving a life is like deserving a bullet in the head.'

'I don't want to hear this,' Cale says, glancing down at the toes of his boots, which are sprinkled with sawdust. 'He's my brother, I love him, and nothing will ever change that.'

'Nothing?' Ewan Redstone asks from his place down in the grass, where only his chest, his shoulders, and face can be seen. His face that is now drenched in sweat and turning the colour of cheese. And his mouth: with every jag of glassy pain that hits Ewan Redstone, so his mouth is cranked open just a wee bit more, revealing more creamy clenched teeth, and more dry pink gum.

'Listen to this, Cale, I never wanted you to know the truth. I was prepared to keep it to myself, to bear it myself. But judging by the position I'm in, I reckon I should tell you, and then we can forget about this. Forget about it altogether. We can just concentrate on getting me out from under here, can't we?' He paused. 'He's not mine.'

'Who?'

'Tommy. He's another man's.'

'That's rubbish,' Cale says. 'Mum was a one-man woman. She wouldn't have dreamed of sleeping with someone else. Jesus, is there any *depth you won't sink to?'*

'Believe what you want, but it's the truth. That's why your mother and I argued that day, five years back, and she walked out on us. I found out, Cale. I found out that Tommy isn't mine.'

'How?' Cale asks. 'How did you find out?'

'I can't go into that right now, it's a long story, and I haven't got the time for a long story. Come on, Son, I'm being crushed to death here! Take these timbers off me! Take them off me now!' He begins to cough, and it is a watery cough that is speckled with tiny droplets of blood too small for Ewan Redstone to know of their existence. But Cale knows. He sees them fly in the air, and watches as they spot his father's cheeks and chin.

'I can't, I won't,' Cale says. 'I can't bear to watch little Tommy suffer anymore. You can stay there. You can stay there for as long as it takes.'

'Stay here for as long as what takes? My death, you mean? Pity's sake, I'm your father! Are you just going to stand there and watch me die? Your own father?'

Cale doesn't answer. He doesn't know if he is just going to stand here and watch...or if maybe he is going to put his father out of his misery. And here is a new addition to Cale Redstone's ever-expanding catalogue of do's that he believed would always remain don'ts. Already he has hesitated - and for several minutes - against his natural instincts to just free his father, because yes, he is, after all, his father, and it is the normal, unthinking reaction for any son to just start lifting the timbers off his old man and get him out from under there.

But now there is something else, the idea in Cale's head, fresh and somehow fantastic, that he can kill his father...and he won't actually be killing him, will he? He'll just be ending his life, the way a vet will end a horse's life when it has stumbled into a ditch, its legs are broken, and there is no other option but to fire a bolt into the poor nag's skull.

'All right, all right,' Ewan Redstone says. 'I won't lay into Tommy anymore. I promise you that. I'll just leave him be. I can't promise to love him the way I love you, but what do you want, miracles? And look, I'm busted up under here. Can't you see that? It's going to take a while for me to get back on my feet again. I can't lay into Tommy in a wheelchair, or on crutches, can I? Be reasonable, Cale. Give your old man a chance.'

'I'll think about it,' Cale says, and right then, at that moment, with the sun breaking through the clouds and with the birds chirruping in the trees and with the early morning dew laying on the grass in the backyard like a thousand tiny pieces of broken glass and with the air tasting clean and fresh in his nostrils, Cale Redstone really does intend to think about it. He intends to think about whether his father can indeed honour his promise and no longer lay into Tommy for no good reason.

But of course his father is a terrible man whose dials are always turned up to ten, whose needles are always in the red zone, whose outlet valve is always whistling with hot, pressurised steam, and when he hears those words, I'll think about it, he can no longer hold back. He suddenly lets fly with a boiling torrent of hate and frustration.

'You'll think about it? The fuck you will, you little piece of shit! You'll get these timbers off me, right this minute, you hear me, boy? If you don't, when I get out of this mess, I'm going to beat you black and fucking blue! You think Tommy's been having a hard time of it? When I'm done with you, sunshine, you'll find your teeth so far down your fucking throat, you'll have to stick a toothbrush up your arse to clean them! Get me out of here! Get me out of here now!'

More blood flies out of his mouth, landing on his face again. And some are not tiny speckles anymore but bright, coin-sized drops.

'I knew it,' Cale says, so strangely calm, his hands so strangely free of sweat, as is his face. There are no trembles, either, not even deep down in his stomach, where there should at least be the odd, light flutter. 'I knew you'd show your true colours in the end. Wouldn't be able to help yourself.'

'I'm fucking dying here!' his father spits. 'What do you expect? Jesus on the cross, all merciful and long-suffering?'

'No. All I ever wanted, all I ever prayed for, is that one day you'd come to your senses over Tommy and stop hitting him with those hands of yours!'

'I'll leave him alone!' Ewan Redstone says. 'I've already told you that, haven't I, that from now on I'll leave him alone? I promised you that, didn't I?'

'I don't believe you, no more than I believe that Tommy isn't your son. And anyway, you're right, you will end up in a wheelchair. For a while, anyhow. You know what? I think Tommy's life will be even more unbearable...if that's possible. I think, when you can't do your work and can only sit around, waiting for your body to mend, that you'll just pick on the boy for absolutely nothing.'

'Listen to me, Cale! For crying out loud, just listen! Tommy hasn't got the hands to work with wood the way you have, and he certainly hasn't got the hands to push a pen all day. After all, to push a pen, the hands need to be working in tandem with the brain. What brain? There isn't one. And it was me who wanted him to go to that special needs school over in Battenford, wasn't it? At least there, he would have been planted in the same garden as all the other cabbages. But no, Elsa Lovell insisted that he was bright enough to join all the normal pupils at Brougham Moor, when the new term begins. Did I have a say in that? No, I didn't. The silly woman decided she knew best.'

'She's a teacher, she does know best,' Cale said. 'When it comes to a child's education, she does, anyhow. If Elsa Lovell said that Tommy was bright enough to go to Brougham Moor with all the "normal" pupils, as you put it, then she must be right. And I just happen to think she's right as well. And Tommy would have been boarded at the special needs school. He wouldn't have been able to take that.'

'Well, I would have been able to take it,' Ewan Redstone said. 'I'd have been able to take it just fine. Fucking useless kid always hobbling around this place, day in, day out, with nothing better to do. Mark my words, Cale, he's a liability. Remember I said that. Remember I said that when he's troubling you more than a puppy that won't stop pissing on the floor. But why am I telling you this? I'm fucking dying under here!'

He begins to whip his head from side to side so that sweat flies everywhere, sweat mingled with blood. His hair, so profuse and dark, is now plastered to his scalp like tar. His brow is pallid and crinkled. His lips, dappled with blood and with pink, frothy spittle, are now peeled all the way up over his teeth, giving him the look of a rabid dog that wants to bite...and to chew...and to tear chunks out of anything it can wrap its jaws around.

He is trying to get his hands out from under the fallen timbers, Cale realises. He watches as his father pumps his shoulders, working them like *pistons, the veins standing out on his neck like cables. But the effort is soon over. His father, ordinarily so strong and, somewhat dishearteningly, predictably tenacious - especially when it comes to doling out the pain to little Tommy - is running out of puff. And fast. Just three or four pumps of the shoulder, a similar amount of tugs on both his arms, and then it is over. His father, the monster that usually can't be stopped, has been stopped. Has been stopped by the pain in his lower regions and the crushing weight, the vast crushing weight, of the timbers that lay across his chest, pinning him down.*

He lies there panting and coughing, his head, that rock-like head, beginning to make a deep imprint in the lush, dewy grass. He gazes up at Cale with eyes that now seem to accept that there has been a huge shift in the balance of power, and here he is, like a toppled dictator whose fate no longer rests in his own hands.

'It's over, Dad,' Cale says. 'Things around here will never change, not while you're still alive. And for Tommy's sake, I won't put up with that anymore.'

'Cale, Jesus. Jesus Christ, Son, listen to me. God, please, just think about what you're doing!' But Ewan Redstone's voice is a thin, almost ineffectual croak, far-removed from the voice that usually booms around this place, barking out orders and threats and ultimatums. 'How will you get along without me? How will you pay the bills? And if I die, you and Tommy will be split up. No way the Social Services will let you take care of him. He'll end up in the special needs school, after all, and he won't thank you for that. Believe me, he won't. You need me, Cale. You need me to keep the status quo.'

'I don't know what the status quo is,' Cale says. 'But if it's anything like how it's been around here since mum left, then I don't want it. You can keep it. And don't tell me you'll change. Whatever you do, don't say that, because I know you can't. I know that nothing *around here will ever change…unless I do something about it.'*

'Letting me die? Is that what you call change?'

Cale considers for a moment, then says, 'No, letting you die isn't change. Change is the chance you take when it comes your way. And I'm going to take it.'

~

The pillowcase is on the clothesline, along with the rest of the household washing. Cale goes over there and unpegs it. It is still damp, quite a bit damp, but that's fine, that's okay. It doesn't need to be dry and neatly-pressed for the job he has in mind.

'What are you doing, Son?' his father asks. But Cale doesn't answer. He simply walks up behind him with the pillowcase held open. He kneels down, coldly kneels down, and slips it over his father's head. After that he quickly ties a knot in it, at the side of his father's neck, so that his father's nose becomes a fin pushing at the case's bright white material. Spots of blood begin to bloom on the case, mainly around Ewan Redstone's mouth. They make Cale think of ink spots on blotting paper.

Ewan Redstone groans, and then, once again, he begins to move his head from side to side. No whipping or thrashing around this time, though. No strength. Just a feeble series of rolls, twice to the left, three times to the right, and then finally he can move his head no more. 'Don't do this,' he says. And are those tears that Cale can hear in his father's voice, tears right at the back of his throat, but there, nonetheless? Yes, Cale thinks so. Wonders will never cease. 'Whatever you've got in mind, please don't do it, Son. You'll only regret it.'

'I don't think so,' Cale says. Sounding oddly calm. Oddly determined, too. 'The only thing I'll regret is that I was unlucky enough to be born the son of a man as evil as you.'

As if to validate this statement, he glances back at the clothesline. Moreover, at the right side pole, to which is attached a short piece of clothesline that Cale's father often ties Tommy to, then leaves him there for several hours, like a dog. One time, he even left the poor boy tied to that line all night, in the pouring rain.

Evil? Yes, Cale's father is evil, all right. No two ways about it. And that night Cale hadn't been able to do anything about it. He'd wanted to. He'd wanted to dash outside, untie his little brother, bring him back inside, dry him off, make him a cup of hot, sweet tea, and sit him by the fire. But he simply hadn't been able to. For Cale, his brother's never-ending torture had always seemed like a film he could only sit there and watch.

Not anymore, though.

No, not anymore.

He heads back into the workshop.

Takes down the mallet that is hanging on a peg next to the bandsaw.

Goes back outside.

'Cale?' Ewan Redstone's voice is now a feeble, husky whisper, but the breeze picks it up, anyhow, and carries it to Cale's ears. 'Where have you been, boy? I don't feel too good. It's like I'm...sinking.'

Cale doesn't respond, just looks down at the mallet in his hand. Begins to spin it, its head rotating in a choppy, irregular blur. His fist is dry, remarkably dry. Not the fist of a boy about to commit murder, that's for sure, even if that murder will not be murder, exactly, more a case of simply bringing the inevitable to a close, and more importantly, releasing little Tommy from his torment.

Cale has no wish to defend what he is about to do. There is no defence. No legal defence, anyhow. He is going to commit murder. That's how any court of law will see it. Just plain old murder. But of course the judge, the solicitors, the barristers, the jury, none of those would have had to face, almost every night, a whack with a stick, a slap with the sole of a shoe, a lashing with a leather belt, a smack with a clothes-brush, just like little Tommy had. Then there is that no-win choice between Hospital and Death.

Which one do you want, Tommy? What's up, the question too difficult?

'I know you're there,' Ewan Redstone says. 'Speak to me, Son. How many times do I have to tell you that I won't hurt Tommy anymore? I gave you my promise on that, didn't I?'

'Your promises mean nothing to me,' Cale says. 'A man who can lie that his own son is not his own son can make a thousand promises and break every one of them.'

Ewan Redstone makes a sound like an air bed deflating, an air bed in which there is not much air left, anyhow. Just the weak, stale air still trapped in it and puffing out in a tired, inconstant sigh. He moves his head again, just a little. The bloody patches in the pillowcase now outnumber the white patches, while around his mouth and nose, there are no patches whatsoever. Not anymore. Just a wet mask, like a gruesome fake beard, that curves around his throat, all the way up to his earlobes. It is a wonder, Cale thinks, that his father can still talk and be understood.

'Hey, Cale,' he begins, and then he has to stop for a moment to accommodate the coughing fit that takes him over. And when that ceases, it is replaced by a horrible bubbly wheezing noise. The pillowcase puffs in and out, tackily. His chest goes up and down so rapidly, so shallowly, that to Cale it is like watching a man not breathe but shimmer, somehow.

'Cale,' he says again, when the gaps between the coughing and the wheezing become long enough for him to fit words into. 'Do you remember the time we went fishing together at Witches Point? You must have been...oh, seven years old, I reckon. Perhaps only six. As we drove there, we saw a rabbit leap over a hedgerow. You remember that, don't you?'

'It was a hare,' Cale says.

'Yes, a hare! God yes, a hare, of course it was!' Ewan Redstone is sounding desperate now. Desperate in the way that he is sinking, and desperate in the way that he is sucking up to Cale like Cale could have said it was an elephant which had jumped over that hedgerow back in the spring of 1954 and his father would have agreed. An elephant, yes, God yes, an elephant, of course!

'You marvelled at that, Cale. Had a smile a mile wide.'

'I'm sure I did.'

'You did, you did!' Another coughing fit. Then: 'You caught plenty of fish that day, sonny-boy. You caught all the fish! Me, I caught nothing. Standing next to you, I was, close enough to catch a cold, and that's all I would have caught that day, a cold. No fish. You had a magic hook that day. A magic hook. Do you remember that, Son? Do you?'

'Yes, I remember,' Cale says in a voice so low, and so faintly choked, it is like a ribbon gliding over a blackberry bush, snagging occasionally on the thorns. He puts a hand, the hand that is not holding the mallet, up to his right cheek...and his forefinger happens upon a single tear that is hot to the touch. Tears. But why the tears? Tears for a man who would tie his own

son to a clothesline and leave him there overnight? Tears for a man who had almost certainly forced their mother to leave home, and in the daytime, too, while Cale and Tommy had been at school, and so there had been no farewell hugs. No farewell kisses, either. Just a motherless house when they got home that day. Not even a letter to explain it all. Only the man of the house, standing there, telling his boys that their mother had gone, and where to, he didn't know, but no need to worry. She'll probably write when she finds a place to live. You wait and see, she'll write.

But she never does.

'Yes, I remember, all right,' Cale says, wiping away that single tear with a quick, almost offended swipe of his hand. 'I remember very well how lovely that day was at Witches Point. But it isn't enough, Dad. It's never been enough. People like you seem to think that one good time is all it takes to fill the memory, like one good picture is all it takes to fill a photograph album. Sorry, but no, that isn't how it works.'

'Yes, a magic hook,' his father goes on, as if Cale has said nothing. 'You could use that magic hook again, couldn't you, Cale? Could use it to get me out of here? Just drop your hook in the water and catch me like one of those fish you caught that day? You could do that, all right. You could do that if you wanted to.'

'If I wanted to,' Cale says. 'But I don't.'

He hears a car then, and his heart seems to stop in his chest.

It goes past, but it could have stopped. It could have been a customer. It wasn't, thank God, but yes, it could have been. 'I've got to get this done,' Cale whispers to himself and to the mallet in his hand. The mallet that suddenly seems to weigh as heavy as a bag of scrap iron.

'Don't hurt me, sonny-boy,' Ewan Redstone suddenly whines, as if he now knows that mallet is in Cale's hand. No tears at the back of his throat now. They are all the way up in the gummy barrels of his nose, and probably pouring out of his eyes, too, under the blood-drenched pillowcase. Then he begins to desperately gabble like a man who knows his time is up. 'Oh Jesus, don't hurt me, please don't hurt me! Help me, someone! My own son is going to murder me! Help me, help me, help me! For God's sake someone help me! HEEEEELP!'

This is it.

No more time to waste.
Cale smashes his father's head in.
No offer of Hospital for Ewan Redstone.
Just Death.

Chapter 3: Don't Believe It

Cale stumbled into the kitchen and drank two glasses of cold water straight down. Did this to quench his thirst, but mostly to take away the bitter taste of puke. After that, he stood there, gripping the sink, thinking he was bound to faint, that the reckless enormity of what he had done would send him crashing to the floor.

It didn't. It did send him into the bathroom, though, and in there his bowels released a thin stream of fluid the colour of sump oil. He waited for it to finish. It didn't. Another stream, then another, until he believed he'd be on the toilet all morning. But then finally it stopped. He cleaned himself up, hiked up his jeans, and washed his hands.

He returned to the kitchen sink. Again the world swung to-and-fro, his vision blurry, his legs wobbly, but after a while the feeling went, thank God, and he stuck his hand in his pocket, carefully pulled out his mother's necklace. He began to clean it, doing this delicately, using a damp pad of lint. The chunks of rotted flesh, clinging here and there, fell off and were washed down the drain. Pieces of the woman who had given birth to him, back in the spring of 1948, at the Our Lady of Divine Grace Hospital in Unity Gate.

He patted the necklace dry with a tea-towel, then walked down to his father's little office, which was no more than a cramped, low-ceilinged room next to the kitchen. He took out his father's keys and opened his writing desk.

There were many drawers in here, drawers which Cale would investigate in a moment, but for now, he opened the top, right-hand drawer, and into it he put his father's wallet, his penknife, as well as the necklace, the Coca Cola necklace, which had been restored to its former, glittering glory. He closed the drawer. Locked the desk. Went back into the kitchen and took off his clothes.

Once again he took out the metal bucket behind the pleated swish of brightly-patterned curtain. Just as he had done earlier, he filled it with hot water, and dumped his clothes in there to steep. Then he put the bucket back behind the curtain and pulled it shut. After that, he went back into the bathroom and washed himself all over. Towelled. Went upstairs and changed into fresh clothes.

After combing a splash of oil into his hair, and re-modelling his quiff, he returned to his father's office. Sat down once more at the desk. His father had been a bad man, a very bad man, but when it came to his work, he had been honest. Straight down the line. A man like him, with his wife's dead body buried out in Sad's Place, would *have* to be honest, wouldn't he? Couldn't afford to not pay his tax, his insurance, his bills, etcetera, and face the prospect of having the bailiffs around.

Cale took out his father's books, which were held together with a thick elastic band, and spent a while going over them. He found them to be in order, just as he expected, although he had no idea what all the figures meant, but with a bit of application, he knew that at some point he'd get to grips with them. Would have to, if, that was, he was going to run Redstone Joinery single-handed. A daunting prospect, that. Every bit as daunting as it must be for Tommy on the brink of joining Brougham Moor School. The Big School. Still, Cale would get through it. Would have to. For himself.

And for Tommy.

He found money in the desk, a bundle of cash right at the back. His father liked cash. Didn't trust banks. He said they whittled away at your money, taking a little bit here, a little bit there, like woodworm making holes in your furniture. Cale picked up the bundle and thumbed through it. It amounted to two-hundred pounds, a lot of money. And the house was paid for, Cale knew that much. His father was proud that he had made Redstone Joinery work. Had made it work so well, in fact, that the mortgage had been paid in less than ten years. So no mortgage worries. Good. No money worries, either, in the short-term, anyhow. And by taking a glance in his father's appointment book - a small red book which had been secured to the accounts book by the elastic band - Cale could see there was plenty of work on the horizon, too, should Redstone Joinery clinch that work.

'I'll clinch it,' Cale said. 'I'll make *sure* I clinch it.'

There were debts to pick up as well, Cale saw. Mr Edward Coates, of 28 Richmond Drive, owed thirty-five pounds and two-shillings, according to the books. A sum which should have been paid, at the latest, on Friday the 22nd of July. It was now Monday the 1st of August.

'Better put that right,' Cale said.

Also, a Mr Brian Digweed, of The Cedars, Spinwell Street, owed the sum of fifty-pounds, three-shillings, and four pence. And his debt was even older. Went all the way back to the middle of June. 'Can't have that,' Cale said. 'Better put that right, too.'

Then he wondered, if briefly, how his father had been so lackadaisical. He had been a stickler for making sure that any debt was paid on time. Probably part of the reason, in fact, why Redstone Joinery had been so successful over the past: no debt, no trouble. But in truth only Brian Digweed's debt had been outstanding for any length of time. And when Cale looked closer, having to squint in the light that was not much good in here, he saw a faint pencil line drawn through the debt, as if his father had half-heartedly cancelled it. So faint that it could just be an accidental thumb scratch, in truth.

'I'll call on Brian Digweed to check it out, ' Cale said. 'I'm sure he won't mind.'

He closed his father's books, snapped the elastic band back around them, then put them back in the desk. The bundle of money, which had been sitting in Cale's lap, went back in there, too. That done, he dug into the desk a little deeper and found a pile of letters and photographs, again held together with an elastic band. He removed the band and discovered that the letters were love letters, written to Cale's father by Cale's mother when he had been away, posted up north, on National Service.

Cale read a few and found them to be heart-breaking. *I miss you, I love you, I can't wait for you to get back.* All the usual sentiments you'd expect to find in letters like this, but as the words had flowed from his own mother's pen, driven by the feelings in her heart, it was still difficult for Cale to read them and not feel hurt. A woman in love - a young and beautiful woman in love - putting her feelings down on paper to the man she would marry and with whom she would have children, and yet that man had murdered her. Had murdered her for a reason that had almost certainly been no reason at all. Just the way that Tommy's clumpy foot, or the way he talked too fast, had been no reason to make the boy's life a misery.

Cale tossed the letters back in the desk. Picked up the photos and looked through them, all of them taken before Cale and Tommy had been born. His mother on her own, his father on his own, but mostly the two of them together, their arms around each other, smiling. Eyes bright. Teeth white. Two young people who had survived World War II, but who would not survive the battleground of their marriage.

He tossed the photos back in the desk, too, thinking as he did, that his father hadn't been able to part himself from his relationship with Cale's mother. Not altogether, anyhow, for here they were, the letters and the photos, all paying recognition to a time that should no longer have mattered to him. Yet for some reason it had. He had killed her, either by strangulation or by a heavy blow, and yet he had kept her memory locked up this desk, like it had meant something to him.

'Just nuts and bolts, that's all it is,' Cale said. 'Like nuts and bolts you keep in a tin but never find a use for.'

Yes, that was it: nuts and bolts that Ewan Redstone had accumulated, they were his, and they would *stay* his, even if they were of no real use to him. Just nuts and bolts that no longer held anything together, but if he'd thrown them away, he would have missed them.

Cale locked the desk and went over to the small, low window in here. Looked out at the backyard, at Sad's Place. 'You were right to take those letters off the door,' he said, speaking to the little girl whose pony had died and so she had renamed Sadie's Place Sad's Place. 'You were right all along.'

At three o' clock, he went down to the front gate. Unlocked it. But he did not pull it open. He crouched behind the hedge, waiting for Tommy to come home. Every now and then a car would go by. None pulled over, but that was his fear, that someone would pull over, paying little attention to the CLOSED sign, and try to put a little business Redstone Joinery's way. It happened. It happened a lot. Passing trade accounted for much of the company's business.

His fear of some passing motorist pulling over was nothing compared to his fear of Sergeant Willoughby suddenly making a return, though. And Willoughby was all worked up at the moment at the thought of another pensioner having his or her life-savings stolen by a bunch of heartless con-men posing as meter readers.

Understandable. But Cale didn't need Willoughby in that kind of a mood right now. If he became frustrated at his lack of success, while driving around trying to find these people, then he might just be back. Back to bend his best friend's ear about it. That best friend being Cale's father, of course, and summer cold or no summer cold, Willoughby was not a man to be dissuaded. And the nasty germs that might be lurking in the air? Willoughby would soon find a way over that, Cale knew. He'd probably put on some old World War II gas mask, meaning to talk to Cale's father that way, caring little about how silly he'd look. Don Willoughby was not just fussy. Not just a little excessive when it came to the issues of cleanliness, either. There was also a side to him that was frankly ridiculous. This Cale gathered from the stories his father used to tell him every now and then.

One time Willoughby bought a tow-rope from an army surplus store in Barford Green. Not just any old tow-rope. This one had been used in Africa during the war to pull heavy trucks out of the sand. The rope had had strands of high-tension elastic running through it, strands that helped the rope to gently take up the strain. Fine for trucks that were stuck axle-deep in sand. Not so fine for ordinary cars on ordinary roads.

One night Willoughby offered to tow a friend home whose car had broken down. Home? They didn't even get close. After tying the rope to both cars, Willoughby had driven off, and he'd almost been in the next town by the time the rope finally took up the slack and began to pull the broken-down car along. So in the end the mission had been aborted and Willoughby's friend had to call the breakdown services, which he probably wished he'd done in the first place.

Almost certainly from the same army surplus store, Willoughby also bought a suit. Like the rope, it wasn't just any old suit, either. This was a pilot's suit, deeply-quilted with copper wires running through it, to which was attached a plug that could be inserted into a plane's dashboard, and thus the suit would heat up and warm the pilot.

Willoughby somehow managed to connect the plug to the battery of a motorbike he owned at the time. He then zipped himself into the suit, climbed onto the bike, started it up, and off he rode into what was a chilly, windy day, believing the suit would keep him warm.

It did. Until it began to rain. The suit got soaked, it shorted, as did the bike, and Willoughby had to push the bike home dressed in a suit that must have weighed a ton. According to Cale's father, Willoughby hung the suit in his garden shed to dry, but six months later, it was still wet. Smelly, too. In the end he threw it away. *But that's Don Willoughby for you*, Cale's father had said. *Nutty as a fruitcake...and the worst of it is, he has no idea. Just thinks he's normal.*

Coming from Ewan Redstone, Cale thought that was the pot calling the kettle black.

Cale saw something that was mainly white, but with the odd flash of red in it, flapping in the distance. It was 3:15. Here came Tommy – Tommy riding that bike of his that was really nothing but a death-trap.

From bits he'd scavenged here and there, Tommy had built the bike himself. Its front wheel was smaller by two inches than the rear, which meant the bike dipped down at the front. No lights on it, either. No brakes, as well, unless you wanted to call the stick that Tommy used to slow it down with a brake. The stick dangled from a piece of wire fixed to the saddle, and whenever Tommy wanted to slow the bike down, he pushed the stick out and it rubbed against the tyre. *Squealed* against the tyre. Effective, though.

Tommy hasn't got the hands to work with wood, Ewan Redstone had said. But his ignorance, perhaps his *deliberate* ignorance, suggested he had known almost nothing about his own son. Nothing positive, anyhow. Had just known the faults, that was all. Well, here was something. Tommy hadn't built the bike out of wood, that was true, but if he could work with metal, then he could certainly work with wood. That was Cale's view, anyhow.

The mainly white thing Cale had seen was the flag of St. George. It was tied around Tommy's neck, and it flapped behind him like a cape, the wind occasionally catching it, twisting it around, so that Cale caught glimpses of the red cross on the flag. When Tommy reached the driveway, Cale sprang up from behind the hedge and pulled the gate open. Not far. Just enough for Tommy and that death-trap of a bike of his to get through.

'What are you doing hiding behind there?' Tommy asked in that gabbling, runaway voice of his. 'You made me jump Cale you made me jump!'

'Get in here,' Cale said. 'Quickly.'

Tommy did and Cale closed the gate. Snapped the padlock shut and locked it. Put a hand on Tommy's back to hasten him up the driveway. 'What's up what are you doing?'

'I need you in the house, and fast,' Cale said, looking around, up the road, down the road, just about everywhere, in fact. Even across at the woods. 'I need you in the house so that we can talk.'

'Talk about what Cale talk about what?'

'I'll tell you in a moment.'

'The workshop's closed why's that?'

'Stop talking and just do as I say.' Cale saw that his brother was looking with fear at the workshop. Tommy probably thinking that because the workshop was closed, then his father must be waiting for him, up by the house, ready to lay into him for something that must be so, so bad. If it wasn't, then why would the workshop be closed?

'Don't worry, there'll be no more Hospital or Death,' Cale said. 'All of that has come to an end for you.' Cale said this clear enough, but Tommy only looked confused. No evidence that Cale's words had registered at all. And why would they? Tommy had been beaten from pillar to post for most of his life. For him, Hospital and Death had become the norm. Sadly.

When they reached the back door, where Cale's work-boots were drying in the sun, Tommy got off his bike and placed it against the kitchen wall. Then he came over to Cale, clumping along on that built-up shoe of his. He crossed his arms over his chest and patted his shoulders. 'I got this from Miss Lovell.'

'The flag?' Cale asked. 'Nice.'

'It was hanging on the classroom wall she gave it to me for working hard and I do work hard Cale I really do.'

'Good, I'm glad you work hard, I'm proud of you,' Cale said. The flag had likely been hanging on the classroom wall since before the World Cup Final. Now that England had won the cup, Elsa Lovell had made the wonderful gesture of giving it to Tommy.

They went into the house, and Cale locked the door. Pulled the curtains closed. Sat his brother down at the kitchen table.

'I'm hot Cale I want a drink!'

Yes, the boy looked hot, and still confused. His eyes were blinking and his mouth sagged.

'Didn't you hear me out there?' Cale said.

'Hear what?'

'No more Hospital or Death?'

Tommy just gazed at Cale, and still there was no recognition. Just that sagging jaw of his, along with eyes that stared at Cale emptily. He scrubbed his hands up and down his face, then let them fall loosely back into his lap. And nothing. It was like looking, Cale thought, at one of those automatons at the fairground into whose mouth a ball had to be tossed to win a prize.

'I want a drink Cale I'm hot!'

Okay, a drink. Cale went to the pantry, took out a bottle of orange squash. He poured a little into a glass, then topped it up with cold water. Handed it to Tommy, who took it in both hands and gulped it down.

'I want another drink Cale I'm still hot!'

Cale filled the glass again. Handed it back to Tommy. Watched as he gulped this one down, as well, realising that what he'd been saying so far to Tommy would not have made much sense to the boy, anyhow. He needed to just come right out and tell him *why* there would be no more Hospital and Death. Just spell it out for him.

'How's that?' Cale asked, when Tommy had finished. 'Better?'

'Much better.'

'Good. Okay, so here's what I'm going to do. I'm going to tell you something that you won't believe, but you'd better believe it because it's true.'

'What's that Cale what's that?'

'There was an accident this morning,' Cale said. 'A pile of wood fell on dad and he was crushed to death.'

But of course that wasn't the whole truth. The whole truth was less to do with an accident and more to do with how Cale had smashed their father's head in. While he'd been burying his father in Sad's Place, Cale had thought long and hard about whether he should tell Tommy the truth, or just say that their father had been crushed to death under the pile of wood. An accident, pure and simple. But saying it had *just* been an accident wouldn't have fit. Had it *purely* been an accident, there would be a funeral. And there would be no funeral. The funeral, if it could be called that, had already taken place, attended by one person who could hardly have been called a mourner.

'Dad's dead?' Tommy said. He'd been waiting for his father to appear, and that was mostly why he'd gulped down those two glasses of orange squash, just in case his father denied him any more drink for the rest of the day. With drink Tommy was a gulper. With food he was a bolter. He also had the habit of storing food-and-drink in his bedroom, at the back of his wardrobe, or even under the floorboards. To Ewan Redstone, Tommy had been no more than a dog to be fed scraps, if and when he felt like it. Which was never that often.

'Yes, you heard me right,' Cale said. 'Dad's dead.'

'Crushed under a pile of wood Cale a pile of wood?'

'Yes. How do you feel about that?' Cale wanted to put his arms around Tommy, and say, *Isn't that just the greatest thing, Tom? You're free of him. No more beatings. No more being tied to the clothesline. No more lapping milk off the floor whenever you spill it. You're free of him. No more Hospital. No more Death.* But at the moment it all came back to Cale's question: how did Tommy feel about that? And Cale could not tell one way or another, because Tommy had gone back to just staring at him again in that silent, gape-mouthed way. Only this time his disbelief seemed to be deepening instead of clearing. It was like he was slipping into some kind of a fit, and dismally this was confirmed when the empty glass slipped out of Tommy's hand and fell, with a crash, to the floor.

'Tommy?'

Tommy's lower lip began to twitch, revealing shutter-quick glimpses of his bottom teeth. The tip of his tongue hung there in the wet, limp darkness of his mouth. His eyes rolled up and his lids fluttered, lids that were such a washed-out pink, that Cale could see his brother's eyeballs floating around under there. He made a hollow, crackling sound at the back of his throat. It came out as *deg!* - dead, perhaps? - and then he began to slip down in the chair, the flag around his shoulders becoming rumpled, and then rolling up over his head like a hood.

Cale stepped forward. He swept the pieces of broken glass under the table with a foot, just in case Tommy slipped all the way down and pronged a bare knee on the shards, because, at the age of eleven, he still didn't own a pair of long trousers. Not even a pair of jeans. Like the food and drink, new clothes came to him rarely.

'Don't believe it don't believe it don't believe it,' Tommy said, over and over. 'Don't believe it don't believe it don't believe it don't believe it...'

Cale took another step forward, at first thinking he would pick his brother up before he sank to the floor. But instead he slapped him. Slapped him hard, and Tommy's eyes sprang open, at first dazed, and then alert. Almost magically alert. Violence. Tommy responded to the sharp crack of violence the way other kids would only respond to words of kindness. It had become Tommy's language, a slap, and double underlined for emphasis.

'Sorry, Tom, I didn't want to do that. But I need you with me. I need you here, not in some other world where I can't reach you. Dad's dead. You heard me right. He's dead.'

'Don't believe it don't believe it don't believe it...'

'Damn it, I'm not going to hit you again!' Cale said. 'Listen to me, and if you can't, then think of the clock!' He grabbed Tommy's face, his pale, hot face that shone with sweat. Turned it towards the clock on the wall. 'The clock, Tommy! Tick-tock, remember? Tick, you speak, tock, you don't? Christ, how many times do I have to tell you that?'

'Don't believe it don't believe it don't...' And then thankfully his eyes seemed to fix on the clock, on its ticking second hand, and with a foggy, mesmerised look in his eyes, he said, 'Don't. Believe it. Don't. Believe it. Don't. Believe it.' The words too measured, too mechanical, but for Cale, it was better than listening to all that a hundred-mile-an-hour gabble.

'It's true,' Cale said, now gently stroking Tommy's face. 'If you don't *want* to believe he's dead, then that's your business, but sooner or later, you'll find out that I'm telling the truth. He's dead, Tom. He's gone. Gone forever.'

'Don't. Believe it. Don't. Believe it. Don't. Believe it.' And so it went on, with Tommy staring up at the clock, saying this over and over, in time with the second hand.

Cale began to worry that what he'd said might just have caused a lockup in his brother's brain. Maybe even a permanent lockup. The news of their father's death had been delivered as reasonably as Cale could make it. No Joy. No satisfaction. He'd kept the joy and the satisfaction out of his voice, even though it had been difficult. But of course it wouldn't have mattered *how* he'd delivered this news to his little brother.

When prisoners were set free, not all of them wanted to walk out the gate.

Most. But not all.

Later that afternoon. Tommy in bed. The England flag pinned to the wall, as it had been in Miss Lovell's summer school. Cale had pinned it there.

'How are you feeling?' Cale asked when Tommy opened his eyes.

'I'm thirsty Cale I want a drink I'm thirsty.' Tommy's voice, as per usual, up and running before his brain had a chance to join in. It was a wonder his tongue didn't just snap off, Cale thought. But at least it was working. For a while there Cale had believed he wouldn't hear that voice working again.

'There's a drink right there,' Cale said, pointing to the rickety chair that served as Tommy's bedside table. 'Do you need a hand?'

'No I'll be fine Cale I'll be fine.' Tommy sat up. He grabbed the glass and drained it. Even then, he poked his tongue in the glass to mop up any stray drops, much like a dog. This was Tommy's third glass of squash in as many hours. He'd be off to the toilet in a minute, and like many kids his age, the toilet would just be something to stand in front of, not something that should be aimed at.

'We need to talk, Tommy. We need to get things straight.'

'I know that Cale I know that I know that.'

'Think of the clock, Tom, *please* think of the clock.' Cale was sitting on his brother's bed that was all broken springs and a thin, uncomfortable mattress with feathers hanging out of it. 'And don't get funny with me, eh? I've had a hell of a day so far.'

'I'm not getting funny Cale I'm not.'

'Sounds like it to me,' Cale said. 'Here, give me the glass. I don't want you breaking that one, too.'

Tommy handed it over. 'It's just that I'm confused.'

'I'm sure you are. That news I gave you would confuse anyone.' Cale put the glass on the chair. 'But before I go on, try and remember what I said about the clock. Is it too much to ask to make it stick in your head?'

'I try to remember but without the clock I forget.'

'Here, take this.' Cale unbuckled his watch. 'Put it on your wrist. Now you can look at it every time your voice runs away from you.'

'Can I have it Cale can I?'

'Yes, it's yours. I'd have let you have it before, but I couldn't because Dad would have taken it back. But he's gone now. So you can keep it. Let's hope it slows your speech down a bit.'

Tommy looked at the watch with thrilled eyes. 'It will Cale it will!' He threw his arms around Cale, their faces pressed together in a warm, tender way that shocked Cale into realising that he hadn't been this close to his brother in years, that they had become strangers staring at each other from opposite corners of life. And that was hell, wasn't it? Time would make other hells apparent, but at the moment the one hell Cale understood was how far apart he and Tommy had become, cut adrift from each other by a man who'd only wanted one boy to live and the other to drown in a sea of loneliness, of loneliness…and pain.

It would have been better, I think, if he'd *been the one trapped under this fallen stack. Then I'd have been given the excuse to end his miserable life and get him out from under our feet.* Those words of Ewan Redstone's, too cruel to understand, aimed at a boy whose only mistake had been to be born the way he had.

Now that he was this close to his brother, Cale could see dirt grimed into Tommy's neck. Could see earwax, too, orange-brown gunk inside his left ear. The boy would be taking a bath in a moment, Cale decided. A proper bath. Hot and soapy. No more of the occasional washes in the kitchen sink that his father would sometimes allow him. From now on he'd have the "luxury" of a bathtub at his disposal.

He gently eased Tommy away, looked down at the watch in his hand, and said, 'You want me to help you with that?'

'Yes please Cale yes please!'

Tommy wrapped the soft, leather strap around his wrist and Cale fastened the little, fiddly clip. 'There, how's that?'

'Neat!' Tommy said. 'A real watch that's all mine!'

'Yep, it's all yours,' Cale said. 'Look after it.'

'I will I will I will!' Tommy gave Cale a look that was too bright, too grateful, for his pale, sleep-puffed faced to carry. His face that even now did not display any real notion that his father was dead, and that if his father walked into the room right now, Tommy would take off the watch, probably claw it off, hold it out to him, and say, *I was just trying it on Dad it's still Cale's not mine honest!*

But that was how life had been for Tommy: a boy filled with guilt when there should have been no guilt whatsoever. And when earlier Cale had carried him up to bed, knowing that Tommy should rest first and then they would talk, he had known even then that when Tommy woke up, it was still going to be almost impossible to convince him that their father was no longer around. No longer around to offer him the heads-you-lose, tails-you-lose, choice of Hospital or Death.

'I love this watch,' Tommy said. 'I love it and I love you.'

'I love you, too,' Cale said. But he almost choked on those words, and had to put a hand up to his mouth to stop himself from crying. 'Yes, I love you, too, Tom. I really do.'

After Tommy had taken a leak, Cale ran him a bath and washed him from head to toe. Cale had kept some of his old clothes in a box under his bed. Not exactly to save them for Tommy; he had long since given up believing they would go to that poor mite. It was more a case that some of these clothes had been Cale's favourites, he had grown out of them, but he hadn't been able to part himself from them.

Cale had cleaned up the broken glass while Tommy had been in bed. Had washed his jeans, too, which had been soaking in that bucket under the sink - the water had been a scummy red-green colour, a mixture of blood and grass stains. Now Tommy was sitting at the kitchen table, using a towel to dry himself between his fingers and toes. While he did this, Cale went upstairs and brought down the box. Placed it on the table. The watch was on the table, too, Cale's watch that was now Tommy's, and when Tommy finished drying himself, he eagerly put the watch back on and fastened it. Without Cale's help, too.

'You like that watch, don't you?'

'It's just the best,' Tommy said, focusing on the watch, his words falling in with its tick. 'And I think you're the best brother in the world, Cale. Really you are.'

'I think you are, too,' Cale said. He delved into the box, which was dusty on the outside, but shrewdly, he'd had the good sense to wrap the clothes in brown paper and to tie the package up with string. He took the package out, snipped the string with a pair of scissors, and opened it. There was a blue Ben Sherman shirt on top with a smart, button-down collar, complete with a white motif of a ship's wheel on the breast pocket. Cale held it up. 'You like this, Tommy?'

'Wow that's nice!'

'It's yours,' Cale said. 'Here, put it on.'

Tommy did. Even though he was leaning on his stick - an old cut-down walking stick that kept him balanced when he wasn't wearing his built-up shoe - he looked quite the smart little grown-up man. His hair needed combing. He was small for his age, too, and being underfed didn't improve the image. Even so, despite the fact that Tommy's right eyelid hung over his eye, and that also his face fell away on that side, there was still a beauty to him that was absurd and yet somehow gorgeous. Looking at him made Cale's heart swell and his eyes shine with tears.

'Now for the piece-de-resistance, whatever that means,' Cale said. 'Dah-dah!' He held up a pair of jeans, and they were not just any old jeans, either. They were Levis, by golly. But Tommy was all at once looking at the back door, which had rattled in the late-afternoon breeze. It was no rattle, though. Not to Tommy, anyhow. To him, that rattle had been the doorknob being turned. By his father's hand. *Which one do you want, Tommy? Hospital or Death? What's up, the question too difficult?*

Cale clicked his fingers. 'Earth to Tommy, Earth to Tommy. Are you receiving me?'

Tommy looked around. Tommy, whose full name was not Tommy Edward Redstone, or Tommy David Redstone, just plain old Tommy Redstone. Unlike Cale who had a middle name, which was the same as their father's first name: Ewan. And that was something Cale was more ashamed of than proud, a name given to him by a father who had seen this son, and this son only, as someone important enough to have a middle name, and all the better that it should be Ewan. A chip off the old block.

'Hmmm?'

'I'm over here, Tom,' Cale said, holding up the jeans again. 'What do you think?'

Tommy's eyes snapped back to the front, and then widened. 'Are those mine Cale are those mine?'

'If they fit, then yes, they're yours.'

'They'll fit I'll make them fit,' Tommy said. He took them off Cale, and he forgot all about his stick, and it fell to the floor with a clatter. He leaned against the table and began to yank the jeans up. He got them around his waist (which was terribly sunken, Cale saw), buttoned them up, but Cale had known all along that they wouldn't fit, and so already he had the answer in his hand, taken out of the package and waiting to be called into service: a handsome leather belt once worn by Cale, but it was now too small.

'Here, try this,' Cale said, holding out the belt to his brother, who was gazing down at the large gap between his belly and the waistband, wondering, no doubt, how he could make that large gap shrink so that the jeans would fit.

'A belt just the job!' Tommy said. He grabbed the belt and began to feed it through the loops, and as most kids do, he missed the loop right at the back, but at least he had gotten all the rest. He pulled the belt tight. Buckled it up. And the jeans - at the front, anyhow - had become pleated and bunched up.

'No need to worry about that,' Cale said. 'Just leave your shirt untucked. That way, the bunches won't show.'

'Good idea,' Tommy said, arranging his shirt on the outside. He bent, picked up his stick, and then stood to attention, which could not in any way be described as standing to attention. Not really. Just Tommy's awkward, leaning version of it. 'How do I look Cale how do I look?'

'Handsome as a prince,' Cale said, and he knelt before his brother, at first in mock reverence, and then, more practically, to put a couple of turn-ups in the jeans, because the bottoms were dragging on the floor.

'Thank you sire,' Tommy said. 'You may rise.' He glanced at his watch, bending his wrist extravagantly, as if the watch was a Rolex, not a Smith's. He watched the second hand sweep, trying to fall in with its motion, hesitantly at first, like someone waiting to jump into the swing of a skipping rope and not wishing to trip. Then, in a grand, plummy voice, he said: 'I see it is close to dinner time, old boy. What are we dining on this evening? Pheasant and caviar, I hope.'

'You said that perfectly, Tom. Well done, you.' Then Cale began to laugh, and following that, he helplessly began to *fall* about laughing, having to clutch his stomach. Tears before bedtime, so they say, but there had been many tears in this house, and mostly they had been Tommy's. Not just at bedtime, either. But now there was only laughter, a laughter so good that it tasted like an over-sweet treacle pudding that would make you sick if you ate too much of it. And Cale and Tommy Redstone ate plenty. And then some more.

No pheasant. No caviar. Cale, however, cooked two plates of egg and chips, complemented by a thick, crusty loaf, and there were lashings of cold ginger beer, too. Cale, who had eaten well over the years when Tommy hadn't, could not remember when he'd last sat at the table and eaten with his brother, and that brought a lump to his throat that was still there, uncomfortably, even when he took a sip of his beer.

The laughter had ceased. Somehow. At one point Cale believed it would never stop, that the two of them would just go on laughing until the moon appeared, big and silver, in the kitchen window, and there they'd be, still laughing away like a couple of stupid planks.

Finally, though, they had fallen into each others' arms, with Tommy's head, smelling fresh and clean, resting on Cale's chest. Both enjoying the closeness, wanting more of it, and in the end barely able to let each other go. More I love you's. More touching, and there was a little grooming, too, from Cale, who went through Tommy's hair for a short spell, just to check it wasn't crawling with nits. Probably it should have been, Tommy's access to shampoo had been pared right down by their father's meanness, but of nits there was thankfully no sign.

When both boys had finished eating, Cale pushed his plate to one side and belched, gently, into his hand. Tommy did not. Tommy, whose manners had fallen away somewhat over the years, belched noisily, and Cale said, 'Don't do that, Tommy. Do it quietly, with a hand over your mouth.'

Tommy nodded, but he smiled deviously, and then, he farted loud enough, and fierce enough, to almost tear a hole in the Levis Cale had given him. 'Sorry about that Cale sorry!' But his apology became a contradiction the moment he began to laugh, and uproariously, his head thrown back, his hair, which needed cutting, hanging down over the chair's back.

'Jesus, put a sock in it,' Cale said. Serious. Frowning. Then he became caught up in Tommy's high spirits and joined in, laughing with that lump still lodged in his throat like a stone.

They laughed until tears dashed their cheeks. The laughter of two brothers, one knowing exactly why he was laughing - at their unexpected freedom - the other laughing for those reasons, too, but not as yet altogether acquainted with the full details. But in due time they would have to get down to those full details, Cale knew, and so he banged the table with a fist, hard enough to make the breadboard and the plates jump. Knives and forks jangled. Glasses of ginger beer sloshed.

The laughter ceased. From both boys. Abruptly.

'Okay, that's enough,' Cale said. 'No more laughing. Not for a moment, anyway. We need to talk, Tom. We need to get things straight, and laughing won't help.'

Again Tommy nodded, and this time it was not contradicted by a belch or a fart. He just stared at Cale, his eyes unblinking, his hands placed flat on the table before him.

'How was the food?'

'Lovely it was lovely Cale.'

'Good.' Cale gave Tommy an assertive look that let him know they could not afford to mess around anymore, not until certain words had been said and the reality had been dealt with. Otherwise they might never get down to the crux of the matter. And the crux of the matter was serious. Dead serious. These two boys were in trouble, one in particular, who was only eighteen and as such still on the fringes of manhood, but that wouldn't stop any court of law from throwing him in jail. And for a very long time. Murder was murder. Forget the ins and outs. Murder was still murder.

'First I want to say I'm sorry,' Cale began, and then he had to take another sip of beer, but still the lump in his throat was there, bigger then ever, and feeling more like a blockage now than something that just felt uncomfortable. 'I should have defended you. I should have stuck up for you.'

'That's okay Cale that's all right I understand.'

'It's not okay, and it's not all right,' Cale said. 'But I couldn't do anything, you know? Much of the time it was like watching a horror film, and if I didn't want to watch it anymore, I could simply put my hands over my eyes. That's how it became for me, Tom: a horror film that I didn't have to watch if I didn't want to. But of course I could still hear the screams, and no one has enough hands to cover their ears, as well, do they?'

'It's okay Cale it wasn't your fault.'

'I know it wasn't my fault. I just wish I'd been braver.'

A moment's silence, interrupted only by the breeze outside, which was becoming less of a breeze and more of a wind that made the window rattle and the curtains flap and twist. Curtains that were still drawn, and in a moment, Cale would have to switch on the light because it was starting to get dark in here. Tommy's face, on the left-hand side, had begun to fade into brown, lumpy shadows that made his lower lip seem too plump, as if it were bruised.

'Let's not talk about that Cale I'm sure you would have helped me if you could have.' Tommy closed his mouth. Stared down at his new watch, not looking at Cale, just concentrating, and tenaciously, on the ticking second hand. Unprompted, too. Which was a first. 'What happened, Cale?' he asked in a normal voice. 'You said that dad was crushed under a pile of wood, is that right?'

'Yes, under a pile of wood,' Cale said, suddenly grasping the chance to confess it all, now that once and for all he had Tommy's undivided attention. 'But that's not all, Tom. Dad might have lived. Probably not, but *had* he lived, then I think it likely he would have spent the rest of his days in a wheelchair.' Cale took a deep breath. 'So I hit him. I hit him with a mallet, and several times. Put a pillowcase over his head and just kept on hitting him until he was dead.'

Tommy looked up from his watch, startled, his eyes opening so wide that they seemed as big as salt cellars. This time there was no *Don't believe it. Don't believe it. Don't believe it.* This time there was still disbelief in Tommy's face, but it was a disbelief that at last was beginning to fade. 'You killed him Cale you killed him?'

'Yes, I killed him. Although maybe we shouldn't *quite* see it that way. I think mostly I just finished him off. And he deserved it, anyway. He got himself into trouble, into big trouble, and he couldn't get out of it. So yes I finished him off.' Cale laughed, not meaning to laugh, just meaning to snort, but it came out all high-pitched and chuckly. 'God, maybe I *am* sort of brave after all. I sat back and watched him tormenting you for so long that when I finally did something, I just went the whole hog and beat him to death. As revenge goes, it may just have been a little...well, excessive?'

'What does excessive mean?' Tommy asked, staring back down at his watch.

'It means that perhaps I went too far.'

'I don't think so,' Tommy said. 'I think in the end either he would have died or me. Probably me.'

'That's what I think, too,' Cale said. He didn't just *think* that, either, he knew it. Hadn't their father killed their mother? And wouldn't Cale almost certainly have been right in his prediction that their father would have killed Tommy sometime during this summer? Yes. And that made a ripple of cold run up his back, the kind you get when you almost walk in front of a car and step back just in time.

'So where is he now?'

'In Sad's Place. I buried him in there and put the junk back on top of him. Locked the door. And it will stay locked. Have you got that, Tommy?'

'Yes.'

'And you won't go in there?'

'No.'

'Cross your heart and hope to die?'

'Yes.'

'Then do it. Cross your heart.'

Tommy ran a finger up the middle of his chest and then across it.

'That's it,' Cale said. 'Now I believe you.' *And the real reason I don't want you to go into Sad's Place is because mum is buried in there, too. He killed her, Tom, he killed her. That's what really happened that day. She didn't walk out. That was a lie. He killed our mother.*

Cale felt the urge to say this but didn't. He would keep that specific horror to himself, along with the memories of that worm curled up in their mother's eye-socket. Then there was the Coca Cola necklace, to which had clung little bits of her rotted flesh. But now it had been cleaned and was locked safely away in their father's writing desk. Where it would stay. Unbeknown to Tommy.

'So what'll happen now?' Tommy asked, still staring down at his watch. 'Someone will find out, won't they? Sergeant Willoughby, do you think?'

'Sergeant Willoughby was dad's best friend, just about his *only* friend, so that'll be a problem, yes. A big problem. But while you were upstairs resting, I came up with a solution. It's a temporary solution at best, but I think it'll buy me some time until I can come up with something better. I'll tell Willoughby that dad's working up north, that he got a big contract up there. If I say it's in Templeton, then Willoughby will understand why dad can't come home at night. And anyway, Willoughby has enough on his mind at the moment. There's a gang of men in Unity Gate. They rip-off old people by posing as meter readers. Willoughby wants them. He wants them badly. So his time's pretty much taken up for the time being.'

Tommy eyes snapped up from the mostly-enchanting dial of his watch. 'Yeah but once he catches those men you'll be done for Cale he'll be over here and he'll want to know where dad is and oh God you'll be in all sorts of trouble - '

'Stop it!' Cale said, again bashing his fist on the table. 'Don't let your mind wander like that. We need to stay calm. If we stay calm, then we've got a chance of getting out of this. And remember that mum went missing, didn't she? No one made a fuss about that. She had friends, too, more friends than dad ever did. But even *they* accepted that she'd just upped and left. No one called the police, did they?'

'No,' Tommy said, lifting his wrist and fixing his gaze back on the watch. 'But when mum left, we still had dad to take care of us. If people find out that dad isn't here anymore to do that, then they'll split us up. I'll be sent to that special needs school in Battenford, and probably you'll be put in prison.'

'None of that will happen, Tom. I won't let it. For years I stood by and did nothing, but that's all going to change. I promise you that. From now on I'll protect and take care of you. Make sure you take a bath, get your hair cut, have clean clothes to wear, and I'm going to make doubly sure that you get an education. You have to remember that I suffered, too. Not as much as you, I know, but dad certainly messed-up my education, because I wanted to go to college and become a draftsman, but nope, he insisted that I become his apprentice. I don't like being a joiner, Tom. It just doesn't toot my whistle or blow my horn, but that's the way it is, and I have to accept that.'

'Well, I know that dad didn't make life easy for you, either, but in a different way. It's just that I don't want you and me to be separated.'

'We won't be, Tom. I'll do whatever it takes to prevent that. We just need to stay calm. Go about our business, same as usual. Act like nothing has changed. You'll need to be strong, though. You know that, don't you? You'll need to keep your mouth shut, too. Keep the fact that I killed dad to yourself. Not let it slip out. Can you do that? Can you?'

'Yes, I can do that, as long as no one comes to take you away, then yes, I'll be able to keep my mouth shut, I'm sure of it.'

God knew that Tommy had kept his mouth shut over the years that he had taken those beatings, some so bad that like their mother he often had to stay indoors until the bruises had gone. And really this was no different. Just a matter of boxing-up the horror, the way that Cale had boxed-up those old clothes of his, and like those clothes, Tommy would have to stow the horror away somewhere where it couldn't be gotten at, unless he deliberately reached for it.

'Good lad,' Cale said. 'Just put your faith in me and everything will be fine. Believe me, it will be.'

'What about the joinery shop, though? Can you run it on your own?'

'It'll be difficult, but yes, I think I can. We've got plenty of work to be getting on with, and plenty in the pipeline, too. It'll mean that I'll have to work long hours, of course. Maybe have to work into the night sometimes, but I'm young, I'm fit, I'll manage.'

'What about the books, Cale? Can you deal with those?'

'I looked at them earlier. It's going to take me a while to get my head around them, but when it came to the joinery shop, dad was at least honest and legal. The books seem to be in order. And I'll make sense of them. Given time I'll make sense of them.'

'You'll have to run the house as well,' Tommy said, all of it perfectly clear, perfectly paced, but then he took his gaze off his watch and stared at Cale wildly. 'You'll have to wash clothes cook clean fetch the groceries order supplies for the workshop pay the bills keep dad's truck on the road it'll be too much for you Cale don't you think don't you think don't you think don't you think...?'

His eyes rolled up, his lids flickered, his head fell back, his body began to slip down in the chair, all this, just like before. His face white in a kitchen that was now bathed in grey shadow, broken only by the intermittent flap of the curtains that allowed sprays of light in and would then choke it off again.

Cale stood up, whacked his knees on the table, and swore. He turned on the light, using the switch that was next to Tommy on the wall by the hallway door. Cale had known, of course, that Tommy's capacity to deal with this situation might again become too much for him. Their father's death, and the way around the problem of his death, would simply prove too much for him to handle. Might even prove to be impossible. But it was understandable. Expected, really, for the boy had been to hell and back. Corny but true, and for Cale "hell and back" did the job, anyhow. It all too effectively explained what his little brother had been through these past five years.

To hell. And back.

Only Tommy was having trouble getting all the way back after such a long and painful ride. One minute riding on the crest of his liberation, the next minute drowning under the weight of it.

'Tommy, snap out of it!' Cale said, grabbing his brother's face, which although pale was once again amazingly hot, as if he'd been sitting all day in the boiling sun. 'Snap out of it, you hear me?'

No response. Tommy falling ever deeper into another lockdown. His mouth was hanging open, and it was so lopsided, it looked as if an invisible finger was pulling it down on that side. His teeth, though, were not dirty. Remarkably clean all told. This despite the fact that his toothbrush hadn't been renewed in years and sat in its own dingy, cracked glass, while Cale's and his father's sat side by side in a glass so spotless, you could read a book through it. The whites of Tommy's eyes shone murkily under the hood of his trembling lids. His legs were thrust out, stiff as his walking stick.

'Shit!' Cale said, knowing that telling Tommy to snap out of it wasn't going to get him anywhere, no matter if he said it a thousand times over. It was just an order, bland as a bark, with nothing tempting in it to make a boy like Tommy listen and take notice. And he wouldn't slap the boy again. He was done with violence. Violence, be gone.

He looked around at the kitchen door, which opened on a small ventilation lobby that served as a place in which to hang coats and to take off dirty shoes so that mud wouldn't get tramped into the house. Through the lobby, Cale could see the back door with its two squares of foggy glass, one at the top, one at the bottom. In the bottom square, there, not looking for it, but somehow knowing that *something* would be there, something that would give him an idea, he looked. And what he saw was the rear wheel of Tommy's bike, the last third of it curved against the glass, its black tyre dark enough to still be seen in the dimming light.

He turned back to Tommy, clutching his face in his hands, and said, 'Tommy, if you come back to me right now, then on Saturday I'll buy you a new bike. How about that, eh, a new bike? The best bike you ever saw?'

For a while there was still no response, just the pale, hot face, the sagging mouth, and the trembling, pinky eyelids. Then, blessedly: 'Uh?' And Tommy began to open his eyes. Just groggy, confused slits to begin with, the irises rolling back into place so slowly that Cale thought they would get stuck halfway down and stay there forever.

'A new bike, Tom? You want a new bike?'

And now Tommy's eyes were opening all the way, his irises becoming brighter until they were that lovely, delectable light-blue colour, and here they were, slipping all the way back down into place. Back to dead centre. Finally starting to fill with comprehension. 'A new bike?' he asked, his voice as light as dust. 'Is that what you said Cale a new bike?'

'Yes, you heard me right,' Cale said, again gently stroking his brother's face. 'Not only a new bike, but a new bed as well, one you can sleep on that doesn't make you ache in the morning. And we'll decorate, too. How about that? We'll buy some paint, some wallpaper, and we'll make the England flag that Miss Lovell gave you the centrepiece. What do you say to that, hmmm?'

'Can we afford that Cale can we?'

'Yes. I found a bundle of notes in dad's writing desk. We'll be fine for money. Stop fretting, eh? You go on like that and you'll make yourself sick!'

'I'm sorry Cale I'm really so so sorry.'

'Don't be,' Cale said, lowering his voice to a whisper. He knelt on the floor in front of his brother, put his arms around what was not a waist, just a withered, underfed slip of flesh, and hugged him. Began to cry. Couldn't help himself. But he let the tears fall silently so that his little brother couldn't see or hear them.

'A new bike wow Cale a new bike!'

'Yes, a new bike,' Cale agreed. 'And a new life.'

Chapter 4: Started a Ball Rolling

The barriers in Tommy's Redstone's life were removed, one after the other, and in quick succession. He had eaten his dinner at the kitchen table, a first in many years, and that was one barrier removed. Now Cale ushered him into the sitting room so that he could watch the television set. Another barrier removed, thank you very much, although to begin with it was difficult for Tommy. Clutching his walking stick and quaking a little, he stood in the doorway as if an invisible force-field would repel him the moment he tried to walk through it.

'It's okay,' Cale said, standing behind him, gently squeezing his shoulders. 'Dad's not here anymore to tell you where you can and can't go, so get moving, hmmm?' He prodded Tommy in the back, Tommy jumped slightly, and then he looked around at Cale with hesitation in his eyes, but finally he moved, anyway, knowing that his brother had promised to protect him, and if Cale said that, then the chances were high that no nasty surprises would be waiting in the wings to hurt him.

Tommy stepped into the sitting room, and Cale watched, both heartbroken and guilt-ridden, as his little brother came to a brief halt in order to familiarise his bare feet with the soft, fluffy carpet in here. For Tommy, soft, fluffy carpet was an alien material. His feet had become used to linoleum, floorboards, tiles, and concrete. None of which were particularly comfortable.

'Nice and warm,' Tommy said, smiling down at the carpet. He walked all the way into the room, then came to a stop so sudden that Cale almost marched into the back of him, and if he had, then the two of them probably would have gone sprawling into the fireplace.

'What is it now, Tom?'

'I don't know where to sit.'

'Sit where you like.'

But then Cale saw the boy looking over at their father's chair, which was a big chunky brown leather monstrosity on whose left arm were overlapping rings made by beer bottles-and-glasses, while on the right arm were several burn holes made by their father's hand-rolled cigarettes. No cushions. Real men didn't have a use for cushions the way women did - that had been Ewan Redstone's view on that matter. In the centre of the chair's back, at the top, was a round, rumpled mark made by Ewan Redstone's head, and this mark was not only rumpled but made shiny with hair oil.

'You don't have to sit there, do you?' Cale said. 'Sit here on the sofa.' Cale patted the sofa, and Tommy took up the invite and sat down...but that was not his problem. His problem, Cale now realised, was not where he should sit. His problem, undeclared but now becoming clear in the boy's eyes, was their father's chair. The way it dominated the room and made even Cale feel as if their father was there, sitting in it.

'I'll get rid of it,' Cale said, and the following morning he did just that, he lugged it into Sad's Place and dumped it in there with the rest of the junk (he also took something out of Sad's Place which he believed would be of a help to Tommy). Just for this evening, though, the chair would have to stay. 'In the morning, Tom. I'll get rid of the chair in the morning.'

'Thanks Cale thanks a lot,' Tommy said.

Cale switched on the television set, waited for it to warm up and for the snow to clear. No *Thunderbirds* or *Batman* or *The Lone Ranger* - too late in the evening for those programmes - but when the picture came up, Cale saw Diana Rigg dressed as the cat-suited Emma Peel, along with Patrick Macnee as the umbrella-wielding John Steed.

'How's that, Tom?'

'Wow *The Avengers* I love *The Avengers!*'

'Great,' Cale said. He left Tommy to it and went outside in the darkness. Took the items off the clothesline (now short of a pillowcase), and brought in his work-boots, too, that had been dried by the afternoon sun and by the freshening, night-time wind. But so much for *The Avengers*. Halfway through it and Cale took Tommy in a mug of hot cocoa, but he found the boy fast asleep, curled up on the sofa. Not even the lovely Diana Rigg in that tight, leather suit of hers had been able to keep the boy awake, so it seemed.

Cale put a blanket over him, not wishing to move him, knowing the boy would get a better night's sleep here, on the sofa, than he'd get in that broken-down bed of his. He kissed his forehead, which was still hot but nowhere near as pale now. Turned off the television. Turned off the light. Was about to close the door when he heard Tommy say in a dreamy but lucid voice: 'You can come back now, Mum. Dad's gone. You can came back and live with me and Cale.'

The letterbox suddenly rattled in the wind, the letterbox to which, even now, Tommy would often go in the morning to see if there was a letter from their mother (which of course there never was), and Cale jumped. Jumped hard enough to tip a little of the cocoa over his hand.

It wasn't until later that he realised Tommy had spoken, not in that gabbling, runaway voice of his, nor in his alternative voice that was governed too slowly, and too precisely, by either the kitchen clock or by the watch that Cale had given him.

He had spoken correctly. *You can come back now, Mum. Dad's gone. You can come back and live with me and Cale.*

Cale in bed. Sad's Place, down below his room, so silvery-blue in the moonlight that it seemed filmed over with a scrim of frost that made its roof twinkle. Cale thinking that Tommy was not a fool. Far from it. Which was why Elsa Lovell had pushed so hard for him to go Brougham Moor School, as opposed to most other people who had simply written the boy off as a nervy, sometimes distracted kid who struggled to regulate his speech.

Their failure to understand him, however, was simply because they never *tried* to understand him. But Else Lovell was an altogether different proposition. Elsa Lovell was like a miner digging for gold, and if she came up with coal, or tin, or copper, then she would just keep on digging until she had a nugget of the shiny, precious stuff in her hands.

Had Cale's father known this? Yes, unquestionably. He had known all along that once Tommy started Brougham Moor School, then his days as a bully would be numbered, that Elsa Lovell would get to the bottom of Tommy's problems, discover they were linked to his appalling home life, and then she'd come gunning for the boy's father. And Ewan Redstone would really need that, wouldn't he, what with his wife's body buried out the back in Sad's Place?

Oh yes, Cale was really getting the picture now. The special needs school all the way over in Battenford? Forget that Tommy would have been planted in the garden with all the other cabbages, as Ewan Redstone had so sensitively put it. The truth was, the special needs school would have been a convenient place to send a boy whose presence around the house was becoming so intolerable to Ewan Redstone that either the school took him, and this very summer, or he, Ewan Redstone, would take him. Would take his life. The way he had taken Natalie Redstone's life.

Ewan Redstone had been getting more than just a little nervy himself, that was the truth of it. Distracted, too. At the infant school, Tommy's welfare had never been much of an issue, not in a place that was falling apart, overcrowded, low on funds, and the teachers seemed relieved when the bell rang and they could get out of there.

Not so at Brougham Moor, though. Brougham Moor, like the infant school, had suffered at one time from the same problems, but Elsa Lovell, the miner that she was, had kept on digging until she'd struck the gold she'd been searching for. In came the funds to build a new library, the gym was refurbished, the old Victorian classrooms were decorated, and soon enough Brougham Moor was a school again, a real school, not a place in which the kids walked through one door and came out of another looking like they'd lost another six hours of their life and couldn't remember where those six hours had gone.

For Ewan Redstone, the infant school had been ideal. Tommy just another kid lost in the crowd. But at Brougham Moor, he would not be. He would be seen, counted, logged, examined, appraised. The infant school had been a lazy monster that had simply opened its mouth and in had walked its food for the day…but Brougham Moor was not a lazy monster. No anymore. For Tommy Redstone, the only monster had been his father. Now the monster had been vanquished…although, in a way, it was still here, its mouth gaping, waiting to feed on any scraps that Cale Redstone might drop, if he wasn't careful.

I'll be careful, Cale thought. *My dad's death has passed the responsibility onto me, but I can handle it. I'll feed Tommy, I'll groom him, I'll even dress him every morning, if that's what it takes to keep Elsa Lovell out of my hair. And I'll make him talk correctly, too. If he can do it in his dreams, then he can do it when he's awake.*

It wasn't a question, either, of Cale *hoping* to make Tommy talk correctly. If he didn't accomplish this, and before the new school term began, then it wouldn't be long, Cale knew, before Elsa Lovell came over to the house one evening to discuss Tommy's speech problems. And with whom would she discuss these? No mother. No father. Just Cale. Elsa Lovell was clearly a woman who cared deeply about her pupils - she had confirmed that already by giving Tommy the England flag off the classroom wall - but summer school was just summer school, after all. A place simply for the seedlings to be bedded in. It was not the hothouse into which they'd be transferred once the school began in earnest.

Just Cale. And Cale could not afford to be "just Cale". If Elsa Lovell came over one evening and decided that all was not right here at number 3 Samuel Lane, then Cale would be in so much trouble, that his best course of action would be to call Don Willoughby and confess to everything before the situation got even more complicated.

There was hope, though, a good deal of hope, Cale believed, not just because he had heard Tommy talking correctly in his sleep, but because, if Cale's mind served him right, Tommy's gabbling, runaway speech had only started up full-time after their mother had gone. He couldn't entirely be sure about this. Cale had had enough problems of his own back then, trying to deal with their mother's sudden disappearance, but yes, if his mind served him right, Tommy as a six-year-old had talked pretty much the way any normal six-year-old would. He had jabbered *sometimes*, but not all the time.

God, it all seemed such a long time ago. It seemed to Cale that he and Tommy had been caught up in this mad existence for so long, pressed as they had been so firmly under their father's tyrannical thumb, that the past seemed to have begun, not on the day they were born, but when their mother departed. A past that had not been a past, exactly, more a clump of hazy, tangled time marked not by the advancing hands of a clock but by the dark rumblings and sharp thunderclaps of their father's temper. When you lived in the eye of a storm, Cale now understood, you gradually forgot how the flowers grew so bright, so upright, so fresh, when the wind wasn't always wrenching them out of the ground and tossing them aside. You just forgot. Simple as that.

He fell asleep and dreamed of Little Miss Orange Dress. Cale, wearing a bright-red shirt and a pair of carpenter's jeans (a miniature duplication of the ones his father wore), walking hand in hand with the girl across the grassy backyard towards Sad's Place, both sets of parents inside the house, the Blunts, the Hunts, the Dunns, whatever, showing Cale's parents around...and hoping for a sale, of course.

The girl's hands are as smooth as wax, her whole *body* is as smooth as wax, it seems to Cale. Her dress floats around her, so thin, so delicate, that Cale can see her legs through it. Her buttocks, too. Even the two little bumps high up on her chest which, on his mother, are large, curvy swellings.

They come to a halt outside Sad's Place. The girl bends over and looks closely into Cale's face. He looks up and sees those eyes of hers that are like gentle but powerful beams of light that draw him in and take him to some other place beyond the flat but explicable confines of this world. In a voice that feels like a feather being gently stroked up his arms and neck, she says, *I have something to show you, Cale. Something for you to see, and...to feel. Come with me.*

In reality she may well have said those exact words, but Cale can't remember, because so much of his past before his mother left seems to have gone, as if she took it with her. There is a shimmer in the girl's voice, though. He can remember that, and clearly, a shimmer that seems to run down her throat, spread across her chest, and make her tremble slightly. Her hair is as dark as midnight, her lips so red they seem almost to be bleeding. She pulls back, becomes erect, and needs not to put a hand into her dress to grab a key because Sad's Place is not locked. She turns the handle, opens the door, reaches inside, slides the bolt across, and then the top and bottom doors are being swung back against the wall.

It is dark in Sad's Place, Cale sees, walking over and peering inside it. And it smells. Of an animal. A smell that is not altogether unpleasant, just strong and sour. At the place where the sun still shines and the shadows begin, he can see straw spread out there, edging the threshold like brown, straggled lace. The girl wraps one warm, waxy hand around his, glances around guiltily at the house, only Cale doesn't know it is guilt. Can only see that bright, chaotic colour has now jumped into her face.

She leads him into Sad's Place...and it is here where Cale's dream begins to swerve off the road and head into the forest of nightmares. There, right back in the shadows, is Cale's father, sitting in that armchair of his (which Cale in real life has yet to dump out here), with its overlapping beer-glass stains on one arm, and cigarette burns peppering the other. Cale's father with his lower half smashed to a mushy, splintery pulp, and still wearing the pillowcase over his head that is now a bloody hood.

You'll pay for this, boy, he says, his breath puffing the hood out and then sucking it back in. *You've started a ball rolling that you won't be able to stop. Remember that, lad. You've started a ball rolling that you won't...be able...to stop!*

A thump from somewhere. This followed by a whimper. Another thump...and then Cale knew what it was, where it was coming from, and he knew that whimper, as well. Had heard it too many times to mistake it for anything else: his brother in distress.

His eyes flew open, he scrambled out of bed, and went out onto the landing. Leaned over the banister, and there he saw Tommy – Tommy coming up the stairs, thumping his stick down hard on the treads.

'What is it, Tom? What's wrong?'

'I woke up in the sitting room and didn't know where I was!' he said, looking up at Cale as if he'd been betrayed. His brother had not protected him, his brother had in fact left him all alone in some strange, dark place, and Tommy was none too happy about that. 'I woke up and saw dad sitting in his chair and he was staring at me and oh Cale it was horrible and...'

Bleary-eyed and not altogether steady on his legs as yet, Cale nonetheless hurried down the stairs, scooped his brother up, settled him in his arms, and carried him into the bedroom in which, just a minute ago, Cale had been having a scary, unsettling moment of his own.

You've started a ball rolling that you won't be able to stop. Remember that, lad. You've started a ball rolling that you won't...be able...to stop!

He laid Tommy on the bed, relieved him of his stick, and rested it against the wall. The bed was a double, spacious and ridiculously comfortable, compared to Tommy's little single that was just about falling apart.

'Why did you leave me down there Cale why?'

'I didn't do it on purpose,' Cale said, on the defensive because he felt a little grumpy after that dream. 'You feel asleep in the middle of *The Avengers* and I thought it best to leave you there. Thought you'd get a better night's sleep on the sofa than in that creaky old bed of yours.'

'Oh,' Tommy said. His face was pale but burning up again, and Cale could see tiny droplets of sweat dotted along the boy's hairline, turning the hair there a shade or two darker. His eyes looked sore, heavy, and there were brown stains under them. He looked so fragile, so small, so *vulnerable*.

'I think you'd better sleep with me tonight,' Cale said. 'For the rest of the week, in fact, until I buy you that new bed. What do you say?'

'Thanks Cale I'd like that thanks.'

'Okay then.' He picked Tommy up and put him in the bed. Tucked the bedclothes around him, neat and tidy. 'Comfy?'

'I am Cale I am.'

Cale got in beside him. Slung an arm around his head, and there, in that place, Tommy became snuggled. Five minutes later and the boy was asleep. Not Cale, though. Cale lay awake for most of the night, thinking that if he got out of bed and peeped through the curtains, he would see his father down there in the grassy backyard, sitting in that armchair of his, smoking a hand-rolled cigarette through that bloody pillowcase, the smoke rising up and drifting across the fat, bright face of the summer moon.

Chapter 5: The Digweeds

Tommy went to summer school on that rickety, boneshaker bike of his, but his hair was all stuck up like the white-brown peaks in a meringue, and so Cale called him back. Told him to comb his hair, which the boy did, despite the fact he used the comb as if he were raking leaves. He got the job done, though, and by and large he looked as smart as a new pin.

'Take care now. I love you.'

'I love you too Cale I love you.'

'Enjoy your day.'

'I will I will.'

'And make sure you keep your mouth shut. Not a word to anyone.'

'Not a word not a single word I promise you that.'

Cale watched him go, and when he was out of sight, he opened the front gate all the way, flipped the sign over from CLOSED to OPEN, and walked back up the drive. The first job? To take that armchair out into Sad's Place. This he did, but it was a struggle - the damn thing was so bulky and awkward to grab hold of that it was like wrestling a dead bear out of the house. Once he got it into Sad's Place, he closed the door, locked it, but that was a struggle, too. His hands had become sweaty and shaky and twice he dropped the key…all the keys…all nine of them, down in the grass.

He was glad to see the back of that chair.

He went across the backyard, passing the blood stain in the grass that had looked like a scorch mark yesterday, as the day had progressed, but now looked like an oil spill - on the face of it. Yet when Cale took a closer look, he saw streaks of dark purple in it, and patches here and there of red, as well. Enough, he believed, to make a suspicious person forget all about oil spills and start thinking about blood.

No suspicious people walked around here, though. Suspicious or otherwise, hardly *anyone* walked around this part of the backyard, apart from Cale and Tommy. And their father. Their father who was now dead and who would not be walking anywhere. Not anymore.

Apart from maybe in Cale Redstone's dreams.

Cale unlocked the workshop and stepped into the gloom that as yet had not been swept aside by a sun that still squatted lazily on the far reaches of the sky.

His father's chamois apron was on the workbench, he saw. Its pocket gaped open, and in it Cale saw his father's tobacco pouch, his matches, and his wooden, fold-up rule. A chisel was next to the apron, the one he'd put down yesterday so he could fetch in that length of eight-by-two that would turn out to be a rogue that would trick him and bring down the stack under which he would be pinned. Under which his hands, both Hospital and Death, would be pinned, as well. Leaving him helpless and at the mercy of a son whose compassion had been drained by the very man who had required it most.

Cale grabbed the apron and hung it out the back, in the storeroom. The chisel he put back in the rack, next to the rest. His resolve to see Redstone Joinery maintain it success without his father at the helm was so strong that the strangeness he felt, he ignored. His father wasn't here anymore to guide him in that curt, abrasive way of his. Wasn't here to help him if he got stuck in a jam. His father was dead. His father had gone to that Great Joinery Shop in the Sky, Cale would have said about anyone else, but not about his father. His father was just dead and that was that. No good dwelling on that, either, not even for a moment. If he did, then the work would stack up around him and before long he'd drown in it. Best to just get on with it, and so that was what he did. He picked up where he'd left off yesterday morning and got down to sanding up the window-frames that, if he got them finished on time, he would deliver to their destination this afternoon.

He worked for two hours, flat-out, and then a car rolled up, a blue Morris Minor, its driver a short, portly man in a jacket with a tartan collar. His eyes floated behind a pair of black-rimmed spectacles. His hair was a knotty, auburn blaze, so thick and wiry.

Cale switched off the orbital sanding-machine he was using. Wiped his hands down the front of his apron. Went out to greet the man. He thought he knew him, had seen him at the very least, but couldn't quite place his face, because many customers came up to the workshop, and it was Ewan Redstone who almost always greeted them.

'Morning,' Cale said.

'Morning,' the man said. 'Is your father around?'

'No, he's up in Templeton hoping to clinch a new contract,' Cale said. He saw the man glance over at Ewan Redstone's dark-green truck, parked there on the far side of the workshop, with Redstone Joinery painted on both its doors in plain, white writing. That look meant nothing, it meant nothing at all, but Cale nevertheless felt the need to clarify. 'He went up on the train.'

'The train,' the man said, probably not caring a jot which mode of transport Ewan Redstone had used to get to Templeton, but saying the word anyhow. He stuck out a hand. It was chubby and smooth and hairless. 'The name's Coates. Edward Coates. I owe your father some money. I called here yesterday, but the gate was shut with the sign turned over to CLOSED. I've never seen that before, this place closed on a Monday.'

'It was the World Cup,' Cale said. 'My father had a little too much to drink over the weekend. You know how it is.'

'I do,' Coates said, smiling and showing a mouthful of small white teeth. 'I had a few drinks myself.'

Cale smiled, too. And now he knew who Edward Coates was. Had seen that name yesterday, written in his father's accounts book. He swept a hand towards the workshop. 'Would you care to step inside, Mr. Coates?'

Coates said yes to that and into the workshop they went. There was a small office in here, of a kind, situated just inside the main door. Mostly it was just a half-glass, half-timber partition, inside of which were two straight-back chairs, a small plywood desk on which sat a dusty, Bakelite phone, and all around, pinned here and there, were delivery notes that Ewan Redstone had kept for reference. To Cale it was just a messy, disorganised array of old paperwork that he would have sort through some time.

'Take a seat, would you?' Cale said. 'Somewhere here is a book of receipts. The moment I find it, I'll be able to - '

'Is this it?' Coates asked, picking up a well-thumbed book that was on the chair he'd been invited to sit on.

'That's the one,' Cale said, smiling again, and if he didn't keep smiling, and all the time, he feared his mouth might abruptly dissolve into the look of someone with something to hide. All about keeping up appearances – that's what he believed. Yes, all about keeping up appearances. And so far he believed he was doing just that.

He took the book off Coates with a hand so steady he almost dared it to shake…and then he pulled out of that idea, that stupid, stupid, stupid idea, just in case his hand did shake, and so badly, the book would slip out of his hand and fall to the floor. He slapped it down on the desk, and much too hard, much too *loudly*, like it was a nervous bird that might fly off if he didn't pin it down. Edward Coates, now sitting in the chair, flinched a little at that.

'Sorry about that,' Cale said. 'I've been using a sanding machine that makes my hands numb.' This was true, the machine, after heavy use, did make his hands numb. That was not the reason why Cale had flapped the book down so hard and so loud, though. Excitement was the reason. That, and the guilt that wanted to escape him and crow to the world that Cale Redstone was a murderer, a murderer, a murderer!

'No problem,' Coates said. 'I'm a jittery person by nature, anyhow. It runs in my family. Like noses.'

'Like noses,' Cale said, grinning. 'Good one, Mr. Coates. Funny.' He opened the book of receipts, snatched up a pen, and poised it. 'I think your bill is thirty-five pounds or thereabouts.'

'Thirty-five pounds and two-shillings to be exact,' Coates said. He pulled out a brown, slightly crinkled envelope. Handed it to Cale. 'It's all there, and I'm more than happy to part with it, too. The doors you made me were first class.'

'Thank you,' Cale said. 'We're a family business. We take great pride in the service we provide. I'm glad you're happy.' He took the envelope off Coates, tipped out the money, saw it was all there, and wrote out the receipt. Signed it. Tore it out of the book. Gave it to Coates.

Coates took it. Folded it. Tucked it in his breast pocket. That was it, the transaction had been done, short and sweet, and Cale walked Edward Coates back down to his car. Opened the driver's door for him.

'Thank you,' Coates said. 'Manners maketh man, so they say. And you have manners. Must be down to your father.'

'Must be,' Cale said. 'I'll pass that compliment onto him.' He thought for a moment, and then ventured to persuade out of Coates a little information that might settle Cale down a little, that might make him feel he could handle running the workshop and not seem like a boy doing a man's job. 'Do you mind if I ask you something, sir? If you're in no rush, that is.'

'Fire away,' Coates said, settling himself behind the wheel of his car and running his hands through that wild, red hair of his. 'What would you like to know?'

'Did you mind dealing with me?' Cale asked. 'I'm young, just eighteen. Perhaps too young for a grown man to feel...well, *comfortable* dealing with?'

'You have no worries in that department,' Coates said. 'You might be young, but you come across as mature and confident. Will your father be away in Templeton for some time?'

'He could be.'

'And he left you holding the fort, did he?'

'Yes.'

'Then pass on my good wishes to him,' Coates said. 'If he gets that contract, he'll have no problem leaving this place in your hands. He must have known that, anyhow, or why would he have gone up to Templeton in the first place, eh?'

'I see your point,' Cale said. 'Thanks, Mr. Coates. You've been a big help to me.'

'Happy to assist.' Coates started his car and reversed down the drive. Backed out into Samuel Lane, and then he was gone. With Coates's payment stuffed safely in his jeans pocket, Cale went back into the workshop. He made a cup of tea, drank it down, and then went back to sanding the window-frames.

By midday they were finished, and Cale loaded them onto the truck. Tied them down. Cale started the truck, it rumbled into life, and off he went to Spencer Peyton's place over in Walnut Grove, which just happened to be around the corner from Brian Digweed's place. Digweed, the man who had not as yet paid his bill, the way Edward Coates had.

It could of course just be a mistake, Digweed may well have paid his bill already, but when Cale thought back to that faint pencil line his father had drawn through the amount Digweed owed - fifty-pounds, three-shillings, and fourpence - he was still undecided as to whether it had been a faint pencil line, or an accidental thumb scratch.

Either way, Cale had to check it out. Had to. If a customer owed money, then it was money that he, Cale, wanted. No one had ever cheated Ewan Redstone out of money.

It wasn't going to start here with his son.

~

Spencer Peyton took delivery of the window-frames, four, of varying sizes, and paid his bill right there on the spot, in cash. A receipt was written out, he and Cale shook hands, and soon enough Cale was back in the truck and driving over to Brian Digweed's place in Spinwell Street.

The Cedars, the place was named, but Cale could see just the one cedar tree, and it was hardly impressive. Just a squat and shabby-looking thing that looked almost ashamed to be there, in the middle of the garden, as if it wouldn't mind being uprooted, cut into pieces, and used as firewood.

Mrs Digweed - presumably Mrs Digweed - was all the way over in a shadowy corner of the garden, wearing pink shorts and a large straw hat. Although she had seen Cale walk through the gate, she paid him little attention. Just gave him a quick glance and then went back to tending her borders. Her legs were long and lovely and Cale, too busy gazing over at those legs, almost walked dizzily into a trellis up which thorny, red roses meandered.

'Shit!' he whispered, and ran a self-conscious hand through his hair. He got himself back on track and went up to the door. Rang the bell. Almost right away the door was yanked open, hard enough so that Cale thought it would explode from its hinges with a loud, splitting bang. It was opened by a man who looked ready to snap if he heard so much as a bird sing. His face was flushed and his eyes were the sort of mad, red shade one would expect to see on a rabid dog. His mouth twitched. His hands flexed.

'What do you want?' he asked.

'Mr Digweed?'

'Yes.'

'My name's Cale Redstone. I - '

'Redstone?' the man asked, his mouth abruptly bunching. 'Not related to *Ewan* Redstone, are you?'

'Yes, my father.'

The man put a hand up to his forehead, somewhat theatrically, as if the world had not just chosen to pull his leg today, but to openly laugh at him. 'Your father?' he said. 'Jesus, just go away, boy. Go away before I do something I might regret.'

In Cale's hand was the original estimate for the kitchen unit that Redstone Joinery had made for Brian Digweed: red-and-black Formica on a waxed pine pedestal. Cale had found the estimate in the workshop office, slapped on a nail among all the delivery notes, and now he held it out to Digweed. 'I just wanted to know, sir, if you've paid for this kitchen - '

Digweed cut Cale off again. 'You're not hearing me, lad. I want you off my property. Please don't darken my door again.'

When your father was Ewan Redstone, a man who had, by nature, been violent, not a man like this man, who simply had a bee in his bonnet for some unknown reason, then your threshold for taking abuse was higher than most people's. This man, Digweed, he could tell Cale to go all he wanted and Cale would not. He had come to get his money, and although he didn't know, this way or that, if the debt was still outstanding, he would stay here until he found that out for sure.

'I'm not leaving, Mr Digweed, not until you tell me if you've paid this bill,' Cale said. 'If you have, then fine, all well and good. If you haven't, then I want the money, all fifty-pounds, three-shillings, and fourpence of it.'

Digweed suddenly marched down onto the doorstep, so that he was standing there menacingly in front of Cale, his hands curled into fists, his shoulders all squared like a roadblock. His eyes not red anymore but blazing as if on fire. 'Why are you here, boy? What's behind this?'

'I don't understand,' Cale said.

'Your father, lad, your father! Why did he send you here to do his dirty work for him? Why didn't he come over here himself, if he wants that money so bad?'

'He's away on business,' Cale said, wanting to shrink but standing firm. In his head he heard Edward Coates say, *You may be young, but you come across as mature and confident,* and that made Cale stand a little firmer. 'He might be away for some time, and so I just wanted to make sure that everything was in order.'

'Away, is he?' Digweed said, picking up on that, and now a strange, twisted smile crossed his lips. He put a hand up to the side of his mouth and called out across the garden: 'Did you hear that, Cynthia? Lover Boy is away on business? How about that, eh?'

Lover Boy?

Cale turned and saw Cynthia Digweed coming across the lawn. Her steps were plodding, reluctant almost, but she came, anyway, perhaps because she could no longer bear to see, and hear, her husband amusing himself with what was, after all, just a boy, and a boy at that who was completely in the dark.

Lover Boy? What did that mean? Cale wondered.

Like many people who hear news they don't wish to hear but know they have to, no matter what, Cale began to understand what had been happening here, as if it were coming to him through a thick, soupy fog. *Lover Boy.* He took another glance at those long, lovely legs of Cynthia Digweed's, and suddenly pictured his father lying between them, thrusting, thrusting, thrusting, and he wanted to block that picture out, and immediately. The more he tried, though, so the more colourful and detailed the picture became, until he saw Cynthia Digweed naked, his father naked, the two of them going at it like rabbits. Horrible. Yucky. Yet quite clearly it had been a reality, the way that Brian Digweed's pain was quite clearly a reality.

'You hear that?' Digweed went on. 'Lover Boy's away on business! What do you think of that?'

'I heard,' Cynthia Digweed said, her voice tiredly quiet. 'I think the whole *world* must have heard.' There was no outrage in her voice, though. She sounded the way she looked: tired...and perhaps a little bored. And what was that on her face? As she approached, and the brim of her straw hat became a little less useful at keeping away the shadows, so Cale saw a plump, yellowy bruise under her left eye. A swelling, too, at the corner of her mouth. One that was split by a cut that was beginning to heal but was still evident.

Digweed turned back to Cale. His eyes, which had been blazing with anger, now blazed with a mad, wallowing cruelty. 'How much do you think my wife is worth, lad? How much?' He suddenly thrust out a hand, grabbed his wife's upper arm, and pulled her towards him. She uttered a frightened little cry. 'How much, boy? Nice legs, wouldn't you say? Nice tits, too.' He grabbed one and squeezed it, roughly. 'Want a feel, do you, like your father had a feel? Why not? Just about *anyone* can have a feel, if they want!'

'Stop it, Brian, stop it!' Cynthia Digweed said, her large brown eyes beginning to mist over.

'Why should I?' Brian Digweed said, turning to his wife. 'I wanted *you* to stop it, didn't I? But you wouldn't, you damn well wouldn't! Just wanted to make a fool of me in front of the whole town!'

'No one knew about it, Brian, I told you that! No one *knew!*'

'How much?' Digweed asked, turning back to Cale. He snatched the estimate out of Cale's hand, read it, and then glared at Cale with eyes so sad and crazy it was hard for Cale to look at them and not feel a little sad and crazy himself. 'You think she's worth fifty-pounds, three-shillings and four-pence? I don't! I wouldn't give you a penny for her! Not one...single...penny!' The hand clutching the estimate was trembling, and trembling so much that the piece of paper made jerky, rustling noises. Digweed's eyes, like his wife's, now brimmed with tears. His breathing was so rapid that Cale thought he could see his heart drumming away under his shirt, *bang-bang-bang-bang-bang*, as quick as little Tommy's gabbling, runaway speech. 'Tell your father that I've already paid this bill,' Digweed snarled. 'Tell him I've paid for it, not with cash, but with my marriage! You tell him that! You tell him!'

Cale nodded his head. All of a sudden the money meant nothing to him, he could not, in fact, care less for it. Just wanted to get out of here, and swiftly. 'I'm sorry that I troubled you, Mr. Digweed,' he said. 'I didn't know. I truly didn't.'

'I'm sure you didn't!' Digweed said, spittle flying off his lips. 'I bet there's a lot of things you don't know about that father of yours! A lot of things!' He scrunched the estimate up and tossed it away.

'Brian, please, no more, just don't say any more, please, please, please!' Cynthia Digweed looked like a woman not just on the brink of tears, but on the brink of wetting her pants. 'No more, Brian, I beg you!'

'It's okay, Mrs Digweed,' Cale said. He was shocked at the sight of Cynthia Digweed's bruises, shocked at her distress, as well, but not exactly surprised by any of it. He had lived with all that...and more. Much more. Ewan Redstone had been the all-time champion when it came to battering people and scaring the shit out of them. 'Your husband is right. There probably *are* a lot of things that I don't know about my father. After all, I didn't know about this, did I?'

She suddenly gaped at Cale. Brian Digwood gaped, as well. He was still breathing hard, his face was still bunched, and his eyes were still on fire, but the flames did not seem quite so hot now. Still hot. But not roasting. And his hands were not fists anymore. They began to slowly unfold until they were just a regular pair of hands.

'Don't look so amazed,' Cale said. 'My father is my father, and so I won't run him down to anyone else who isn't family. However, if he had an affair with you, Mrs Digweed, then I can't stand by him for that. I see marriage as a sacred thing, you see. I know that must sound sort of odd, coming from the mouth of a baby like me, but I suppose that's because I'm nothing much like my father, anyway. When I get married, it will be for good, and I will never stray. Not ever.'

Brian Digweed wanted to laugh. Cale could see it in his face, cracks that appeared, just for a second, and then closed again. 'Are you really Ewan Redstone's son?' he asked, staring at Cale as if examining him. 'You can't be. Surely not.'

'I am…but please don't tar me with the same brush. I came here simply to enquire about a bill that may or may not have been paid. I didn't come here to cause you and your wife any more trouble. I can see you've had enough of that already. I'm sorry.'

Brian Digweed nodded his head, then gazed down at the ground. When he raised his head again, he looked almost normal, as if the demon gnawing away at his soul had been cast out. He swiped a wrist across his watering eyes, and said, 'All of a sudden I feel terrible, just terrible. I shouldn't have shouted at you like that. It's none of your business, this trouble between your father and I. Will you shake my hand?'

'Yes,' Cale said. He paused. 'On one condition.'

'The money? I'll pay it.'

'I don't want the money,' Cale said. 'Not any more.'

'Then what do you want?' Cynthia Digweed asked, looking confused.

'For both of you to promise me that you won't throw away your marriage because of my father,' Cale said. 'He's not worth it, believe me, he isn't. Furthermore, while we're on the subject of promises, I think I can make one to you: that you won't see my father again.'

'How can you make a promise like that?' Brian Digweed asked, looking even more confused than his wife did. He also looked hopeful, absurdly hopeful, like Cale was building a bridge over a gap that just a few minutes ago Digweed had seen as impossible to span.

'Leave that to me,' Cale said. 'But you can take my word for it that you won't see him anymore.' He turned to Cynthia Digweed, who was now looking up at Cale as if he had come from another planet. Another *galaxy*, maybe. 'How do you feel about that, Mrs Digweed?'

'Well, it's...' She began, and she stuttered a little, and then she started again. 'Well, it's over with your father, that's the truth of it, and I can't say it was much of an affair to begin with, anyhow. Not really. Just something that happened...and shouldn't have.'

'You don't have to do this,' Brian Digweed said, letting go of his wife's arm, and then slipping his hand gently around her waist. 'You don't want to embarrass the boy, Cynth.'

'*Am* I embarrassing you?' Cynthia Digweed said, staring up at Cale in that oddly spellbound way of hers. 'I hope not.'

'No, you're not,' Cale said. 'Your husband, though. For his sake, maybe you should keep this kind of talk just between yourselves. It is kind of personal, don't you think?'

'Yes, I suppose it is.'

'And all I wanted, anyway, was to know how you'd feel if you didn't see my father around anymore? Would it be good, or would it be bad?'

'It would suit me just fine,' Cynthia Digweed said, leaning back against her husband and giving him one of those smiles that said that maybe they could work this out after all. Not exactly lovey-dovey, as smiles went, but Cale got the impression it would get there in the end.

'It would suit me just fine, as well,' Brian Digweed agreed, and his hand crept around his wife's waist a little further, all the way around to her tummy, in fact, and he pulled her close to his chest. 'What did you *do* with him, lad? Hit him over the head and bury him somewhere?'

They all laughed at that, Cale more than anyone. Cale laughed, as a matter of fact, until there was a stitch starting up in his side and he had to make himself stop before it got any worse. 'Very good, Mr.

Digweed. Very witty. Seriously, though, he'll be working up in Templeton for a long, long time. He might even stay up there for good. It's a possibility.'

'Let's hope it's a possibility that becomes a reality,' Digweed said. 'What about Redstone Joinery?'

'It's in my hands now,' Cale said, 'although I'd rather you didn't shout that from the rooftops. I don't want people around here thinking that Redstone Joinery will be a soft-touch because it's now being run by an eighteen-year-old.'

'Oh, I'm sure no one would think that,' Cynthia Digweed said. 'In fact, with you in charge, business will probably boom!'

'Indeed!' Brian Digweed chimed.

'Stop it, you're embarrassing me,' Cale said, holding up his hands. 'I'm just glad this didn't end up in fisticuffs on the lawn. For a moment there, I thought it would.'

'Now I'm the who's embarrassed,' Brian Digweed said, the red beginning to flow up out of his shirt collar and clench his face like burning moss. 'I did sort of get all heated up there, didn't I?'

'He always gets heated up,' Cynthia Digweed said. 'All men do from time to time, don't they...?'

'It's Cale.'

'Cale,' Cynthia Redstone said.

'Cale,' Brian Digweed said. He smiled and stuck out his free hand.

'You have to promise me first, remember?' Cale reminded them both. 'Promise me that you won't throw away your marriage?'

'Oh yes,' Digweed said. He glanced down at his wife, and rather tenderly, too. 'I'm sure, given time, that we can work things out, don't you think, Cynth?'

'Yes, I'm sure we can.'

'Okay then, I promise,' Digweed said.

'And you, Mrs Digweed?'

'I promise, as well,' she said.

'Great!' Cale said. He shook Brian Digweed's hand, and there were smiles all round, large, relieved smiles. The situation had been defused. Yet Cale couldn't quite keep his eyes off Cynthia Digweed's pale and still nervous face…and the plump, yellowy bruise under her left eye…and the swelling at the corner of her mouth, the cut there healing but still fairly discoloured…and the way her blouse had been pulled out of shape around the breast that her husband had grabbed so roughly.

'Mr Digweed?'

'Yes?'

'Can we have a word, do you think? In private, over by my truck?'

'Of course we can. No problem.' Digweed seemed a little unwilling to take his hand off his wife's waist, though, and the fact she was gawping up at him with eyes starting to fill with love, and perhaps with lust, made it all the harder for him to let her go. But he did. Finally he did. He let her go, his fingers slowly trailing down her hip, and then he was standing next to Cale, ready to walk up the drive, over to the truck.

'Nice to meet you, Mrs Digweed,' Cale said.

'Nice to meet you, too, Cale. And thank you.' She gave him an acutely grateful look, as if Cale had pulled off a minor miracle, the minor miracle being that Cale had somehow calmed her husband down, and so there was something close to awe in her eyes, as well. An awe that for the most part saddened Cale. So pretty, this woman. Unmistakably intelligent, too. Yet she seemed almost woozy with the prospect that she and her husband would likely patch up their differences and have another stab at their marriage. Fine. That wasn't Cale's business. Not strictly, anyhow. He had intervened purely because he couldn't bear to think of his low-life father being responsible for a couple parting company. All the same, if Cynthia Digweed didn't mind being used as a punchbag from time to time, then there was nothing Cale could do about that. He wasn't a marriage guidance counsellor, for goodness' sake. Nonetheless, the fact remained that he had seen too much of that slap-happy stuff being doled out to his mother, and to Tommy. It was hard for him to just stand back and let it go.

'Cheerio,' he said to Mrs Digweed, smiling. He nodded at Brian

Digweed, and together they walked up the drive, out of the gate. Digweed swung the gate shut, and now Cale and he were standing between the truck's front nearside wheel and the high, neatly-trimmed privet hedge that bounded the Digweeds' property. Nice and quiet here. Secluded. No prying eyes.

'If it's about the money, then I told you that I'm happy to pay it,' Digweed said, looking nonchalantly up at a sun that was now warm and bright, as it had been yesterday. 'No trouble about that whatsoever.'

'I'm sure,' Cale said. 'What I'd like, though, Mr Digweed, is to take my payment in another way.' He clarified this, not with words, but with a sudden, hard punch to Brian Digweed's midsection. *Whump!* And Digweed, who'd still been gazing up at the sun, let out an *ooof!* noise, and promptly sank to the ground on one knee. You know how a deckchair will simply fold up if you don't put it up just right? That's how Brian Digweed went down. Like a deckchair.

He began to cough and splutter.

'Don't hit your wife,' Cale calmly told him, and then he blew on his knuckles the way cowboys do on their guns, after firing them. 'My old man used to hit my mother, until she could stand it no longer and walked out on him. Don't let that happen, Mr Digweed. Take good care of your wife. Who knows? She might just take good care of you and find no need anymore to seek comfort in the arms of other men. You get my drift?'

Digweed, clutching his stomach, did not look up or say anything, just nodded his head. Probably *couldn't* say anything anyhow, he was coughing and spluttering that much…and making horrible, gargling noises, too, as if he were about to puke. Under his dark but thinning hair, his scalp gleamed a bright, stoplight red. His shoulders were shaking. His shirt had come untucked and lay in a ruffle around his hips.

'Well, all right then,' Cale said. That was all he had to say, and do, on the matter. Short and sharp - the best and most efficient cure. He opened the truck's door and got inside. Started the engine. And off he drove. He looked in the rear-view mirror and saw Brian

Digweed, still down on one knee, suffocating just about in a thick, brown cloud of exhaust fumes.

Good. Very good indeed. The prick.

Chapter 6: Thank You for the Trees

How many other woman had Ewan Redstone messed around with? Cale wondered. Just Cynthia Digweed? Or had there been others?

And did it matter? Did it really?

No, Cale supposed it didn't. If he gave the subject elbow room, he'd just be giving it a weight it didn't deserve. His father was gone now, anyway, he was out of their lives, out of he and Tommy's lives. What was more, he had spoiled a big enough chunk of their lives already, without spoiling it beyond the grave.

His messing around days were over. Brian and Cynthia Digweed had perhaps not believed that completely, even though they had been willing to accept the notion as far as they *could* accept it. In time, though, they would accept it, and completely: Ewan Redstone's messing around days were indeed over.

For good.

No doubt about it.

Cale drove into town and bought two bags of groceries, the bags mostly filled with fresh fruit and vegetables, which Tommy had seen little of over the past few years, and it was a wonder the poor lad didn't have scurvy, Cale thought. He bought a watch, too, to the replace the one he had given to Tommy. Yesterday, he could have taken his father's watch off his wrist and worn that, as his father wouldn't be needing it anymore, but the idea of wearing an item of his father's so close to his skin…well, it frankly disgusted him, and so he had buried the watch along with him.

On his way back home, just outside of town, Cale heard a horn honk behind him. He looked in the rear-view mirror and saw a car weaving around, a car whose headlights were flashing, too. A car that was black and shiny. Sergeant Don Willoughby's Humber Sceptre.

Cale pulled over. Got out of the truck. Behind him, Willoughby had pulled over, as well, but he did not get out. Not right away. Too busy putting that cap of his on straight. Perfectly straight. Once it was, he then got out, but he did not walk over. Just stood there, indecisive.

'How's it going, Cale?'

'Fine,' Cale said. He began to walk over to Willoughby, but Willoughby abruptly thrust out his hands, and then began to take panicky, retreating steps.

'Don't come any nearer!' he said. 'Not until I know it's safe!'

All of a sudden Cale began to believe that Willoughby knew something. He couldn't know anything, he simply couldn't, but now that the seed of doubt had been planted in Cale's head, it began to flourish there and prickle the corners of his brain. His heart began to race. His scalp tightened. His vision blurred until there were multiple Don Willoughby's standing before him, overlapping one another.

But of course the chances were this had nothing to do with Cale's father...and everything to do with Brian Digweed. Possibly Digweed had flagged Willoughby down, had told him about how Cale had punched him, and now Willoughby was here to get Cale's side of the story.

'I'm talking about you and your father's health,' Willoughby explained. 'Do you and he have a cold, a bug, whatever, after all, or are you clean?'

Cale stopped ten feet from Willoughby, who was still on the retreat, and now almost up by the rear of his car. His shadow stretched along the road, all the way up to the very tip of Cale's boots. 'Jesus,' Cale said, relieved. 'I didn't know what you meant right then. My health?' He laughed nervously. 'My health is fine. So is my dad's.'

'No colds, no flu, no nothing, then?'

'Nothing,' Cale said. 'We just felt under the weather, that's all.'

'Thank God for that,' Willoughby said, dropping his hands. 'The last thing I need right now is an illness. I'm up to my armpits in this business with the con-merchants.'

'Oh yeah, the con-merchants,' Cale said, beginning to relax, but so slowly that his heart continued to race and his sight was still blurry. 'How's it going? Any progress?'

'Some,' Willoughby said, 'but not enough. I'll nail them, though, you bet I will. Sooner or later I'll come across them, and when I do, it'll be wham!' - he slapped a fist into his palm, sharply - 'I'll have them behind bars as quick as that.'

'I'm sure you will,' Cale said. 'You're a man not to be dissuaded.'

'You're right there,' Willoughby agreed. 'I am indeed a man not to be dissuaded. I didn't get these stripes here off a cornflake packet.' With two fingers, he proudly tapped the three chevrons high up on his arm, those chevrons that indicated he was a sergeant, and deservedly so. He smiled. For a long time he smiled. Then: 'How *is* your dad, by the way? If you're on your way home, tell him I may pop over later for a chinwag.'

'Sorry, no chin-wagging today,' Cale said. 'Maybe not for a while.'

'Why's that?'

'Dad's gone up to Templeton. He got a phone-call last night, from a contractor wanting to put a whole lot of work his way. He must have offered dad a fair bit of money, too. He took off this morning on the train. Left me to run things at this end.'

'Did he?' Willoughby said. 'Well, you're a capable young man, I must say. I know because your father tells me that from time to time. Any idea when he'll be back?'

'No, but he said he'd phone tonight and let me know. I'll pass the message on, when I get it.'

'You do that,' Willoughby said. But then he looked distracted. Kind of fed-up all of a sudden, too. He put a hand up to his face, cupped his chin, and began to drum a finger against his jawbone.

'Something up?'

'It's nothing, Cale, nothing. I'd just be making a fuss for no good reason.'

'Tell me,' Cale said. 'If I can help, then I will.'

'Well, it's that business with the birds' shit,' Willoughby said. 'I found another splodge on the car this morning. Three splodges, actually: two on the bonnet and one on the roof. It's beginning to depress me.'

Willoughby *looked* depressed, too. Down in the mouth, the way most other men would only look if their wife had left them (or had perhaps come back) or their pet dog had died. There were signs of sleepless nights under his eyes, as well, the skin dark, puffy. Understandable, given that a disgraceful little crime was going on at the moment, and because Willoughby's mother was old and there was always the possibility she could be the next victim, he had taken it personally. But even that, Cale believed, was not the *real* reason why Willoughby's sleep had been scratchy of late. It was the birds, those Filthy Stinking Flying Shit Machines that just kept crapping on his car. Willoughby had taken *that* personally, too.

Like it was deliberate.

'What you want is the trees outside the station to be cut back, is that it?' Cale said.

'That's exactly it!' Willoughby said, snapping immediately out of his depressed state. He pointed a finger at Cale. 'That's exactly it, with big jangly bells on! Not *all* the trees, though, you understand. Just the ones that overhang the parking bays. I'd get a tree surgeon to do the job, but there's only one in Unity Gate, Trevor Somerville, and he's working out of town at the moment. Just like your father. What do you say, Cale? You reckon you could do it? I'll pay.'

'I don't want money,' Cale said. 'You're a friend of the family.'

'Christ, but you're a good lad,' Willoughby said, clapping Cale on the shoulder. 'I've heard people say you're a dick, but I don't happen to think you are. Why? Because dicks are useful, that's why. That's a joke, by the way.'

'Nearly,' Cale said.

By mid-afternoon Cale had cut back the trees. It took him an hour, that was all, all of it done with an old saw that was in the back of the truck, along with a hammer and a stiff broom.

He dumped the severed branches outside the police station, next to the rubbish bins. He heard the blast of a car horn then, and glanced around at the road that ran past the station. What he saw was little Tommy on that death-trap bike of his, swerving to avoid an oncoming car. Tommy on his way back from summer school…and riding like a maniac.

'That boy's going to kill himself one day!' Cale said. He dropped the last of the branches on the pile and ran towards the road. The car, a pale-yellow Ford Anglia driven by a woman in a bright-green hat, pulled over. She leaned out of the window, raised her fist, and shook it at Tommy. The boy did not see this, however. Red-faced, he just went on racing up the road. Then he was gone.

Cale came to a halt some way short of the Anglia - he had no wish to associate himself with this incident. Moreover, he had no wish to associate himself with the woman, who looked about ready to knock someone's head off, if anyone so much as came near her. She seemed thoroughly hot and bothered under the stiff angles of her hat.

Furthermore, if she discovered that Cale was Tommy's brother, she'd probably not only knock Cale's head off, but give him a lecture on why the boy ought to be given cycling lessons. Which was not such a bad idea, Cale thought. Lessons: the boy could take lessons. And the purchase of a new bike was in the offing, was it not? Absolutely no chance of Cale letting Tommy loose on a new bike that he might just wrap around a tree on its maiden run. No chance whatsoever.

He turned and went back to the station. Grabbed the broom out of the back of the truck and began to sweep up. Thinking about lessons. Thinking also that when he got back home, he was going to give Tommy hell for the way he rode that bike of his.

All of a sudden Don Willoughby's Humber swept into the car park. Somewhat untidily, too. Brakes squealing. It came to a shuddering halt at an angle. Not in one parking bay or another. Intersecting two.

Willoughby got out. Pretty much *stumbled* out. Caring not this time that his cap was on nice and straight. The cap was not even on his head, but in his hand. His other hand, meanwhile, was clapped to his forehead.

Blood was running through his fingers.

Cale dropped the broom and rushed over to him. 'What happened, Sergeant Willoughby? Christ, what happened?' Cale's eyes darted to the car, hunting for signs that Willoughby's shiny Humber was not so shiny anymore but crumpled somewhere, where it had been involved in a smash-up. Or perhaps he had swerved, the way the driver of the Anglia had swerved to avoid Tommy coming the other way, and he had driven the Humber into the side of a building.

Tommy, oh good God! When Cale got home, he was really going to let rip at that brother of his.

'The bastards,' Willoughby groaned in a thick, muzzy voice. 'I caught up with them, Cale. I caught up with the con-merchants. Three in total. Dressed in black leather jackets, they were. Rings in their ears. Dark, curly hair, too. Gypsies, I reckon. They jumped me. Coshed me over the head and left me lying in the road.'

'Crikey, where was this?' Cale asked.

'Up the hill, past Walnut Grove.'

'Are you hurt anywhere else?'

'No.'

'Then let's get you inside,' Cale said, putting an arm around Willoughby's waist and leading him towards the station. His tunic, normally so immaculate, was dusty at the back, Cale noticed. His trousers were a little damp in places, too, as if he'd fallen on his knees into a puddle.

Cale and Willoughby took no more than four steps, and then two constables came clattering down the steps. One was handsome but with a bad case of pimples, while the other was as ugly as sin but with skin as smooth as silk.

'Here, mind out the way,' the ugly one said to Cale.

'Yep, we'll take over,' the handsome one said, and all of a sudden Cale was relegated to just a spectator. The constables supported

Willoughby, one either side, and walked him up the steps into the station. Willoughby's chin was now sagged down on his chest, his blood spotting the car park as if large drops of red rain had begun to fall.

Cale stood there for a moment, and then picked up his broom. Began to sweep up the last of the leaves and twigs. He half-expected a load of policemen to come pouring out of the building, on their way up to Walnut Grove, to see if they could catch the offenders. Gypsies, Willoughby had said, although Cale doubted they would be genuine *Romany* Gypsies. Romany Gypsies were decent people, he'd been led to believe, people who wouldn't hit anyone with anything unless provoked.

No policemen came out, though. Just...nothing

Nothing at all.

Cale put the broom back in his truck. Slapped the dirt off his hands. Then he walked up into the station, which was a flat-roofed building with two large, blue lamps either side of its double doors. He went inside, but not before wiping his boots on the mat provided; he'd been climbing trees, of course, and his boots were filthy.

There was a constable behind the reception desk who reminded Cale somewhat of the actor Sid James: the pruned skin, the wiry, corrugated hair. He was holding a pen and making notes. It was hot in here, pretty much sweltering. The windows behind the constable were open, but the aperture was filled with vertical metal bars. Through the bars, Cale could see a small courtyard in which was a wooden bench and a few pots that thronged with flowers. Nice. A place, Cale supposed, that the men, and perhaps the women, drank coffee, smoked cigarettes, and had a chit-chat during their breaks.

The constable was wearing a white shirt with the sleeves rolled up. When Cale walked in, he looked up but said nothing. Not right then, anyhow.

Cale ambled across the tiled floor, which no doubt had been spotted with more of Willoughby's blood, and so someone had mopped the floor and now it shone wetly and smelled tartly of disinfectant. He went up to the notice board and looked at the notices pinned there. There seemed to be notices about everything imaginable, but nothing on what he needed.

The constable suddenly asked: 'So, how did it go with the trees? All done?'

'Yes, all done,' Cale said, turning around and smiling shyly. 'There should be no more trouble with the birds.'

'Only the Sarge has trouble with the birds,' the constable said. 'Birds are just birds. They have to do their business somewhere, don't they? Ever seen a bird with a roll of toilet paper under its wing?'

'Can't say I have,' Cale said, wanting to snigger but holding it back, just in case the constable had not been making a joke, exactly, more a serious comment on Willoughby's fussiness, which of course could be a real bone of contention in this place. 'How *is* Sergeant Willoughby, by the way?'

'He'll live,' the constable said. He's out the back being patched up by a young constable. A young *female* constable. WPC Jenkins. Nice-looking.' He put his pen down and looked up. 'You're Ewan Redstone's boy, right?'

'Right.'

'How is the rascal?'

The rascal, Cale thought. Such a flattering term for a man who had killed his wife and who had then spent the next five years inviting his youngest son to chose between Hospital or Death. Then there was the fact that on many an occasion he had been banged up, overnight, in a cell in this place for fighting in public houses. Mustn't forget that. The rascal.

'He's fine,' Cale said. 'Up in Templeton. Working.'

'Is he now? And he left you to run the show, did he?'

'Yes.'

The constable nodded. Picked up his pen. Went back to writing. On his desk, propped against a vase, was a framed photograph of Bobby Moore, the England Football Team captain, holding aloft the Jules Rimet Trophy: the World Cup, of course.

Cale looked around. To his left was a green corridor with a polished dado rail running at waist height along the walls. A *dildo* rail, his father had called them. Funny, ho-ho-ho. Three doors, he could see, as well. One marked Interview Room # 1, the other marked Detention Room. Then there was Willoughby's office at the far end. Beyond that would be the cells, Cale presumed. A couple of other rooms, as well, no doubt. Interview Room # 2 would be down there somewhere, he supposed - as there was a # 1, there was bound to be a # 2. And still he could see no one readying themselves to go out and look for the people who had done this to poor old Willoughby. No one at all. Strange.

Cale turned back to the constable, and said, 'It's none of my business, I know, but shouldn't people be out there looking for Sergeant Willoughby's attackers?'

The constable put his pen back down. A fountain pen, it was: silver-topped with a gold nib. He looked up, and said, 'Let me tell you something, lad. I think you've been watching too many episodes of *Z Cars* and *Dixon of Dock Green*. This place here is just a piddling rural sub-station. There's me, an old fart just three years away from collecting his pension. Then there's Constable Thornley, Constable Arkwright, WPC Jenkins, and finally there's the Sarge. You've seen me. You've seen Thornley, I'm sure. Can't miss him. He's the one with the pimples. You've seen Arkwright, and you've seen the Sarge. You think between us we could tackle three men armed with coshes? Who might even be armed with *guns*?'

'You think they might have guns?' Cale asked.

'It's a possibility,' the constable said. 'That's why we've called in the Heavy Mob.'

'The Heavy Mob?'

'They're the boys up at the main station in Upperlands.' He glanced up at the clock above the notice board. 'They'll be here in, oh, twenty minutes, I reckon. Then you might see some action. After they've spoken to the Sarge, of course. Taken the details off him.'

Cale nodded. 'Maybe the Sarge - I mean Sergeant Willoughby - maybe he shouldn't have gone after those men in the first place. Not on his own, anyway.'

'There's a truth to that,' the constable said. 'But the Sarge is not a man…' He stood there, trying to think of a way to finish his sentence.

'To be dissuaded?' Cale offered.

'Very good,' the constable said, nodding. 'A man not to be dissuaded. I like that. I was about to say he is not a man who can stay out of trouble, but under the circumstances, a "man not to be dissuaded" is probably a little more kinder.'

Up with the pen. A bit more writing. Down with the pen. 'So why are you hanging around here, anyway, son? Waiting to *see* the Sarge, are you?'

Cale nodded at the notice board. 'Mostly I was hoping to find something here on cycling proficiency. Any courses being run in the near future, do you know?'

'There could be,' the constable said. 'Who needs the lessons?'

'My brother. He rides a bike like a bad circus act.'

The constable smiled. 'Tell you what. I'll leave a note here for the Sarge, telling him to get in touch with you. Does he have your phone-number?'

'Yes, he has both, for home and for the workshop.'

'Well, that's fine then, isn't it?' the constable said. He picked up his pen, lowered his head, and once again returned to scratching away in his notepad.

Cale stood there for a short while. In the end, he said, 'Give Sergeant Willoughby my regards, would you? Tell him I hope he gets better soon.'

'I'll do that.'

Cale turned. Began to walk out. It was then that Willoughby appeared, along with PC Thornley (he of the pimples) and WPC Jenkins who, even in her uniform, was just as nice-looking as the old constable had said: big brown eyes and a small, button nose.

She, along with Thornley, went up to the desk and began to quietly talk with the old constable, who again had to put his pen down and refrain from writing. As for Willoughby, he walked up to Cale, indicated that he would like to step outside, and so they did. They stepped outside and into the blistering heat.

There was a large, gauze pad on Willoughby's forehead, just above his right eye, held in place with a bandage. No blood seeping through the pad, but Cale, nonetheless, could see a coffee-coloured coin of darkness underneath it. Blood, perhaps. Or iodine. Or maybe a mixture of the two.

Willoughby's cap was tucked under his left arm. He looked odd without it on his head, Cale thought. Sort of pathetic. Like a court-marshalled soldier. His hair poked up, here and there, as if he'd just gotten out of bed after a heavy night on the drink. The lights in his eyes were on, but they did not exactly shine. Just two dim bulbs, really.

'How are you feeling?' Cale asked, his voice low and considerate.

'A little sore,' Willoughby said. 'A little *embarrassed*, too.'

'Why embarrassed?'

'I was out of my depth, Cale. I shouldn't have gone looking for those men in the first place. Betts told me that. He's the constable on the desk. The somewhat *wise* constable. At least he likes to think so. He told me I'd get into trouble, if I went out on my own, and I did. I should have called in the Heavy Mob right at the start of all this.'

'Well, I just happen to think you were very brave,' Cale said. 'Never might old Constable Betts in there. Some people just sit back and let things happen. I know about such things. I sat back myself one time, and I regret doing that. But I did something about it in the end. Oh yes I did something, all right.'

Willoughby, with the middle finger of his right hand, had begun to tenderly rub the surface of the gauze pad, distracted, as if Cale had said nothing. And probably that was good. If Willoughby had been a little more attentive, he might just have pressed Cale about that time when he sat back, and then finally decided to do something. And what would Cale have said?

He would have lied, that's what. Would simply have invented something. Like how he eventually got off his backside and decided to ask a certain girl out to the pictures, instead of just admiring her from a distance. It would have been along those lines, anyhow.

'How do I look?' Willoughby asked, his vanity coming back to the fore, although it was fair to say that Don Willoughby's vanity was never far away from the fore, anyhow. Just like his cap, it was always in the neighbourhood somewhere, just waiting to be pulled on and squared. 'I look like a fool, I bet.'

'Nah, you could never look like a fool,' Cale said. 'What you look like is a police sergeant, and a courageous police sergeant, at that, who was assaulted in the course of his duty.'

Willoughby smiled as best he could, but it was slightly wan and staid. 'You're a kind lad, Cale. A kind lad indeed. And look at the trees!' he added, looking up and gazing around, his eyes becoming a little more brighter. 'You made a great job, I must say!'

'No more Filthy Stinking Flying Shit Machines,' Cale said. 'Not until the branches grow back, anyhow.'

'Well, that won't be for a while,' Willoughby said, and he seemed to be fine, seemed to be snapping out of his depression a little...and then he saw his car, his beloved Humber Sceptre, sitting there askew across two parking bays.

He began to grind his teeth together. He made a lengthy, rasping noise low down in his throat. He reached down and touched the long, thin pocket that ran up his trouser leg, the pocket in which he kept his truncheon. 'Let me tell you something, Cale. If I'd been given a little more time, I would have drawn this, and I would have beaten em with it, beaten em, beaten em, beaten em. Beaten all three of em to a pulp! Do you believe that? Do you?'

'Of course I do,' Cale said. 'You are not a man to be dissuaded.'

'You're damn right I'm not.' Willoughby suddenly spun around on his heels, and in jiffy, he whipped his hat out from under his arm, clamped it on his head, and squared it off. Never mind the gauze pad strapped to his head. He just squashed the cap down over it, and he didn't flinch, never mind groan, even though it must have hurt him to do that. The peak was now pulled down over his eyes, and it cast them into their usual, restful shadow. Restful for Willoughby, that was. For everyone else staring into that line of darkness, it was mostly unsettling. A little, anyhow. 'Let me tell you something else, as well, Cale.'

'What's that?'

Willoughby loomed over him like a schoolteacher, his chin jutting out, his jaw mashing. 'The Heavy Mob will be here in a short while.

Bells ringing, lights flashing, all of that palaver. You know what I think to that? Fuck em - that's what I think! Let's see how *they* get on with those rough-tough gypsy boys, shall we? Let's see if *they* come out of it without a scratch!'

'I'm sure they won't,' Cale said. 'I reckon some will get biffed over the bonce, just the way you did. Maybe *all* of them will.'

'That's what I think, too,' Willoughby said. 'That's *exactly* what I think. So good luck to them, eh? Good luck to them with - '

'Bells on?' Cale said.

'Yes, with bells on!' Willoughby agreed, nodding his head. 'With big loud clanging bells on!' He winked an eye at Cale, and Cale saw this, even though the peak of Willoughby's cap was almost touching the bridge of his nose. He winked an eye, and then he jerked his head to the side, a gesture that was meant to look chummy, but all it did was make Willoughby look like he had a nervous disorder. He winked his eye again, jerked his head. Did it again. And again. Four times in all, and then he straightened. After that he huffed, open-mouthed, on a tunic button and gave it a little polish with a shirt cuff. 'You know what, Cale? It seems that you and me, we are on the same wavelength, don't you think? Singing from the same hymn sheet, and all of that?'

'Yes, I suppose we are,' Cale said.

'No suppose about it, we are, we are!' Willoughby said. 'Just like your dad, you. He's something of a bad penny at times, I know, but he's always been there for me. That's the thing about your dad, he's always been there. And he always listens to what I have to say, as well. A good man is Ewan, by and large. Don't know where I'd be without him, actually.'

'Yes...well...I'd better be going,' Cale said, looking down at his boots. 'I'm in charge of Tommy at the moment while dad's away. And he can be a bit of a handful.'

'Anything I can do to help out?' Willoughby said, gazing around at the pruned trees. 'I owe you one, remember? You've only got to ask.'

'Well, there is something,' Cale said. 'I spoke to Constable Betts about it, while you were being patched up.'

'What's that?'

'Cycling proficiency,' Cale said. 'Any courses coming up?'

'Tommy, is it?'

'Yes.'

'A mad one on that bike of his, isn't he? All over the place.'

Cale nodded, and rather glumly. 'Outside here, on his way back from summer school, he nearly rode into an oncoming car. He's got no awareness. He needs to be sharpened up.'

'I'll see what I can do,' Willoughby said. Then, in a low and confidential voice: 'That bike of his, it's pretty duff, don't you agree? Barely roadworthy. And no lights or brakes.'

'It's a shambles,' Cale conceded. 'That's why I'm going to buy him a new one. There'll be a condition, though: that he learns to ride it properly.'

'Does your *father* know you're buying him a new bike?' Willoughby asked. 'Never known Ewan to spend money on Tommy.'

Right then, Cale looked up into Willoughby's face, and he wondered just what Willoughby knew. Could it even be possible that he knew Cale's father had murdered Cale's mother? Surely not. Yet he knew about Tommy, all right. Knew that money had seldom been spent on the boy. That could just be an observation, though, based on what Willoughby had seen. And just what *had* Willoughby seen during his friendship with Ewan Redstone? Had he seen how frightened Tommy had been around his father? Had he seen the bruises that showed up, every once in a while, on Tommy's arms and legs? Had he seen Tommy's clothes, virtually rags?

And did Cale want to torment himself with this, or what? Because that's exactly what he was doing, tormenting himself, the way he'd be tormenting himself if he thought any deeper about his father messing around, not just with Cynthia Digweed, but probably with other women, as well. Tormenting himself. *Pointlessly* tormenting himself. So he locked it off right there. Just shut the door on the subject and bolted it. What Willoughby knew, or didn't know, mattered not a whit anymore. It was time to look forward. Not backwards.

'No, my father doesn't know I'm buying Tommy a new bike,' Cale said. 'It's nothing to do with him, anyway. I'll be buying it out of my own money.'

'Oooo,' Willoughby said, jokingly offended. 'Quite the little independent, aren't we?'

'Sometimes you have to be,' Cale said. 'No choice in the matter.'

'I don't know what you mean by that, precisely,' Willoughby said. 'But good on you, anyway, Cale. You buy the bike. It's your money. You can do what you damn well please-y. And about the cycling proficiency? I'll find out about it and let you know. The constable who runs the course, his name is Barrows, or Burrows, something like that. He operates out of the main station in Upperlands. Tours the schools at certain times. I'll try and find out when the next tour is.'

'Thanks,' Cale said. 'That would mean a lot to me.'

'I can see it would,' Willoughby said. Willoughby, who was becoming more like the Willoughby that Cale recognised, not the one who'd been hit over the head and left bleeding in the road up by Walnut Grove. 'My, but you're growing up, Cale, and so fast! Seems like yesterday that you were just a boy!'

That's because I was, Cale thought, and then three cars came racing into the car park. They screeched and smoked to a halt. Men jumped out, some in uniform, others in plain-clothes. Doors were slammed, *bang, bang, bang,* with a timing that made Cale think of shotguns going off.

'I'd better go and greet these fellows,' Willoughby said to Cale from the corner of his mouth. 'No doubt I'll be in hot water for single-handedly tackling the gang that did this to me.' He touched his cap at the place under which was the gauze pad that pretty WPC Jenkins had applied to his wound. 'See you later, Cale. I'll be in touch. And thank you for the trees.'

'That's okay,' Cale said, and off he went to his truck. *Thank you for the trees,* he thought.

To him it sounded like the title of a hymn: Thank You for the Trees.

Martin Price

Chapter 7: Of Mice and Men

The truck was a big old thing with a bull-nose front and a glazing-bar up the centre of its windscreen. A huge exhaust pipe, too, that created as much pollution as an open sewer, along with a steering-wheel as big an ocean liner's. And there was Cale, sitting behind it, the truck rumbling out of town, into the country, but with Cale unable to enjoy the view because he was thinking about something his father said yesterday during the protracted throes of his death: that Tommy would become a liability to Cale, that he would, in fact, trouble Cale more than a yapping dog that wouldn't stop pissing on the floor.

There was a chance that prophesy might come true, as well. At the time Cale had been aware of that, completely aware, but what Ewan Redstone had failed to understand was that Tommy, despite his disabilities, was essentially just a normal eleven-year-old kid. Excitable, yes. Dramatic, yes. A short attention span, yes. Jabbered too much, as well, only with Tommy it was like listening to a record being played at the wrong speed.

Still just a normal kid, though, when you got right down to it. Not exactly a monster from Outer Space. And how many kids could cycle on the public highway, anyhow, without irritating some driver or pedestrian somewhere along the way? Not many. Kids were just kids. They were the sudden, playful breeze that blew your newspaper inside-out. Or the ice you slipped on and bashed your head. Or the shower of rain that snuffed out your bonfire. But kids just the same. Mostly just a rash on the back of your neck that itched every once in a while, but that was all.

Even so, over the coming weeks, Cale would have to shape the boy into something he could send out into the world and be more or less confident he would come back in one piece and not be dragging a whole load of trouble in his wake. And the cycling proficiency course would be a start. A big start.

For the time being, however, Cale just wanted to know that Tommy had made it home safely, that he hadn't gotten himself into another tangle further up the road somewhere, the consequences of which might well be a lot more serious than just some hot and bothered woman shaking a fist at him.

No broken bones, please - that's what Cale was thinking. No broken bones. Not today. Not ever. Broken bones would mean hospital, another kind of hospital, not the pet-name of a certain brutal man's left fist, but the place in which physical repairs were made...and then would come the questions. The names of the boy's parents, please? And if no parents, then the name of his guardian? The address? The telephone number? And the questions would go on like that, becoming deeper and more complex, until Cale would find himself in a corner he wouldn't be able to get out of.

A visit to the doctor would be okay, just as long as Tommy wasn't seriously ill. A visit to the dentist would be okay, as well, all the time Tommy's teeth were in good order and no major work needed to be done. Not the hospital, though. If Tommy ever had to be hospitalised, then that would be that. Cale would simply have to confess to everything...and where would that lead? For Cale it would lead to jail, or borstal at the very least. For Tommy it would mean spending the rest of his youth in care or with foster parents. Or maybe he'd just be dumped in the special needs school over in Battenford after all, and then pretty much forgotten. Not even a family of any kind to come home to...and that was not an option Cale cared to think about. Therefore, it was not just about Cale's *shaping* the boy, it was also about making him understand that he had to be responsible...if only for the time when he was out of the house. In the house, and Cale could take over. But outside? That was a different matter altogether.

He put all that to one side, though, when he parked the truck and went into the workshop. Here was Tommy, safe and well, and moreover, he was not in the house watching the television, but out here, in the little office, minding the phone. *Responsibly* minding the phone. All at once the boy's near miss with the Ford Anglia didn't seem to matter so much. The cycling proficiency, either. He didn't even tell Tommy about how Sergeant Willoughby had been hit over the head, and in a little town like this, that was big news.

The fact that Cale had punched Brian Digweed in the stomach was not such big news. Just regrettable, for the most part. And Cale found it remarkably easy, not just to put that to one side, but to forget all about it. One of those awkward little incidents that happened from time to time, they shouldn't, but often they did.

'Hi Cale how's it going?' Tommy asked. He was drinking a bottle of lime-flavoured fizzy pop that looked to Cale like some mad scientist's brew. Chomping on a chocolate bar, too. Sitting in his father's chair also, which was tipped back on its rear legs and resting against the wall.

'Hi, Tom,' Cale said. In his arms were the grocery bags, overflowing with fruit and vegetables. He put them down on the desk. Then he squinted at Tommy, and doubtfully. 'Are you okay in that chair?'

'Why shouldn't I be Cale why?'

'It's dad's. I thought it might give you the willies.'

'Only that chair in the sitting room gives me the willies Cale.'

So here was the real reason why Tommy was out here and not in the sitting room, watching the television: that big brown leather armchair with the beer bottle rings on one arm and the cigarette burns in the other. Nothing to do with responsibility at all. Just Tommy scared to go into that room while their father's chair was still in there, and so he had come out here.

But maybe Cale was being a little hard on the boy. After all,

Tommy could just have sat in the kitchen, listening to the radio until Cale had returned, or ridden his bike around the backyard, or gone down to the common field at the bottom of their garden and mucked about in there to pass the time. His choices had been various, but he had chosen to sit in here and mind the phone. Didn't have to. But he had.

'Well, you'll be pleased to know that I've moved dad's chair out into Sad's Place,' Cale said. 'Did it this morning, straight after you went to school.'

'Thank God for that,' Tommy said, clearly relieved, and then he shrugged his shoulders, as if he didn't much care, anyhow. 'Anyway it's not like I wanted to watch the television or nothing.'

'Of course not,' Cale said. 'You'd rather help me out, wouldn't you?'

'That's right Cale that's right.'

'So, did you take any calls?'

'Three calls Cale three I wrote them down.' Tommy dropped his half-eaten chocolate bar into his lap. Reached out, his lips stained green with the lime and brown with the chocolate, and with a grubby hand, he turned a piece of note paper around so that it faced Cale.

The writing was poor, more than just a shade below standard for an eleven-year-old, but it was readable, all said and done. Three calls, all right. The writing may have been poor, but at least Tommy had had the good sense to jot down the callers' names, their addresses, and their telephone numbers.

'What did you say to these people, Tom?'

'That you'd call them back when you got home,' Tommy said.

'And they understood you?'

'I used this,' Tommy said, looking down at his watch. 'Tick tock I used the clock.' He gave Cale one of his brightest, lopsided grins. 'Did I do all right Cale did I?'

'You did great,' Cale said. 'Well done, Tommy. You've been a big help to me.'

'Have I Cale have I?'

'Yes.' But then Cale nodded down at Tommy's lap. 'You're not being much of a help to me eating a chocolate bar, though, are you? And drinking that sugary chemical shit, either? Here, eat this instead.' He produced a banana and gave it to Tommy. At the same time, he made him hand over the rest of the chocolate bar, which he did, and with no dispute. 'Where'd you get the money for a chocolate bar and the fizzy pop, anyhow?'

Tommy flushed and bowed his head. 'Off the kitchen table Cale I found some change on there this morning.'

'You should ask before you take,' Cale said. 'It's only good manners.'

'I'll ask the next time I promise.'

'All right, just make sure you do,' Cale said. He smiled, trying to relax a little. 'Anyway, how did it go at summer school today?'

Tommy looked up. 'It was good Cale fine no trouble.' He looked around then in an almost comically surreptitious way, his eyes flicking to the left, flicking to the right, just to make sure no one was around to hear what he had to say next. He put a finger over his lips and whispered: 'I kept my mouth shut about dad Cale not a word to anyone.'

'Wild horses wouldn't have dragged it out of you, right?'

'Right Cale wild horses not a chance.'

'That's just what I thought,' Cale said. He watched as the boy suddenly peeled the banana, his fingers a flashing blur, until four long flaps of yellow skin lay across his bunched hand, and then he began to eat the fruit. His head moving jerkily, he quickly bit into the banana. Began to quickly munch away at it, too, like one of those little marmosets in the South American jungle, his teeth clicking together, *clickety, click, click, click.*

When their father had been in charge around here, the opportunity for Tommy to pig-out on sugar rarely presented itself, but when Cale looked down into the waste basket under the desk, he saw several chocolate bar wrappers in there, and realised that Tommy had been making up for lost time with the piggiest pig-out of all.

On the desk was the bottle of lime-flavoured fizzy pop, its sides plastered with chocolate. Two red-and-white straws poked out of its mouth, bent and soggy. 'Let's have that, as well,' Cale said, pointing at the bottle, then turning his palm upwards and wagging his fingers back and forth. 'Give it here, Tom. I think you should stay off that stuff.'

'Why's that Cale why?'

'Because I don't want to be taking you to the dentist all the time,' was Cale's reply to that, and on its own, it was a good enough reason, anyhow. 'You keep drinking that stuff and soon you'll be eating with nothing but stumps.'

Tommy, again without dispute, pushed the bottle across the table towards Cale and Cale picked it up. Dumped it in the waste basket along with the half-eaten chocolate bar.

'How's the banana?'

'I like it Cale I like it.'

'Good. From now on choose fruit over chocolate, Tom. It's healthier.'

'I will Cale I will.'

Cale nodded his head. 'Now go indoors and clean yourself up, eh? Take these with you.' The moment Tommy finished eating the banana, Cale gave him the bags, although he had to wait a while, not just for Tommy to finish the banana, but for him to dump the skin in the waste basket. When Tommy had done that, he took the bags off Cale and began to walk away. He took just three steps, though, and then turned around, his eyes peering through the rumpled, frilly leaves of a cabbage. And Cale could see a strange, dreamy look in the boy's eyes that suddenly made him feel wary.

'What is it, Tom?'

'I've been thinking Cale.'

'About what?'

'About mum.'

'What about mum?'

'I thought maybe she could come back home now that dad's gone.'

'We don't have her address,' Cale said. 'Don't even know which town she lives in. She could be in Timbuktu for all we know.'

Tommy's eyes began to glitter in a way that suggested he was no one's fool. 'Maybe we could put an advert in the paper Cale what do you think?'

'Not such a bad idea,' Cale said. 'But what would we write? Two boys looking for their mother, Natalie Redstone? Would like her to come back home to number three Samuel Lane, Unity Gate? Sorry, Tom, but it wouldn't work. It just wouldn't.'

'It would it would it would!'

'No, it wouldn't,' Cale said. 'What if someone saw that advert, some nosy parker, and it got them thinking? It could happen, Tom. If the wrong person saw that advert, someone who knew we were being cared for by dad ...well, they might start thinking that something was wrong around here. And they'd be right, wouldn't they? After all, why would two boys whose mother ran off and left them five years ago be trying to get in contact with her?' He waved a hand at the boy. 'No, it's too dangerous. Much too dangerous.'

'Oh fiddlesticks!' Tommy said, stamping his feet like a four-year-old. 'How can we get mum back then? *You* think of something!'

'I *can't* think of anything,' Cale said. 'What do you want me to do, magic mum out of thin air? I can't do that, Tom. At the moment, I've got enough to think about, more than enough, and you're not helping me. Jesus, stop messing me around, would you? Dad's been out of our lives just a day and already you're giving me hell.'

A quiver beset the drooping corner of Tommy's lower lip. Tears dribbled over his lids and ran down his face, glistening there. He began to tremble, and the grocery bags began to tremble with him. 'I'm sorry Cale I'm sorry really I'm sorry.'

'I should think so, too,' Cale said, still annoyed, but almost immediately he relented for Tommy's sake. After all, the boy had taken enough shit over the years and piling on a little more wouldn't help matters.

Cale relaxed his shoulders...as best he could, anyway; they were knotted and stiff with tension. Last night he hadn't slept well, had scarcely slept at all, in all honesty, thinking that if he drew back the curtains his father would be down there in the backyard, sitting in that chair of his, smoking a hand-rolled cigarette through the bloody hood of the pillowcase. And now here was Tommy kicking up a stink in the tradition of many kids who thought their troubles were greater than those of their elders and wanted to make that known as loudly and unreasonably as they could.

He went over to Tommy, put his arms around him, and around the grocery bags, as well, out of which poked carrots and bananas and oranges and green beans...and the cabbage, too, of course, in which all of Tommy's face was now buried, apart from his ears and the top of his forehead. The bags, made of heavy brown paper, made soft crinkling sounds.

'Look, I'm sorry as well,' Cale said. 'We've been through some hard times together over the years, and at the moment, we're going through another hard time. Not the same as it was when dad was here. No, God forbid, we don't want those times back. It's just a time of adjustment, that's what I'm saying. We've got to get used to another way of living, and we can't do that by upsetting each other, can we?'

'I didn't mean to upset you Cale I didn't honest.'

'I know you didn't. You want mum back. So do I. I want that more than anything. But we can't place adverts in newspapers, Tom. If we do, the chances are we'll just bring more trouble down upon ourselves, and I think we've got enough of that already. You agree with me, don't you?'

'Yes I agree with you I didn't think Cale I just didn't.'

Cale kissed the top of his brother's head, which still smelled fragrantly of the shampoo he had washed his hair with last night. 'Well, now you know,' he said. 'So let's make this work as best we can, hmmm? Who knows. Maybe in time we can think of another way of getting in contact with mum.'

'Yes another way another way another way,' Tommy said in that unique and continual way of his, like bullets being spat out of a Gatling gun, and all the time he made gentle snuffling noises into the cabbage, and right then, Cale looked out of the workshop window, which was filmed over with dust, but even so, he could still see Sad's Place through that window clear enough. Thinking about what he found buried in there yesterday: their mother. The woman who had not run off and left her sons, but in reality had been murdered by her own husband, and now two-thirds of her face had been eaten away, the rest just a baggy, slushy mess sloughed off to one side. A worm now nestled in one empty, bony eye-socket, as if it had taken up residence in there. Her once smooth and slender throat around which had lain the Coca Cola necklace now just rotted fibres and rotted strings and rotted leathery webbing.

You can come back now, Mum, Tommy had said last night in his dreams, and with perfect, evenly-spaced clarity. *Dad's gone. You can come back and live with me and Cale.*

But sadly that was never going to happen.

Never.

Cale worked late into the evening, after returning the phone-calls and making arrangements with the three potential customers to come to their homes and estimate the work. He then got cracking on the next job in line, a pair of French doors for a customer over in Birdhouse, the next town up. He was reasonably confident with French doors, had made quite a few pairs in his short time as a joiner, and wouldn't need to consult his father's leather-bound manuals in the house to get them right.

After several hours of milling timber, making sure it was nice and straight, ready to be mortised and tenoned, he then went out the back into the storeroom, to check on supplies. The last job of the night.

He needed to make sure there were enough nails, enough screws, enough dowelling rod, enough glue, enough hinges, enough latches, because without the hardware there would be no joinery, and hence, the outstanding orders in the book would be delayed. And there could be no delays. Delays meant a backslide. A backslide meant sloppy service. Sloppy service meant you got a bad name, and more often than not, once you got a bad name, that was when your business went into freefall and then folded.

And Cale Redstone could not allow that to happen. Redstone Joinery was his employer. It would ask no questions, it would meddle not in his affairs. As long as he kept its wheels turning, he knew it would provide him with a living that would not be monitored by anyone else but himself. Independence, that was the key. As long as Cale maintained his independence, then he'd be fine.

No one would suspect a thing.

He seemed to have enough hardware, for the time being, anyway. He took off his apron, hung it on the hook next to his father's apron, which would not be going around his father's waist anymore, and switched off the lights. Switched off the mains power, as well. Finally he locked up the workshop. He glanced through the door's upper glass and saw the bandsaw in there, looking like a big, round-shouldered brute standing in one corner, silently brooding. Just looking at it sent gooseflesh rippling up and down Cale's arms and made the hairs bristle on the back of his neck.

The evening was balmy, the moon a bloated purple colour, as if, before the sun had gone down, it had stolen some of its heat, and yet Cale shivered.

He went into the house, not walking but hurrying a little. He washed his hands, his face, and made a beef stew dinner, which took an age to prepare, but he got the recipe out of his mother's old cookbook (which was still in the cutlery drawer), so when the dinner was finally ready to eat, it tasted wonderful: the meat tender, the vegetables flavoursome. Like last night's dinner, he set out a crusty loaf to go with it. Just like last night, there were lashings of cold ginger beer, as well.

He may have been anxious to get out of Sad's Place after he had dumped his father's armchair in there this morning, but he had stayed long enough to grab a book, just about the only book, in fact, that wasn't damp and yellow. Was very much still readable. Once dinner had been eaten, he handed it to Tommy.

'What's this?' the boy asked, puzzled.

'A book. I want you to read it. Out loud.'

'Of Mice and Men,' Tommy said, opening it up. A quick, indifferent glance, and then: 'I can't read this Cale it's too difficult!'

'Read it, Tom. If you don't, Miss Lovell might just show up here one evening, wanting to know why you talk that way, like a steam train thrashing along a track. I think, if you read that book, it'll help to regulate your speech.'

'I've always talked this way Cale always.'

'No, I don't agree. When you were little, around four years of age, you used to call that necklace of mum's the Cowa Cowa neckis. I used to kid you about that, and that was when I came up with the idea of the clock: tick, you speak, tock, you don't speak. It was a bit fussy of me, I admit, given that you were so young, but I've always tried to speak correctly myself and I wanted the same for you. Do you remember saying Cowa Cowa neckis, Tommy?'

'Sort of.'

'And do you remember the necklace itself?'

'Yes the Coca Cola necklace.'

'That's right. But there were still times - '

'Gold with red stones.'

'Yes, gold with red stones. Anyway, back then there were still times when you could string words together with the right spaces between them. When mum was here, much of the time you talked normally. I can't *swear* to that, things have become a little broken up in my mind, but I'm as sure as I can be that you didn't always talk that way. It was dad, I think. He beat you down so much, made you so nervous, and that's when you began to talk so fast like that.'

Tommy, it seemed, did not need the history lesson. Just looked down at the book, and said sulkily: 'I can't read this Cale I can't!'

'Don't push me, Tommy. If you don't read that book, you might have to go to the special needs school after all. They won't question your speech in that place, you see. They'll just accept it as part of your disability.'

'I've got a wonky leg and face Cale not a wonky brain.'

'Don't tell me that, I know, don't I? So does Miss Lovell. That's why she might come over here one evening, hoping for a cosy chat, because she'll know you're not a fool. And who will she want that cosy chat with? Your parents, that's who. Only your parents won't be here, will they? It'll just be me. On my own. Looking like some stupid animal caught in a car's headlights. Blimey, Tom, stop thinking about yourself and read the damn book, would you?'

'Can't you find me an easier one to read?'

'Oh, hang on,' Cale said. 'I'll just go into our own private library and pick out Jack and Jill Went up the Hill, shall I? Or maybe the Cat Sat on the Mat? You just help yourself to the brandy and the cigars, old bean. I won't be a jiffy.' He paused, gazing at Tommy harshly. 'I've only got that one book, Tommy. Read it.'

Tommy wrinkled his face, and when Tommy wrinkled his face, it looked twice as...*ugly* was the word that shot into Cale's mind, but no way would Cale ever use that word to describe his brother's face. Not ugly, no, never ugly. When Tommy wrinkled his face, there just seemed to be a hundred wrinkles appear, as opposed to the dozen that might appear on a person's face which hadn't been botched-up by a pair of forceps. His face looked twice as *animated* - that was the word Cale had been searching for. Animated.

'Don't look at me that way,' Cale said. 'I'm not playing around, Tom. Read the book or I won't let you watch the television. Not tonight. Not ever. Not until you read that book.'

'I've worked hard at summer school today Cale I'm tired!'

'I'm tired, too. Read the book. Don't make me tell you one more time, or I'll lose my temper.'

Tommy pushed his empty dinner plate to one side and spread the book on the table. In a moany, whimpering voice, he said, 'Some of the words here are long Cale really long.'

'I've read the book myself,' Cale said. 'It gets easier. Just a bit flowery at the beginning, that's all. Stop making excuses. Get on with it.'

'How many pages?'

'Four. Then you can watch the television.'

Tommy nodded his head and shuffled forward a little, so that he was arched over the book, his walking stick resting against him like a tall, thin pet that had fallen asleep that way. He began to read out loud, hesitantly at first, which Cale had anticipated, given that the first couple of pages were all about twinkling yellow sands, and golden foothills, and giant sycamores, and grey, sculptured stones, and rabbits hurrying noiselessly, and stilted herons, but when Tommy got past that - his speech so slow at times it almost came to a complete dead halt - and he got into the dialogue between George and Lenny, his speech picked up speed, sensible speed, and it began to knit together almost flawlessly.

Many nights Cale believed he would have to sit here listening to Tommy read, thinking that Tommy would spend much of that time just stumbling and bumbling all over the pages, but would you believe it, already there was an immediate improvement in the way he talked, and if Cale could somehow get him to transfer that over to his everyday patter, then yes indeed, they would soon be in business and Cale would be able to relax a little and not have to live in fear of Elsa Lovell coming over to the house.

'Okay, you can stop now,' Cale said, beaming happily, but Tommy either didn't hear or didn't *want* to hear. He just kept on going, telling Cale about how Lenny could pet his dead mouse with his thumb while he walked along, and George telling Lenny that he wouldn't be petting no dead mouse while he walked along, he had to remember where they were going now.

'Tommy, it's okay, you can stop now,' Cale said. 'You've read enough.'

'Oh, but this is just so *good*!' Tommy said. 'I could read this all night! Better than the television!'

'Wow!' Cale said. 'You've got it, Tom, you've got it at the first go!'

'What?'

'Can't you hear yourself? You're talking properly with the right spaces between the words, and not looking down at your watch, either. Well done, Tommy, well done!'

'Did I really Cale did I really talk with the right spaces between the words?'

'You did…just a moment ago you did, anyhow,' Cale said, a little deflated. 'Now you're back to gabbling again. Never mind, though.

Already we're making progress, aren't we?'

'Perhaps,' Tommy said, lowering his head. Then he looked up and gave Cale a passionate, bright-eyed stare. 'Can I read this tomorrow Cale can I?'

'Tomorrow, and the day after that, and the day after that, until you can talk properly without having to read that book at all. It's all about regulation, you see, Tom. I was right, wasn't I? I was right to think that if you spoke someone else's words, instead of your own, then you'd have no choice but to speak in the correct manner. It worked. It slowed you down to the right pace. Now all we need is to get you to do that without the book.'

'Whose book is this anyway?' Tommy asked, closing it and regarding its pictureless hardback cover. Just the title, in faded gold writing, and the author's name. That was all.

'It must have been mum's,' Cale said. 'I found it - ' He paused, not wanting to tell Tommy that he found it in Sad's Place. If Tommy knew that, he might start thinking that more of their mother's personal stuff was out there, and he'd go poking around. 'I found it under the stair cupboard,' Cale lied. 'I had to go in there this morning to fetch the vacuum cleaner, in order to clean up the carpet where dad's chair had been, and there it was, lying in a dusty corner.'

'Why didn't she take it with her I wonder?'

'Let's not go into any of that at the moment. I've had a long day and I've still got dishes to wash. We can talk about this some other time. Now, you want to watch the television? I think some cowboy film starring John Wayne is on tonight.'

'Can I read this in the sitting room Cale?' Tommy's eyes were still on the book, keenly on the book, like he had discovered some marvellous object that had captured his heart and now his heart was held in its hands.

'No, leave it there. The book is a joint assignment, Tom. You read, I listen. That's the way it is.'

Tommy put the book down and pushed it to one side, a little reluctantly, but with no obvious disagreement. Just with reverence, really. He gave it a longing look, and then he got down from the table.

Grabbed his walking stick, stirring it out of its sleep. Gripped it and began to head out into the hall.

Again the back door rattled, as it did yesterday while Tommy had been putting on Cale's old, hand-me-down clothes. Rattled like someone had put a hand on the knob and was about to twist it. And Tommy' eyes went to it, jumpily. He said, 'Are you sure dad's dead Cale?'

'Dead as a doornail. It's just the wind, Tom.'

Tommy hobbled off into the sitting room. Nothing more was said between them…until, that was, Don Willoughby came knocking at the door.

And that set a ball rolling that couldn't be stopped.

Chapter 8: Cowboys and Indians

It was a cowboy film on the television, all right: the volume right up, guns banging, arrows twanging, horses whinnying, wagon trains crashing, the Red Indians making that warbling battle-cry of theirs, cowboys shouting yee-ha, women and children screaming. All sorts of calamity. Tommy in the sitting room, nailed to the gogglebox, as their father used to call it.

Cale, meantime, was up to his elbows in soap suds, scrubbing his way through pots and pans and the like, and there he was, looking out through a chink in the curtains at the moon that was like a warm penny. He couldn't be sure, but he didn't know of too many cowboy films in which two of the actors spoke British English, but over the commotion, that's just what he heard: two people speaking British English.

He missed the first part of their conversation, could only hear the accent, and so he moved towards the hallway door, which was open a little. Put his ear to the gap. The long, sharp knife he had used to cut the bread with was in his hand, its blade now wet and sparkling with soap suds. He was curious to hear those voices a little more clearly, and try to put a face to them. Not even vaguely did he think he was about to be thrown, headlong, into making yet another decision so soon after killing his father.

Another horrific decision.

The first voice was that of an adult, and although the tone was intimidating, the words were, without a doubt, just a joke. To Cale they were, anyhow. Just a leg-pull. Just a have-on. Just a silly old innocent tease.

'I know what's been going on around here, boy,' the voice said. 'You may as well confess and come quietly. If you do that, there'll be no need to put the handcuffs on you. I'll just take you down to the station, make out a report, throw you in jail, and tomorrow we'll put you up in front of the judge.'

'No don't take me away and put me jail!' the other voice said, a voice that was young, completely terrified, and even though this had to be a joke, just had to be, the owner of that voice did not get it. It was Tommy, of course, a Tommy who was gibbering helplessly and suddenly, into the bargain, he was digging a great big hole for he and Cale to fall into. 'Cale didn't mean to kill dad it just sort of happened he fell under a stack of wood and he would have died anyway!'

Cale jerked the door open, and there was Don Willoughby, a Don Willoughby who'd almost certainly come calling about the cycling proficiency (and much earlier than Cale had expected; he thought Willoughby would be in touch sometime later in the week), and now he was in the house because Tommy had *let* him in the house. Tommy must have heard Willoughby knocking on the door, but Cale hadn't, the noise in the sitting room had been an outright din (it was still an outright din), and yes, here he was, in the house, and whatever good humour had been on his face when Tommy had answered the door, it was not there anymore. Willoughby's eyes shone like penlights under the brim of his cap. His mouth was a thin, unsmiling crease. He was mashing his jaw together, which was Willoughby's trademark twitch whenever a problem arose and it needed a prompt resolution.

'Don't take Cale and me away and put us in jail!' Tommy went on as if he were going mad. Just mad, mad, mad. He was staring up at Willoughby like Willoughby was a hangman. Or maybe the Grim Reaper. 'It wasn't Cale's fault - '

'That's enough!' Cale suddenly barked at the boy. 'Don't you dare say another word! Get back in the sitting room! Now!' Cale was shaking, the knife was shaking, too, its blade glimmering, its shadow so big on the wall, it seemed as if Cale were holding a sword, not a knife. Soap bubbles dripped off its tip and dotted the floor. He was panting hard, his heart whammed, but somehow he brought his voice back down to a reasonable, almost normal, pitch. Not that anything about him *felt* normal. In point of fact, he felt like going a little mad himself. Just mad, mad, mad. 'Get back in the sitting room, Tom! At once!'

Tommy did. Using his stick in a speedy reverse motion, a motion he had used many times before to retreat from his father whenever his father brandished both Hospital and Death at him, he backed through the doorway, his eyes drenched with tears, his face so white, he looked like a stick of chalk with clothes on.

His jaw flapped up and down but nothing came out. Had it, then almost certainly it would have been an apology, because the boy had begun to realise in some bleary way that Willoughby hadn't come here to throw them in jail...but how could he have known that for sure? He couldn't. The poor boy had no idea that Cale had been talking earlier with Willoughby about cycling proficiency, and that Willoughby's threat was just a joke made for the reason that Tommy had almost hit a car today. So here was Tommy, looking up at Willoughby with wet, pleading eyes, then looking down the hall at Cale with wet, apologetic eyes, and somewhere in the middle was a mess that he couldn't make head nor tail of.

Things had gotten out of hand - that was all Tommy Redstone seemed to know. All of a *sudden* things had gotten out of hand. He backed all the way into the sitting room and closed the door.

'You'd better come through,' Cale said to Willoughby.

'After you,' Willoughby said. 'And get rid of the knife. I don't want that thing coming between us.'

Cale turned and began to walk into the kitchen. More guns banged in the sitting room, and a tomahawk, as well. Cale could hear the whoosh-thud of a tomahawk as it sank into someone's skull. A white man's skull, no doubt. And Don Willoughby? Cale could hear him bringing up the rear, the town's police sergeant, a distinction he had not earned by faffing about, and what was more, he really was a man not to be dissuaded. If there had been any shilly-shallying on Willoughby's behalf, then it had now been replaced with an urgency every bit as sharp and unsophisticated as the knife in Cale Redstone's hand.

'What the hell is going on here, anyway?' Willoughby asked. 'Can you tell me that, Cale? Tommy's not the easiest kid to understand, especially when he starts talking like that, but did he say that you killed your dad? Did he *really* say that?'

Before Cale could respond, Willoughby said, 'Was that a lie? Your father up in Templeton? Was that a lie all along?'

Cale had to think…and quickly. If he got into a dialogue with Willoughby, then it would be over. He would confess to everything, because people like Don Willoughby were expert at getting people to see sense, to be reasonable, to just own up to their crimes. That was their job. It wouldn't even be a concern to him that Cale was his best friend's son. That fact would probably make Willoughby even more determined to get straight to the bottom of this, and never mind tip-toeing around the edges.

The moment Cale believed Willoughby was directly behind him, his mind was made up. He felt sick to his stomach, and seemed to somehow be drowning in air rather than water, but of course, this was about Tommy, this was *all* about Tommy. He would protect him. He would take care of him. That was the promise Cale had made to the boy. In turn, the boy had agreed to keep his mouth shut, to say not a word about how Cale had killed their father…just as long as no one came along to take Cale away. And in Tommy's mind Don Willoughby had come along to do just that, to take Cale away, to take them *both* away, and so Tommy had opened his mouth without even pausing to think.

So much for wild horses.

It wasn't like Cale could accuse his little brother of letting him down, either. If anything Cale had let Tommy down by not telling him about the cycling proficiency. If he had, then the boy might just have stood a chance with Willoughby's teasing. Not much of a chance, but a slim chance at least. But oh well, it was too late for any of that now. Too late for Cale Redstone to get out of this with words instead of violence.

He spun around, and in a flash, he stroked the knife across Willoughby's windpipe. Willoughby's hands shot up to his throat, but there was no blood. Perhaps Cale had only nicked Willoughby's windpipe like a shallow razor cut.

Then he saw blood, all right.

A lot of blood.

It began to trickle through Willoughby's fingers and run down the backs of his hands, into the cuffs of his tunic. He made a surprised open-mouthed gargling sound, and then sank to his knees, much like the way he had sunk to his knees, Cale supposed, up at Walnut Grove, after being hit over the head by one of those con-merchants.

Just put your faith in me and everything will be fine, Cale had told Tommy, and although this was not exactly what Cale had had in mind (far from it, actually), he guessed that everything *would* be fine, or could be *made* fine, just as long as Willoughby died right here and didn't put up a resistance that might get him out of the house, down to his car, and then onto the radio, calling for help.

God, here Cale was, taking a man's life, taking *another* man's life, something that prior to murdering his father he had not believed he was capable of. All right, his father's life, yes, that had pretty much been a requirement, for Tommy's sake…but this…?

A friend of the family, am I? Willoughby's face, now twisted with pain, seemed to say. *Is this how you treat a friend of the family?*

Willoughby fell forward into the kitchen, onto the floor, and Cale closed the door, just in case Tommy heard the scuffle, unlikely because there wasn't much of a scuffle to begin with, and if there had been, then the boy probably wouldn't have heard it, anyway, above the din of that cowboy film in there. More guns banging. More horses whinnying. More wagon trains crashing. More screams from women and children afraid for their lives, and as soundtracks went, Cale supposed it couldn't have been more appropriate. After all, there was nothing refined about the way in which he was putting Don Willoughby to death. It was right up there with a tomahawk to the white man's skull.

Willoughby rolled over onto his back and began to grope for his truncheon, the truncheon he hadn't had time to pull out up at Walnut Grove and defend himself with.

'No, don't do that!' Cale barked in a voice that sounded so hot and coarse. 'Just die, don't struggle!'

Just die, don't struggle? He was appalled to hear such desperate and cold-hearted words pouring out of his mouth. Not that Don Willoughby paid any heed to those words. He was not about to just *die*...God no....he would struggle...he would struggle for sure...he was a man not to be dissuaded, and so he groped for his truncheon, he got the pocket undone, and now his fingers, greasy with blood, reached into that pocket. Began to slide the black, polished weapon out of there.

'I'm going to get you for this,' Willoughby said. 'I'm going to get you for what you've done to me, and for what you've done to your father...whatever that might be. Where is he, Cale? What have you done to him? What have you done to my best friend Ewan?'

All those words from a man whose windpipe had been cut, and there was so much blood now, it was like he was wearing a red bib around his neck.

'Leave that alone!' Cale said, looking down at Willoughby's hand as it groped for the truncheon. 'Just leave it alone and die!'

But of course Willoughby still paid no heed to that. He got the truncheon halfway out of its long, slender pocket, and Cale struck once again, by chopping the knife down on the back of Willoughby's hand.

'Ooo, bastard!' Willoughby said, flinching, and then he gazed down over the ridge of his chest to confirm that yes, his hand was now sliced deeply, just the way his windpipe was.

His hat fell off and his hair poked up out of the bandage that pretty WPC Jenkins had wound around his head to keep that large gauze pad in place above his right eye. The gauze pad with that coffee-coloured coin of darkness underneath it.

Anger in Willoughby's face now, so *much* anger that he almost seemed to be bursting apart with it, and yet what good was anger when you were dying? That was the philosophical wing of sense that all at once seemed to flutter across Willoughby's eyes. What good was anger? He was dying, his body was sending up warning flares to affirm that, and now it seemed he had no choice but to alter his approach.

'Radio in for help, boy,' he grunted, clasping at his throat. 'God's sake, radio in for help!'

'I can't do that,' Cale said, starting to blubber now. Tears slipped down his face. His quiff, drenched with sweat, now lay against his brow, glued there in a downward pointing arrow. He let the knife fall out of his hand, its blade frilled with blood, and it fell to the floor with a clatter.

'Please, do as I say, boy, do as I say!'

'I can't, I'll go to prison, and Tommy will be put in care! I can't, I can't!'

This was becoming spookily like yesterday: he and his father out in the backyard with the sun beating down and his father refusing to die as if he were a fly trapped but still moving under a swatter.

Cale could not allow that to be repeated. Simply could not. And so he yanked the truncheon out of Willoughby's hand, his hand that was bloody, and likely it would be numb, as well, as most of the tendons had either been cut or partly cut, and for the most part it wasn't like Willoughby even seemed to *know* that Cale had done that, anyhow, had yanked the truncheon out of his hand. He was just too busy pleading with Cale to radio in for help, for God's sake please radio in for help, and that was when Cale brought the truncheon down hard and sharp on Willoughby's skull. Brought it down once...twice...three times, the truncheon's shadow, with every backward swing, swishing across the pantry door.

Then it was over. Sergeant Don Willoughby, he of the three chevrons high up on the arm of his tunic, was all of sudden, thank God for that, dead. No more did the radio seem so important to him.

He had been dissuaded.

⁓

He didn't need to think because already he had a plan...a plan for Tommy...a plan for Willoughby's dead body, too...and so he got right down to it. If he needed to think, then it was only to marvel at how cunning and resourceful a person became when they were up to their eyeballs in the kind of trouble that would earn them a lengthy jail sentence, should that trouble be discovered.

He slid the bloody truncheon back into Willoughby's pocket. Put his hands under Willoughby's body, and even though Willoughby had been tall, strong and fit, his gracefulness seemed to have given him, even in death, a lightness that made him not such a labour for Cale to carry.

He picked him up and took him outside via the back door. Went down to Willoughby's precious Humber Sceptre, parked there in the drive, and after a bit of fumbling about, he got the passenger door open and sat Willoughby in the seat. Willoughby's hat, around whose rim was that black-and-white chequered band, pinned to which was the badge of the Hampshire Constabulary, was clamped under Cale's arm.

He pulled it out and jammed it back on Willoughby's head. Snugged it down over the gauze pad and over the three fresh injuries, the three fresh *fatal* injuries, that now decorated his forehead. Exclamation marks not written in ink but stamped there by a blunt instrument.

Still weeping but slowly getting himself under control, Cale got the keys out of Willoughby's trouser pocket. Didn't even bother to direct his gaze to the ignition, to see if they were there. Keys in the ignition? A man like Don Willoughby would never have left his keys in the ignition, no more than he would have walked around with his dick hanging out.

Cale grabbed the keys, closed the passenger door, went around to the driver's door, and got in. Started the engine. Drove the car up the side of the house, out into the backyard, and parked it behind the workshop, adjacent to the timbers under which his father had become trapped yesterday, and then Cale had re-stacked them back here, out of the way.

He turned off the engine. The radio hissed, then. A loud, strident crackle followed this, and then a woman's voice broke in: 'Base to Humber One, Base to Humber One, are you there, Humber One?'

Cale froze. He thought of all those cars that had come screeching into the station's car park this afternoon, filled with the Heavy Mob from up at HQ in Upperlands. Those men would be out on the road right now in all probability, still on the lookout for the men who had assaulted Sergeant Willoughby. This, Cale knew, was not exactly the ideal evening to be in unlawful command of a police car with a dead policeman inside it.

Not that *any* evening would be ideal for that.

'Base to Humber One,' the woman went on, that woman who was likely to be WPC Jenkins, she of the brown eyes and the cute, button nose. 'Are you there, Humber One? Sarge, can you hear me? Pick up, would you?'

Cale wanted to rip the radio out but couldn't because if he did, he would arouse suspicion. Perhaps suspicion of some sort had *already* been aroused. Had Willoughby, the man who would not be dissuaded, gone out looking for the con-merchants, yet again, when he had been given implicit orders not to? That wasn't just likely, Cale thought. It was a given, in all probability. That being so, it was a foregone conclusion that the Heavy Mob would be on the lookout for Willoughby, as well. The meddler.

Cale glanced over at Willoughby, who was slouched there in the passenger seat, that bib of blood around his neck not a bib anymore but flowing down his chest like a barber's apron. Cale got out of the car, slammed the door shut, and ran back into the house, trying to stay calm but aware that time might already have run out for him.

He picked the knife up off the floor, washed it, washed it meticulously, in spite of his haste, and put it back in the cutlery drawer. Cleaned the floor then, after filling the bucket once again from under the kitchen sink, and using the string mop that was propped outside the bathroom.

He poured the bloody water down the drain outside. Rinsed the bucket. Rinsed the mop. With that out of the way, he checked his clothes. No blood. He could see no blood there at all. Quite how he had gotten away with that, he didn't know.

He went out into the hallway and stood in front of the mirror in which his mother used to stand and put on her hat when it was windy outside. He ran his hands through his hair. Pulled his quiff back into shape. Straightened his clothes. Cleared his throat. Went into the sitting room then. The film had quietened down, had quietened right down, just two cowboys, downing shots, and chatting together amiably in a bar. And here was Tommy. The moment Cale walked in, the boy's eyes went straight to Cale's wrists, where he expected the handcuffs to be. No handcuffs. The boy, leaning on his stick, suddenly looked up at Cale as if Cale had walked out of a blazing building and shouldn't have.

'It's okay, Willoughby's gone, and he won't be coming back,' Cale said in a low, perfectly stable voice. 'I told him you've been having bad dreams lately, that you dreamed that dad fell under a toppled stack of wood, and that I finished him off with a mallet. When I told Willoughby that, he understood and laughed. Did you *hear* him laugh?'

'No Cale I didn't no.'

'Well, he did, he laughed. He laughed like it was just the funniest thing in the world.'

'And now he's gone Cale just gone?'

'Yep, just gone,' Cale said, and he held out his arms. 'Come here.'

Tommy fell into Cale's arms, weeping. Cale felt like strangling the little mite, but he relaxed his hands, his hands that still felt as if they were clutching that truncheon of Willoughby's, and he began to stroke the boy's hair. So small, so thin, so delicate, he couldn't hurt the boy, he would *never* be able to hurt the boy. Could only hold him and soothe him and protect him and not let him know (*categorically* not let him know) that Don Willoughby was now dead, too, like their father was dead. Dead because Cale had made him dead. If he told Tommy that, the boy, Cale knew, would sink into another of his lockdowns, his mouth hanging open, his eyes rolled up, his face ashen but boiling hot to the touch. If that happened, then it might be the lockdown that this time Tommy might not snap out of. Third time unlucky.

God, but this was a mess, and a mess which had been a blessing yesterday morning - the opportunity for Cale to get rid of the man who had been the bane, not just of little Tommy's life, but of Cale's life, too, in many respects - but right now Cale could not see *any* of this as a blessing. Only as an almighty cock-up.

Later on tonight, though, in bed and with Tommy asleep beside him, he would understand that Willoughby's trait of not being dissuaded would undoubtedly have trapped Cale in due course. Willoughby's friendship with Ewan Redstone had been too close. Willoughby would have rumbled that *something* was up, and sooner rather than later.

'I let you down Cale I'm so sorry I just couldn't help it.'

'It's okay,' Cale said. 'It was my fault, anyway, *all* my fault. I should have told you that I spoke to Sergeant Willoughby today about cycling proficiency lessons. I saw what happened, you see. I saw how you almost hit that car on your way back from summer school.'

Tommy pulled away from Cale and stared up at him with watery, ashamed eyes that were fringed with confusion.

'I was cutting back the trees in the station's forecourt,' Cale explained. 'That's how I saw you.'

'Oh,' Tommy said. Then: 'Was that why Sergeant Willoughby called Cale just about that?'

'Yes, just about the lessons. At least, I *think* that's why he called. In the end we didn't talk about that, we never got around to it, but yes, I think that's why he called.'

Tommy suddenly bawled: 'I thought he was going to take you and me away Cale and throw us in jail!'

'No, he was joking,' Cale said, gently squeezing the boy. 'Throwing us in jail was *never* on his mind. Anyway, he's gone now. We were lucky, Tom, dead lucky. The next time we might not be. That's why we need to have a chat sometime about how you ride that bike of yours, about how we can make you ride it in a more responsible way. And we'll talk about responsibility in general, I think. Now that dad's just a dead body buried out in Sad's Place, you need to be responsible, and for the whole time you're out of the house. I can't have you drawing attention to yourself like that, the way you did today. I just can't.'

'Yes I know that Cale from now on I'll be responsible I promise.' He gave Cale a look of anticipated disappointment. 'I suppose you won't be buying me the new bike now.'

'No, I'll still buy you the new bike, if anything - '

'Yes!' Tommy punched the air.

' - it'll help you to ride better and to gain a bit of road sense. It'll have lights and proper brakes, for a start.'

Ecstatic, smiling broadly, Tommy put his head back against Cale's chest and snuggled into him. He had been soothed. He had believed the lie Cale had spun, and *Please, please, please, just let that be the end of it*, Cale thought. *No more trouble. No more mess to fall into that can only be gotten out of with murder.*

He felt sick. The moral issues aside, he *still* felt sick. Was this how it felt when you murdered someone? His father's murder was not a good yardstick. It had been an act, cold and blunt, committed out of necessity (committed so that he and Tommy could simply get a life), whereas Willoughby's murder had been done of out desperation. There was a difference, a huge difference. Willoughby's murder had been thrust upon Cale like a hand-grenade dumped in his hands from which the pin had already been pulled and there had been five seconds to make a decision: just stand there and let it go off...or toss it away.

He had chosen the latter. Had chosen not to take the blast himself, but to pass it onto Don Willoughby, and Cale felt terrible having done that. No choice, though. Again: was this how murderers felt? And was there *really* an issue, anyhow, when it was kill or be killed? Eighteen years of age and the rest of his life in prison? Well, that was a death, wasn't it? Of a kind. So no, there was no issue. Any issue had been stamped out by Cale Redstone's lack of choice.

Only this feeling now, this terrible *gagging* feeling, that if he didn't get out of here and tie up the loose ends of this rotten business with Don Willoughby, then he was going to puke all over his brother's head.

'I have to go now, Tom. I have a little more work to do out in the workshop. Will you be okay in here on your own for a while?'

'I'll be fine Cale fine.'

'I love you.'

'I love you too Cale I love you very much.'
'The watch, Tom. Tick-tock, look at the clock?'
'I keep forgetting Cale I just keep forgetting.'
'I know you do. *Fuck* it, I know you do.'

Chapter 9: Wild Horses

The moon was no longer that warm, bloated purple colour. It now had the tawdry if eye-catching look of a silver-plated medallion. Its upper half was thickly crested with woolly clouds, and under these clouds shadows twisted in long, hypnotic tendrils. An owl, fat, orange-eyed, flew across the moon's face, hurriedly flapping its wings. In its claws was a chubby, fawn-coloured mouse that would still be alive had it not made a dash from behind Redstone Joinery over to the big black shiny car that was parked there in a dark, leafy corner of the backyard.

Parked there with a man slumped inside it, a man whose throat was dribbling blood into his upward-facing palms.

The mouse had gotten right up to the rear bumper, but had paused instead of going all the way under the car. Had done this, perhaps, to scent the air, or to sniff at the succulent grass, or maybe it had been briefly distracted by the moon's cheap, melodramatic glow. Whatever, the owl had taken its chance. It swooped down from the roof of Sad's Place and snatched the mouse up in one swift, premeditated motion. Crushed it to death in the effortless clench of its talons. Then bore it away.

This was followed by a bang, the bang of the back door as Cale slammed it shut behind him, then dashed over to the car, his face pale and greasy, his gaze darting towards every dark corner in which a detective might be standing, waiting for the moment to step out and snap the handcuffs on him.

With a trembling hand, he pulled open the driver's door. 'Base to Humber One, Base to Humber One, come in, Sarge, flaming *hell*, come in, would you?'

That was the voice, the now impatient voice, that greeted Cale as he sat in the seat and started the engine. No headlights. He left those off the way he had left them off when he moved the car from the driveway to here. No reason to stoke a fire that was burning bright enough already. And the radio? He wanted to grab the cord and yank it out. Wanted to do that more than ever now.

However, if he did that, then WPC Jenkins's mood would change in a blink from impatient to alarmed. If the radio went dead, any police officer worth their salt would immediately think something was up. Something up that shouldn't be up.

Sticking close to the boundary fence, Cale drove up to the crest of the hill down which he had sledged as a child and had crashed into the cattle fence at the bottom, gashing his forehead so deeply that the wound had needed stitching in hospital. Once over the crest, he put the gear-stick into neutral, switched off the engine, and now the car began to freewheel. Better that way. Quieter.

Down the central part of the hill, it was reasonably smooth, but here, at the edges, it was either bumpy or potholed, and halfway down, Don Willoughby all at once fell forward and his face smacked against the dash, and hard. More precisely his *teeth* smacked against the dash, and hard.

Wincing, Cale glanced over and saw Willoughby's face now turned towards him. His top lip, stuck to the dash, was drawn up on one side into a snarl. The teeth behind that snarl were either missing now, or snapped, or chipped. Stuck to his bottom lip was a fragment of tooth so white, it could have been mistaken for a flake of boiled fish. His arms dangled down into the footwell, his fingertips brushing the carpeted floor. His cap was aslant, it creased his right ear, disclosing a large section of the bandage, out of which poked blades and fingers and hooks of dark, soggy hair. His eyes stared over at Cale like dull glass.

Cale's stomach rolled and rumbled. He belched and tasted bile. There was a gate in the fence. He steered the car towards that gate, the same gate through which Little Miss Orange Dress must have ridden her pony, Sadie, in order to get into the common field beyond.

At the bottom of the hill, Cale brought the Humber to a stop.

Got out. Ran over to the gate. Didn't expect to just swing it open. Its hinges would surely be rusted stiff, and grass would be growing around the bottom of it, holding it back, but when he unlatched it, it swung open like a gate that had been well-maintained. A minor miracle given that no one, so far as Cale knew, was responsible for its maintenance. Certainly his father had never done any work on it. Hadn't so much as given that gate a squirt of oil or a lick of paint.

He got back in the Humber. Started the engine. Drove through the gate. The common field was really a large heath that was choked with purple heather, scruffy trees, thorny bushes, and ragged grass. Rabbits abounded here. Badger sets were not uncommon, if you knew where to look, and the ponies, you didn't have to look for those. They were everywhere. Wild ponies with tatty, tangled manes, knobbly knees, and tails so long they brushed the ground.

It was not unusual to spot a deer, either, if you rose early enough and were gentle on your feet. People walked their dogs in this place. They flew kites on windy days. They rode bikes. They ate picnics. Courting couples also came up here on Friday and Saturday nights to canoodle in their cars. It was neither a Friday nor a Saturday. The only courting here tonight was being done by Cale. Courting not a girl but trouble. The kind you kissed and it reacted by handing you a life-sentence. Killing a police officer? They threw the book at you for that, Cale knew. The book, and the shelf it had been taken down from.

'Base to Humber One, Base to Humber One,' WPC Jenkins broke in again, and once more it startled Cale into a freeze. She sounded exasperated now. Pissed right off, in truth. 'Listen, Sarge, if you're there, then pick up the mike and respond, eh? The boss is losing his temper out there. He knows you clocked off at seven. Knows you ought to be at home right now, out of uniform, but Zephyr Three spotted you at nine-thirty on Sackcloth Road. In the Humber. In uniform. I recommend you return to Base before he blows a fuse.'

The boss. WPC Jenkins had not given the boss's name. Likely it would be Detective Inspector Someone or at least Detective *Sergeant* Someone. Out there. The boss was losing his temper *out there*. Where "out there" was Cale did not know, but he guessed it would be around the town somewhere. The boss, around the town somewhere, along with the rest of his men, searching for the villains who had hit Willoughby over the head.

Conclusion? That indisputably Willoughby was doing the same thing, but doing it without authorisation, on his own, with no back-up. He had broken off briefly to visit the Redstone place (something Base as yet seemed to have no knowledge of), but Willoughby had probably done that on purpose, to cover himself. If he got hauled over the coals, he'd simply say that he'd been having a chat with the Redstone boys, Cale and Tommy, about cycling proficiency. That was all. And hell, that amounted to *official* business, didn't it? That's why he had been wearing his uniform...and if they didn't believe him? Okay, fine. Why not phone the boys and ask them if he, Willoughby, had been there? Simple.

'Sarge, for Christ's sake, pick up, would - ' WPC Jenkins got that far, and then...

'Here, give me that.' There was the clattering, hollow sound a mike often makes when someone either bashes it or drops it, and then the intruding voice - male, clearly in charge of the radio now - said, 'Are you there, Willoughby? It's DI Cutlass here. I want you back here at the station immediately. The chief is going bananas out there. If you get attacked again, then it's his view that it'll be your own fault. He gave you *specific* orders this afternoon that this case was not yours anymore but ours. Don't defy him on that. If you do, you'll find those stripes of yours in the wastepaper basket by tomorrow morning. That's not a threat, either. That's a promise. Are you getting this...what?'

A pause. It seemed that DI Cutlass had been distracted by someone or something. Cale expected him to take his finger off the OPEN button, but he didn't...and then Cale remembered that radio set, the one on the desk under the station's courtyard window. Old. A relic, in truth. Probably no button on it that you simply released and the signal went the other way. Just a metal switch that you had to make a conscious effort to flip up or down.

'What is it, Arkwright?'

'A note, sir. I found it on the Sarge's desk.'

'Hand it over.' The sound of paper crinkling. DI Cutlass reading the note. Then: 'You think he could be there?'

Arkwright: 'He could be. The boy was around here today. He cut back the trees outside. Did that as a favour for the Sarge.'

Cutlass: 'Cycling proficiency? Why would Willoughby be up there, at this time of night, talking to the boy about cycling proficiency?'

Arkwright: 'Well, the Sarge has something of a soft spot for the family. He gets on well with the boy's father. I believe Ewan Redstone is working away at the moment. Maybe the Sarge went up there, not just to talk about the cycling proficiency, but to check on the boys. Two of them: Cale and Tommy. Tommy's a cripple.'

Jenkins, offended: 'Wash your mouth out, Glen. That's not nice.'

Arkwright: 'Sorry, Charlotte. I couldn't think of another name.'

Jenkins: 'Try disabled.'

Cutlass, irritated: 'Never mind any of that. We'll give Willoughby another half an hour, and then we'll phone the Redstone place. Do we have the number?'

Jenkins: 'I'm sure we can dig it out, sir. In the meantime, do you want me to keep on trying, or do you - ?'

Cutlass: 'No, you make the phone-call, Jenkins. I don't have the patience. Not when it comes to Don Willoughby, I don't. Why did he want the trees cut back, anyhow?'

Arkwright: 'Birds' shit, sir.'

Cutlass: 'Eh?'

The signal went dead. Cutlass had finally flipped the radio's switch, it seemed, and was probably now handing the mike back over to WPC Charlotte Jenkins. In a moment Jenkins would be back on the airwaves, telling Willoughby to respond. He wouldn't. He was dead. Dead and right here next to his killer, the one, the only, Cale Redstone.

'Half an hour,' Cale said. His lips were shims of numb fat. His face a shiny, pallid mask in the soft, cool glow of the dash-lights. His eyes wide and full of dread. Sweat that had a cold and oily feel to it ran down his wrists, trickling onto his knees. 'I've got half an hour...and that's all!'

Hold on, though. The time factor aside, Cale had known, back at the house, that Willoughby's obsession for finding the men who had hit him over the head might just work in Cale's favour. It had been Cale's plan to slowly drive the Humber across the common field to Sackcloth Road, a back road close to which he would be able to park the car, but he would leave part of it showing so that Willoughby's body would be discovered sooner rather than later. If Cale did that, then the iron would still be hot when it came to laying the blame. The police, when they came across Willoughby's dead body, would almost certainly think he had found those men again, only this time he had gotten more than just a whack over the head. This time those men had gone one step further and put an end to Willoughby.

Cale gazed over at Willoughby, whose top lip was still pulled up into that impotent snarl by the dash, with several teeth smashed out and sprinkled on the floor around his feet and around his dangling fingertips. A slow drive across the common field to Sackcloth Road? Wasn't much chance of that, not anymore. Just half an hour until either WPC Jenkins or PC Arkwright or maybe even DI Cutlass himself phoned the Redstone house, and that was all.

'Hold on tight, Sergeant Willoughby,' Cale said, taking his foot off the brake. 'You might just find the going a little hairy.' He stamped on the accelerator, the Humber took off across the common field, and Willoughby who, let's be honest about this, had no chance of holding onto anything, never mind tightly, was thrown back in his seat so abruptly that blood from his mouth and slit throat sprayed in an arc all over the car's roof. His cap flew off and landed on the back seat.

The car hurtled through bushes and saplings, flattening them with effortless disregard. Alarmed rabbits fled this way and that, and because Cale could not risk using the Humber's headlights, he, like the rabbits, saw approaching objects at the last moment and could only pray that his young, quick reflexes would keep him out of trouble.

The field was bumpy and potholed, as the hill had been down its flanks, but nevertheless, Cale could still tell the difference between a bump, a pothole, and something alive over which the nearside wheel had seemed to roll. A rabbit - it just had to be. An old rabbit that perhaps had been too slow to move out of the way in time. Or maybe it had been a youngster, just a little baby. Cale swore he heard it squeal and its bones snapping...but that just *had* to be imagination. The Humber was quiet, even at full throttle. Not much in the way of creaks and rattles coming from the chassis or coachwork, either. Just the deep, heavy thud of the wheels as they occasionally left the ground, and then slammed back down again.

Had he heard that small animal squeal and its bones snapping after all? No, he thought not. Probably just the dials of his awareness turned up so high that he could even hear his blood rushing through his body and the saliva in his mouth sloshing against his tongue. Everything seemed to be louder, somehow: the crackle of the bushes, the jet-engine roar of the air, the saplings that were too whippy to break with a loud snap...but Cale heard them break as if they were trees being felled.

Sweat dripped off his elbows into his lap. Hunched over the wheel, he stared wide-eyed into the gloom, the common field flashing by either side of him.

'Base to Humber One, Base to Humber One, come in One, come in.' WPC Jenkins again, but sounding a little more relaxed this time, though. No impatience anymore. Perhaps because DI Cutlass was no longer standing behind her, making her nervous. And definitely no exasperation. Yet her voice, as sweet as it was, sounded to Cale as if it were booming out of a loudhailer. 'Respond if you can, Sarge, would you?'

But the way Cale heard this, it made him want to clamp his hands over his ears: *'RESPOND IF YOU CAN, SARGE, WOULD YOU? RESPOND! RESPOND!'*

Another bump, big enough to make the car temporarily take

flight. This followed by a pothole deep enough to make Cale's teeth rattle and his eyes bobble. Then Willoughby was flung forward again, and even harder than before. His nose caught the force of it this time. Wham, it hit the dash, and Cale heard the policeman's nose crunch and then split open like a walnut. Ghastly. He glanced over and saw so much blood flowing out of Willoughby now, it was like he had become a gargoyle spouting blood instead of water.

'*RESPOND, SARGE, RESPOND!*' WPC Jenkins's voice seeming so loud that if she were shouting like that for real, then she'd wake up in the morning with no voice at all. Just a sore throat.

Another bush, the biggest so far, appeared in front of Cale, a bush with meaty, twisted branches and yellow flowers. The car, on the offside, ran halfway through this bush, its branches brushing violently against the window, and then, when the bush had been fully parted down the centre, Cale saw in the darkness what he thought at first was a large smooth brown rock.

No rocks down here in the common field, though. Not that size, anyhow. In the distance, Cale caught a faint glimpse of the one lamppost at this end of Sackcloth Road. Good. Almost there. Beside him, meanwhile, Willoughby's face had begun to hammer against the dashboard. That, Cale thought, was even ghastlier than the blood that poured out of him. And that thing that looked like a rock but couldn't be?

Cale swung the wheel to avoid it, but the wheels became briefly caught in a shallow ditch, and then he saw, he *finally* saw what it was. Not a rock. But a pony. Its eyes dumbly horrified as it peered around its fat, brown rump. Its mane hanging down its neck in silvery, entangled strings. Didn't move. Didn't even *try* to move. It was just standing there in its own little world of stupid, frozen terror.

'Get out the way!' Cale screamed at it. 'Please, please, please, get out the way!'

The steering wheel began to respond again, and Cale swung it hard. Too late, though. It was *always* going to be too late. Had the pony been a rock, then Cale would have scuffed it and likely put a dent in the car. That's all. Nothing would have lost its life.

But the pony did.

Cale struck its left, hind leg and the poor animal came crashing down in a heap.

Cale braked. Willoughby's face no longer hammered against the dash. It seemed to be eating it. Dust and bits of undergrowth sprayed past the windows. Something was torn from the underside of the car and was hurled out into the darkness. Part of the exhaust pipe, probably. The car came to a halt, and Willoughby's face hit the dash one more time, making a sound like a wet fish slapping against a boarded jetty.

He slouched against the door with his face turned to Cale. His mouth was a gaping, bloody hell-hole. There were bruises on his cheekbones, and one that was every bit as plump as the one Cale had seen on Cynthia Digweed's abused face. His hair was a crazy, oily spray. The gauze pad had slipped down over his right eye like a pirate's patch.

Cale got out of the car, thinking he could arrange Willoughby's body to make it look as if he'd been killed here, not somewhere else. How would he go about doing that, though? And did he have the time?

No, he didn't.

He turned and ran back to the pony, and there it was, cast askew in the gnarled, sun-stiffened branches of an old, ugly bush, and all around it was blood, and green piss, and brown, smelly shit. It was still alive. Just. Its hind legs were nothing but bent, jumbled sticks. Its ears twitched slowly. Its nostrils blew loosely in and out. Its lips were drawn back in pain over its piano-key teeth. And the moon had flung cold, silver glitter into its black, afraid eyes.

Cale clapped his hands to his face, and said, 'Oh God, I'm sorry, I'm just so so *sorry*.' And then movement in the darkness. Slow, wary movement. Cale looked up and saw a pony in the gloom, and another, and another, and another, until there were six, maybe more, standing there in a semi-circle and watching him. The biggest, a male with broad, muscular withers, was not so slow and wary. It moved decisively towards Cale, came to a stop, and scraped a hoof on the ground. The look in its eyes said, *Go now and leave us in peace with our dying companion. That's the least you can do. Go now.*

'Yes,' Cale said, nodding, ashamed. 'I'll do that, yes, I'll do that.'

Off he went back to the house, sprinting, his arms pumping. He looked back only once and saw the ponies gathering around their dying companion and beginning to gently nudge at it with their noses. Beyond that, he saw Willoughby's Humber Sceptre with Willoughby slouched inside it.

Like someone sitting in a dark room with the curtains open.

Chapter 10: Cutlass

Back at the house. Panting outside the kitchen door. Bent over. Hands gripping his knees. Then he heard the phone ring and went into the house as a fireman might into a burning building: shouldering everything aside. He made it into the hallway...and there was Tommy, on his walking stick, rubbing his eyes like he'd dozed off and the ting-a-ling of the phone had woken him up. He was heading for the phone, about to pick it up, and Cale, in a voice that sounded much too agitated and much too loud, said, 'Leave it, Tom! Don't touch it! Just leave it alone!'

'Fine,' Tommy said, shrugging his shoulders. 'No need to get your knickers in a twist.' He went back into the sitting room and closed the door.

Cale muttered: 'I'll twist you in a minute,' then picked up the phone. Breathing normally now. Hoping above all else that his voice would sound normal, as well.

'Hello, Cale Redstone here.'

'Hi there, Cale,' a woman said. WPC Jenkins, it was. Just a moment ago pleading with Willoughby to pick up his mike and respond. Now here she was on the phone to Cale, and he sounded as normal as he hoped he would sound. 'Sorry to bother you at this time of night, but we have a problem.'

'How can I help?' Cale asked.

'It's Sergeant Willoughby,' Jenkins said. 'Did he call over at your place this evening?'

'No,' Cale said, and without a pause, because a pause meant indecision, and indecision might just mean you were keeping something to yourself. 'Was he meant to?'

'I'm not sure,' Jenkins said. 'We found a note on his desk, written by Constable Betts. Cycling proficiency. Ring any bells?'

'Oh yes,' Cale said. 'I spoke to Constable Betts, and to Sergeant Willoughby, about that today. Sergeant Willoughby said he'd get back to me when he had some news. He made no arrangements to call and see me this evening, though.'

'Damn,' Jenkins said.

'Like that, is it?' Cale said.

'Pretty much,' Jenkins said. 'We can't find him. Still, I shouldn't be telling you that.'

'Why not?' Cale said. 'If Sergeant Willoughby's missing, then I'll do what I can to help. Does this have anything to do with what happened to him this afternoon, do you think? You know, when those men hit him over the head up at Walnut Grove?'

'I sincerely hope not,' Jenkins said. 'It's probably nothing, anyhow. Knowing the Sarge, he's probably stuck up some country lane somewhere, gassing with someone. We'll find him.'

'I hope so,' Cale said.

'So do I,' Jenkins said. 'Goodnight, Cale. I hope I didn't disturb you.'

'You didn't. Goodnight.' That was it. Nothing more to say. Well, there wouldn't be, would there? Not to a kid. Just question, answer, question, answer, and then goodnight. You didn't get depth when you were a kid...or still *considered* to be a kid. What you mostly got was spoken to like something might snap inside you if you were pushed too hard or given too much.

He put the phone down. Went out into the kitchen. He thought about making a cup of hot, strong coffee, but his legs folded underneath him before he could make it to the kettle, and down he went on his knees as if in prayer.

In point of fact, he *could* say a prayer, couldn't he? It wouldn't hurt. But when Cale Redstone moved his lips, no words came out. Only laughter. The kind of laughter that people let out in place of tears.

'Cale? Cale Redstone?'

Cale, back in the workshop, working on those French doors he was making for that customer over in Birdhouse. He'd been out this morning for a couple of hours, visiting the people who'd called yesterday while Tommy had been manning the phone. And he now had more work to add to a list that was long enough already.

There was an old, dusty wireless on a shelf outside the office. Music was playing but Cale had mostly switched it on for the news, which was broadcast on the hour and half past the hour. No news as yet on Willoughby. It would come, though. By the end of the day it would surely come. And now Cale had a visitor: a tubby man, crew-cut, white shirt, sleeves rolled up.

He recognised the man's voice straight away, that of DI Cutlass. What he did not recognise was his physique or looks. Last night he'd imagined Cutlass to be tall, slim, dark-haired, handsome. He was none of those.

Cale wiped his hands on his apron and went over to Cutlass. 'That's me, Cale Redstone. What can I do for you?'

'Detective Inspector Roy Cutlass.' He shook Cale's hand. 'Can you spare a moment?'

'Of course. You want to talk in the office?'

'No, here's fine,' Cutlass said. He leaned against Cale's workbench. His short hair, his very short hair, was blond. His nose was broad and freckly. He went to put his hands in his pockets, perhaps believing it would give him a more relaxed air, but decided not to. He wrapped one hand around the edge of Cale's workbench, instead, and gripped it. The other he left hanging at his side. He said, 'I believe your father's working away from home at the moment, is that right?'

'Yes, up in Templeton.'

'How old are you, Cale?'

'Eighteen.'

'And you have a brother, right?'

'Yes, Tommy. He's at summer school right now.'

'Can't be easy, can it?'

'What can't be easy?'

'Disabled, isn't he?'

'I wouldn't call him disabled,' Cale said. 'He's got a wonky face and one leg shorter than the other. He's not a vegetable.'

'Don't take offence,' Cutlass said. 'I'm just saying it must be difficult running this place and looking after your brother.'

'He's my brother,' Cale said plainly. 'I love him. It's not difficult.' No shakes in Cale's voice, although there perhaps should have been, given that his sleep last night had been dogged by visions of that pony dying in its own green, steamy piss. Visions of Willoughby, as well, of the blood that had tipped out of him as if from a jug, and his head hammering against the dash. No shakes, though, thank God. Not even slightly. Maybe if Cutlass hadn't started on about Tommy, there would have been, but as it was, Cale had fallen into a mood of protective resentment.

'We seem to have gotten off on the wrong foot,' Cutlass said. 'I'm not here to give you a hard time, Cale. I just want to make sure you can handle the news I'm about to give you.'

'What news would that be?'

'You got a phone-call last night, I believe. From WPC Jenkins?'

'I did. She was looking for Sergeant Willoughby. Thought he might have called here.'

Cutlass nodded. 'We didn't find him, Cale. Not last night, we didn't, anyhow. He was found a couple of hours ago. Dead.'

'Christ,' Cale breathed, sounding suitably shocked. 'Where was this?'

'There's a chunk of common land over by Sackcloth Road. Probably part of it runs behind this place here.'

'It does. Was that where he was found?'

'Yes. In his car. His throat slit and beaten to death with his own truncheon. There's a dead pony down there, as well. At the moment we're a long way from finding out what happened. That'll take a while, I imagine. He was found by a woman walking her dog.'

Cale bowed his head. Put a hand up to his brow. Again, suitably.

Cutlass said, 'I'm sorry, Cale. I know Sergeant Willoughby was a good friend of your father's.'

'A very good friend,' Cale said, sniffing. No crocodile tears. But the dust in here got to him from time to time and made his nose run. Which was nothing but a help in this situation. 'My father will be devastated.'

'I'm sure he will be,' Cutlass said. 'You want me to telephone him and break the news?'

'No, I'll do it. It'll be easier on him if it comes from me.'

'Probably it will be,' Cutlass said, pointing to the wireless. The Beatles were singing about how they wanted to become a Paperback Writer. 'I came here to break this news before it came on the radio - friends and family have a right to know before the rest of the world. I've already paid a visit to Willoughby's cousin, George. Poor man's in bits. And WPC Jenkins is with Willoughby's mother right now, comforting her. I love my job, but this part? Hate it. Always have.'

Cale wiped his nose on the back of his wrist. 'When will the funeral take place?'

'Not for a while,' Cutlass said. 'At some point Sergeant Willoughby's body will be taken up to HQ to be picked over with a fine-tooth comb. His vehicle, as well. That'll take some time. Then there's the crime scene. Never seen anything like it. Bone-dry ground and tyre tracks crossing it this way and that. It's hard to tell the fresh ones from the old. Doesn't help, either, that ponies and deer have been walking all over the place. And the murder itself? It's not even clear yet if Willoughby was killed in the car or outside of it. Blood splashed everywhere. I think we'll be working down there for quite some time.'

'Any idea who did this?' Cale asked.

'We have a *big* idea,' Cutlass said. 'Yesterday, Willoughby was assaulted by some men - '

'I know that,' Cale said. 'I was at the station yesterday when he came back with his head split open.'

'That's right, of course,' Cutlass said. 'Cutting back the trees, weren't you?'

'I was.'

'Anyway,' Cutlass went on, 'we believe the men responsible for that are the same men responsible for killing Willoughby. No reason to think any other way, really.'

'These are the men who've been cheating the old people out of their savings, aren't they?'

'Yes. They've been pulling the same stunt over in places like Rosewater and Portercross and Wentworth. Posing as meter-readers. They won't be in any those towns now, of course. Likely they've fled the area altogether. Maybe even the *county*.' He paused. 'The annoying thing is, we had four cars out on the road last night. And who came across those men? Sergeant Willoughby. On his own. No partner. Also, we didn't really expect them to be around here anymore, anyhow. Thought they'd have gotten out of here after assaulting Willoughby the first time around. How wrong can you be, eh?'

Another pause. Then: 'Most of us just wish Sergeant Willoughby hadn't gotten into this in the first place. Hadn't turned it into his own crusade. The funny thing is, HQ was about to give him two more constables to help him out. They were due here tomorrow. If he'd just waited, he probably wouldn't be dead right now.'

'Did he know about that?'

'Oh yeah, he knew, all right. But Willoughby wasn't a man - '

To be dissuaded? Cale thought.

' - blessed with a lot of patience. A good sergeant, I must say. Knew his job from back to front. Impulsive, though. Perhaps a little *too* impulsive.' Cutlass flushed. 'Maybe I shouldn't have said that.'

'It's okay,' Cale said. 'My dad thought him a bit mad, anyhow. Well, maybe not mad, as such. *Unusual*, is probably closer to the mark. But he cared for him. I know that much.'

'I'm sure he did.' Cutlass began to gaze around the place, at the machinery, at the tools hanging on the walls, and at the work that was currently in progress. 'How come your dad's working away from home, anyhow? Seems like a profitable business he's got here.'

'It's profitable, to a degree,' Cale said. 'By that, I mean that it only provides us with a steady income. That's what dad says, anyhow. We don't earn enough here to take a holiday, that's for sure. That's what dad wants, a holiday. When this job in Templeton came up, he mostly took it so that we could afford to take a break in the sun somewhere, me and him and little Tommy. He's a good father.'

'Sounds that way,' Cutlass said. 'I wouldn't mind a break in the sun myself, but that won't be happening, not with a murder to solve. And Unity Gate is going to get pretty busy over the next couple of weeks, I can tell you. Radio people, newspaper people, television people. They'll all be here. A murder is one thing, the murder of a policeman is quite another. I just wish the government hadn't abolished hanging. Whoever did this deserves to swing.'

Cale heard a pony whinnying down in the common field.

He touched his throat and swallowed hard.

⁓

Later that day, he got to thinking that if the con-merchants came forward to protest their innocence, then they'd wind up in trouble, anyhow. None of them would be put in jail for murder, certainly. But for fleecing many of the old people in the area, and for assaulting Willoughby up at Walnut Grove, then yes, they might just be put in jail. Therefore, would they risk coming forward? Likely not, Cale reasoned. Likely they'd think it better to just lay low for a while, or maybe even disband altogether. Something else that would work, or *should* work, in Cale's favour.

When Tommy came home, he did not come into the workshop to chat with Cale. He just propped his bike against the house and went indoors. He looked like someone with a little black cloud over his head that was showering him exclusively with rain. Cale went in after him and found him pouring cold milk into a glass.

'Something wrong, Tom?'

'No I'm fine Cale just tired.'

'Did you hear about Sergeant Willoughby?'

'Yep we were told at school we had to say prayers for him but I didn't I just put my hands together bowed my head and thought about that new bike you're going to buy me.'

Cale asked: 'Doesn't it bother you?'

'Nope I didn't much like him anyway.' Tommy took a drink of his milk. Did this steadily, too. No gobbling it down. Already a big improvement in his manners. He removed the glass from his mouth, then raised his watch to his eyes. Counted himself into the regular rhythm of the second hand, and said, 'He played that nasty joke on me last night, Cale, and it wasn't funny. It nearly got you and me into trouble, into *big* trouble. Also he must have known that dad was a bastard to me, and yet he did nothing about it. Nothing. He must have seen the bruises on me, and how thin I was, and he would have seen you and dad sitting at the kitchen table, too, eating dinner without me. Some policeman, wasn't he? Fuck him, he deserved to die, that's what I think!'

Cale didn't know if he was taken aback at the swear word, or at Tommy's opinion that Willoughby deserved to die, or at the way the boy suddenly slammed his glass down on the table and just stomped out of the room. He wanted to tell him to come back here, and to wash his mouth out with soap and water...but that would have been a leaf straight out of Ewan Redstone's book of punishments. And Cale Redstone would never look through *that* book to get any ideas.

He let the boy go. Probably for the best. And Tommy had been right about Willoughby, anyhow. A man who could see a tiny speck of birds' shit on the bonnet of his car, but not the suffering that little Tommy had been going through. The *obvious* suffering.

But Willoughby *had* seen it. Of course he had. Had seen it and possibly at times had been revolted by it. In Ewan Redstone, however, Don Willoughby had found a friend, had found a *good* friend. A drinking partner, a shoulder to lean on, an ear to bend when he, Willoughby, had needed to get something off his chest. Why put that on the line, just because Ewan could be a bit carefree with his hands at times? And no one had been killed, had they? That was how Willoughby must have seen it, at least for the most part, that no one had been killed. Except people *did* get killed, didn't they? They got killed in the heart and in the soul until the blood in their veins no longer ran warm but cold with bitterness. And boy, was Tommy bitter right now. Very bitter.

Yes, best to let him go, all right. Best to let him go and work it out on his own.

In the meantime Cale had work to do. He went back into the workshop. Spent a while sorting through that jumble of receipts his father had stuck all around the office on a multitude of nails. That done, he returned to working on the French doors. He worked until the little bright children came out into the vast playground of the night sky, and there they twinkled. In one corner sat the moon: the fat boy that no one wanted to play with.

Chapter 11: The Press Conference

Moina Furneaux: she was on her way like a comet that Cale could not as yet see, even if he'd been looking through the world's most powerful telescope. Out there, though. Out there and heading this way. Not a witch on a broomstick, exactly. But still someone with plenty of tricks up her sleeve. Manipulative, shameless, and wickedly charming, she was a woman not only attracted to trouble. She took pleasure in it. *Gloried* in it.

Deadly.

Cale bought Tommy the new bed to replace the bug-infested box of feathers he'd been sleeping on since he was an infant. He fetched it back from town on the back of the truck. He bought paint, as well, to decorate Tommy's room with. And a new rug to put on the bare boarded floor. And a new school uniform for the boy. And new shirts and underwear and socks. And new towels. And a new toothbrush. And the bike - he bought that, too. Bought it from Harvey's, the main cycle retailer in this part of the world. A cream-and-green model, it was, with lights, front and back, three gears, and brakes that were not a piece of wood you jerked against the rear tyre to bring it to a halt.

When the salesman wheeled it out of the back, smelling of new rubber and fresh paint, Tommy clapped his hands to his face and shrieked so loudly that the salesman winced, put his hands up to his ears, and clamped his eyes shut.

On the way back home, Tommy didn't sit in the passenger seat but kneeled on it, backwards, so that he could look out of the truck's rear window at the bike that Cale had tied down to stop it from moving about and getting all scratched up. The boy was fine, now. Since the day he slammed the glass of milk down, swore, and stomped off, there had been no more of that. And thank the heavens for that! For a moment there, Cale had been worried that the boy might be going down with some affliction that might turn him into a crazy handful that Cale would not be able to cope with, and that would be all Cale needed on top of two murders that chipped away at his brain like an ice-pick. Thankfully, though, Tommy was in fine fettle. Back to his old predominantly cheerful self.

Just outside of town and Cale pulled over. He pressed a half-crown into the boy's hand, and said, 'In you go, Tom. Short back and sides.'

Tommy gazed down at the large, silver coin, and then gave Cale a look that someone might give if they were reeling in a big fish and didn't want to lose it: distracted and none too pleased.

Cale pointed at the barber shop outside of which they had stopped, with the truck half up the kerb, half on the road. 'Get in there and get a haircut. I'll wait.'

'Oh Cale not now I want to ride my new bike!'

'Get your hair cut, Tom. If it gets any longer, you'll look like the fifth Beatle.'

Tommy got down out of the truck, slammed the door shut, hard enough to rock the cab a little, and went into the barber shop. Not happy. Not happy at all. But that was tough luck in Cale's mind. The boy needed a haircut. He needed feeding up and sharpening up, as well, if, that was, he was going to fit in at Brougham Moor School.

And Cale was set on *making* him fit. Summer school was over. The next time the school bell rang, it would call Tommy in for maths, English, geography, history, and the rest of it. The *serious* rest of it. Summer school had been a doddle, in the main. It was time for Tommy to knuckle down…and it all started here with a haircut.

It seemed to Cale that since his father's death he'd barely had time to draw a breath. He made joinery, and when he wasn't making joinery, he was either delivering it or fitting it. However, he somehow found the time to give Tommy a lesson or two on road awareness. Hand signals, for the most part, as well as telling him to ride his new bike close to the kerb and not to weave all over the road. These instructions seemed to sink into the boy's brain, as well, perhaps because he began to understand, in some small way, the pressure Cale was under, and he had the decency at least to pay attention.

They talked about responsibility, too. This over dinner one night before Tommy got down to reading out loud his daily ration of Steinbeck's Of Mice and Men. Although Cale hadn't told Tommy about DI Cutlass's visit to the workshop, and never would (something else Cale had kept from the boy…and now his list of secrets was beginning to grow), he made it clear to him that he should think long and hard before opening his mouth and maybe putting his foot in it once again. Tommy understood this…and this time he seemed to get the message. It was in his face, a depth of comprehension that told Cale that Tommy was perhaps starting to mature a little. Tommy finally grasping that sometimes you just had to sit there, tune in, and listen.

He got the message about accidents, too. That message being that if Tommy ever wound up in hospital, then Cale would almost certainly be in the kind of trouble he wouldn't be able to get out of with weasel words, a blag, or just plain old lie-telling. His time would be up. You could fool some of the people some of the time, but not all of the people all of the time.

~

The boy's room was decorated. Cale worked all night to get it done, from seven in the evening, all the way around to five in the morning. Blue and white walls, the rug that was orange, and finished off with the England flag, pinned above Tommy's bed as the centrepiece. Tommy was delighted with the result. He threw his arms around Cale. Gave Cale a long, affectionate hug that made it all seem worthwhile. And Tommy was putting on weight. Not much. Still thin. But where there had been bone and not much else, flesh now clung to him, here and there, in modest but healthy clumps, and to Cale, the boy at last felt softer to the touch. Not like a blade he might hold and get cut for his efforts.

Time marched on. The investigation into Willoughby's death moved into its third week, and the gang of con-merchants/murder suspects had not been found. Nor had they come forward to protest their innocence, just as Cale had thought. The police were becoming frustrated. DI Roy Cutlass, looking pale and tired, appealed on the television for people to come forward with any information they might have, but so far nothing. The well was proving to be a dry, old hole. Most of the reporters (at the beginning there had been so many that they, along with their vans and cars, brought the town to a complete standstill at one point), had now left Unity Gate and returned to the city. The same reporters who, at the start of all this, would have stopped a dog in the street, if they could have coaxed a remark out of it.

The week prior to that appeal by Cutlass there had been a press conference, which had been held in Unity Gate Memorial Hall. Packed and hot, it had been in there, but Cale had managed to get inside, though, and he stood at the back, amid all the cigarette smoke. He saw Cutlass behind a desk, along with his boss, a man named Chief

Superintendent Warren Gaines, as well as another detective by the name of Jack Bradshaw. The three men, composed on top but clearly hot and bothered underneath, had delivered statements and updates on Willoughby's murder, and now the questions came in, thick and fast. Questions that were mostly answered by Warren Gaines, because it was he, after all, who was leading the enquiry.

'Are you any closer to finding the gang that allegedly did this to Sergeant Willoughby?'

'We have men working around the clock to find them. In the meantime, we have extensively interviewed the victims who were swindled out of their savings and pensions, and we will, I'm pleased to say, be able to release photofit pictures of the men in the next few days. You, the press, will receive copies, just as soon as we have them.'

'Are you sure these men did it?'

'We can't be sure of anything, only that it was these men who assaulted Sergeant Willoughby earlier that day.'

'What if they *didn't* kill Sergeant Willoughby? Could they freely walk into Upperlands HQ without fear of being arrested for the crimes they're guilty of?'

'Immunity, you mean?'

'Yes.'

'No. As yet no terms like that have been offered.'

'Is it a possibility?'

'At the moment, no.'

'In the future, perhaps?'

'Perhaps. You have to understand that the crimes they're guilty of are serious enough. We can't at this stage offer these men immunity from those crimes. That would be unrealistic...and a farce, to put it bluntly.'

'What about fingerprints? How many were found at the scene?'

'Several. It was a police vehicle, remember? A police vehicle is often driven by many people and ridden in by many people. The prints have been taken and we are still in the process of exclusion.'

'And is there other evidence, such as hair, or even fluff, maybe, from the killer's garments?'

'Whatever's found in that car will be closely examined by our laboratory people.'

'Do you have any idea if Sergeant Willoughby was murdered in the car or outside of it?'

'We're almost certain now that he was murdered outside of it.'

'You said in your statement that he was killed by a combination of two weapons, but you didn't specify exactly what those weapons were. Can you?'

'Yes. I can reveal that a sharp knife was used to cut Sergeant Willoughby's throat. He was then beaten about the skull, several times, with his own truncheon.'

'Why wasn't this made known earlier?'

'Because we weren't in a position to make it known. You have to appreciate that Sergeant Willoughby's face was badly disfigured. His nose was broken and most of his front teeth were smashed out. We couldn't be sure to begin with if these injuries took place during the murder or sometime after. We now believe they took place sometime after.'

'How exactly were they caused?'

'Probably by the car's dashboard.'

'Can you explain that a little deeper?'

'Yes. It would appear that Sergeant Willoughby, after he was murdered, was put in the passenger seat of his car and then driven to the scene where his body was found. The journey appears to have been something of a stop-start affair. It seems that Sergeant Willoughby's body was thrown forward many times during the journey, perhaps due to heavy braking.'

'So the car could have travelled quite a few miles, could it?'

'It could have, yes. But we're almost certain that it didn't travel outside of Unity Gate.'

'How can you be sure of that?'

'Sergeant Willoughby was seen in his car, in the Sackcloth Road area, at around nine-thirty that night. We have now established that his death took place somewhere between that time and midnight. It's a broad time-scale, we know, but the car's odometer has been thoroughly checked by police mechanics, and it is their opinion, their *professional* opinion, that while the car may have been extensively driven that night, it did not leave the town's boundaries.'

'So Sergeant Willoughby's car was regularly serviced, was it?'

'Every police vehicle is regularly serviced. Sergeant Willoughby was extremely proud of his car and it's fair to say that his was serviced beyond requirements.'

'What about the place where he was killed? Have you no idea at all where that might be?'

'Still no idea.'

'There would be signs of blood at that place, wouldn't there?'

'Going on the amount of blood that Sergeant Willoughby lost that night, then yes, there would be signs of blood. And there has been no substantial rain that we know of to wash it away. Of course, the killer, or *killers*, could have washed the blood away. It's a possibility.'

'Is there a chance he could have been killed in a building?'

'Yes, there is a chance of that. But there is also a chance he was killed in another vehicle before being dumped back in his own.'

'What about the common field? Have you been able to ascertain anything from that place?'

'Not a great deal. The direction from which the car came is our biggest problem, as far as that place goes. The common field can be accessed from many different directions. The dry weather hasn't been much of a help, either - it's difficult to tell the new tracks from the old. The fact the place is frequented by courting couples has also made it somewhat time-consuming. We're still appealing for people to come forward who regularly use that place, so that we can check their vehicles' tyres and thus eliminate them from our enquiries.'

'A pony was killed that night. Doesn't its death give an indication as to which direction the vehicle came from?'

'Not especially. The killer could have driven around the common field in a circle. For example, to look for a suitable place to dump the car, and then he hit the pony during that procedure. So no, the pony's death really gives no indication to the direction at all.' A nod of the head from Chief Superintendent Warren Gaines to the two detectives sitting either side of him. Then: 'I think we've just about covered everything for the time being, ladies and gentlemen. Thank you for coming here today. I hope we've been of some assistance to you.'

The funeral took place nineteen days after Willoughby's death. The full police funeral, too, with Willoughby's gloves laid out on the coffin, along with the cap he was always pulling down over his eyes and squaring off just perfectly.

Cale bought a wreath of red-and-cream flowers and laid it on Willoughby's grave when it came to his turn. He then stood on the gravel path outside the little chapel at Lavender Hill Cemetery, waiting for George Willoughby to come along. George shaking everyone's hand, and saying thanks, thanks for coming, but mostly that was just automatic; he looked and sounded like someone who'd bashed his head, double-hard, and was still dazed by it. He came to Cale, said thanks, thanks for coming, and just when he was about to move on, he turned back to Cale, and said, 'Your dad's here, isn't he?'

'Yes, George. Out the back, having a cigarette.'

'Of course,' George said, like he had seen Ewan Redstone but had somehow forgotten. He then went on up the line of people who had come here to pay their respects. Shaking their hands. Telling them thanks, thanks for coming.

Cale let out a deeply-relieved breath and went back down to his truck. On the way he saw DI Roy Cutlass standing under an oak tree, next to a gravestone. Expressionless. Cale raised a hand to him, but Cutlass did not raise one back. Like a cardboard cut-out, he was.

Cale climbed up into his truck and drove off. Someway down the road he pulled over, jumped out, dashed around to the base of a tree, put his hands on his knees. Opened his mouth. He thought back to that dream he'd had: Little Miss Orange Dress leading him into Sad's Place. And there had been his father, sitting in that armchair of his, the pillowcase snugged down over his head and stuck to his face with tacky blood. *You've started a ball rolling that you won't be able to stop*, he had said. *Remember that, lad. You've started a ball rolling that you won't...be able...to stop!*

Cale Redstone threw up. Yet again.

'I know we only had dinner a couple of hours ago, Cale, but I'm still hungry. Can I have some cheese and crackers?'

'Yes. Cheese, fridge. Crackers, pantry.' Cale so tired he could barely keep his eyes open. His tongue was like something that had turned-turtle in his mouth and died. He hadn't read a newspaper for days. Hadn't watched the television, likewise. His father's books, now his, were in his lap. Finally he had gotten to grips with them: how to make sense of them and how to fill them out. They needed updating, but the pencil required to do that was on the table, and as yet, Cale had no interest in picking it up.

'I'm making tea as well. You want a cup?'

'No thanks.'

'I got rid of my old bike today,' Tommy said. He was poking around in the fridge for the cheese. Not so long ago, he had been doing the same thing, when his father had come home early from a dental appointment...so his father had said, but looking back, he may well have been humping Cynthia Digweed all afternoon. He had caught the boy in the act, and in his fright, Tommy had spilled a bottle of milk all over the floor. Solution? In true perverse Ewan Redstone style, he had made the boy get down on his knees and lick the milk up like a cat. Every last drop of it. Once again the horror show that Cale Redstone had only been able to watch, never influence.

He had influence now, though. He had saved the boy, had given him back his life. Now, here he was, eating better, gaining weight, gaining confidence, gaining good manners, and gaining something else, as well, that Cale had begun to think he might never gain. Tommy was now eighty pages into the Steinbeck book. He loved the story - everyone did, it seemed to Cale - and he read it out loud as well as any adult. However, after reading his allocated four pages every evening, he would soon fall back into that Gatling-gun patter of his that could only be slowed and then regulated by the watch, tick-tock. But. Two hours had gone by since Tommy had read his most recent allocation. And -

'I took it down to the dump this afternoon,' Tommy said, pulling his head back out of the fridge with the cheese dish in his hands. He closed the door with an elbow, then hobbled over to the table. 'I was glad to get rid of it, too.'

'You were?' Cale asked. 'I thought you'd have found that hard. After all, you built that bike with your own two hands.'

'Only because I had to,' Tommy said. 'But now I've got my new bike, haven't I? And what a bike it is! The kids at Brougham Moor will be dead jealous!'

'I'm sure they will be, Tom. I'm sure they will.' He gave Tommy a smile that did not exactly stretch Cale's mouth to its teeth-baring, smile-at-the-camera limit. Just a tiny, sluggish smile, really, that denoted pleasure, to a degree, but mainly tiredness.

Tommy saw this, and said, 'You look worn out, Cale. Why don't you go up to bed? I'll finish up down here.'

'I can't, I've got these books to do.'

'Leave the books, they can wait.' Tommy not only maturing but being assertive, as well. No longer the kid who most days would have stuck his head up his own arse if he thought it would make him invisible to his father's smoking, brooding glare. He was now able to make decisions, not just for himself, but for others, too. Taking the bull by the horns, Ewan Redstone would have said. Funny, but with that man out of the way and pushing up daisies in Sad's Place, that's exactly what Tommy was doing: taking the bull by the horns.

'Well, are you going, or what?' Tommy asked. 'Bathroom's that way, clean teeth.' His finger was pointing to the right. 'Bedroom's that way, sleep.' His finger then pointing upwards. 'Chop-chop!'

'I'm going, I'm going,' Cale said. He carted the books into the office. Locked them away in the desk. Used the bathroom. Went up to bed. Fell into a sleep so deep that if someone had walked into that room, had looked at Cale's pallid and drawn face, and at his hands folded there on his chest, they might just have believed they had walked into a morgue.

Martin Price

Chapter 12: Beg Me!

Tommy's first day at school. Windy. The sky strewn with clouds but the sun finding places of ingress through which to send its rays, and here and there, they hit the ground in golden, whirling spotlights. And no bike. Cale took Tommy to school in the truck, to lend support, and to calm the boy's first-day nerves. But mostly it was *Cale's* nerves that were acting up - he half-expected Tommy to start gabbling again. All the good work undone because Tommy would suddenly realise the magnitude of this day and allow it to get the better of him. Still talking normally, though, so far. Had been since that day he went to the fridge to fetch the cheese out of there. Just about a full week ago.

When they reached the school gates and Cale had parked the truck, Tommy got out, as did Cale, and they stood there for a moment at the roadside. Tommy looking natty in his new blazer that was baize-green with the Brougham Moor motif on the breast pocket. Long grey trousers that were neatly pressed. Built-up shoes that were highly polished. His shirt white and properly rounded off with the green-and-yellow Brougham Moor tie that Cale had knotted for the boy because he could not as yet do that for himself. Hair combed. A brown leather satchel slung over his shoulders and resting on his hip.

Cale held the boy, thinking he would tell him, *Good luck, everything will be fine, don't worry, it'll be a little scary for everyone, not just for you*, but when he wrapped his arms around him, he suddenly began to cry. There, standing behind the huge, dusty cowl of the Foden truck, and suddenly bawling his eyes out.

'Oh, but I'm so *proud* of you, Tommy. I never thought I'd see this day. I thought you'd just end up out of my life the way mum is, and the way dad is, too. But here you are, going to school! Going to *big* school!'

A little surprised by this, Tommy looked up at his brother with that face of his that was all sloped on one side and with an eye in there somewhere that was partly obscured by the droopy, wrinkled flap of flesh that hung over it. A kid with more spine in his little finger than most had in their whole bodies, the way Cale saw it. Delicious, too. Cale could bite into him, and maybe suck out a little of what made him such a gutsy little character. There was not a child in the world born to be beaten, and neglected, and chained to a post like a dog. Children didn't just *deserve* love, it was surely as natural to give them that as it was to water the seeds you planted, something to be given without a thought. A shame Ewan Redstone hadn't seen it that way. A terrible shame. But he was gone now. He no longer blackened the world. Gone and good riddance.

'Don't cry, Cale,' Tommy said. 'You'll make *me* cry.' His voice small, hushed, and all too conscious of the hustle and bustle that was going on around them, and anxious, perhaps, that someone might see his big brother with tears splashing down his cheeks and holding onto Tommy for dear life.

'Do I have to apologise for breaking down like this?' Cale asked.

'No,' Tommy said. 'It should be me in tears. Without you, I wouldn't be here, standing outside this school in my new Brougham Moor uniform. I'd either be dead or at the special needs school over in Battenford. You got me out of hell, Cale. You made me feel good about myself again when I thought I never would. Can't even remember if I *did* feel good about myself. I love you, Cale. You're the best brother anyone could wish for.' He glanced up at Cale, his one good eye as bright as a glowing bulb. 'And have you noticed something?'

'Your speech?'

Tommy nodded.

'Of course I noticed,' Cale said. 'I just didn't bring it up in case I put the curse on it and it sent you backwards.'

'No backwards for me,' Tommy said. 'These days I only look at my watch to tell the time. It's going to stay that way, too. I promise you that.' He stood on tip-toes then, to plant a smacker on Cale's wet face…and Cale heard loose change clinking somewhere down in Tommy's pockets. Not the school dinner money. Cale had put that in a brown envelope, had sealed it, and stuffed it right down in Tommy's satchel. The clink was the rattle of coins moving freely around.

Had Tommy been stealing again? And was stealing the right word, exactly? Perhaps. All the same, Cale thought it kinder to think of it as filching or maybe nicking. Although both those words were just fancy, softer ways of saying that, yes, all right, Tommy *had* been stealing, no two ways about it. But it really wasn't about that, anyhow. It was about Tommy buying sweets with that money and blasting himself off into space on a rocket fuelled by sugar and chemicals. And the boy had enough problems, didn't he, without adding to them?

This was not the time to be ticking him off, though. Another time for that, and another place. Cale received the kiss from his brother, hugged him one more time, and after drying his eyes, he said, 'Good luck today, Tom. This is your moment to shine, you know that, don't you? This is your moment to let everyone know you have a right to be going to that school and not to some place where the kids are dealt with like babies in nappies. You go in there, hold your head up high, and do your best. Anyone wants to take the mickey out of your leg and face, then you just think about how stick-and-stones can break your bones, but names can never harm you.'

'I know that already, Cale. And I'm happy with who I am, anyway. I'd rather be me, crippled in the body, than some kid crippled in the brain.'

'I couldn't have put it better myself, Tom.'

And so it was that Tommy went to school with all the other kids. Joined with them, mixed with them, and when the bell rang to call them in, Cale watched him go with a lump in his throat. Fresh tears slipping down his face. Waving. All the time waving. Waving when Tommy had stopped waving back and there was nothing to wave at anymore but a pair of doors that flapped in the wind.

Tommy read the remainder of Of Mice and Men, and at the end he wept, as many readers do, and for that duration he was easy to handle. After that, though, he started to become like a boat that sprang a leak somewhere, Cale would plug it, and then another leak would spring up someplace else.

A good kid, a *great* kid, but all the same it was becoming clear to Cale that Tommy had been affected a lot deeper by his father's violence and inhumanity than Cale at first thought. At school he was a gem. He got on with his work, no complaints so far, and although no homework had been handed out to date, Cale believed that when it came to that time, Tommy would do it, and without a grumble - he loved Brougham Moor, and Brougham Moor loved him, so it seemed.

But at home things were coming undone, and because almost all of Cale's time was given to his work (had to be, he had no choice in that matter), he could not always be there, handing out the counsel to Tommy, and the encouragement, and the physical love. On many occasions, Tommy was left on his own for much too long. It was then that he would steal any loose change he could find, sneak out of the house, buy sweets and fizzy drink with it, and Cale, at the end of the night, would find the boy skulking around house, or out in the garden, roving around in the moonlight. All wound-up. Glassy-eyed. His head flicking from one place to another. Looking like he wanted to gnaw on a brick or maybe snap the legs off a chair.

The television was still something of a new-fangled thing to Tommy, and if there was a night of *Thunderbirds, Dixon Of Dock Green, The Lone Ranger*, and *The Avengers*, then Cale was able to relax a little, knowing the boy would be in front of the gogglebox and not getting into trouble.

Those nights were rare, though. When the TV schedule was all political debates, and news shows, and deep, intellectual plays (which, during the week, it mostly always was), it was then that Tommy would go hunting for loose change, and if he couldn't find any, then he would start poking his nose into places it shouldn't be. Mainly into their father's bedroom, along with the office.

So far he hadn't been able to poke his nose into the writing desk, he didn't have the keys, and because of that, Cale never let them out of his sight. Always in his pocket, they were. But it was a real pain, that. Sometimes he just wanted to drop them on the table - they grew heavy after a while and dug into his thigh - but if he gave the boy half a chance, he would take those keys and unlock the writing desk. No doubt about that. Would do that especially if Cale just happened to be in the bath and the boy could guarantee himself a good half hour of uninterrupted time.

And what would Tommy find? The photos of their mother and father, the love letters, their father's wallet, his penknife. And the necklace, of course. The Coca Cola necklace, that chain of gold set with eighteen garnets that had probably been worth more than Natalie Redstone's entire wardrobe and the contents of her handbag put together. Given to her by a man who had loved her at one time, had maybe even *worshipped* her at one time, but even that hadn't been enough to stop him from taking her life. And if Tommy *saw* that necklace, he'd soon realise that his mother had not ridden away from here on a bus five years back. Instead she must have taken a ride on the back of Ewan Redstone's fists, and they, of course, went to only two destinations: Hospital or Death. Why else would she have left that necklace behind?

The end of another long, exhausting day for Cale. He locked the workshop and went over to the house. There were woodchips in his hair. Dust lined his nose. His eyes felt full of grit.

Here was Tommy's new bike, leaning against the wall. Not

looking so new anymore. The front mudguard was kinked, the rear reflector disc was chipped, and there were scratches on the frame, some so deep that Cale could see the bare metal underneath. No accidents, though. In the scheme of things, Cale guessed he had to be grateful for that, if nothing else.

He went indoors. Washed his hands. Saw Tommy's school blazer thrown carelessly over the back of a chair. There was a rip in the breast pocket, Cale noticed, a small one, but nonetheless a rip that was edged with ragged, broken threads. One of the buttons had fallen off, too. And there was a stain down the front of the blazer. Dried custard, it looked like. And what was this? Poking out of a pocket was a Bar-Six wrapper, and when Cale put his hand into that pocket, he found more wrappers. Black Jack and Fruit Salad wrappers, in the main. Penny chews that were just *loaded* with sugar.

Boys will be boys, Cale tried to tell himself, but at the moment the boy in question was becoming less of a boy and more of dog that did nothing but bother him. What was it Ewan Redstone had said while he'd been trapped under those fallen timbers? Something about how Tommy would bother Cale like a yapping dog that wouldn't stop pissing on the floor, wasn't it?

Yes, that was it: a yapping dog that wouldn't stop pissing on the floor. Mean words. Yet regrettably there was a truth to them that Cale could not ignore, only acknowledge. But he was tired, dreadfully tired, and the last person he wanted to pick a fight with right now was Tommy…wherever he was. Probably in the sitting room, watching *Thunderbirds*, perhaps imagining himself living on Tracy Island and sipping drinks by that pool that slid back to reveal a launch silo for Thunderbird 3…or was it 2, or 5? And the hell it mattered, anyhow. At the moment Cale Redstone's tongue was loose in his mouth, like a ferocious dog that wanted to bite. Holding it in there took an almighty effort, too. More of an effort that Cale wished to give it.

The table was littered with empty fizzy drinks bottles. Tommy not even trying to hide his addiction. Just out in the open with it like an alcoholic in the park. There were more wrappers here, as well, along with half a bag of Maltesers. Cale believed that if he looked in a mirror, he'd see smoke streaming out of his ears. That's how angry he was becoming.

He filled the kettle and slammed it down on the stove. Lit the ring beneath it with a match, *floomf!* If he still felt this way after the kettle had boiled, then he would have it out with Tommy, would tell him to get back in line, or else. If, on the other hand, he had calmed down by that time, then he would say nothing. Would just let it go, until he could find the right time to jog Tommy's memory about his responsibilities. How he should stick to them and not let Cale down. Got that?

But then Cale saw the cutlery drawer. Open. And the office door. Also open. Looking at one, then the other. Eyes going back and forth. Putting two and two together and wanting to come up with any number apart from four.

A cold hand seemed to go around Cale's heart and squeeze it. He went down the hall and into the office. Expected to see the writing desk open, the leaf hung down on its brass arms, resting there...and gaping. But the leaf, with the lock at the top, was still up. And shut. But it didn't look good. Never before had the office door been left open like this, so something in here just had to be up.

Had to be.

Cale went over to the desk. Gave it the once over. He found the infringement right away. Couldn't miss it: a fan-shaped scratch between the lid and the lock, a sign he didn't have to look at twice to know that Tommy had tried to jemmy the desk open with a knife. Probably a blunt, thick-bladed dinner knife. Hunting for more loose change, just had to be. And how desperate was that, eh? And dunderheaded, too! You didn't try to lever open a desk knowing that if you did, you'd break the lock. How *obvious* would that be?

Cale swung around...and saw one of his father's leather-bound manuals lying on the floor, under the book shelves. The page that Tommy had left the book open at was marked with sticky, brown thumb prints. Droplets of fizzy drink spotted the book, also. Like the boy had laid on the floor to read it, and couldn't have cared less about the mess he made.

Cale clenched his fists. Rolled his lips into his mouth and gripped them between his teeth. Cords stood out on his neck. He made a low growling noise that made the tiny, ultra-sensitive bones in his ears vibrate. That kid. That *bloody* kid. No so long ago Cale had wanted to suck in a little of what made the boy so plucky. Now he just wanted to...wanted to...wanted to...oh, just wait until he got his hands on him!

He stalked out of the office and into the sitting room. Flung open the door so hard that it bashed against the wall, *ka-bam!* And here was Tommy. Not watching the television. The television wasn't even on. Just sitting there, hunched forward in his chair, he was. Elbows plonked stiffly on his knees. Hands cupping his face.

He was high on sugar, that was clear: his eyes had that alert, pin-sharp look to them. They jerked towards Cale, almost *jumped* towards him. His head moved in small, stop-start movements. His body trembled so fast that you'd hear it before you saw it, like a bee's rapidly beating wings. Tommy once more the old marmoset in the jungle, his dirty, sticky fingers resting on his cheeks and jittering there.

But it wasn't *just* that look in his eyes that bothered Cale. More the tears he could now see running down Tommy's face. His mouth had that emotional, on-the-edge look to it. It was a look you mostly saw at funerals, and sometimes in hospital corridors. A look that broke into a thousand pieces the moment words were spoken.

'What is it, chum? Bad day at school?' Cale trying to sound friendly despite his anger and only sounding cold. Didn't feel friendly in the slightest. Just poised to let rip at the boy.

'Yeah, a bad day,' Tommy said, sadly. 'Miss Lovell, Cale.'

'What about Miss Lovell?' Cale asked.

'She collapsed in her office this afternoon...and she died. Just - ' All of a sudden he opened his mouth and let out a horrible, piercing wail that made Cale want to put his hands over his ears, just like that cycle salesman did that day in Harvey's.

'Died,' Cale finished for the boy. 'Just died. Marvellous!'

He wondered if things could get any worse.

And discovered they could.

Yes. They could.

~

It was a heart attack. Elsa Lovell, the champion of Tommy's cause, fell down and died like an old horse in a field. There was a funeral, a memorial service, too. Prayers were said at Brougham Moor, the school that Elsa Lovell had dragged, almost single-handedly, into the twentieth century. Most of the kids didn't know the history - and for some, school would be a turnstile between childhood and adulthood, nothing else - but all of them were bright enough to appreciate that someone special had passed away, and they paid tribute to her with great respect.

A temporary headmistress was drafted in until the school's governors could find someone to fit the bill on a more permanent basis. The rumour was this might take some time, because the new term was just three weeks in and all the suitable candidates were employed. So what of the temp? Couldn't *she* fill the post?

Cale would come to know this woman. In time he would understand that while she may have been good at her job, it was not in her best interests to hang around a place too long, mostly because she was a stormy petrel, and a woman of questionable morals, too, who knew, when the guns came out, that it was time to fly off before she got shot. And her name?

Moina Furneaux.

Just a week into her stint at Brougham Moor and she came calling at number 3 Samuel Lane. Late evening, this was. Cale, desperately tired, as was the norm these days, and wearing nothing but a towel around his waist after stepping out of a hot bath.

Tommy was up in bed and fast asleep, having had a long day at school, followed by a few hours helping Cale out in the workshop. Tommy had been a good help, too...for a change. He had primed window-frames and doors, had swept up and bagged the wood-shavings that were apt to pile up rather quickly if you didn't watch out, and for the final hour, he had sharpened all of Cale's chisels. Did a fair job, too. Not bad for a kid about whom his father had said, *What brain? There isn't one.*

Maybe Ewan Redstone should have directed that insult at Cale, because today Cale had messed up a flight of stairs, and so badly, they were beyond salvage. Just an ordinary, straight flight, at that. Nothing fancy. Yet in his tiredness, he had read the measurements wrong, had mistaken a five for a three, and over the course of thirteen risers and treads, he had made a flight of stairs that came in well short of the mark. It would cost him to put that right, too. Cost him in time and in money. Money, he had. Time he did not.

Time just lately was a shadow he was always chasing.

The doorbell rang, *ding-dong*, and for the third, persistent time. Cale walked towards that sound like a zombie. *They've come for me*, he thought, and it frightened him, the almost casual acceptance he heard in that thought. Very nearly a willingness. *Yes, it was me, I killed Sergeant Willoughby, and I killed my father, as well, while we're at it, so cuff me, take me down to the station, charge me, just do it, just get on with it.*

But of course that was not what he wanted, just what his brain, steeped in exhaustion, wanted. If he was put in a cell tonight, there would be no more workshop to run, and therefore no deadlines to meet. And in trying to meet those deadlines, he was starting to make mistakes. Today the stairs, tomorrow, who knew? Maybe everything he made from here on in he would fuck up until he lost his ability altogether. No longer Cale Redstone, carpenter/joiner, but Cale Redstone, the village idiot.

He grasped the doorknob with fingers that were covered in cuts, some fresh, some crusted, and at the base of his fingers, there were blisters full of watery pus. He wanted a cigarette. The police might be on the other side of that door. If they were, then he guessed it was almost a condition that he should be smoking a cigarette, even though he had never tried one and in truth didn't want to. It just seemed like a good idea right now: a puff on one of those long white tubes that had become affiliated, it seemed, with anyone who was up to no good and smoked it like a signal that said, *I'm here, I did it, come and get me.* But no such long white tube for Cale Redstone, he was not a long white tube kind of a guy, and so, in that one way, he was not sending out those signals.

But...there were other signals. His fingernails, for one. Fingernails which he had chewed right down past the quick and into the pink, tender flesh beyond. And that tiny clutch of pockmarks on his right cheek, the little gift left there by the chicken-pox when he had been a boy? He had taken to scratching those, and now they hurt. *Burned.* And eczema. There was now a light-brown patch of it on the base of his spine, slightly rough and flaky. He had never suffered from eczema in his life...but now he did. Amazing what a little stress did to the body. Next he'd have shingles or trench foot or ingrowing pubic hair, whatever.

He opened the door and looked out, his wrists wanting to come together, cooperatively, so that the handcuffs could be snapped on without the order being given. But he kept his wrists at his sides because there were no cuffs.

Just a woman.

And she was no police officer, that's for sure.

'Hello there, Cale,' she said. Her voice was soft and low, but so cold it made him shiver. She put a hand on his chest - that part of her was warm, at least - and gently pushed him back into the house. Closed the door. 'I'm Miss Furneaux, Tommy's new headmistress. You can call me Moina.'

Red hair, she had, some of it piled up high, as was the fashion, the rest sweeping into her face, framing it. Dark, loveless eyes. Large breasts that she could expose and it wouldn't make much of a difference: her blouse seemed more of a trick than something she actually wore. Her hips were broad but not fat. There was a gold chain around her right ankle, Cale saw. An anklet, did you call it? Whatever, he thought it a strange, tinselly piece of jewellery for a headmistress to wear. He estimated her to be forty, possibly older. But all of that was secondary, for the most part. She was in his house, and he didn't *like* her in his house.

She gave him the creeps.

'What do you want?' he asked.

'Don't shout at me,' she said, glancing up the stairs. 'You'll wake the boy.'

'I'm not shouting.'

'Yes, you are.' She smiled at him. Of warmth, he saw none. Just the look a small, sadistic animal might flash at him before sinking its teeth into his face. 'My, you're on tenterhooks this evening, aren't you, Cale?'

Cale thrust out his chest in a feeble show of authority. 'I'll ask the questions around here. You're Tommy's headmistress, so what? That doesn't give you the right to just walk in here.'

'Then tell me what I should have done? *Flown* in here? On my broomstick?' She kicked off her high-heeled shoes, one, tra-la, two, tra-la, and there they lay, at the bottom of the stairs. Bright-red and sprinkled with glitter.

'Jesus, just make yourself at home, why don't you?'

'Oh, put a sock in it,' she said, flapping a hand at him. 'Start thinking about the power I have and the power you don't. Can you do that? Can you *grasp* that?'

'Right now I can't grasp anything,' Cale said. 'The only thing I know for sure is that I'm losing my patience.'

'I wouldn't lose your patience, if I were you. If I were you, I'd have all the patience in the world for someone like me. Because I can bring you down, Cale Redstone. How? I'm good at sniffing out the troubles people have and then using them to my own advantage, that's how. That doesn't make me a bad person, though. It just makes me...well, *resourceful*. Yes, resourceful - that's how I'd put it. Nothing wrong with being resourceful, is there, Cale? Especially when *you* can reap the rewards, as well.'

'What rewards might they be?'

'We'll talk about those in a moment. Let's go into the kitchen, shall we?' Then all of a sudden they were *in* the kitchen, as if a magic wand had been waved, and here they were, now standing under the bright, unshaded bulb in the centre of the room, face to face. *Hey presto!*

No magic about it, though. Just Cale Redstone being moved about like a chess piece and unable to stop it. *Powerless* to stop it. The tiredness, that was it. The constant tiredness that made him want to fall down and die the way this woman Moina Furneaux's predecessor had done just that in her office.

Moina Furneaux's hair flamed like a brazier. Her skin was creamy-smooth and surprisingly unwrinkled for a woman her age. Her breasts floated in front of Cale, and he found them tempting, only because he saw them as pillows on which to lay his head as opposed to objects he might like to cup and maybe suckle. Just pillows to snuggle into and fall asleep.

Her eyes bore into Cale, but not the way Little Miss Orange Dress's eyes had done that when he had been small and she led him by the hand into Sad's Place. There had been a kindness in that girl's eyes…and in her heart. But that was not present in Moina Furneaux's eyes. Hers were just cold, scheming dots that sent chills to all the corners of Cale's body.

'Tommy,' she breathed softly. 'Let's talk about Tommy, shall we, Cale? What is he?'

'Hmmm?'

'What is he? We know he's a deformed cripple, we know that much. I'm talking about what's going on up here.' She tapped her forehead with a fingertip. 'What is he? Autistic? Hyperactive? Borderline Personality? A combo of all three, perhaps? Never mind, the ins and outs don't matter much to me. What matters to me is that he is in my school…and I don't *like* him in my school.'

Her school? Already *her* school? Good God.

'My school is for pupils who are sound in body and mind. Am I discriminating? Of course I am. A spade is a spade, that's how I see it. I don't mince my words, the way some might. After all, if I see a black man in the street, then he is a nigger, to me, anyhow.'

'That's just being racist,' Cale said.

'Am I being a racist when I call myself a white honky slut?' Moina

Furneaux asked. 'No. I'm just saying it like it is. I *am* a white honky slut, the way your little brother is a crippled retard.'

Cale, astounded, both at the way she spoke of his brother, and at the way she spoke of herself, as a white honky slut. He guessed that would be funny under any other circumstance, but at the moment, Cale was having trouble getting his act together. A lot of trouble. The only clear thought his confused, intimidated brain could muster was that this was a headmistress. A headmistress? Like leaving a cat in charge of the fish stall, he thought.

So close to him now that her nipples that showed through her blouse brushed against his bare chest. Dark, erect tips that poked into him. 'How did he get into my school, anyhow?' she asked. 'Someone pulling strings they shouldn't have, methinks. Elsa Lovell, was it? Got him into her little summer school, I bet, and before the governors knew it, his admission form was approved, rubber-stamped, and hey-ho, what do you know, little Tommy Redstone was in the big school proper. A page right out of my own book, I must say. Still, like all books, the pages can be torn out.' She narrowed her eyes at him, and whispered: 'I can have him out of there, Cale. Just one phone-call and he'll be whisked off to the moron school over in Battenford where he belongs.'

'You can't do that,' Cale said. He suddenly wanted to grab this horrid, browbeating woman and give her a shake. 'His work has been up to standard, I know it has.'

'Up to standard? No, not up to standard. Just satisfactory, that's all. You know what satisfactory is, Cale, don't you? Satisfactory is the difference between mediocrity and excellence. I don't like mediocrity. Mediocrity is the reason why most people in this country spend their working lives building roads that lead to nowhere. I say pooh to mediocrity.'

'Pooh, perhaps. But Tommy is never going to be another Einstein, anyway. He's just a kid who deserves a fair crack of the whip.'

'I don't give people fair cracks of the whip. I am not a fair person...unless, of course, my back is being scratched in all the right places. Are *you* going to do that for me, Cale? Are you going to let me be…resourceful?'

'What do you want?' Cale asked in a voice that sounded so unlike his own. Just a bleary, docile drone. And no power. That word again: power. It seemed to have been torn out of his personal dictionary the way this woman Moina Furneaux was threatening to tear Tommy out of Brougham Moor.

'What I want is to live here,' Moina Furneaux told him. 'Not at the weekends. I fuck at the weekends. No, I just want a room during the week.'

'Why's that?'

'Because the school has given me a place to live in that could only be improved if someone set alight to it, that's how bad it is. A flat. In Twelve Trees Road. I hate the place. And I doubt I'll ever get my hands on Elsa Lovell's house. It's owned by the school, it should be mine, but her old cunt of a husband is still living there, and they won't throw *him* out in a hurry, not with his wife just passed away. So what's the answer, Cale? *Are* you going to scratch my back so I can scratch yours?'

'I don't want you scratching any part of me,' Cale said with a defiance that sounded so pathetic, it was almost ridiculous. 'Anyhow, don't you think my mother and father will have something to say about that? You think they'll say yes to a woman like you living under their roof?'

Moina Furneaux looked around with fake observation. 'Your parents? Where are they? Hiding under the stairs? Or maybe under the sink there, behind that ruffle of curtain? Don't make me laugh. This place hasn't seen a woman's touch in years. What happened? Did your mother finally come to her senses and run away from her useless husband and her crippled, thick-headed son? Well, it happens, doesn't it? This world is full of women who can't bear the sight of their men any more and finally take off for a better life.'

'You're just taking guesses,' Cale said, but he was stunned, all the same, at her insight. She hadn't got it spot on, of course. But it was close. So close, as a matter of fact, that she had hit upon what Cale had believed for years: that his mother had run away.

'I don't *just* take guesses,' Moina Furneaux said, rolling her eyes. 'I make guesses based on what I've found, after doing bit of digging around. You think I'd come over here without doing my homework first? I'm a teacher, Cale. I set the homework, and I know how to get it done when it comes at me from the other direction.'

'And what did you find?' Cale asked. But knowing. Knowing all along that Moina Furneaux would have found *something*, and something that would almost certainly help her to get her toe a little further in the door. A door that Cale was doing his best to keep shut, this despite the fact this woman was like a battering-ram, all dressed-up in fluffy, tarty things.

She said, 'I found out, after looking through Tommy's old school records, that your mother last attended a parent/teacher evening back in 1961. Five years ago. Your father? Fine. You'd have more luck finding the average father in a knitting circle than you would at a parent/teacher evening. But mothers? Mothers are mostly always there, come hell or high water. I had a chat, too, with one of Tommy's old teachers. She said that Tommy's mother was just about the most attentive mother she ever met. Wanted to know how her little boy was doing from just about every angle. Strange, wouldn't you say? A woman like that just upping and leaving? A woman so clearly in *love* with her little cripple boy? It's the best I can come up with at the moment, but - '

She paused and startled Cale by beginning to sniff at the air. Cale wanted to grab her breasts and give them a good, hard squeeze, just to jerk her out of doing that with her nose. Sniffing like that. But he couldn't - he found her fascinating and repulsive at the same time. Like watching something he wanted to take his eyes off but couldn't. A man poking needles into his cheeks, perhaps. Or a bearded woman. Or two dogs humping in the street.

Finally she stopped sniffing. Gave him a sly, self-satisfied look. 'I smell blood, Cale Redstone. A woman bleeds for most of her life, so she knows the smell of blood. Did he kill her?'

'What?'

'Did your father kill your mother?'

'Jesus, what kind of a woman are you?'

'The kind who knows that murder happens every day, in some place, at some time. The kind who knows there are *thousands* of people buried under floorboards, and nailed behind walls, and no one knows because no one cares, that's why. We all just look in the mirror, and say, "I'm fine, fuck the rest". That's how it goes, Cale. That's why people die and their killers get away with it: "I'm fine, fuck the rest".' She looked at him with a steadiness that was like a gun in the hands of an expert marksman. 'So, did he kill her? Did he?'

'I have no idea what you're talking - '

'Stop that!' she snapped at him, but even then, her voice was still soft and low and distinctly cold. 'If I go to the police right now, I think they'll listen to what I've got to say. Why not? They've got a dead copper on their hands, so I've heard, and they're no closer to catching his killer than they were at the start of it all. So I go down there, I tell them that I believe Tommy Redstone's mother may have been bumped off, and before you know it, they'll be up here to take a look around. You want that, do you? You want them up here, poking their noses into your business?'

'No,' Cale said, not wanting to say no, it would make him sound guilty, maybe not of murder, but of something. He couldn't help himself, though. He said no almost right away.

'No, of course you don't,' Moina Furneaux said. 'And we *all* have secrets, don't we? Maybe some are not so bad, but what secrets do, when they come out, is draw attention to the dark side of our lives, a dark side we don't want others looking into. Would it be fair to say that?'

'Yes.'

'Yes,' Moina Furneaux said. 'We all have secrets, and we all have a dark side.'

He could smell her breath, cool enough but with a peculiar tart edge to it. Not entirely disagreeable. Just different. It made him think for some strange reason of semen that had been cooled in a fridge.

'I have no wish to *know* your secrets, Cale. No wish to look into your dark side, either. I just want a place to live, five days of the week, where the mice don't wear overalls and gas masks. Are you going to assist me, or what?'

'I can't,' Cale said. 'My father's working away up in Templeton at the moment. But when he comes back - '

'Oh, please, don't string me along for a fucking fool!' Moina Furneaux said, reeking of a perfume so cheap, it tickled Cale's nose and caught at the back of his throat like a fishbone. 'Your father's not up in Templeton. You want me to start making those educated guesses of mine again? Fine, I'll do that. It'll give me even more fuel to throw on the fire.'

'No, don't do that,' Cale said, pleading with this woman when he didn't want to. Only wanted to put a hand over her mouth to make her stop. She was like pieces of glass rattling around in his head.

'And you need me, anyhow, don't you, Cale? It's been tough just lately, that's what I think. All that work to get through, out there in the workshop, and the little cripple boy upstairs who just won't behave himself when you want him to?'

'Yes, that's true,' Cale said, again not wanting to say this, but helpless to stop it. It just leaked out of him, a cork in the bottle of his emotions that could be pulled out all too easily and thus it allowed Moina Furneaux to get to the drink inside.

'He gives you more grief sometimes than a wagonload of monkeys, doesn't he?'

'Yes...he does...at times,' Cale said tamely. 'It's the sweets, you see. He sometimes takes money - '

'Steals, you mean?'

'Yes...steals. He steals money and buys sweets...and they change him. Change him from a good boy into a bad boy.'

'Yes, sugar can do that to some kids,' Moina Furneaux said. 'It gets into their system like rocket fuel.'

'Yes, like rocket fuel!' Cale agreed, and much too loudly, and then he laughed like a raving idiot at the circus. 'And he misses his mother, as well.'

'I'm sure he does.'

'Most mornings, when he gets out of bed, he goes to the letterbox, hoping to find a letter on the mat, waiting for him. Even after all these years, he still thinks he'll find a letter there from his mother. But of course there never is.'

'No, there never is. And what about you, Cale? *You* miss her, too, don't you?'

'Yes,' Cale said. He felt like death on the end of some horrible, twisting rope. Tears began to prickle his eyes. His throat clicked like a death-watch beetle. The colours ran out of his world the way they sometimes did when he got a bad headache and the only cure was to lie down, close the curtains, and wait for the colours to slowly bleed back.

'You just want her to hold you, don't you? Want her to run her lovely, sweet-scented hands through your hair, put a kiss on your head, and tell you that everything is going to be all right, there, there, my boy, no one will hurt you anymore, not with me by your side. Am I right, Cale?'

'Yes,' Cale said, and now it began to rise to the top, the pain, the loneliness, the responsibility of running the workshop all on his own, and Tommy, too, of course. Trying to keep that boy from going off the rails, and at times incapable of doing that.

Then there was the guilt, the guilt that ate into Cale, the guilt that wanted to drive him mad, the guilt that came to him in the night and turned his hours of rest into hours of unrest. He would sometimes hear his father's frightened voice shouting, *Help me, help me, help me! For God's sake, someone help me! HEEEEELP!*, as Cale flew at him with the mallet, about to whack it down on his whining, hooded head. And Sergeant Willoughby, his hands held up to his slit throat, and saying, *Radio in for help, boy! God's sake, radio in for help!* And the nightmares, too: ponies assembled around his bed and staring at him with dark, vengeful eyes; his father sitting in that chair of his, smoking a hand-rolled cigarette through the bloody hood; Sergeant Willoughby, his uniform splattered with birds' shit that dripped on the floor and turned into blood that pooled there, around his feet. All of that, as if that was not enough, and then there was Tommy. It *always* came back to Tommy, like it or not. That brother of his about whom Cale would not hear a bad word, despite the fact that Moina Furneaux had said more bad words about him than he cared to hear, and to be honest he wanted to rip her throat out for that...but he couldn't. Because the awful, perceptive bitch had gotten him in a corner, that's why. Had said all the right things at the wrong time, or all the wrong things at the right time, and either way it amounted to Cale feeling that he ought to go down on his knees and thank her for coming here when she had. Thank her for *saving* him!

He had to fight that, too. Actually had to fight the compulsion to thank this woman, and generously, when really she had muscled her way in here and bolted herself to the floor, the way she must have done that at Brougham Moor. Like an octopus to a rock.

'Yes, well I'm here now,' she said to him in that soft but somehow dreadful voice of hers. 'I'm not your mother, I know that, but it's not like I'm all tits and arse, is it? It may look that way, but look how gentle my hands are, Cale. Feel them. Go on.'

He did when she held them out to him. And they were gentle. *Lovely* and gentle.

'My kiss is sweet, too. Here.' She stood on tip-toes and kissed him on the cheek, and it felt strangely enjoyable, too, like a kiss from the girl of his dreams. 'If you let me stay here, then I can take the burden off your shoulders, Cale. I can keep Tommy in line while you get your work done. I'll even give him some extra tuition, if that'll help. Probably it won't. But we can try, can't we?'

'Yes, we can try,' Cale said, and it felt like he *was* in a dream. He began to think that perhaps he hadn't taken a bath at all. Instead had gone up to bed at the same time as Tommy, had fallen asleep, and now he was dreaming. Yes, that had to be it. Dreaming. Just dreaming.

'But first you have to *ask* me to stay,' she said. 'I'm a little disappointed that you were against that, Cale, when it was clear from the beginning that I only wanted to help. Wanted to help you, and to help Tommy.'

'Yes, I know that now,' Cale said, already trapped by this woman. Couldn't fight it. Just couldn't, even though every dissenting voice in his head screamed at him to get her out of here, to pick her up if he had to, anything, just to get her out of here and close the door on the manipulative bitch!

He couldn't, though. He needed her. Needed her more than she needed him, quite possibly. Because without her this brave new world he had made for he and Tommy would come tumbling down. He needed help. Not tomorrow. Not the next day. Or the day after that. He needed help now, before he took his fingers off in the bandsaw, or dropped a pile of wood on his feet and broke his toes. Or, God help him, before he ran a child down in the road in that truck of his.

It could happen. For he was in the grip of a tiredness so out of control, he was really an accident just waiting to happen. What did it matter that help had come to him in the form of a she-devil? It was either that or watch everything fall apart as if it were held together with nothing but string, bent pins, and spittle.

'So ask me,' Moina Furneaux said. 'Don't just stand there, gawping. Ask me.'

'Okay,' Cale said. 'Will you?'

'Will I what?'

'Will you come and live with me and Tommy?'

She would say yes. That was, after all, the object of this exercise, for her to say yes after he had made it clear that *he* wanted her to live here, not the other way around. But what she did was say no. Just like that. No. Then she shrugged her shoulders, like this was some sort of a game

'No?' Cale said.

'No,' Moina Furneaux said. 'If you want me to stay, then beg me.'

'Beg you?' But already he was going down on his knees, even though his mind was still in debate. Going down, and as he did, he turned his hands to his face and saw how lacerated they were, how bruised, how blistered. And God how they *ached*! Ached because they never stopped milling wood, day after day after day after long, miserable, never-ending day.

Going down, going down, going down, and when he reached the halfway point, she abruptly pulled him into her breasts and held him there, his face pressed against them, his top lip stuck there, the way

Don Willoughby's top lip had been stuck to the Humber's dash, pulling it up into a sneer.

'Beg me, Cale,' she said. 'Go on, beg me!'

'I beg you,' Cale said, just wanting to fall asleep, just wanting to huddle into those big, soft breasts, and in them he would doze forever. And ever. And ever. But she put a hand in his hair right then, and yanked him up until he was staring levelly into her cold, cold eyes.

'Again!'

'I beg you,' Cale said. 'I beg you, I beg you, I beg you!' Tears not just prickling his eyes now. They flowed down his face, freely as rain.

'Good lad,' Moina Furneaux said, and then she let go of his hair. 'Now go and fetch my bags out of my car.' She laughed. 'But not like that, eh?'

She was looking down at his hips, his hips to which no bath towel clung anymore. It lay around his feet, he saw, in a damp, rumpled horseshoe. He picked it up. Hurriedly. Fastened it back around his waist. Then he went out and fetched her bags. Understanding now that a boy became a man, not when he could grow a beard, or when he could buy a legal beer, but when he knew how to handle a woman. And Cale Redstone didn't.

But when DI Roy Cutlass came calling one hot, October afternoon, Cale soon came to the conclusion - as he watched Moina in the workshop, drenched in blood, and feverishly working at the bandsaw - that *no* man would have been able to handle a woman like Moina Furneaux. No man.

Chapter 13: Miss Fur-Knickers

'We've got a guest,' Cale said, pouring himself a coffee. His hands trembled but he tipped the coffee into his cup, successfully, without spillage.

'Who?' Tommy asked. Not much interest, though. There was a bowl of cornflakes on the table, doused in cold milk, heavily sprinkled with sugar, and he just wanted to tuck into them. But then he looked up, his eyes all of a sudden bright and attentive. 'Is it mum, Cale? Is mum back?'

'No, not mum,' Cale said. He cut that thought out of the boy's head before it could take hold. 'Miss Furneaux.'

Tommy shook his head as if dazed. 'Miss Fur-Knickers? What's *she* doing here?'

'Miss Fur-Knickers? Is that what you call her?'

Tommy nodded. 'Just about everyone at school calls her that. Have you seen the way she dresses?'

'Yes. Well. I've seen the way she *doesn't* dress, if that's what you mean. But anyway, her. I put her in dad's bedroom. From now on, she'll be staying here during the week.' *At the weekend she likes to fuck,* he thought, but of course did not add. 'At the weekend she'll stay at her flat over in Twelve Trees Road.'

'I don't understand,' Tommy said. 'How did this come about?'

'I'd rather not go into that,' Cale said, embarrassed by the fact that last night he'd been rolled over so easily by Moina Furneaux. He'd been tired, of course, there had been that, and as excuses went, it was sufficient. More than sufficient. After all, you could pretty much roll anyone over when sleep had become to them like a rosy apple too high up in the tree for them to pluck. And it wasn't like it had been *just* that. She had known things - things anyone else could only take a guess at and be wildly off the mark. Not Moina Furneaux, though. Moina Furneaux - old Miss Fur-Knickers herself, apparently - had been so close to the mark, that had it been an exam, she would have received a B+ at the very least.

I set the homework, and I know how to get it done when it comes at me from the other direction.

Not just a load of hot air, that. When Moina Furneaux did her homework, she delivered, so it seemed, and in style. In here now, and sleeping in Daddy Bear's bed, thank you very much.

'So what are we going to do?' Tommy said. 'Just let her get away with it?'

'She hasn't *gotten* away with anything, not really,' Cale said. 'It was me who said she could stay here. I could have said no when she came calling last night.'

'So why didn't you?'

'Because...' It was on the tip of his tongue to just tell Tommy that Moina Furneaux could have Tommy out of Brougham Moor, that all it would take was one short phone-call. But why tell him that? He'd just be letting Tommy know that he was the barrel over which Cale had been bent last night. No point telling him - it would set the boy against Moina Furneaux, and furthermore, it would make him feel worthless, when right now, at Brougham Moor, he had never felt more worthy in his life. 'Because,' Cale said, 'she'll be another pair of hands around here...and I could use them.'

'What about me, Cale? Haven't *I* been any use to you?'

'Yes, you have. But you can't cook a dinner, Tom, or clean up, or wash clothes, or make a bed, the way an adult can. And look at me. Jesus.' He held out his hands that were cut to ribbons and ached like a bastard. His eyes next. He pointed to those, drawing attention to the dark puffiness underneath, and to the fact they were faintly bloodshot. Nevertheless, he had slept last night. It had been good, unbroken sleep, as well...notwithstanding the fact that one swallow did not a summer make, of course.

Tommy gave Cale a remorseful look. 'Yes, okay, it's been difficult for you just lately, I know that. I only wish I could do the things grownups can, but I can't.' He lowered his head then, ashamed. No need to feel ashamed, though. Tommy had lent a helping hand, and on several occasions. Last night, for example, he'd primed those window-frames, swept up the shavings, bagged them, and then sharpened all of Cale's chisels. Useful. The problem was that inside the house he was not so useful. Pretty much an ornament, all told.

'I don't *expect* you to do the things that grownups can,' Cale said. 'The only thing I expect is for you to get your head down at school. School is everything, Tom. For you, anyway. For me, it's just about plugging away in the workshop and earning the money we need to stay independent. If we stay independent, then we stay out of trouble. I think I said that a while ago, didn't I? Or something like it?'

'Yes,' Tommy said. 'But what about Miss Furneaux? What if *she* finds out about dad?'

'No problem. I told her he's working up in Templeton.'

'No, not that. What if she finds out' - he glanced around, just to make sure they weren't being listened to - 'you know, that you bumped him off?'

'How will she find that out?'

'By looking in Sad's Place, maybe?'

'She won't,' Cale said. Such a discovery probably wouldn't matter much to that twisted woman, anyhow, but for Tommy's sake, Cale went through the motions. '*I've* got the key to Sad's Place, haven't I? And it's right here.' He patted his chest, then opened his shirt to show Tommy the key, that long, old-fashioned, rust-speckled piece of metal with its large, toothy end that was now on a piece of string around Cale's neck (he had rigged this up last night before going to bed, now that Moina Furneaux was staying in the house). 'No one's going to get it, Tom. No one.'

After the way Tommy had tried to force open the writing desk, that would serve as a warning to him also, that Cale was tightening security around here. Here was the key to Sad's Place, the one key, the *only* key, and if anyone wanted it, they would have to take it off him.

Physically take it off him. And the key to the writing desk? That was on the string, too. Trust no one: that was Cale's motto now. Even with Tommy.

'Fine,' Tommy said, nodding at the key. 'But I'd still be careful of Miss Furneaux, if I were you. She has the teachers wrapped around her fingers. The *men* teachers, anyhow.'

The *male* teachers, Cale wanted to correct the boy, but this was not the time to be picky. And it was hardly much of a surprise that, anyhow, to hear that Miss Fur-Knickers had the male teachers wrapped around her fingers. Pretty much what Cale expected, after what had happened here last night. That was done with, though - the knot had been tied and it could not be untied. Uppermost in Cale's mind for the time being was Tommy's reaction to all of this. 'Have I let you down, Tom?'

'Let me down? How?'

'By allowing Miss Furneaux to live here?'

'No, not really,' Tommy said. His voice was low, temperate, understanding. 'It was a worry to me at the start of all this that running the workshop and the house on your own would be too much for you. I'm *pleased* someone is here to give you a hand. I just wish it wasn't my headmistress.'

'You don't have to tell anyone about it, though, do you? You know, that she's living here?'

'Don't worry, I won't be. Embarrassing or what. Miss Fur-Knickers? Crikey.'

Cale smiled in spite of himself. 'What's up, don't you like her?'

Tommy thought for a moment, and then said, 'She's just, well...*weird.*' Then he gave a theatrical little shudder, as if someone had walked over his grave. 'Anyway, she won't be at the school for long. She's only a temp. Probably she'll be gone by the end of the term.'

And she was. Just not the way that Tommy had imagined it. Or Cale for that matter.

October and the sun still a hot, shining ball that refused to be rolled off the sky. Ten days since Moina Furneaux had moved in, and Cale was back on top of his work again. Back on top, and ahead of it, in many respects. Great. And Tommy? Some days the brightest pin you could tack to your lapel and be proud of, and then there were other days, especially when he was on the sugar, when Cale just wanted to give him a shake that might help tighten the screws in his head that seemed to come loose every now and again.

Still, these past three of four days, Tommy's behaviour had been excellent. Dare Cale believe it but the boy actually seemed to like Moina Furneaux. All makeup, and crazy hairdo, and long, painted fingernails, but Tommy seemed to find something in her that he liked. Great, also. But things, *despicable* things, were happening underneath the crackled glaze that Cale could not see through...mostly because he wasn't looking. Just getting on with his work, and on many occasions he still worked late into the night, but at least he didn't have to deal with the household chores when he knocked off. Moina took care of those. She cooked the dinners, dusted, vacuumed, washed the clothes and bedsheets. Even took down the nets and curtains one afternoon and gave those a wash. Just about fit enough for the bin, they were. Ragged, moth-eaten things. But that evening Moina darned them, and somehow made them respectable enough to hang back in the windows again.

'They turned the water black,' she told Cale, sitting there at the kitchen table with his mother's sewing basket on her lap. 'Like tar. That's how filthy they were.'

His mother had been the last to wash those nets and curtains, so he wasn't exactly amazed when he heard that from Moina. Still, Moina's look had not been black like that water, but kind, it must be said. Bigoted, manipulative, foul-mouthed, and bawdy, she was. Stick a few more choice adjectives in there, too, they'd probably fit the bill. However, when it came to keeping house, Moina simply got on with it when she didn't have to, and uncomplainingly. Just gave Cale that look a woman will sometimes give a man that said, *When God created woman, man got a bargain.*

So it seemed, too...on the surface, anyhow. Cale hated to think it, he was still mortified at how easily she had gotten passed him that night, as if he'd been a sentry fast asleep at his post, but give the woman her due, she not only made his life easier, but exceeded all of his hopes. And she could cook, as well: jam roly-poly, carrot cake, apple pie, fruit flan, and a wonderful wild berry tart that made Cale's tongue tingle every time he put a spoonful in his mouth.

Then came the party games. One night Cale went into the sitting room, thinking he'd watch the news and maybe the *Rat Catchers* afterwards, starring Gerald Flood as the redoubtable Peregrine Pascale Smith, and then go up to bed. But when he walked in the room, he found Moina and Tommy playing games such as Jack's Alive, and Coffeepots, and My Aunt went into Town, and Chinese Touch, and Mother Magee.

Cale joined in, and couldn't recall when he'd had a better night. The air peppered with Moina's original brand of expletives, which were, for instance, "Fuck em, bandy!" and "Ride me, Sailor!" and her all-time favourite, it seemed, "Truss me up and stuff me like turkey!" However, when he put all that aside, along with the blouses she wore that you could spit through, what you got on the face of it was basically a decent woman who somehow existed next to the smutty, blackmailing cow who had stolen in here that night, threatening to take Tommy out of Brougham Moor if Cale did not submit to her demands.

Nevertheless, he would soon find out that Moina Furneaux, as good as she was at making a home - and at bringing a little entertainment to that home - was not a woman to be second-guessed...or boiled-down...or kicked into a cocked hat. She took sandwiches and cold lemonade out to Cale when she came home for lunch. Ironed his shirts. Polished his work-boots. Opened the windows in his bedroom to air it, and remembered to close them again before it got too chilly in there. She let him have the best chair in the sitting room, and asked him first before switching stations on the television, and sometimes she even brought him in a bottle of beer, along with a side-plate of savoury nibbles. Nice. Bliss, actually. But even the hardest of women knew how to soothe a fevered brow, to cook a tasty meal, and to make a bed so that when a man got into it, he drifted straight off to sleep. That stuff was inbuilt. It came to a woman the way that tinkering with an engine came to a man, no matter what. And you certainly did not take that as a weakness. Just took it as part of what made most women tick, anyhow. Their natural readiness to serve.

Cale knew none of that, though. For what a boy knew, a man had forgotten, and what a man knew, a boy could not acquire. Only time, and time alone, stood between the light of a boy and the beacon of a man...and for Cale Redstone time was running out.

However, while the gates of a hell that were yet to open still remained closed, he made the best of it. He watched Moina run out of the house one morning with a bucket of cold water and throw it all over Tommy. A cheeky but harmless remark had sparked this off. Just a light-hearted leg-pull, but Moina didn't let it go at that. She paid him back with a dousing that made her laugh, that made Cale laugh, and made Tommy laugh, too. Eventually.

'Ah, that's not fair!' he protested at first. 'Look at the state of me!' Dripping. His hair plastered to his head. His jumper sagging off him. 'Is this funny?' he went on complaining. 'If it is, then *I* don't see it!' But in the end he saw it all right, as most people do when laughter was all there was and nothing else.

None of them laughed like Cale, though. He laughed when it was funny, and he still laughed when all the funniness had gone, and he went on laughing when there was absolutely nothing to laugh at anymore...except perhaps at himself. His face. He suddenly swung around and saw it in the workshop window, a face that was red, contorted, howling. A face, he thought, that belonged, not to a carpenter/joiner, but to someone who had escaped from the madhouse.

Taking advantage of the unseasonably warm weather, Moina Furneaux found a shovel in one of the broken-down sheds at the back of the workshop, a shovel with a rotted handle and a blade full of rust. That didn't stop her, though. Wearing gumboots and a bikini so small she might as well be naked, she set about creating flowerbeds under the kitchen window as well as up the side of Sad's Place. Next to her were two crates of flowers she must have bought on the way home from school.

An amazing woman, really...when you put the bad in her to one side. All of this, and a house to run, a school to run, and heaps of paperwork to get through, and still she found the time to give Tommy the extra tuition. *What is he? Autistic? Hyperactive? Borderline Personality? A combo of all three, perhaps?* Her less than flattering opinion of Tommy that night, along with calling him a deformed cripple, and a couple of times since then she had referred to him as Thicko Spasmo. This, when she and Tommy seemed to be hitting it off, and grandly.

Yet behind his back she continued to speak ill of him. It pissed Cale off, that. A lot. But without her, he knew he'd be in all sorts of trouble by now. A case of forgiving the sins to enjoy the benefits. Even though it hurt him to do that.

A puzzle, she was. Undoubtedly. One moment next to a saint, and then, all of a sudden, she'd be taking cheap shots at Tommy, then after that the fun-time girl would come out. Then there were the times when she was like a bird with its head tucked under its wing. Thinking. But not thinking anything that Cale wished to know about. It would be dark in there, he knew. The kind of dark in which horrible things wriggled and squirmed. But to doubt her intelligence would be to doubt the sun on your face, or the wind in your hair. Her intelligence Cale witnessed one night when she gave Tommy a biology lesson that left Cale thinking she should not be an itinerant headmistress but lecturing at Oxford or Cambridge. Yet not all the waters of her mind seemed to flow in the same direction. She fucked at the weekend, using her words, her words that were upfront and in your face. She fucked at the weekend, did the white honky slut. Jesus. Not exactly what you wanted to hear from a woman, was it? Even so, for all of that, not one man called at number 3 Samuel Lane. Not one. Moina Furneaux kept that side of her life strictly private.

'Hi, Cale, how's your bum for spots?'

Cale turned and saw Tommy there, munching on an apple. 'My bum's fine, thanks.' He nodded at the apple. 'Are you feeling all right, Tom? Haven't got a fever, have you?'

'Uh?'

'The apple?'

'Oh,' Tommy said, looking down at the half-eaten fruit in his hand that was dripping juice everywhere. 'Miss Furneaux gave it to me before she went back to her flat. Told me to eat it all up. So I am.'

'Good for you. So she's gone, has she? Back to Twelve Trees Road?'

'Yep. Just you, me, and the whole weekend ahead of us. What are those?'

'Fishing rods,' Cale said. He was in one of the sheds from which Moina had gotten the shovel the other day. Now he decided to have a poke around himself. And here were the rods, one his, one his father's. Up in the rafters. Made of split-cane with fancy, brass eyes, and when Cale turned the reels, they spun perfectly. He took them down. Grabbed a cloth and wiped the dust off them.

'Are we going fishing?' Tommy asked, suddenly joyous. 'God, I've never been fishing in my *life*! Are you taking me, Cale? Are you?' Jumping up and down like a jumping bean. Holding his crotch as if he might wet himself. 'Oh, please, Cale, please! Take me, take me!'

Cale gave Tommy a less than patient look. No longer behind in his work, of course, and his books were up to date, and just about all of the customers had paid their bills, too. No need to go chasing them for their debts, thank goodness. His mind was still on his work, though. Checking out the sheds had just been a minor interruption in what was otherwise a brain that operated these days on one level and one level only: work, get it done. And when the work behind it came to the fore, then get that done, too.

The work, however, no longer disabled him. He was sleeping better, not great, still suffered from the bad dreams, but yes, he was sleeping better now that Moina Furneaux was here. His hands were still cut to ribbons, but he could do precious little about that. It was the price he had paid for losing the other pair of hands that used to help him out around here. His father's hands, Hospital and Death.

Still, it was a Saturday, wasn't it? Moina Furneaux gone back to Twelve Trees Road. Just Cale and Tommy. And what had Cale and Tommy done together since their father's death? Not much. As a treat, just before Tommy began his first term at Brougham Moor, Cale had taken the boy to see *Goldfinger* at the Embassy Cinema in Unity Gate. Afterwards, Tommy hadn't been able to stop chattering about the gold-painted lady on the bed, and the laser that had threatened to cut James Bond in half, and Oddjob. Oddjob had been Tommy's favourite character in the film, moreover, that bowler hat of his that, when thrown, could cut a man's head clean off. When they came out of there, Tommy had mimicked Oddjob by throwing an imaginary bowler at people in the street, and would then shout out, *Gotcha!*, and then make a thud noise as their heads rolled off and fell to the ground. Funny, but somewhat annoying, after a while.

Another time they played football in the back garden, with Tommy putting on his own World Cup commentary, such as 'Moore to Charlton, Charlton to Ball, Ball to Peters, Peters to Hurst…and oh yes, would you believe it, Hurst has scored with the most wonderful shot you've ever seen! The goalie didn't stand a chance! In the top corner, thank you very much!'

Not much else, though. For Tommy, the house had become something of a prison, and for Cale the workshop had become likewise.

Now here was Tommy requesting that Cale take him fishing, and when Cale looked into the boy's eyes, eyes that would surely pop at a refusal, he couldn't help himself. He said, 'All right, Tom, we'll go fishing. I could do with a break from all this shit, anyway.'

'Yes!' Tommy said. 'Whoopee! Whoopee! Whoopee!' Then he wet himself, just like that. The front of his jeans abruptly darkened, and Tommy looked down at his crotch, embarrassed. Dropped his apple. Began to grope at himself to try and stop the flow, but of course he couldn't, because a child's plumbing was no better than a leaky tap. 'Ooops.' It trickled out from beneath his turn-ups and began to pool there on the boarded floor.

'All right, no problem,' Cale said. His tone was kind, and there was patience there, too, finally. Albeit a touch artificial. 'Go inside and clean yourself up. While you're doing that, I'll dig for bait, and make a packed lunch, as well.'

Off the boy went, back to the house. Head down to begin with. Shoulders rounded. Ashamed of what had happened and just as perplexed by it. Halfway across the back garden, however, and he started to run, and to leap, and to shout, 'Hurrah, hurrah, hurrah!', like nothing had happened.

Cale put the rods down, and began to hunt for his father's fishing basket. It would be in here, too, somewhere, full of hooks and lures and reels of line. He stared into the gloom at the back of the shed, where the dust was deep, where the mould, hairy and moist, jealously hugged the timbers, and where cobwebs dangled from the rafters, shimmering.

His father's fishing basket? He didn't find that. Not right then he didn't, anyhow.

But he found his father.

He was crouched behind an old chair with a busted straw seat. Grinning up at Cale. His teeth filthy with blood. 'Aaah!' Cale cried, and fell back against a stack of cardboard boxes that broke his fall. He struggled to his feet, his heart-rate doubling, tripling, even. His balls scurried up inside his belly, the only place that seemed to be warm right now. The rest of him had turned ice-cold. A bubble that contained much of his sanity tried to float away from him, but Cale grabbed it before it could do that. Before it could float away, out of his reach.

He went back to the place where he had seen his father who had not been his father - of course not, don't be silly - but even so, Cale still took it one small, timid step at a time. His chest tight. His eyes so wide, they seemed to press against his brain, uncomfortably. A tea-chest was here, and in it, Cale would find the basket he'd been looking for, but for now, he grasped the chest and peered over it.

What he saw was a blackboard down there, behind the busted chair. A blackboard on which had been drawn a simple chalk face. Probably Tommy had drawn that face when he had been an infant. A round face with inexpressive dots for eyes, sunbeams of yellow chalk for hair, and a mouth filled with teeth that where, for some unknown reason, as red as the lips that surrounded them.

Where have you been, boy? that face seemed to say to Cale. *I don't feel too good. It's like I'm sinking. Sinking.*

Cale did not fall back this time but stepped away, one pace, two paces, three paces. Brought his hands up in a slow, trembling arc, and placed them on his cheeks. His fingertips pulled at the skin under his eyes and made his face look as if it were melting. 'Yes I need a break,' he said. 'I need a break away from all this shit, all right.'

He found the basket and grabbed it up. Same for the rods. Then he got out of there.

Many people discover over the course of their lives that birthdays, Christmas, summer holidays, those days that are etched indelibly into the calendar, can be something of a disappointment, and that it is the off-the-cuff days that really bring joy to the heart. Those days when you put on a raincoat, go walking in the woods, and listen to the rain as it drips off the trees like a secret message. Or when you charge down a beach and run into the sea like a lunatic with all of your clothes on. Or when you make love to someone on the back step with a brisk wind using your arse as a bagpipe. Or when you bump into an old friend on a street corner, you embrace, you swap the history, you laugh, and when you part, you walk away feeling energised, and yet a little confused as to how you could have lost contact with such a nice fellow. Life really was a mystery. The best you could do, Cale understood, was jump at the chances that came your way, and when they didn't, you went out and made those chances happen. On this occasion he had done that. And he was glad that he had.

He and Tommy spent a wonderful day at Witches Point. They caught two skinny, oily mackerel that wouldn't fill a half-decent sandwich, but it wasn't what they caught out of the sea that mattered, but what they caught in love and togetherness. They found each other that day, they really did. They found each other properly, away from the ghosts of Samuel Lane, just like the old friends who bumped into each other and then wondered how they lost contact in the first place. They playfully ruffled each other's hair. They grabbed. They slapped. They kissed. They told jokes. How long's the next bus? About fifty-feet! What do you call an Irishman hanging off a light bulb? Shaun-delier! What do you call a man with a shovel in his head? Doug! My girlfriend's a red-head: no hair, just a red head! Crap jokes, they were, but they had both boys in stitches. They watched the clouds go chugging by on the sky's wide blue road. They watched the sea as it lashed against the pier, then receded in a plume of foam and with a sound that was like hailstones on a tin roof. They ate ham sandwiches that smelled of raw fish and of the worms that Cale had found for bait in the flowerbeds that Moina Furneaux had made back at the house. They drank hot coffee. And when the day was over, they walked back to the truck, arms around each other, and carrying their rods and tackle. Tired. Aching. But content in a way that Cale had not felt for a long, long time. The same for Tommy, most likely.

Tommy said, 'The Red Indians, they sometimes become blood brothers, did you know that?'

Cale said, 'Yes.'

Tommy said, 'Can *we* become blood brothers?'

Cale said, 'Yeah, why not.' Didn't even think about it. He took the sharp, fish-gutting knife out of his father's basket, made a little cut in his forefinger, wincing, and then did the same to Tommy's. *Ouch*! But no tears from the boy. Not even the tiniest quiver of the lower lip. He just stood there in the shadow of the hulking truck with sea salt stuck in his hair, his cheeks wind-slapped, and with an almost comical look of bravery on his face. They pressed their fingers together and held them there for a while. It was done: blood brothers. An odd way to finish the day, for Cale, it was, anyhow. And sadly it would become horribly prophetic. The truck, the blood. The truck. *And* the blood.

Chapter 14: Splendiferous

A late afternoon with Tommy out on his bike somewhere, and the world about to tilt and then tip Cale Redstone right off the edge. In the meantime: 'There's a glass of cold lemonade out here, Cale. A tuna sandwich, too, if you want it.'

Moina Furneaux, that was, standing outside the workshop in that bikini of hers that left nothing to the imagination. Just four triangles of thin material, it seemed. Wearing her red glittery high-heeled shoes, the gold anklet, as well, and thoughts of a sexual nature began to run through Cale's head, thoughts he didn't especially want, not when a forty-something headmistress just happened to be the focus of these thoughts.

Before all this trouble blew in, Cale used to go to the Spennymore club in Unity Gate. The Spennymore was a youth club in which the kids met on a Friday night to play records, to dance, and to drink warm beer. And of course there were the usual hormone-driven groping sessions in which most of the kids indulged at the end of the night. There was never any actual *sex*, the girls just weren't loose enough for that, and so these sessions usually ended with Cale making a mess in his underpants that he'd have to clean up when he got home. It *was* sex, though…of a kind. And a relief. Just lately, though, there hadn't even been any of that. Frustrating. It made him realise he really ought to get a social life again.

'Couldn't bring it in for me, Moina, could you? I'm rather busy.'

'I was hoping we might have a chat,' she said. 'Can we?' Her voice was soft and low, as was customary, but this time there was no coldness in it. None at all. A little warmth there for a change that Cale found difficult to resist.

'Okay, then. Just give me a minute.'

Moina acknowledged this with a nod of her head, then went back to the garden. Cale, meanwhile, finished fixing a particularly delicate piece of laminate to the edge of a kitchen unit. Once done, he went out the back, into the storeroom, took off his apron, washed his hands, and then joined Moina on the back lawn. It *was* a lawn, too, not a patch of neglected, ankle-high grass anymore. After creating the new flowerbeds that day, Moina had returned to the sheds, and after a bit of digging around, she had come back with an old lawnmower: a Qualcast that was rusted to buggery. No motor. *Hand-draulic*, as Ewan Redstone would have put it. After borrowing a file out of Cale's toolbox, along with a little grease, she soon got the blades spinning again, though. Got them sharp, too. An hour after that, and there it was, one lawn. No bowling green, admittedly, but one heck of an improvement, all the same.

There were two deck chairs out here, Cale saw, next to the flowerbeds that now blossomed with winter pansies. A low table, too, between the chairs on which Moina had set out the food and the drink. She was eating an apple, although not in the usual fashion. Using a sharp knife, she was, to cut segments of the red, shiny fruit that she would then slide into her mouth. Nothing wrong with that, fine. Just that the knife was the one Cale had used to slit Willoughby's throat with. He kept meaning to throw it away but thus far had not gotten around to it.

He sat beside her. Hard to believe it was October with the sun still hot enough to tan the skin and to leave a throat parched. But there it was. He began to eat his sandwich and to drink his lemonade, in which ice cubes crackled and clinked. All the time, from the side of his eye, sneaking little glances at Moina. Couldn't help it. Looking at the way she would cut a thin slice of apple, slip it into her mouth, and then crunch it up with her white, even teeth. The knife in one hand, the apple in the other, both resting on her tummy in which no baby had ever grown, that was clear, because it was flat, taut, and no stretch-marks were tattooed there. This woman, not exactly beautiful but beguiling, nevertheless. Eyes that were still those dark, scheming dots, but occasionally Cale glimpsed a mellow depth in them that Moina seemed to suppress most of the time with a thin but strong layer of superficiality. Her way of blocking out the warmth and locking in the ice, he supposed.

When Cale finished eating his sandwich, he looked at her directly. 'That was nice, Moina. Thanks for that.'

'You're welcome.'

He wiped the breadcrumbs off his hands. 'You wanted a chat with me. About what?'

'Just wanted to know if I've passed my trial period. Have I?'

'What trial period would that be? There wasn't one.'

'I'm being humble, Cale. Pleasant. Trying to mend a few bridges I may have burned on the way in here. Is that okay?'

He shrugged his shoulders. 'Fine by me. What makes you that way, anyhow, Moina?'

'What way?'

'So hard.'

'*Am* I hard? I don't think I am. I just know what I want and how to get it.'

'I understand that. What I don't understand is that you're a headmistress, and that makes you a cut above the ordinary woman in the street. An intellectual, you know. But sometimes you can be just so cruel. Take Tommy, for example - '

'No, let's not take Tommy,' she said, and sharply. 'I don't *care* about Tommy. Don't care about you, either. Why should I? In a couple of months the school will have found a permanent replacement for me, and I'll be out of Unity Gate. Gone. Goodbye. Cheerio. Ta-ta. Don't judge me, Cale.'

'I'm *not* judging you.'

'You are. The act of questioning is an act of judgment in itself. Most people ask questions in order to form an opinion of a person, and then, when they've gotten enough answers, they pigeonhole them. Okay. That's all right. Just human nature, love it or leave it. I prefer to leave it.'

'So what do we talk about? If I can't question you, then why am I here?'

'Because I'm a bad girl with an ulterior motive, that's why. Mostly I just want you out here so you can fuck me. What do you think?' Straight out of her mouth, no messing about. Just the way she had called herself a white honky slut that night. 'Well?'

'Well, what? Don't be ridiculous.'

'I'm not *being* ridiculous.' She tilted her head and gave him a provocative look. 'Or is it that you're a poof?'

'A poof?'

'Yes, a poof. After all, a good-looking boy like you, and no girlfriend? That doesn't make sense to me. *Ought* to have a girlfriend. Yes, you must be a poof.'

He couldn't believe what he was hearing. Startled at first. Startled numb and then startled into anger. 'I am *not* a poof. I just haven't had the time for girls just lately.'

'Boys your age make time, don't they? All that juice swilling around inside of them? It's got to go somewhere, hasn't it? Where's yours going, Cale? Down the toilet? All over the bedsheets?'

'Don't talk that way, I don't like it!'

'*Why* don't you like it? Don't you want to fuck a nice, juicy hole?' She stood up then, abruptly but elegantly. Dropped the apple on the deck chair. The knife, too. Began to undo her bikini top. 'Or is it that you'd be fucking an older woman, and if you fucked an older woman, it would be like fucking your own mother?'

'Don't you *dare* bring my mother into this! You're disgusting, you know that? A woman with your brains and yet you act like a slut! Incredible!'

'Incredible? Why's that? Oh, I get it. You think a woman with brains should lead a good, ethical life, is that it? Keep her legs shut and her hands on her hanky? Sorry, but that's a little too boring for me. A brain isn't a passport to purgatory, Cale. A brain you use when you need it, and then, when you don't, you lock it away so it can't escape and spoil the rest of your time. Now, let's fuck em bandy, shall we?'

Her top now undone, she took it off, and out popped her large, plump breasts. The top fluttered down onto the deck-chair and joined the apple there. The knife, too. The knife whose blade was shiny and wet with juice.

'We can't, Tommy might come back!'

'Tommy? I don't think so. When he's out on that bike of his, he doesn't come back until the sun goes down. Stop playing for time, Cale.' Now for her panties. Down they went, two pieces of material that were like paper held together with weak glue. Then she was out of them and she tossed them aside. Naked. Just standing there in nothing but her high-heels and with that gold chain around her ankle. Cale swallowed hard. Put his glass of lemonade down and got to his feet. A little unsteadily, too. Sweat poured down his face. His heart flapped against his ribs like a bird in a cage.

'Sorry, Moina, but I can't do this. Jesus. Don't make me.'

'Do I *have* to make you? Surely not. Don't you like what I've got?'

'Yes...I like it...of course I do...it's just that I can't go through with this...I just can't. And I've got work to do.'

She laughed. It sounded derisive. Almost heckling. 'You've got work to do right here, Cale. Get on with it.' She grabbed herself, then. Grabbed her neat little thatch of pubic hair and gave it a vigorous upwards tug, and Cale's eyes went to that, they went to that place that opened briefly, and in there he glimpsed pink, moist flesh. Oh God, a sight for sore eyes that had been! There it was, though, a glimpse of that place that could drive men mad, and some, he suspected, *did* go mad. Just off their tiny minds.

'I thought you only fucked at the weekend?' His voice sounded all timorous and squeaky, as if a mouse, perhaps hidden in his pocket, had asked that question.

'For you, I'm making an exception. Come here, gorgeous.' A hand outstretched, a forefinger beckoning. Her voice still soft and low, that never changed, not ever, but the coldness was back, along with a gruff, shivery edge to it.

He began to walk backwards. Feeling a fool for doing this. A big fool - none of the boys at the Spennymore would turn this offer down. None of them. Be in there like rats up a drainpipe. For Cale, however, the mental block was Tommy, because, oh fuck it, it was *always* Tommy, day after day, week in, week out. Tommy, Tommy, Tommy, Tommy. To think about him was to see him - that's how it was for Cale.

Whenever he thought about the boy, he saw him, either stumping along on that cane of his, or riding up the drive on his new bike that did not look so new anymore. Tommy. Not the entire reason why Cale had slammed himself into reverse, but as the boy owned the largest share of the reasons, so that gave him a dominance in Cale's mind that Cale could not get rid of. He suddenly pictured himself in a sexy clinch with Moina Furneaux. Then he pictured Tommy suddenly there beside them, mouth agape, shocked as if he'd seen a ghost. And thinking no doubt: *Is this really my big brother here, making love to my headmistress, Miss Fur-Knickers herself? Can't be! Just can't be!*

If that wasn't enough to make Cale wilt, then nothing would.

'It's Tommy, Moina. I can't do this, not with the idea stuck in my head that he might just catch us.'

'He won't. I've already told you that. Come here. Don't walk away from me.' Her voice came to him like threads that first clung to him, here and there, and then began to draw him in. He continued walking backwards, however, in spite of that. In spite of her deadly charm, her deadly voice, and the even more deadly sight of her body. Forty-something. He still didn't know her age...she gave nothing away...not a thing...not a damn thing. Tight as a drum when it came to talking about herself. Had to be forty-something, though. Oh God Jesus yes. Maybe even *fifty*-something!

Even so, there was no clear hook in Cale's mind on which he could hang the hat of estimation. All he knew was that her body was like nothing he had ever seen on a woman of such an age. Her hips swayed like a hypnotist's watch. Her boobs wobbled but it was a subtle, entrancing wobble. Long, shapely legs. A belly-button that was really a neat little thing, not an ugly knot of gristle. No turkey neck for this woman, either, and wrinkles, sags, dewlaps? Forget it, he couldn't see any of that. However, if Cale yielded to this, he'd be yielding to a woman who'd pretty much been his housekeeper these past few weeks, and no one would have it off with their own housekeeper, would they?

And oh would you believe it but her hips were not just swaying anymore, they were *mincing*. He wanted to laugh at her - that was just nerves to begin with - but then he realised that laughter would likely be his most effective defence against her. His objections were no defence, all but useless against a woman who was clearly used to reeling in her men with little or no fuss whatsoever. The male teachers at Brougham Moor, for instance, who probably went over to her place in Twelve Trees Road on Friday and Saturday nights like the well-worn moths to the well-worn flame. But laughter? Yes, laughter might just do the trick, for Cale knew one thing if not much else: that the vanity of a woman was mostly as thin as the tissues she carried around in her handbag. Moina Furneaux would be no different. Her weakness just had to be her vanity. Had to be. That, and her sexuality. Laugh at one, and you'd laugh at the other.

But then –

'You're beginning to make me angry, Cale. You keep backing away like that, and I might just have to remind you there's a police station not too far from here. The officers inside it? Well, let's just say if you don't head your cock over here, then they might just want to cock their heads at what I've got to say. Get my point?'

'You're blackmailing me again!' He shouted that out. Couldn't help it. It just sprang out of him.

'I use what I want to get what I want. Call it blackmail, if you wish. Me? I just dip into my bag of resources and pull out whatever tool I need to crack the problem. And *you* just happen to be the problem, Cale. Don't take it personally.'

Don't take it personally? Jesus. Hard not to when personally it was him personally she wanted to hump, and in a personal kind of a way.

He took two more backwards steps, and then the heel of his left boot struck the corner of the workshop. His reached behind him and placed his hands on its boarded outer skin, the way someone would do that if they were shuffling along the narrow ledge of a tall building. *Help me!* that desperate posture said. *Help me find a way out of this!* His head swam. His chest blew in and out, and he could hear the keys, the one that fit Sad's Place, and the one that fit the writing desk, jiggling against his breastbone. His palms left sweaty imprints on the boards as he worked his way along them towards the open door.

Out with a hand. He grasped the doorframe. Began to pull himself into the workshop as a man might pull himself towards the safety of an outcropping using a deep, vertical crack for aid. Yet all of this was a waste of time…and he began to understand that. There *was* no safety, that was the truth of it. If Moina Furneaux went down to the police station in Unity Gate and told the officers in there her suspicions, then yes, they'd be up here and sniffing around, all right. Make no bones about that. For Cale it was either fuck the crazy headmistress…or fuck himself. And in the process he'd be fucking Tommy, as well. Tommy, always Tommy. At the moment, though, Tommy's dominance in Cale's mind was no longer an annoyance but a reminder of why Cale had to hold onto what he had and to not let go.

You got me out of hell, Cale, Tommy had said outside the school that day, in the shadow of the big, rattlebox truck. *You made me feel good about myself again, when I thought I never would.*

For Cale to put that in danger just because some old bird wanted to fuck him, and who, in a couple of months' time, would not be around anyhow, was simply absurd. It was easy to have morals when your world was all roses in the garden and toasted crumpets by the fireside. Not so easy when you lived your life on the edge of a knife that could slice you in two if you made one false move.

Absurd? Yes, absurd, all right. And the centre of that absurdity, for the time being, anyhow, was Moina Furneaux. Here today, gone tomorrow. So why bother? On the great, unfurling scroll of life, Moina Furneaux was but a spilled drop of ink. Nothing more, nothing less. Let her have her way - that's what Cale began to think. And when he realised she was now on the drive, completely stark-naked, in full view of Samuel Lane, along which a car could pass at any moment, or even someone on foot, he decided to get this over with.

He slid inside the workshop. Moina followed. He closed the door. Locked it. And then she was on him. Like a vampire, for the want of a better expression. But that's just how she was. Like a vampire.

The beginning of one memory combined with the end of another that Cale, right now, could not recall, and really didn't want to. He *would* recall it, though. Among the ghosts that would press their faces against the workshop's windows, and cackle in the storeroom, and cast their shadows against the walls, he would recall every single piece of that memory...and more. It would awaken him, would allow him to finally see through the cracked glaze, and that in turn would impel him to pick up the mallet once again and carry it up the stairs, where the curtains would tumble and twist in the wind, and far off somewhere the thunder would rumble.

The end of that memory, it had something to do with Little Miss Orange Dress, more precisely, her voice that had sounded like she was huffing warmly on a frosted window: *That's it, all the way in, yes, right up there.*

However, when Cale thought of that, it became all mixed up in what Moina had said while she'd been having sex with him across the workbench. A bit like trying to remember a tune while the radio played another. *That's it, oh yes, that's nice, I like that,* and then, savagely, *Oh truss me up and stuff me like a turkey, boy! Yes, ride me, ride me, ride me, sailor, ride me, FUCKING RIDE ME!*

Now here he was, still lying on the workbench, among the shavings, the sawdust, the litter of nails and screws. Moina no longer here. Gone back to the house, or perhaps to her deck-chair in the garden.

Something of her was still here, though: a long red hair that was stuck to Cale's face, and he wiped it away. The same with her lipstick, which he could taste on his lips, and now he drew an arm across his mouth to take that away, too. Then there was her perfume that clung to him like smoke. That other perfume, as well, that natural perfume people deposit on each other after making love. He could smell it all over him. Not entirely horrible. Just overpowering. Like Moina herself.

He was in a daze, and when he stood, hoisted his jeans and fastened them back around his waist, he was still in a daze. Just couldn't clear his head, like something in there had been knocked out of shape and he couldn't straighten it back out. He looked at his work, at the kitchen unit that he ought to complete but didn't want to. So he went back outside for no reason that he could think of, it was done, this squalid business, and what could he say, anyhow, to make it seem less like rape and more like lovemaking?

Nothing.

Nonetheless, he went back outside, and there she was, Moina, in the deck-chair, just as he thought she might be. Sitting there like nothing much had happened. Back to sunning herself in this dazzling, late-afternoon heat that showed no signs of abating. In her bikini again. Eating the rest of her apple. Aloof and relaxed and carving herself slices of that red, juicy fruit with the knife that Cale had swiped across Don Willoughby's throat that night.

Her gaze was turned up to the sun...and then, when Cale's shadow fell across her, she did not turn to him, as perhaps she should have done. Instead she lowered her gaze and looked right past him, towards the clutter of broken-down sheds and to that place from which Cale had cleared last year's freight of autumn leaves, along with a load of other useless crap, so that he could stack the timbers there that had fallen and crushed the life out of his father. And of course many of those timbers had been stained with blood...and still were.

Cale turned and looked in the same direction. What he saw was a man. Blond, cropped hair. A broad nose. A face covered with freckles. A white shirt with the sleeves rolled up. Smiling and waving, but in that cranky, overstated way that suggested he might have more than just a pencil and notebook in his pocket. A bomb, perhaps. It was DI Roy Cutlass, who was the destruction in Cale's rear-view mirror that he now had to turn around and look at. And regard. And face-up to.

From behind Cale, Moina Furneaux said, 'Who the hell's that? Doesn't he know there's such a thing as a front door?'

'Clearly not,' Cale murmured. 'It's Roy Cutlass. Detective Inspector Roy Cutlass.' *And I'm in trouble*, he wanted to add but didn't. Just waited for Cutlass to close the gap, and soon enough he did. Soon enough he was across the lawn, and smiling like he'd struck oil and wanted to share his good fortune with anyone who'd listen.

'Hi, Cale! And hi to you - '

'It's Moina,' she said. 'Moina - '

'Furlough!' Cutlass finished, tapping the wide, fleshy tip of his nose. 'The new headmistress at Brougham Moor, right?'

'Close,' she said. 'Like close to being completely wrong. The name's Furneaux. F-U-R-N-E-A-U-X. And I'm the *temporary* headmistress at Brougham Moor.'

'Right,' Cutlass said. 'Just testing.' And he laughed. *Brayed*, actually, his hands on his portly stomach and guffawing into the air. He went on laughing like that until it tapered off into an embarrassing, stop-start hitching noise: ha-ha...ha-ha...ha-ha. No one laughing but him. No one. Just two people waiting for him to stop faffing around and get on with it. So he did. He cleared his throat, and said to Cale: 'Mind if I have a word with you, son? Don't want to spoil your time with Miss Furnish there, but it's rather important. Over here will do.'

Cale nodded.

'Splendiferous,' Cutlass said, turning and walking back across the lawn.

To Cale Moina mouthed: *What does he want, do you know?*

Cale could only shrug, though. No time to explain. He trailed after Cutlass, all the way over to the brow of the hill down which Cale had taken Willoughby's car that night. That car of his whose dash Willoughby had fallen against, and smash, he had lost most of his front teeth.

Cutlass stopped. Cale joined him, and as he did, so Cutlass slung an arm around his shoulder. All chummy. Like the hug of a boa-constrictor. Together they stared down the hill at the gate that opened onto the common field, the same gate Cutlass must have climbed over before walking up the hill and into Cale's back garden.

'So what's that woman doing here, Cale? That woman wearing nothing but a smile, just about. Hasn't she got a place of her own to go to?'

'I'd rather not talk about Miss Furneaux, if you don't mind,' Cale said. 'After all, I don't think she's the reason why you're here, is she? I think Sergeant Willoughby is. Best we stick to him.'

'Very well,' Cutlass said. He took his arm off Cale, reached into his pocket, and pulled out a tape-measure. One of those retractable, spring-loaded ones that Cale was very familiar with, as he used one himself from time to time. Cutlass began to juggle it back and forth in his hands. 'The fact is, Cale, this case isn't going too well. Been several weeks now since Sergeant Willoughby's death, and still no breakthrough. Read the papers, do you?'

'When I can.'

'Then you'll know that me, my boss, Warren Gaines, and my colleague, Jack Bradshaw, have been taking something of a roasting just lately. Fine. I can handle it. We all can. And what do journalists know, anyway, about the complexities of a crime? Nothing, just about. There are people, highly-skilled people, working around the clock in the laboratory, in the motor shop, or simply knocking on doors, questioning people. A great deal goes on, and they never seem to take any of that into account: the hard work that keeps people like me awake at night, trying to piece things together to make a little sense of it all.'

Cale nodded. Ran a hand through his hair, realised it was all stuck up after Moina had had her hands in it, and smoothed it back down. He could smell her, could *still* smell her. Wondered if Cutlass could smell her, too: that personal smell that sticks…and lingers. Not that it mattered, of course. His making love with Moina Furneaux perhaps found guilty him of a weakness, but not of a crime.

'Still, last night I actually slept for a few hours,' Cutlass went on. 'You know why that was, Cale?'

'No.'

'Because,' he said, pointing the retractable tape at Cale, 'I suddenly realised that everything leads back to this place. *Everything*. I should have seen that from the beginning, but at the time, we had a lot to get our teeth into. Too much, probably. The gang of con-merchants, for starters. We still haven't found them, and likely we won't. Not now. It's my experience that you either catch these people in the first few weeks, or whoops, there they go, out of your hands. Probably they've got new identities and don't look anything like their photo-fits anymore, but never mind. I'd like to put them in front of the beak for what they did to many of the old people around here - fleecing their pensions and savings like that - but I'd swap all of that, would *happily* swap all of that, just to catch Sergeant Willoughby's killer.' He looked at Cale with hot, deliberate intensity. '*You* know who that killer is, don't you, Cale?'

'I don't know anything,' Cale said, shaking. Glad that Cutlass's arm was not around his shoulder anymore because he would feel those shakes. Would feel them running up and down Cale's body like a low electrical charge. Nonetheless, he kept a straight face, and a straight, clear head, as well. As best he could, anyhow. 'Really, I don't.'

'Okay, then,' Cutlass said. 'Looks like I'm going to need a little more patience, and what's a little more patience, anyhow, when there's a lifetime of satisfaction heading my way, hmmm?' He grasped the tape-measure's hooked tip, pulled on it, and out came the measure itself: a thin, yellow tongue marked in feet-and-inches.

He snapped on the lock to keep it in place. 'Come with me, Cale. I want to show you something.' Cutlass walked across to the shabby hedge that bounded the Redstone property, and Cale followed. When they got there, Cutlass crouched down. Using the extended tape, he pointed out to Cale two tyre tracks that were imprinted in the grass. Still there because it had not rained significantly enough to fluff the grass back up. 'You see these?'

'Yes.'

'These are tyre tracks. You know that, of course. Any fool would. Want to know how far apart they are? Take a guess. You're a carpenter, likely you've got an eye for that.'

'Four feet. Maybe four feet, six inches.'

'Not bad. Actually, they're four feet, five and a half inches apart. Take a look in the Rootes handbook for a Humber Sceptre and that's exactly what it gives as the measurement between its tracks: four feet, five and a half inches. Worn tyres and bad tracking can cause discrepancies, of course, but as I'm using a well-maintained police vehicle as my reference, I don't think such discrepancies would come into play.' He stood up. 'How many vehicles do you have here, Cale?'

'Just two at the moment: my dad's truck and Miss Furneaux's Morris Minor.'

'Well, I think we can safely say these tracks here weren't made by your dad's truck, or by Miss Furneaux's Morris minor. The truck's would be wider, the Minor's would be smaller. Does your dad have a car?'

'No.'

'How did he get up to Templeton, then?'

'By train.'

Cutlass nodded, but he didn't of course believe that. Just nodded for the sake of it. 'How's your dad doing, by the way?'

'Fine.'

'He wasn't at the funeral. Why's that?'

'He was too busy. Couldn't make it down.'

'Not even for his best friend? I think *I* would have made it down for my best friend's funeral. Nothing would have stopped me.'

'Not everyone's the same as you, Detective Cutlass. We all deal with death in different ways.'

'Like lying, you mean? Like telling George Willoughby that your father was there, out the back of the chapel, having a smoke, when he wasn't?'

'I told George that so as not to upset him,' Cale said. 'I was being diplomatic.'

'You're being *fucking* diplomatic, in my view, Cale. As diplomatic as it gets. Still, I'll get to the bottom of this, one way or another. My teeth are into you, son. And I won't stop until I've taken a great big mouthful. Got your father's phone-number in Templeton, have you?'

'Back at the house, in the office.' Not just shaking now. Cale was trembling enough to make his teeth rattle and his bones feel like they were turning to powder. He dug his nails into his palms until it hurt, and that seemed to take away the shakes. For now, at any rate.

'Back at the house, is it? I'll get it off you in a moment. Then I can have a nice, long chat with your father, can't I?'

'If you want.'

'Oh, I want,' Cutlass said. He smiled, but there was no mirth in it. None at all. 'My, but I reckon you're a chip off the old block. Like your father, are you?'

'I'm *nothing* like him.'

'I wouldn't be so sure about that,' Cutlass said. 'I gather he used to be quite handy, especially with his fists…until he was barred from just about every pub in Unity Gate.'

'My father changed his ways.'

'Only because he had to.'

'He was never officially charged with anything.'

'No, he wasn't. Why? Because his best friend was Sergeant Willoughby, and Willoughby was supportive of your father, even when he really shouldn't have been. When I think, in fact, that he probably came close to flouting the laws for the sake of your father. *Bending* them a little, anyhow. Still, that was Sergeant Willoughby, a loyal man, and I think that was his weakness, the fact that when he made a friend, he stuck by that friend, no matter what.'

Cutlass looked back down at the tracks again. Thinking. A hand up to his mouth, a finger tapping against his podgy cheek. Then: 'It's a crying shame I can't take an imprint of these tracks. Too much grass, not enough dirt. I'd put my wages on it, though, that they were made by a Dunlop tubeless. That's the make of tyre they fit as standard on a Sceptre. It'll take a Goodyear whitewall, too, but we don't fit those. Too flashy. Yes, I'd say they were made by a Dunlop tubeless, all right. A Dunlop tubeless that runs all the way to that gate down there. See them, do you? See how those tracks go all the way to that gate down there?'

'Yes.'

'So how do you explain that, son? How can you see that and still keep your mouth shut about what happened that night?'

'Easy,' Cale said. 'I didn't do anything that night but watch the television with my brother. I spoke to WPC Jenkins when she phoned to ask if Sergeant Willoughby had called at the house. But apart from that - '

Yes, you were watching the television, I heard that already. What about Willoughby, though?'

'What about him?'

'He called here, didn't he? I know he did. Want to know *how* I know? Well, here goes. I found a note at Willoughby's house, dated the day he was murdered. He must have written it at the station, sometime after he was assaulted up at Walnut Grove, and then took it home with him at tea-time. I found it in his bureau.' Cutlass dug into his pocket and pulled out a scrap of paper that was tattered at the top, having been torn out of a spiral notebook, by the look of it. 'Here, read it.'

'You read it,' Cale said. He wasn't being awkward. Just afraid that he would start shaking again if he took that scrap of paper off Cutlass. 'Whatever it says, I'll take your word for it.'

Cutlass nodded. He held it up, and said, 'It says, and I quote, "Must phone Barrows/Burrows at HQ when I get home. Have a chat with him about fixing a little private bike-riding tuition for Tommy Redstone." Stop. Unquote.'

He folded the note. Back into his pocket it went. 'You know what, Cale? Willoughby did indeed make that phone-call. Only the man he spoke to isn't named Barrows or Burrows, it's PC *Burrell*, double R, double L. He's the man in charge of all that safety shit for kids. Tours the schools and other such places. So I had a chat with Burrell myself, just to find out if Willoughby *did* phone that day. He did. That very afternoon, in fact. Burrell also told me that he had been willing to come up here, to your house, to give Tommy the private tuition that Willoughby requested. Wouldn't normally do that, but for Willoughby he'd make an exception. Willoughby had said great, but he told PC Burrell he'd have to check it was okay with you and Tommy first. He'd either phone the Redstone place, or pop in. But he didn't phone, did he, Cale? He popped in.'

'No, he *didn't* pop in,' Cale said. 'I've already told you that, haven't I, that I didn't see Sergeant Willoughby that night?'

'I think you did,' Cutlass said. 'I think there was some sort of argument - I don't know why, only you can tell me that - and you went at Willoughby with those hands of yours that are just like your father's. Hands that are quick to lash out and start punching.' He paused. 'Just the way you punched Brian Digweed that day, outside his house.'

Cale's mouth dropped open. 'How do you know about that?'

'Small world, isn't it?' Cutlass said. 'Brian Digweed just happens to be an acquaintance of mine. We're not close, nothing like that. Our paths cross every now and then on the golf course. I knew he was having marital troubles, that his wife had been having an affair...and well, what did I discover when I ran into him just a few days ago? That the man she'd been having an affair with just happened to be your father. Brian got a little drunk back at the clubhouse. He told me about that, and not *just* about that. He also told me about how you punched him in the stomach that day outside his house.'

'Damn right I did,' Cale said. 'Did Brian Digweed also tell you that he beat his wife so hard, he split her lip and bruised her eye?'

Cutlass seemed stunned by that, but his eyes, nevertheless, stayed fixed on Cale, and evenly. 'No, he didn't tell me that. That shocks me. Still, why would you get mixed up in Brian and Cynthia Digweed's troubles? Just came to collect an overdue payment, didn't you?'

'Yes, I did, but the fact is, I just can't abide men who hit their women. I had enough of all that when I was a kid, and my fa - ' He paused for a moment in order to get his brain back in gear. And to tie his loose tongue back in his mouth. 'I just don't like that kind of thing, that's what I'm saying. It gets my back up.'

'Why's that, Cale? Your father used to hit your mother, did he? That's what you were going to say, isn't it?'

'No.'

'Rubbish!' Cutlass snarled that into Cale's face so fiercely that Cale jumped back a step. 'Where *is* your mother, Cale, while we're on that subject? Do you know?'

'She left home, five years back.'

'I say rubbish to that, as well. Did she change her name?'

'Not that I'm aware of.'

'So why can't I find her?' Cutlass asked. 'Natalie Redstone, isn't it? I've made a hundred phone-calls these past few days and I can't find that name anywhere. Unless she's now living in the Outer Hebrides. What happened, Cale? Did your father do away with her?'

'Stop it!' Cale said. 'Don't say those things?'

'Why? Because the truth hurts?'

'No!' Hot tears began to trickle down Cale's face. Many times just lately he had felt small…and alone…and needy. This again was one of those times…but in spite of that he still stood his ground. 'She just ran away, that's all I know! Leave me alone!'

'Leave you alone? No chance. But I *can* switch to a different angle…for the time being, anyhow.' Cutlass thumbed back the lock holding the tape-measure in place, and with an urgent, metallic snap, it sprang back into its casing. He dumped the tape in his pocket.

'Let's take another walk,' he said. 'Come with me.'

They went back up onto the lawn, and then Cutlass turned right at the sheds, and now, here they were, at the back of them, where the shadows were deep and it was noticeably cooler here. Here at the place where the bloody timbers were stacked.

'These here,' Cutlass said, pointing at the timbers. 'You see those stains down there, on the bottom three or four planks? Can you tell me what made them?'

'It looks to me like a mahogany wood-dye,' Cale said, wiping his eyes.

'Doesn't look much like a mahogany wood-dye to me,' Cutlass said. 'What it looks like is blood.'

'Well, it could be,' Cale said. 'After all, it's not unusual for my Dad and I to cut ourselves. It's part and parcel of the job. One of the downsides.'

Cutlass gave Cale a look of counterfeit admiration. 'Nice.

Somehow you're still just about holding it together, aren't you? But let's face it. There isn't a cut in the world that would generate *that* much blood...unless it just happened to be a cut from here to here.' He ran a finger from his groin, all the way up over his belly, then up to his throat. Following that, from his back pocket, he pulled out two small plastic bags. A pair of tweezers, as well, the type a woman would use to pluck her eyebrows with. 'Mind if I take a sample?' he asked, looking down at the bloody timbers. 'I would have taken one a moment ago, but I needed you here as a witness, and at the time, you were...well, otherwise engaged.' He waggled his eyebrows, and lewdly.

'You saw?' Cale asked, flushing.

'Yeah, I saw,' Cutlass said. 'I took a look in the workshop window, saw what was going on, and went back behind here until you'd finished mauling each other.' He flashed a toothy grin. 'What was it like?'

'Eh?'

'Fucking the headmistress?'

'That's none of your business.'

'You're right, it isn't.' He went down on his haunches. Using the tweezers, he grasped a loose, blood-stained splinter, pulled it away from the plank, and put it in one of the bags. Sealed the bag. Put it back in his pocket. Same with the tweezers. One bag left. He opened it up. 'Mind if I take a sample of your hair, as well? Just a few strands will do.'

'Why do you want those?'

'We found a few fair hairs in Sergeant Willoughby's car. Some were Willoughby's mother's - she still has some fair hair among the grey – another came from George Willoughby's wife, Ruth, and another came from a young mechanic up at HQ. There's still a couple of fair hairs left that we'd like to look at under the microscope.'

'And you think they might be mine?'

'I'd put my house on it,' Cutlass said. He reached out with a hand to snatch a few of Cale's hairs, but then -

'You leave that boy's hair alone!' Moina Furneaux said. Moina Furneaux suddenly standing there in the shadows in a stance that seemed peculiar to Cale but as yet he could not fathom exactly what that peculiarity was. 'Do you have the authority to do that?'

Cutlass turned, and jumpily. Understandable, Cale thought. Moina Furneaux would make *any* man jump. 'I'm a detective, ma'am. Of course I have the authority.'

'I don't think you do.' She walked forwards until she was standing before him. 'You're not any kind of qualified scientist, are you? And anyway, shouldn't you have another officer, detective, whatever, with you? You know, just to make sure everything is above board?'

Cutlass smiled, but nervously. 'Look, I'm just taking these samples so that we can run a few tests. If they show promise, then naturally, I will send the relevant people up here to do the job officially.'

'I don't like it,' Moina said. 'There's something fishy about this. You know what? I think you came up here, on your own, because you got an idea in your head that you didn't want to share with the rest of your colleagues. What does that make you, Detective Cutlass? In my mind that makes you nothing but a glory boy.'

'I'd watch that mouth of yours if I were you.'

'I don't have to. I'm not the one you're after, Cale is. And right now, I'm the fly that just flew into your ointment.' She gave him a challenging look. 'Okay then, so why don't you arrest me? Charge me with something, snap the handcuffs on me, and put me in the back of your car. You can't, can you? Your car isn't around here, but over in yon field where you left it before walking up here and making that less-than-honest entrance of yours. What does that say about you, Detective? It says that you had no *intention* of arresting Cale in the first place. Just decided to come up here on your day off and likely even your wife doesn't know you're here.'

'Madam, you're getting right out of line with all of this,' Cutlass said, but she wasn't. She had in fact hit the nail squarely on the head, or thereabouts. Cale could see it in Cutlass's face, the ticks, some nervous, some angry, that were now dancing in his eyes and on the edge of his lips. 'If I were you, I'd go back to tanning that body of yours that someone like me would rather not see so much of.'

'Speak for yourself,' Moina said, aiming her gaze at the place where Cutlass's belly spilled over his waistband. 'But let's not get into Jack Says This, Jill Says That, shall we? Let's stick to what's happening here. And just *what* is happening here, Detective Cutlass? Came up here with a few desperate, hair-brained ideas, did you, hoping that Cale would crack, because basically he's just a boy and he's *bound* to crack? But so far he hasn't, has he?'

'My ideas are neither desperate, nor hair-brained,' Cutlass said. 'I'm not sure if Cale killed Sergeant Willoughby, or if his father did. Or if they did it together. I just know that all the evidence points to this place right here in Samuel Lane. And you're right, it *is* my day off, and I didn't tell my wife, or anyone else, for that matter. I just came up here - '

'To bully a confession out of the boy?'

'No, I did not. I am not a bully. However, if Cale *did* confess, it would save me a hell of a lot of time and bother.'

'I'm sure it would. After all, this crime has been going on for too long, and from what I've read in the papers, several pairs of nuts are about to be crushed, if someone doesn't solve this murder, and soon. Your job on the line, is it, Detective? You and Bradshaw and Gaines?'

'That has nothing to do with you.'

'Oh, I think it does. If I ran a school the way you are running this investigation, then I'd be out of a job. I'm the kind of person who could happily fuck your dog and then, ten minutes later, have my arm around some poor kid who's failed his exams. But that's just the right and the left hand of the human being, Detective Cutlass. Good work with one, bad work with the other. However, I know one thing. I would never, and I mean *never*, compromise my principles just to grab the limelight. And that will be your downfall, Detective Cutlass, that huge ego of yours.'

Cutlass appeared to hear none of that, however, at least not from the part where Moina said she could happily fuck your dog. He looked down at her red, glittery shoes, perhaps at the anklet there, too, and then back into her face, framed by that wild, red hair of hers. 'You'd happily fuck my *dog?* Excuse me? Is that what you said?'

'I did,' Moina said. 'I did this, as well... '

It was then that Cale finally managed to fathom that peculiarity in Moina's stance that up until now had eluded him: that her hands, throughout this, had been behind her back.

Then he saw the quick and deadly gleam of the knife as Moina brought it out from behind her, and Cale watched, helpless, as she thrust it up into the soft, flabby place between Cutlass's jaw and throat. His tongue was pinned to the roof of his mouth in a horrible instant.

'Glag!' he said. Followed by 'Urgle!' And then his hands went up to his throat just as Willoughby's hands had done that back in some past nightmare that Cale had experienced both in reality and in his dreams. He watched as Moina, both hands on the knife now, stood under the shelf of Cutlass's chin (she looked to Cale like a woman under a showerhead that sprayed blood instead of water), and forced the knife further up into the roof of Cutlass's mouth...and then into his brain. There was a pop noise, much like the noise an empty crisp bag will make if you fill it with air, twist the top, and then slap it between your hands. Cutlass's belly jiggled, and jiggled so much that Cale could hear the loose change rattling about in his pocket. Thought he could even hear Willoughby's note in there, as well, rustling.

Cutlass's eyes first began to fill with blood, and then that blood trickled over his lids and poured down his face. His hands went down to Moina's wrists, he grasped them, he tried to get them off the knife, but Moina was having none of that. She kept her hands firmly on it, and just went on applying more upwards pressure. Her teeth gritted. Her feet firmly planted. Her eyes as mad as cursed beads.

'Aggle!' Cutlass said. 'Aggle, *ahaaarg!*' He began to tip backwards, his head jittering, his eyelids fluttering, as the circuits in his brain issued their warning signals, circuits that were complaining, failing, and then folding up completely. He pissed his pants, the way Tommy had done that on the day he and Cale went fishing. Let out a long, trumpeting fart after that, and the air behind these sagging, mouldy sheds was suddenly filled with a smell that Cale could not just taste but actually *feel*, stinging his eyes.

The little plastic sample bag sailed out of Cutlass's hands and landed atop a small drift of brown, slimy leaves. The bag in which several strands of Cale's hair would have been put, sealed, and then taken up to the lab at Upperlands HQ for analysis, had Moina not stepped in when she had.

Cale wished she hadn't. Was then glad she had. Couldn't make up his mind. Just knew that appreciation exchanged places with opposition several times over. Overlaying this unresolved moral stalemate were the brutal images he had to watch no matter what. Moina Furneaux murdering the detective with the same knife Cale had used on Sergeant Willoughby that night. One dead cop...and another about to follow.

Cutlass let go of Moina's hands, and now gravity turned tipping into falling. Down the detective went, and hard. He hit the stack of timber with a crash that made several planks jump up and then slap back down again with a loud bang. Outstretched, his legs that were wet with piss began to tremble, his feet began to rattle on the ground, and then, all of a sudden, nothing trembled, nothing rattled, because the policeman was now altogether utterly still. His arms fell limp at his sides, his bloody eyes and face staring upwards but seeing none of the clear, blue sky that lay in the narrow lane between the sheds here.

And the knife? Breathing hard, Moina finally let go of it. The knife now belonged to Cutlass entirely, his to deal with however he wished, if his brain could have made a decision, but of course it couldn't. His brain was dead. As was the rest of him. And so there he lay across the timbers, another victim of number 3 Samuel Lane that even Cale had now begun to see, not as number 3 Samuel Lane, but as Sad's Place. Not just the name for that little stone stable with its blue, paint-peeled door. The whole *property* was now Sad's Place.

Detective Inspector Roy Cutlass: another victim of Sad's Place. Splendiferous.

Chapter 15: The Bandsaw

'Snap out of it, Cale,' Moina said, clicking her fingers in front of his face, and then waving a hand across his eyes. 'Don't throw a funny on me, boy.'

'It's okay,' Cale said, leaning against a shed to whose boards moss clung in soft, squelchy clods. 'I'll be all right in a moment.' But he didn't think he *would* be all right. Not in a moment, anyhow. Possibly not ever. He couldn't tell Moina that, though. She needed him to be one full half of the team that would have to sort this mess out, and quickly.

Moina said, 'Are you with me yet?'

'Yes.'

'All right, then.' She gestured at the stacked timbers. 'I want to know what those stains are down there. Don't even *think* about lying to me, either. I want answers, and fast. Tell me. What are they?'

'Blood.'

'Whose blood?'

'My father's. I killed him.' Even though he was still in a daze, which in fact he had been since having sex with Moina, he explained everything, and without hesitation. He told Moina about how his father had fallen under those timbers, but not here, out by the side of the workshop. Back in August, that had been. A couple of days after the England football team had won the World Cup. He told her about how Ewan Redstone had become trapped under the timbers, and how that had given Cale the chance to end his father's life by bashing his brains in with a mallet. Had done that because, since Natalie Redstone's sudden exit from this place, Ewan Redstone had made little

Tommy's life hell. Always beating the poor boy, and when he wasn't beating him, he was tormenting him in some terrible way or another.

It hurt Cale to recount this, already they seemed like distant memories he'd rather forget, but in another way, he was glad to get them off his chest. Such a relief, in truth, that he would have fallen into Moina's arms, had she not been covered in blood. So much of it that it even lay in the dips of her shoulders, either side of her neck. Pooled there.

'You don't seem surprised by what I've told you,' Cale said.

'I'm not,' Moina said. 'I pretty much knew things for Tommy, and for you, had been difficult around here.'

'Not difficult, *horrendous*,' Cale said. 'When that wood stack fell on my dad, I soon realised I had the chance to get rid of him, to get him out of our lives, once and for all. It was still hard to kill him, though. After all, he was my father, and no one kills their father lightly, do they? Just something I knew I had to do. For Tommy. And for me.'

Moina nodded her head, and then the urgency, sharp as a smack, jumped back into her eyes. 'So what about your mother? What happened to her?'

'My father killed her, just as you suspected. We didn't know that at the time, Tommy and me. Dad told us that she upped and left and we believed him. That was five years ago. Then I found her body.' He nodded towards the garden that was still bathed in bright, warm sunlight. 'She's buried in that old stable over there. The place Tommy and I call Sad's Place.'

'Sad's Place?' Moina said, but then: 'Oh, I get it. Yes, two of the letters are missing. Used to be called Sadie's Place, from what I can make out.'

'That's right,' Cale said. 'Sadie's Place.'

'So how did you end up *finding* your mother?' Moina asked.

'Because I buried my father in Sad's Place,' Cale said. 'I started digging a hole to put him in…and that was when I came across her.'

'And because you killed your father, you couldn't go to the police, right.'

Cale nodded.

'Horrible, just horrible,' Moina said. 'Does Tommy know she's in there?'

'God, no. If Tommy knew that, it would break his heart.'

'I'm sure,' Moina said, and although there was sympathy in her voice, the urgency in her eyes remained there, clear as a flame. She glanced around at DI Cutlass's dead body. 'Any room in Sad's Place for one more?'

'No, it's too small in there,' Cale said, fiddling with the keys around his neck. 'We'll have to think of something else.'

Moina said, 'Just the way you thought of something else when it came to Sergeant Willoughby, eh?'

'Yes.'

'That's okay,' Moina said. 'I don't want the details. I don't *need* them. Likely Willoughby came here that night wanting to know where your father was. Perhaps he didn't believe he was up in Templeton, the way *I* didn't believe that. There was an argument, most likely, followed by a struggle, and you killed him. Am I on the right track?'

'Close enough for a *Crackerjack* pencil,' Cale said.

'Then,' Moina went on, 'you drove his body down to the common field, hoping the police would believe those other men had killed him. And they *did* believe that, didn't they? Even Cutlass. At least for a while.'

'Yes, for a while,' Cale said.

Moina nodded her head, glanced back at the dead detective, and said, 'Well, we can't dump him down there, can we, like you did with Willoughby? Got to come up with some other plan.' She went back to thinking with that smart but tainted brain of hers, and when she lowered her head and pressed the heel of a hand against her temple, Cale, once again, was reminded of a bird with its head tucked under its wing. A bird delving into the far corners of its brain.

After a short while, she looked up and stared at Cale, her eyes unblinking. Here in the cool shadows with this half-mad, half-brilliant woman, who was streaked with blood, and in places, it actually *dripped* off her, the way raindrops will drip off a house when the clouds have passed but you can still hear the sound of those drops splashing on the ground.

'I've killed before,' she admitted to Cale in that gentle but cold voice of hers. 'I ran this guy through with a knife because he stole money out of my purse while I was sleeping. Killed him stone-dead. I put him in my car, drove him over to Blackthorn Wood, and buried him there. Ten years ago, that was. Are you surprised? Probably not.'

Cale tactfully shrugged his shoulders, but in truth, he was not surprised in the least to hear she'd killed before. More surprised she'd confessed to that, for up until now, he'd gotten little out of her.

'Never mind, it was a long time ago,' she said. 'Old hat. Here's what we're going to do.' She went over and pulled the knife out of Cutlass's throat, and so casually, it was like she had pulled nothing but a needle out of a pincushion. Then she laid the knife at Cale's feet. 'In a moment, I want you to take that into the house and wash it clean. Then I want you to clean all the blood away from around here. Got that?'

'Yes.'

'Then I want you to find something you can throw over that wood stack there. A tarpaulin, perhaps. Do you have one?'

'Yes, in the storeroom.'

'Okay, then.' She bent down and picked up the little plastic sample bag that Cutlass had dropped. Tucked it down the front of her bikini bottoms. 'But first we need to get Cutlass into the workshop.'

'Why into the workshop?'

'Well, we can't *bury* him, can we?' Moina said. 'Not at the moment, anyhow. At the weekend, we can take him over to Blackthorn Wood and bury him there. You can bury a body in that place, mark the spot with a flashing light, and still no one will find it.'

'So why can't we do that right now?'

'Think,' Moina said, tapping her head. 'Cutlass's car will almost certainly be found in the next few hours. If one of his colleagues has the slightest idea that Cutlass was onto you, then it's reasonable to assume that he'll grab some men and be up here to take a look around. Let me tell you something, Cale. If you're not here, they'll turn this place over, until they find something they can pin on you. They *will* find it, too. They'll find *something*.'

'You think Cutlass *did* tell one of his colleagues?'

'Probably not. He was out to grab a little glory for himself, that's what I think, and the look on his face when I said that makes me believe I was right. Still, you can never be too sure, not when it comes to the police. Best to err on the side of caution.'

Cale said, 'I'm thinking about those woods over the road. Couldn't we bury Cutlass in there?'

'I don't think so,' Moina said. 'Firstly, it's too close. Secondly, I'm not lugging a dead body over that road in broad daylight, along with a couple of shovels. No, we'll have to go with my idea.' She explained her idea to him...and Cale thought he was going to faint. Could feel himself tipping towards blackness, but managed to pull himself back by ramming a couple of knuckles into his mouth and biting down on them until the feeling passed. Once it had, he pulled them out, and said, 'Moina, you can't do that! You don't even know how to operate that machine!'

'Stop fussing. I'm a quick learner. Here, grab his shoulders. I'll take his legs. Let's go.'

'What about the mess? There'll be blood everywhere!'

'I'll deal with that.'

'Can't we just put him in the boot of your car?'

'I've got a Morris Minor. Back then, when I killed that other guy, I had a Vauxhall saloon, but even then it was tight. And Cutlass is bigger. Much bigger.'

'I can take him in my truck.'

'*You* can't take him anywhere,' Moina said. 'You need to be here, in case the police come, remember? And what do we do, anyhow? Prop him in the front seat between us, like a drunk uncle? Nice idea...just as long as you don't mind half the town seeing him sitting there. He could go in the back, of course, but the back is uncovered. And what about the blood? By the time we reach my place, it'll be spilling out of him and running all over the road.'

'Maybe we could plug the holes,' Cale said. 'Plug his mouth and throat?'

'Yeah, and why don't we do a little embalming, as well, while we're at it? No, we'll go with my idea. That's the end of it.'

'Oh but Christ, Moina, this is awful! What am I running here, a butcher's shop?'

She suddenly thrust a finger under his chin, a finger that felt as cold and sharp as a six-inch nail. 'You should have thought of that before you killed your father,' she rasped. 'Don't you know that one thing always leads to another? Every mug in the world knows *that*! Now let's get moving.'

There had to be another way, had to be, but if there was, then Cale couldn't think of it. Just felt as if he were being chased along an endless road by a savage dog, and along the way he could find no place to turn into, and hide, and think. And Moina, it seemed, was loving this. A strange word to use, that, loving. Yet it was not just apt but almost too perfect to change it for any other. She was *loving* this. He could see it in the way she trembled, not with nerves but with excitement. Put another way, had there *been* another way, then he believed Moina would not even have considered it, anyhow, because, dare he think it, this was what she wanted! Oh fuck! This was what she actually wanted! To cart Cutlass's dead body into the workshop and…

'Come on, stop wasting time!' she snapped at him, and Cale, with a jolt, went over to help her with the dead detective. Grabbed his shoulders, while she grabbed his legs, and together, they lugged him around to the workshop.

'Oh, the big fat bastard,' Moina said, dumping Cutlass's legs down onto the floor. Cale dumped his end down among the shavings and the sawdust, and went back to the door. Closed it. Locked it. Gazed out through the dusty glass on top. His head was on fire, it seemed to him. On fire with guilt…and with dread.

Moina called out, 'I've already told you that Tommy won't be back until it's nearly dark, haven't I? Now get over here and show me how this machine works.' Her bikini bottoms were damp with sweat, and damp with blood, as well, that made them droop slightly around her bottom. She was staring impatiently at the machine.

'You'll need the support,' Cale said, feeling sick to his stomach. The support was hanging on the wall outside the storeroom. Made of timber and plywood, and with two folding legs at one end, a pair of clips on the other, it could be attached to the bandsaw's metal bed to provide support for long, heavy lengths of timber. Cale took it down and carried it over to the bandsaw. Clipped it to the bed, and then unfolded the legs. Made sure they were firmly in place. 'Now you'll be able to cut him up, and safely,' he told her in a voice that sounded like a weak puff of air. 'Want to lift him up onto here?'

Moina nodded. They picked Cutlass up, just like before, and after a bit of grunting and groaning, finally they got his body up onto the support, and there he lay, his feet dangling off the end, the top of his head pointing towards the bandsaw's looping, fearsomely-sharp blade.

Set into the roof were half a dozen plastic sheets, corrugated, see-through. A few summers back, his father had fixed them up there to allow a little extra light into the workshop...and it was a little extra light that Cale could have done without, thank you very much - he could see enough already, and all of it was awful. A godforsaken nightmare! Nonetheless, the dead detective was about to be cut up into little pieces, and Moina couldn't wait to get going, it seemed. She was staring eagerly at the two buttons on the bandsaw's control panel: GREEN for go, RED for stop. Hardly a difficult machine to operate. No even when you added in the brake that you pressed with your knee to bring the blade to a halt.

'Explain,' Moina said, nodding at the controls.

Cale did, and it didn't take long. After that, he adjusted the height of the guard. Adjusted the guides, as well, through which the blade passed. Did this just to make sure everything was in order, and while he did this, he tried to come up with a way that might spare poor old Roy Cutlass's dead body from being turned into mincemeat.

'Is that it, are we done?' Moina asked. 'Or are you just fiddling around with all that for the sake of it?'

He turned to her, wanting to grab her, to shake some sense into her, but there was nothing to grab hold of (only her bikini top with its spaghetti straps)…and what was more, there *was* no sense that he could see to shake into her, anyhow. Just Moina Furneaux being Moina Furneaux. Basically a bag of horrors.

Despite this, however, he said, 'Listen, Moina, there must be another way. Must be.'

'Yeah, there is. We just stand here with our thumbs up our backsides until the police arrive. Does *that* sound like a good idea to you? Doesn't to me.' She nudged him aside, rather irritably, and went through Cutlass's pockets until she had everything out of him, or off of him. Handed them over to Cale: a wristwatch, a wallet, the tape-measure, scraps of paper, old sweet wrappers, and some small change. 'Put those in the glove-compartment of my car,' she said. 'This, as well.' She pulled the plastic sample bag out of her panties and slapped it on top of the stuff in Cale's hands. 'And hurry it up!'

Cale did as she said, and at double speed. When he returned, he saw that Moina had the bandsaw going already, that it was slowly cycling up to full speed, and now she was looking Cutlass up and down the way a butcher might to work out the most efficient way of slicing up the carcass before him.

After once again locking the door, Cale covered all the glass that faced the driveway with old dust-sheets that he got out of the office. Hung them up on nails or wedged them into cracks or clamped them between window rebates. Did that just in case someone walked up the drive and tried to look in. That done, he went into the storeroom, grabbed half a dozen of the heavy-duty plastic sacks that normally he filled with wood-shavings, and put them on the floor close to Moina so that she could grab one when she needed it.

Moina glanced up at him, and he saw that she was wearing the pair of clear-plastic goggles that were hanging on a hook at the side of the machine. She had put them on to avoid getting blood and bone in her eyes. Sensible, that…although the word sensible could really only be applied, he thought, to this specific act of safety and not to any other part of this grisly business.

That wild, red hair of hers, it had now become bunched here, and skewed there, by the goggles's straps. The skin either side of her nose had become stretched, giving her the appearance of a pilot being buffeted by a strong wind. Her eyes made him think of beetles trapped under glass beakers...and that made him want to scream. Above the deafening, spinning roar of the bandsaw, Moina nodded down at the tubby corpse that used to be a living-breathing detective, and shouted out: 'You think he might get a little cut up about this?'

She laughed.

Cale didn't. Cale went into the storeroom, closed the door, and thought that half the world was mad...and that he could now be counted among their number.

He did everything she asked him to, from cleaning the knife, to washing away the mess out the back of the sheds, to putting a tarpaulin over the timber-stack, that timber-stack to which death now seemed to be attracted, as if every one of its timbers had been cursed by Ewan Redstone.

Cale hadn't been able to use the storeroom door, what with all those dust-sheets hanging there. Instead, he had gotten in and out of the workshop by means of the small window above the metal sink.

The final job was not one Moina had given him. He got in his truck, drove it around the back of the sheds and took it down the hill in an attempt, not to remove the Humber's tracks - he wouldn't be able to remove them, not as such - but he *would* be able to drive over them, weaving here and there, and hence, make it harder for anyone to identify them the way Cutlass had with that tape measure of his.

Cale wished he'd done this before, but the thought hadn't even crossed his mind. Doing it now was much like closing the stable door after the horse had bolted. However, as he seemed in the mood for proverbs, he decided to throw in another one as well, while he was at it, which was: better late than never.

The job done, he drove back to the house, parked the truck, got out, then stood in the driveway. On guard. Leaned back on the bonnet of Moina's little pale-blue car with his arms folded and with his legs crossed at the ankles. Trying to look relaxed, but whenever he heard the bandsaw cutting through another piece of Roy Cutlass, he winced.

He still felt sick to his stomach, as well, and although he hadn't as yet puked, he thought it only a matter of time before it came out of him in a hot, baking rush. His face was deathly pale. It seemed to grip him like a mask made for someone else. And his hands, which he'd scrubbed with soap and water, and several times over since handling the piss-stained policeman, still seemed to reek. Not just of piss, but of the farts which had trumpeted out of him, from time to time, even in death.

Across the road, a bird flew out of the trees, and Cale jumped as if a gun had gone off. He did the same whenever a car went by, too, because, in his tormented, melting mind, every car was a police car full of men who had come to arrest him.

He watched the sun sliding down the sky, while all around him the shadows grew a little longer, a little thicker, a little creepier. He tried to think and couldn't. His brain seemed to have been switched off like a light.

When Moina called out to him, he had no idea how long he'd been standing there, and if he'd looked at his watch, it wouldn't have told him anything, anyhow, because time for Cale had become meaningless, the way that dreaming about his mother returning home had now become meaningless, because she was dead, not living somewhere else.

'Pssst!' Moina said, with a hand up to the side of her mouth. 'Get over here, Cale, and help me out!'

Cale turned and saw Moina peeking out of the workshop door. Just about dark now, and she cast almost no shadow. Her face was pale, shiny, bare of makeup. No blood on her that he could see, either, and he expected it to be *dripping* off her, and even worse than before. Just saturated. However, he could see not one little drop, and then realised she'd taken a wash - he could smell the strong, disinfectant whiff of the coal-tar soap in the storeroom. She had washed her hair, as well, and tied it back with a piece of string. No bikini, either. That had been exchanged for a pair of overalls that were much too big for her, a pair of Ewan Redstone's old ones, they looked like, but at least they were clean.

She looked tired, worn-out, actually. And when Cale walked all the way into the workshop, he realised why that was. The dust-sheets had been taken down and stored away. The bandsaw support had been unclipped, scrubbed, folded, and hung back on the wall. The bandsaw itself was spotless, as was the whole workshop. *Impossibly* spotless, one would say. No sign of blood anywhere, this despite the fact the lights were on and the teeniest speck of blood would have showed up, had it been there. The workshop looked back to normal, like no atrocity had been committed here. He couldn't even *smell* the blood, just the strong, tart smell of the cleaning fluids that Moina had used. Everything looked just fine...apart, that was, from the bags that were sitting near the door.

Six in all. Tied at the top. Stuffed full of Roy Cutlass's body parts.

Cale took one look at these and ran into the storeroom with a hand over his mouth. He puked into the sink, and up came the tuna sandwich that Moina had made him earlier, along with the lemonade. When all of it was out of him, he put an arm on the sink, rested his head there, until he could stand again without his legs turning to rubber. Then he ran the taps until all the sick had been washed down the plughole. Filled a tin mug with cold water after that. Drank it down. Went back into the workshop, and not just warily. He was frightened stiff that if he looked at those bags again, which he'd have to - wouldn't be able to get out of that one - he might just lose control of himself completely. Just go running off up the road, screaming, and disappear into the sunset, never to be seen again.

Moina was standing next to those six bags as if they were filled with nothing more offensive than firewood, or perhaps cast-off clothing for the charity shop. 'How do you feel?' she asked.

'Great,' Cale said. 'Don't think I'll ever eat meat again, but that's no bad thing, is it?'

'Suppose not,' Moina said. 'So how about you give me a hand to get these bags out to the car. Come on, time's tight. Chop-chop!' She clapped her hands, and Cale came running as if she'd rung a bell.

'Did you do as I asked?' she said.

'What?'

'The mess out the back, did you clean it up?'

'Oh yes. Spick and span out there.'

Moina gave him a slap of approval on the back. As she did, Cale looked over at the bags again, specifically at the one nearest the door. Didn't look for long, though. Just long enough to see, through the bag's clear plastic, a flap of wrinkled skin with an eyebrow on it, two chubby white fingers, a piece of freckled leg covered with velvety, fair hair, and a blue eye that stared at him like a small, weird fish.

'Don't you dare!' Moina warned him. 'You puke up again and we'll be here all night! Get a grip!'

'I'm trying,' he said, holding his stomach. 'What's the plan?'

'The plan is that I'll check to make sure the coast is clear, while you carry the bags out and load them into my car. All right with that?'

'Yes,' Cale said. Then, turning his head to one side, he bent, picked up a bag, and held it against his chest. Immediately he became educated in one important detail outside the sickly haze that filled head: that body parts were heavy, incredibly heavy, and twice he had to shift the bag higher, just to keep it from slipping through his arms.

While Cale got to grips with the bag, Moina opened the workshop door fully and gazed down the drive, passed the open gate at the far end that was now just a series of brown, interlaced paint-strokes in the darkness. 'Okay, all clear, let's get moving.'

Cale went passed her, down to the car. Halfway down and Moina overtook him to get to the car before he did, and then she unlatched the boot. Cale dumped the bag in there, and the moment he did that, he realised the boot would only take four bags, perhaps five at a squeeze, and so he told Moina that.

'No matter,' she said. 'I'll put one in the passenger footwell, if I have to. That'll be all right. It's dark, just about. No one will see.'

He looked at her face. Despite her tiredness, portrayed by the dark stains under her eyes and the worn creases around her mouth, he once again saw that excitement in her eyes. Could hear it in her voice, as well, the little pleasurable trembles. Loving this. Loving every aspect of it, even down to the thought of driving this horrific cargo down to her flat in Twelve Trees Road and storing it there until the weekend, when they would, at last, be able to take it over to Blackthorn Wood and bury it.

'Next one,' she said, hooking a thumb back at the workshop. 'Get to it, boy.'

He did. He lugged the rest of the bags down to the car, stacked them in the boot, and when it came to the final bag - which just happened to be the one with Cutlass's head in it, but not all of it, the lower half with a little of its damp, hairy scalp still attached to it - there was no more room, and so it would have to go in the front, just as he'd expected.

Cale put it in there, and there it sat, with Cutlass's mouth facing the front and sort of smirking at the glovebox. Cale had witnessed some hideous sights these past couple of months, but he thought this topped the lot - the lower half of Cutlass's face smirking away like that underneath the clear plastic, while at the back, his hair was neatly shaved into his nape. A nape that was sticky with a grey, lumpy substance. And blood. And bits and pieces of gore.

'Okay, we're done,' Moina said, slamming the door shut on that awful sight, and thank God. 'Remember, if the police come, just act normal. I don't *think* they'll come. I'm still of the opinion that Cutlass was carrying out his own little investigation outside of the one

that the police as a whole are investigating. So keep it closed, yes?'
Then she pulled an invisible zip across her mouth.

Cale nodded.

Moina got into her car. Started the engine. Leaned over the
passenger seat and wound down the window. 'By the way, when
Tommy gets back, if he's hungry, you'll find a shepherd's pie in the
fridge that just needs to be heated-up in the oven. I fucking spoil you
two boys, don't I?'

'You do,' Cale said.

He suddenly felt sick again.

Chapter 16: Little Miss Orange Dress

After Moina left, Cale sat in a deckchair and watched, without interest, as the ground gobbled up the last of the warm, blue sky. Shuddering. His hands dangling loosely between his legs. Now and again he scratched his face, as well as the base of his spine, because he itched in those places. He was unable to access his brain. It seemed to have shut up shop altogether and gone to bed...and maybe that was just as well. No police so far, and if they came, he would say nothing, and if they took him away, he would say nothing about that also. Would just go with them because that's what children did when they were lost and needed someone to hold on to.

He gazed over at the light that streamed out of the workshop, cold, somewhat misty-looking. He heard a car go by, and a motorcycle, and a lorry, and another car. A train's whistle tooted down in the Unity Gate shed, and when it stopped, Cale thought he could still hear it in his head, whistling maddeningly in there. Underneath that, he thought he could also hear the noise of people talking. If it was, then he couldn't make out what they were saying. But he answered them all the same - it would be rude not to. 'Oh right,' he said, and laughed. 'Jolly good for you,' he said, and laughed again. Then he went back to staring at the darkness that washed up the lawn and slicked around his feet like an oily tide.

When he gazed over again at the light streaming out of the workshop, he saw that it had created two stretched, spinning wheels on the driveway, along with a hunched figure who was pedalling like mad, and panting hard. Tommy, no less. When the boy turned the corner, what he was riding, Cale saw, was not the clean, shiny bike that Cale had bought for the boy at Harvey's, but the heap of junk that Tommy had turned it into: a sad, battered contraption with balding, muddy tyres, broken lights and reflectors, and mudguards that were bent out of shape to the point of falling off.

Innocent of the fact that Cale was there, Tommy got off the bike, let it fall to the ground, and went over to the kitchen door. Put his hand on the knob.

It was then that Cale jumped to his feet, and said, 'Hey, boy! Where do you think *you're* going?'

'Oh, hi there, Cale,' Tommy said, surprised. And then fright took command of his face as he cast a guilty, sideways look at the bike on the ground. 'What are you doing out here in the dark, anyway?'

Cale advanced on him, angry enough to tear holes in the thickening gloom with his bare hands. Pointed down at the bike with a sharp, jabbing finger, ready to let rip at the boy, but when he saw Tommy's face, which was turning white while the ground turned black, he backed off. Became suddenly agreeable. 'What am I *doing* out here?' he asked. 'Just waiting for you, that's all.'

'Am I late, Cale, is that it, am I late?'

'A little,' Cale said. 'But that's okay. Hungry?'

'I could eat a scabby horse!' Tommy said.

'I bet,' Cale said. 'Let's go inside and see what Old Mother Fur-Knickers prepared for us earlier.'

'Old Mother Fur-Knickers!' Tommy said, looking up at Cale and laughing. 'Blimey O' Riley.'

Tommy took a bath, and after that, he ate Moina's shepherd's pie, which had looked delicious, but Cale had not been able to stomach even a mouthful of it. While Tommy ate, Cale had stood at the kitchen window, his ears tuned to the front doorbell, his eyes fixed on the garden, watching out for the police to come up the hill, the fanning lights of their torches preceding them, no doubt. But by the time Tommy went to bed - after asking Cale where Moina was, and he didn't just ask this once, but several times over - and Moina came back from Twelve Trees Road, there was still no hint of the police...and Moina said that likely there wouldn't be. Not yet, anyhow.

'How can you be so *sure* of that?' Cale asked, watching as she stripped off his father's old overalls and tossed them into the wash-basket under the table. Her bikini was in one of its pockets, he saw; he caught a glimpse of a thin, bloody strap twisting through the air. And now she was naked, although Moina's nakedness no longer embarrassed him, if ever it had. In fact, it occurred to him that she looked odder in clothes than she did out of them, like an alabaster figurine that wouldn't look right if you painted it.

'I can be sure,' she said, 'because I watched the television back at the flat - the news, actually - and Cutlass's car has been found. It was found this afternoon, around four o' clock. You know what *I* think? Reading between the lines, I'd say that Cutlass was halfway to a mental breakdown, anyhow, over this case, and what the police think is that he's simply gone missing. His wife seems to be of the same mind. She mentioned that he hadn't been sleeping well just lately, and that he'd been unusually quiet.'

'That fits,' Cale said. 'He certainly *looked* halfway to a mental breakdown this afternoon...didn't he?' He looked at her for validation, because, in all honesty, Cale would not have known what a man looked like who was close to a mental breakdown, anyhow, but Moina said nothing. Didn't even nod or shake her head. Just asked him to put on the coffee pot while she ran a bath. 'And maybe *I'm* close to a mental breakdown, too,' Cale murmured to himself. 'But how does a person *know*, exactly?'

'Hmmm?' Moina asked, poking her head around the door, now that she had started running the bath, and steam frothed around all around her.

'Nothing,' Cale said. 'Just talking to myself.'

'First sign of madness,' Moina remarked, and then she went back into the bathroom.

'Wasn't that just the best!' Moina twittered, clapping her hands together, and kissing him on the cheek, and then slipping her tongue into his mouth momentarily…and Cale flinched, but Moina wouldn't have noticed, anyhow. She was suddenly all hyped-up on the bloodthirsty exhilaration of the day, it seemed to him, and here she was, smelling sweetly of soap and shampoo, and acting like a little girl on her birthday. 'That's the best day I've had in a long, long time! Takes me back to my days on the farm when my brother Ernie and me - ' And then she said no more, just cut her words dead in their tracks, picked up her coffee, and began to drink it. Her head down like a machine whose power had all at once been switched off.

'Your brother?' Cale asked. 'You have a brother?'

'*Used* to have a brother,' Moina said, keeping her head down. 'But that was a long time ago. I'd rather not talk about it. Is Tommy around?'

'Up in bed.'

'Did he eat my shepherd's pie?'

'Yes.'

'Maybe I'll go up and give him a kiss. Goodnight, Cale.'

'Goodnight. And Moina?'

'Yes.'

'Is Cutlass…you know…all tidied away?'

Moina nodded. 'Like pretty maidens all in a row.'

He went out to the workshop, switched off the lights, went into the office, and sat there. The warmth soon began to drain out of the air. A chill began to tickle his skin, and goose-bumps rose on his arms and around his neck. He thrust his hands between his thighs, for warmth, and for comfort. In the distance he swore he heard thunder. Maybe he did, maybe he didn't. He snatched up the phone, and startled himself by doing that. Held it to his ear, and without dialling any number, he said, 'Hello there, Mrs Nipples. Just phoned to say I've made that new door you wanted, and I'll be over tomorrow to give it a good banging. How's that with you?' Then: 'Good evening, Mrs Funnyfanny. I've got that new window of yours. Can I come over in the morning and give you a good fucking?' And then: 'Is that you, Mr Smallcock? Just called to check the measurements of your wife's fat backside. Is it fifty-three inches, or fifty-five? Can't for the life of me remember.'

No laughter, however. Not even a smile. He just put the phone back in its cradle, leaned back in his chair, and grabbed his coat off the hook behind him. Settle it over his cold, aching body. Got in touch with his brain once more, to see if it would allow him to think again, but no, his brain was still having none it - all thought, it seemed, had been locked behind a door to which the keys around Cale's neck, or the ones in his pocket, would not fit. And so he closed his eyes, slipped down into his chair, and just when he believed that sleep would not come, that he would sit here all night just staring into space, it did come...but not for long. He was woken up by the rumble of thunder across the hills somewhere, and by rain hammering on the roof. The warm weather just lately had become a little too ripe, like a fruit ready to burst, and now finally it had.

On legs shot full of pins and needles, he went to the door, eased it open against the wind, and what he saw, when he looked out with eyes that were still half shut - and faintly sticky, too - was rain coming down in crazy, flapping sheets, rain that beat at the driveway and turned the deep wheel ruts there into streams, rain that beat on Moina's old car and made it rattle, rain that beat on Cale's truck and turned the flatbed at the back into a pounding, metal drum. He saw lightning cutting across the sky, zigzagging back and forth, but not close, somewhere over Rosewater way, he reckoned. Heading this way, though, he was sure of it.

He looked up at the house and saw water spilling over the gutters like dangling, silver chains. The wind blew cold against his face. He was clutching his jacket to his chest, and now he put it on, buttoned it up. Couldn't decide if he should run into the house or simply stay in here. His brain was still refusing him right of entry to even the simplest of decision-making tools...but then a decision of sorts was taken for him.

He heard a crash. Out the back. In the storeroom. And off he went to investigate, lurching through the darkness that was lit by sporadic cracks of lightning. He bashed the back of a hand against his workbench, and said, 'Fuck it.' His knee struck the kitchen unit he'd been working on this morning, and he pushed it aside so roughly that it toppled over and smashed to the floor.

When he reached the storeroom, he paused there for a moment with an ear to the door, listening. He heard nothing. He opened the door and switched on the light. He vaguely expected to see that the window had blown open, perhaps because he hadn't closed it properly after using it to get in and out of the workshop while Moina had been cutting Roy Cutlass up into little pieces. Vaguely expected also to see a pile of smashed glass in the sink and maybe littered all around it, but the window was still latched. There *was* no broken glass, and so he began to look elsewhere.

What he saw was a tobacco pouch on the floor, his father's tobacco pouch. Somehow it had fallen out of Ewan Redstone's old chamois apron that was hanging there on the hook. The pouch was open, and tobacco had spilled out of it. The cigarette papers, as well. And the smell of smoke. Cale detected that the moment he opened the door, but only now did it register. The smell of smoke, more directly, the smell of his father's hand-rolled cigarettes. Unmistakeable, that smell. Sickly-sweet. Like burning rose petals. And Cale gasped so hard that his heart seemed to gasp as well, and a hand went up to his chest, as the hand of a woman might who has heard such terrible news that she takes hold of the locket around her neck.

'Daddy?' he said, and although that should have surprised him, him calling out like that to a man he had hated, when he said that word, *Daddy*, his throat suddenly locked up, and he felt tears running down his face and into the corners of his mouth. 'Is that you, Daddy?'

Daddy did not reply, though. Whatever Daddy had to say on the matter had already been remarked upon, not in words, but in the mischief that Cale saw more evidence of as he walked further into the storeroom. A pot of glue, overturned, and white, gooey strands of the stuff running down the shelves. Boxes of door hinges scattered all over the place, and lying among their protective wrappings of brown, waxed paper. Handfuls of nails flung here and there. Rolls of laminate slashed to ribbons. Hooks and latches and brass screws and brass cups - those too had been messed with and dumped in all the wrong places. And while Cale tried to make sense of all this with a brain that still refused to work, he looked back into the workshop, and what he saw were three huge shadows, overlapping one another, and pressing against the dusty, whitewashed brickwork, and against the windows in which spider webs shimmered.

Cale heard a chuckle, too, a horrible, grating chuckle, and said, 'Oh Jesus, crikey, God's sake!' in a broken, tear-choked voice. He closed his eyes for a while. Kept them that way for perhaps ten seconds, and then he opened one eye, just a wee bit. Looked and saw, with relief, that the shadows had gone. No more strange voices, either.

The rain went on slapping against the roof, and his gaze flicked between the storeroom and the workshop, back and forth, back and forth, until finally it settled on the little office in the far corner there, and in his own mixed-up way, he came to the assumption that he must still be asleep in there. Would have believed that, too, had he not wiped a hand down his coat right then and felt raindrops on his palm. Just a few, the few that had gotten through the door while he'd been standing there, looking out, but enough, nevertheless, to let him know that he certainly wasn't asleep.

He rubbed his eyes that were still half-closed. Couldn't persuade them to open up all the way, and so he made rings out of his thumbs and forefingers, placed them over his eyes, like fake glasses, and tried to prise them open that way. As he did, he looked over at the windows...

There were three men looking in at him: Ewan Redstone, Don

Willoughby, and Roy Cutlass, their faces drenched with rain. Cale wanted to scream, and he opened his mouth to do just that…then realised that actually he *didn't* want to scream, not in the slightest, because really he didn't feel any fright at all. Instead he felt peculiarly drawn to those faces, especially to the warning that seemed to be etched in their round, gawping eyes.

He removed his ringed fingers from his face, and the men were gone. Raised them again, and here they were, back again, and peering in at him. Down, gone. Up, and back they came. Why was that? And would his damn brain open up just a little and let him use it?

Stiff-legged, he walked over to the windows. Once more he curled his fingers, placed them over his eyes, and here they were again, the faces, only now the men joined to those faces were pointing across the garden.

All three men pointing like prophets.

To Sad's Place.

'What is it?' Cale asked. The question barely out of his mouth, and then he saw the upper half of the stable door swing open, followed by the lower half. Not happening for real, of course. The doors looked more like slabs of mist he could walk through than solid boards, and struts, and nails. And what he learned right then was that he would never run away from a ghost. Always believed that if he saw one, he would, positive the need to run would be far greater than the need to look. Far, far greater. Yet the way he was standing here, stock-still, seemed to refute that. And was his ability to reason like this proof that his brain was now up and running again?

Yes, that seemed to be so, thank God, and what should have been an alarming experience now seemed to be a beneficial one, one that had shaken him out of the trance he'd been in since Roy Cutlass's death. He glanced out at the men again, his curled fingers still up to his eyes, and what he saw was Little Miss Orange Dress now standing in the doorway of Sad's Place. Not a hair out of place, and her dress, just as gauzy and bright as he remembered it, did not even minutely twitch in the wind and the rain. And why would it? She was not, after all, the *real* Little Miss Orange Dress, who would by now be in her late-twenties, but some kind of otherworldly carbon copy of that girl. That girl who had walked him by the hand that day into Sad's Place when he had been a toddler, while the Blunts, the Hunts, the Dunns, whatever, had been showing Cale's mother and father around the house.

His mind went back to that now, went back to the dream he'd had that night, on the day he'd killed his father, that dream which had not been a dream but a memory. No more cross-threading, or cross-patching, or cross-pollination, or whatever the correct term was. No more mixing dream with memory, and memory with dream, the way he'd done that after having sex with Moina Furneaux, with her all the time wanting to be stuffed like a turkey and to be fucked bandy. The memory was pure now, as pure as the photo you found and thought you'd lost, and when you looked at it, at that little snippet of time, captured and frozen there, it all came back to you, as clear as sunlight.

Through those curled fingers of his, Cale followed the direction of the three men's pointing fingers, and yes, there was Little Miss Orange Dress. Cale, as well, wearing his bright red shirt and the little pair of jeans that his mother had made for him to the exact pattern of his father's carpenter's jeans, even down to the long, thin pocket on the leg, made to accommodate a wooden, folding rule.

He watched. And remembered.

His hand is in hers. Her dress floats around her, so thin, so subtle, and Cale can see her legs through it. Her buttocks, too. Even the bumps on her chest that will become bosoms when she grows up into a woman. She bends over and looks into Cale's face. He looks up and sees those eyes of hers that are like gentle but powerful beams of light that draw him in and take him to some place beyond the flat but explicable confines of the world.

I have something to show you, Cale, she says. Something for you to see and…to feel. Come with me.

She leads him into Sad's Place, after first glancing guiltily up at the house. It is dark in here, it smells of an animal, and there are clods of muddy straw sprinkled here and there on the dirt floor. Webs hang from the rafters, and old bits of leather, and old bits of string, and old bits of chain, and a long length of rope, and while Cale is looking up at these odds and sods, and at the holes in the roof slates through which the sun shines in buttery, dusty rods, the girl has hiked up her little orange dress, has pulled down her panties, but Cale doesn't know that because Cale has been instructed to close his eyes, if he does she will give him sweeties back at the house, and so Cale does as she requests, and then his hand does not feel as if it is in hers anymore but in some moist place that is like a mitten, and then the girl is saying in a faint, trembling voice, That's it, all the way in, yes, as far as you can get, *and Cale pushes, and the girl groans, and Cale pushes further, and the girl groans a little more, and then, in a voice that sounds almost exultant:* That's it! All the way in! Right in there! Yes, yes, yes! *And then, when it seems that this will never end, all this pushing, all this groaning, it all of sudden comes to an end with the "mitten" suddenly relaxing around his hand, the girl slides his hand out of there, and Cale can now open his eyes, she tells him, and when he does, there are dark shades of guilt on her face again, and she says that she's sorry, that she's so, so sorry, and that if he promises to say nothing about this, then he can have all the sweets in the world, if he wants them, would he like that, would he?*

'So that's it,' Cale said, dropping his ringed fingers from his eyes and snapping back into himself. The three rain-lashed men at the window had gone. It was just Cale again, thinking about how he had taken the sweets from Little Miss Orange Dress that day, and then, because the wrongdoing hadn't seemed like much of a wrongdoing, anyhow, he forgot about it, the way most kids do when it doesn't seem like much has happened to cry over. Just toddled off to find his parents with a strawberry-flavoured lolly in his mouth, and a bag of fizzy sherbet in his hand.

Still, this was not about Cale.. This was about Tommy. The Tommy who, over dinner, had kept on asking: *When will Moina be back, where is she, do you think she'll be late, Cale?* And so it had gone on, until Cale had told the boy to take a leak, to brush his teeth, and to get up to bed.

This the boy had done. And some time later, Moina had done the same, had gone up to bed...and early for her. Too early. Even allowing for the ordeal of having to slice up a dead policeman with a bandsaw.

'So that's it,' Cale said again, nodding. With a chewed fingernail, he absently scratched the pockmarks there, on the right side of his nose. After that, he shoved a hand down the back of his jeans and itched the eczema there. Again he did this without paying much attention. His attention was elsewhere. Looking out of the rattling, rain-drenched windows, he was, up at the house, moreover, at the small, sash window there that looked down on the clothesline that was swinging to and fro in the wind.

In his head, he heard Moina say about Tommy: *Maybe I'll go up and give him a kiss.* Which was all well and good...except Moina Furneaux didn't do that mumsy kind of thing. At least not to the Tommy's of the world, the little cripple boys with their wonky faces and their gammy legs that disgusted her, just about.

My school is for pupils who are sound in body and mind, she had said that night in the kitchen, as they stood there together, under the unshaded bulb, Cale in nothing but a towel, Moina wearing a blouse that had been like sculpted fog. And then Cale remembered something else, as well: him telling Moina that Tommy stole money and bought sweets, and that the sweets, they changed him. Changed him from a good boy into a bad boy. And although Moina's reaction to that had been to say that sweets were like rocket fuel to some kids, it seemed to Cale now, looking back on that night, that Moina, whenever the mood took her, would have gladly lit the blue touch paper to Tommy's addiction...if, that was, it spelled a means to an end.

And what would that end be, precisely?

'I wonder,' Cale said, and he turned away from the windows in

which no faces were framed anymore, and he went back into the house.
Angry.

Chapter 17: The Return of the Mallet

He went up the stairs, thinking that the abuse hadn't ended with his father's death, it was still going on, just in another form, and yes he was angry about that, angry enough to want to rip Moina Furneaux's scheming, low-life head off and use it as a football.

However, despite this, all he *really* wanted was to send her back to Twelve Trees Road where she belonged. Never mind the mice and having to breathe through a gas mask. Never mind that she could have Tommy out of Brougham Moor and into the special needs school over in Battenford. Cale would listen to none of that. Wouldn't *need* to. Moina Furneaux knew enough to put him in jail and he knew enough to do the same to her. She could go to hell, and he would have her out of here, right this minute, and be done with it.

He passed the window on the landing in which the curtains flapped and twisted in the wind. The storm was overhead now, and it felt to him as if the grumbling, spitting clouds were hugging the house...and beginning to smother it. A ground-shaking cannonade of thunder rolled across the sky, and lightning printed the stair-rods on the walls in prison-like bars, or perhaps zoo-like bars. And that fit - it had begun to *feel* much like an animal house around here just lately.

He was running almost, but as he knew this house from top to bottom, right down to the last nail in the skirting and the last screw in the hinges, he made it up the stairs, across the landing, and without making so much as one single floorboard creak. Or even squeak a little. He got to Tommy's bedroom door, taped to which was a piece of paper on which the boy had printed in bright-red crayon: England 4 West Germany 2, Yippee! Then Cale put a hand on the knob, gently turned it, opened the door a little, poked his head around it, and what he saw he expected to see…although this in no way blunted the spectacle. In fact, it seemed to make it sharper, the way an accident will seem sharper when you know it's bound to happen and nothing can stop it.

He saw Moina kneeling on the floor, wearing not a stitch, her backside like some large, exotic fruit ripening on a forest floor. Saw the shadow of her red, haystack hair bobbing madly up and down on the wall, too…and there was Tommy, lying on the bed, his pyjama bottoms around his ankles. His face was hot and greasy. His eyes were glazed. He was making faint, shivery sounds. He looked as if he'd died and gone to heaven.

Except he hadn't. The litter of empty sweet wrappers all over the place, and the empty bottles of fizzy pop to go with them (some with the straws still poking out of their mouths like wilting flower stems), suggested that Tommy was simply sky-high on sugar, and that the act Moina was performing on him, which just happened to be one of the acts she had performed on Cale down in the workshop, probably felt to him as if it were happening in a dream.

Dream or not, however, that was it, Cale had seen enough. He marched into the room, and said, 'So this is what you meant when you said you were giving Tommy a little extra tuition, was it?' He intended to fling her to the floor and tell her to get out of here, to go, to just get out and to not come back, but before he could do that, she quickly spun around, her face growing long with shock and horror.

Her feet paddling, her fingernails digging into the carpet, she pushed herself up against Tommy's bed, and now her knees were pressed up against her breasts, making them bulge against her arms. There was spittle running down her chin in which Cale saw tiny flecks of red lipstick, and she wiped it away with a trembling, guilty wrist. The look in her eyes told him that she hadn't expected to die that night, that almost certainly she believed that many years of this low-life behaviour still lay ahead of her. But then Cale saw those expectations flow out of her, as if the plug of her life had been pulled. How he must have looked to her right then in that closing instant of her life, he didn't know. Mad, probably. Although he didn't think she would have had much time for any of that, anyway, for thinking. His appearance, along with his state of mind, wouldn't have mattered much to a woman who was looking up at a boy with murder written all over his face.

She didn't say anything, either. No protests, and certainly none of those drastic, worthless apologies that some people blubbered just to buy themselves a little more time. Had she said something, then knowing Moina, it would just have been her brand of mocking defiance, anyhow, such as: *So what? You caught me gobbling off your little cripple brother, big deal. Don't go making mountains of molehills.*

And so he brought the mallet down on her, the mallet that he couldn't remember picking up. The mallet that he thought was just a bare hand he had swung at her to slap her further away from his little brother, but when he heard the crunching, popping noise, followed by the sight of blood splashing up the walls and all over that new bed he had bought for Tommy back in the summer, he realised that *no* bare hand could have made that noise. Or caused that sort of damage.

He watched, confused, as Moina slumped to the floor, and what he at first denied, he soon accepted when he saw the hole in her left temple that was gushing blood. Her eyes became dark, rolling blanks. Her legs shook, as did her arms, and the rings on her fingers clinked together daintily. Her breasts wobbled, those same breasts that Cale had cupped out in the workshop with a lust against which his shame and loathing had not been able to compete. Blood oozed through her chattering teeth and slipped over her bottom lip. She was not quite dead...but she was getting there.

Cale gazed at the mallet in his hand, barely able to believe it was there, and then he let it drop to the floor. Wanted to drop to his knees, as well, and try to help Moina in a way that he knew he couldn't. She was finished - that was obvious. Just one blow, that was all it had taken, but that had been enough to snuff out her lights. It was over. All bar the waiting. The waiting that Cale Redstone didn't want to do but knew he had to.

He looked over at Tommy. Saw that he had backed himself into the corner where his bed met with the wall, and he was screaming out of that drooping, twisted mouth of his: *'Oh God Cale, what have you done, what have you done, what have you done?'* Pulling crazily all the time at his pyjama bottoms, to get them back up around his waist.

He was spaced-out on the sugar, and spaced-out, too, on the extreme, flat-out horror of it all. Screaming. And while he screamed, the storm went on whacking away outside. A slate became disunited from the roof and slipped down into the gutter. A dustbin went rolling across the lawn and smashed into the house. The clothesline clattered against the metal poles to which it was attached. Rain splattered so hard against the window that it sounded to Cale like a wild animal that wanted to get in here. He put his hands up to his head, pressed his palms against his temples, as if, by doing that, he could squeeze out all the pain that was like a big, infected boil inside him.

When that didn't work, he suddenly turned back to Tommy, his jaw set, his eyes fiery. 'SHUT THE FUCK UP!' he bellowed. 'JUST SHUT... THE FUCK...UP!' And the boy did. Immediately. He got his trousers up, fastened the cord around his waist with shaking, disorganised fingers, and then, still jammed into the corner, he sat there making a *zizz-zizz-zizz* noise over his teeth. His eyes were leaking. His face was horribly bunched. His hands fluttered up and down in the electrified air as if they were butterflies that could not find a leaf on which to settle.

'Good,' Cale said, nodding with approval. His tone was all of a sudden so calm and reasonable, it surprised him, and then it pleased him, because it indicated, perhaps, that he might just be able to think straight enough to put a plan together. 'Okay, fine,' he went on. 'I've made a terrible mistake, haven't I? But it's done. I can't change it. So now I need to come up with a way out of this.'

'Zizz-zizz-zizz,' Tommy said to that, and Cale held a hand up to the boy, just to let him know that the *zizz-zizz-zizzing* was all right, tolerable, anyhow, but that he shouldn't even *think* about screaming again. Please, no more screaming.

Then: 'Yes, I've made a terrible mistake, all right. But on the other hand, so did you.' Cale's words were now directed at Moina, whose body was still shaking but the shakes were getting weaker, more of a ripple. Her eyes began to close, those eyes in which Cale had never seen love, or the shadow of love, or even the *ghost* of love.

However, while there was still some semblance of life there, albeit the kind that no longer received and then returned, Cale said, 'Christ, Moina, did you *have* to do that to Tommy? What for? He's just a boy, that's all. And that's all I am, too, just a boy. What is it with you people? Why can't you live a life without having to tear up the lives of others? My father was like that. That man could stir up trouble in an empty room!'

With a foot, Cale lashed out with frustration at an empty drinks bottle, one of those that Moina must have brought into the house, unbeknown to Cale, and given to Tommy, to get him loaded up on sugar before making another of her vile approaches on him. It skimmed across a pile of well-thumbed comics and football magazines, making them riffle, and then it crashed into a poster of Jimmy Greaves that was taped to the wall. Smashed there in a hundred jagged, twinkling pieces.

'I'm sorry, Cale,' Tommy said. 'I couldn't stop her…I couldn't make her go away…I couldn't get her to leave me alone…I wanted to tell you she was doing that to me, honestly I did, but I couldn't, I just -'

'Stop!' Cale said. 'I don't want to hear any of this! Spare me the details, please!' He was breathing hard, gasping really. His chest rose and fell under his wet, heavy coat. His hands dangled at his sides, leaden. His hair was damp and it tumbled over his forehead in sloppy, pepper-coloured curls. When he looked over at Tommy, though, at the brother he loved with all of his heart, he melted and gave the boy a look of kindness. 'Christ, Tom, it's not your fault. *None* of this is your fault. It's mine. I knew she was bad. I knew she was just about capable of anything. But I had a workshop to run, a workshop that was just about killing me, and when she came along that night, she was like a godsend that God Himself did not send.'

None of that could slap Tommy all the way back into the real world, though. Not only were his hands still fluttering, his head was jerking, too, at the sound of the thunder, and at the sight of the lightning that now flashed almost continually against the window, but mostly his head jerked that way due to all the sugar in his veins. Sugar that turned him into a rebel for the most part and made him almost impossible to control...unless, of course, you just happened to be Moina Furneaux with a wet, warm mouth. And who's fault was that? Not Moina's, if you wanted to point the finger. Moina, as sick as she was, had simply taken advantage of the boy's addiction, as a thief will take advantage of a deserted shop. No, this was all down to Ewan Redstone, who had turned Tommy's diet into such a hit-and-miss affair, that the boy took whatever came to him, an apple or an orange, if it was offered, but if it wasn't, then he went straight for the sugar. No contest. Just off with the wrapper, or off with the stopper, and Tommy got his hit.

'What are we going to do, Cale, what are we going to do?' Tommy asked, and then, entirely out of context with the worry and fright on his face, he suddenly laid down on the bed, pulled the sheets up under his chin, and that was it, he was out again, sparko, and staring up at the ceiling. His head rolling from side to side. His eyes bobbling. His fingers twitching on the bedspread.

'*We're* not going to do anything,' Cale said. 'It's up to me to sort this out...and I will.' He looked down at Moina Furneaux, still shocked by what he'd done, and still confused, too, although mostly the confusion had now been taken over by the urgency to come up with a plan to get rid of her.

He watched as she blinked, once, twice, a third time that was not really a blink, more an agonised clench, and then her eyelids closed all the way down. Eyelids to whose lashes a tear seemed to cling to every individual dark, curled filament. Her body jittered one final time, her fingers splayed, her back arched, and she let out a long, gravelly sigh over the rim of her blood-stained lips. Her body stiffened, seemed to lengthen a little, too, as if it were being stretched on a rack, and Cale swore, below the roar of the storm outside, that he heard her joints popping and clicking.

Then it was over. Her body relaxed, and it may have been the light in here, which ranged from total darkness to bright blue flashes that lit up the room in blinding, startling flares, but Moina Furneaux seemed all of a sudden to double in size, turning her thighs into overflowing saddlebags, and her belly into a big, cheese-coloured sponge. Her breasts were no longer the firm, bulging hillocks that Cale had eagerly squeezed out in the workshop this afternoon but wrinkly, sagging bags of flesh that slid under her armpits as if to hide there, embarrassed. Her pubic hair no longer seemed dark, lush and well-tended, but more a straggly tuft of greying weed. Her red, piled-up hair, undoubtedly dyed, had turned into a messy, knotted heap through which Cale could see patches of her scalp, white as chalk. Funny, but he thought only love was blind, but now it seemed that anyone, or anything, could fool your heart if you weren't paying close enough attention.

He looked down at her red, glittery shoes, and saw that they were not so red and glittery anymore, that in fact they were scuffed, they were torn, and in places he saw that the soles had peeled away from the uppers. And that gold chain around her ankle, the anklet she wore almost all the time, as if it meant as much to her as a wedding ring would to a new bride? He knelt down, took hold of it in his fingers, and saw that it was nothing but cheap metal coated in gold-coloured paint. She had money, she could have bought herself a real gold anklet from a quality jeweller, but on reflection, he guessed that Moina Furneaux had been cheap in just about every aspect of her life, and in doing so, she had bought herself a cheap death.

He scooped her up and carried her into her bedroom, which had not been her bedroom but Ewan Redstone's, although that man, had he been alive, would not have recognised it, what with the bright materials flowing out of the drawers, and the chains, the necklaces, the beads, hanging off the mirrors, and the shoes, the boots, the strappy sandals that littered the floor. And the bed. Ewan Redstone would not have been seen dead lying under the frilly, pink sheets and the flowery quilt that Moina had so favoured.

Cale dumped her down on the bed, grabbed one of her coats out of the wardrobe, but not the furs, of which there were two, and they were smelly, sleek things, anyhow, in which he wouldn't wrap her because the fur would make it harder for him to get a grip on her. Instead, he selected her raincoat, a navy-blue one with a belt on it, and he dressed her in it. Buttoned it up. Tied the belt. As he did this, the keys on the string around his neck clinked together, and he thought: *Keys!*

He opened Moina's handbag, sitting there on her bedside table. Dug out her ring of keys. Took off the latch key that fitted this place, the one Cale had gotten cut for her at a hardware store in town, and tossed it down on the bed. Put the rest of the keys in his pocket and went back into Tommy's room. Knelt beside his bed, above which was pinned that England flag that Elsa Lovell had given him at summer school.

Cale tenderly pushed the boy's hair away from his forehead, his forehead which was sunburned, where he'd been out all day on his bike, and Cale found it hard to believe that that day, and this night, were part of the same twenty-four hours, now that the sky was a raining, blasting sea of mayhem.

He held the boy's hand. 'Tom?'

'Hmmm?'

'I've come up with a plan. I'm going to take Moina's body down to her place in Twelve Trees Road. Going to take her down there in her car and then walk back. Did you tell anyone at school that she was stopping with us?'

'Hmmm?' Tommy said again, and in such a bleary, faraway voice, that Cale had to give him a gentle shake.

'Tom, listen to me. Did you tell anyone at school that Moina was staying with us?'

'No.'

'Are you sure?'

'Yes.' He rolled his eyes. 'Blimey O'Riley.'

'Never mind Blimey O'Riley. Just make sure you don't answer the phone if someone calls, or the doorbell, if it rings. Just stay right here in bed until I get back, okay?'

'Okay,' Tommy said, and then, unexpectedly, he slung an arm around Cale's neck and began to weep. Cale soothed the boy, by stroking him and by shushing him, but overall, this was largely useless because the boy undoubtedly felt responsible for what had happened here. Perhaps felt responsible, too, for what had happened to their father. After all, had Tommy not been around, then none of this would have happened. Cale Redstone would just be an ordinary kid getting along with his ordinary life. But of course what was done was done, and Cale bore no grudges for that. How could he? He loved Tommy. Loved him so much that he had killed their father to stop him from killing the boy. Better a world *with* Tommy than without him. But Tommy, it seemed, felt differently to that.

'Oh Cale, what have I done?' he said. His face was awash with tears. His eyes were big glass marbles. 'I think you would have been better off without me to drag you down. I've caused you nothing but trouble, haven't I? Dad dead, and now Moina. And I'm the one to blame, aren't I?'

'Don't say such silly things,' Cale said. 'I killed dad because, if I hadn't, then he would have killed you. And Moina? It's not your fault I let that terrible woman into this house. That's my fault. *All* my fault. I should have been man enough to stop her, but I wasn't.'

'That's because you're *not* a man, Cale. You're just a boy like me. And how can two boys get a life when all the grownups want is to spoil everything? I hate grownups. If that's how I'm going to turn out, like dad, and like Moina Furneaux, then I don't *ever* want to grow up! I'd rather die right now while I'm young and to hell with it!'

He put his head against Cale's damp coat, buried his head in there, and went on sobbing. For a kid seen as an idiot by just about everyone, he certainly knew how to get his point across. Cale could not have put it better himself. How *did* two boys get a life when all the grownups wanted was to spoil it? Was murder the only answer? If it was, then

Cale wasn't so sure that *he* wanted to be a grownup, either. Better to go out of this world, he thought, with much of your innocence still intact, than let age lay you open to all that darkness out there...except maybe Cale and Tommy had seen too much of that darkness already.

Two boys, two *brothers*, who had perhaps crossed the line of no return.

Cale let his brother's hand fall back on the bed. He stood up, and said, 'I'm going now, Tom. I don't want to, but I've got to. You understand that, don't you?'

Tommy nodded.

'Try to get some rest, if you can, eh?'

Tommy, still weeping, gave Cale a look that said he would if he could, and he turned over on his side, his hands clasped together and wedged under his face. Difficult to think the boy would do that, would just lie there and try to rest with that storm crashing away outside and with that bloody mallet lying there on the floor, but he left the boy that way, anyhow. Because he had no choice.

'I love you, Tom,' he whispered, and out he went, walking away from one hell and into another.

Chapter 18: Soulmates from a Soulless Place

He doubted that hell, however, could be defined as one place or another. Hell, he came to believe that night, as he drove to Twelve Trees Road, was not a place of brimstone, of slave-driving demons, and of lost, screaming souls, but simply a life over which you had no control. And that had been Cale Redstone's life as far back as he could remember, a life over which he'd had no control. And his plan? There was no plan. A plan suggested that a degree of clever thinking had been applied in order to bring about a favourable outcome, but the truth was, Cale was just about incapable of anything that even came *close* to clever thinking. He simply wanted to get Moina's body out of the house, and that was that.

The bad weather had cluttered the streets with debris, such as dustbin lids, roof tiles, paper, branches, leaves, but not with people. As Moina's flat was up one short flight of stairs, he had been able to drag her out from the back of her car and then lug her into the place without anyone seeing him.

Lit by the lightning flashes that continued to spit down out of the sky, he carried her over to the shabby couch in here, and sat her down, facing the television, with her hands in her lap. He had plugged the hole in her head with a rag he found in Moina's glovebox, likely the one she had used to clean the windscreen with on cold or rainy mornings. It had stopped the blood from dripping all over the road, the pavement, and up the stairs.

Cale put her keys on a low table beside the couch, alongside Roy Cutlass's stuff that Moina had taken off him before slicing him up. Moina's remark about the mice in here appeared so far to be a myth, although Cale would not have been surprised to *see* a mouse. Or a rat for that matter - it was truly a dump in here. And her remark about having to breathe through a gas mask? That at least was not a myth. Much of the wallpaper was peeled. There seemed to be rising damp, falling damp, and in the middle of all that, mildew grew on the walls in black, weeping clumps. There was some stuff down there, too, in one corner, on top of the skirting board. Silvery and plump and covered with short, dark hairs. It made Cale's skin crawl just to look at it. But he doubted that was responsible for the smell in here. The cooking fat that clung to the walls, and to the ceiling above the gas stove, seemed to be responsible for that. Cooking fat that hung down in places like snot.

Then there was Moina's bed. He looked over at it, then almost at once he looked away, disgusted. That bed had seen so much activity that it had collapsed. It teemed with fleas that he could see leaping, too, even in the darkness, and it was drenched in bodily fluids that in places had dried to a crust, whereas in other places it was still damp. Ropes, fashioned into wrist restraints, hung from the scratched headboard. A whip lay across the bed like a dead snake.

Trying to make sense of any of this was just about impossible. Moina had proclaimed the curtains filthy at Cale's house when she had taken them down, washed them, and darned them. Yet the curtains in this place were far, far worse. Just rags that seemed to be held together with grease, dust, and cigarette smoke. He guessed that trying to work some people out was just about pointless, though. His father had been a headcase, Moina Furneaux had been a headcase, and although that was making light of the problem, better that, Cale thought, than trying to ride the carousel of analysis that would just send him around in circles.

Rain sprayed against the window. Lightning flickered again, and Cale saw the sacks in which Roy Cutlass's body parts had been stuffed. In a wardrobe, they were, and despite the fact the door handles had been tied together with string, the sacks were so heavy that they bulged against the doors, pushing them open slightly. *Like pretty maidens all in a row*, Moina had said about those sacks, but Cale didn't think so.

Only Moina could have used the words "pretty" and "maidens" to describe how those sacks in there were stacked. He saw a finger in one of them, around which was a gold wedding band. The finger was curled a little, as if motioning to him. No thanks. It was time for Cale to go.

Except –

He bashed his foot against something that was under the couch, a corner of it poking out. He bent down, pulled it of there, and saw that it was a book. More precisely a photo album.

He opened it up.

And wished he hadn't.

"Me and Ernie pissing" had been scribbled in pen alongside one of the pictures in here. Ernie had been Moina's brother, of course, and the act in which he and Moina were participating told Cale that Ernie had been every bit as sick as his sister.

"Oh Rex, you dirty fucker!" was the caption of another picture. Rex was a sheepdog, and if someone had asked Cale to describe what had been happening in that picture, he would have told them to take a look for themselves, because *he* wasn't about to describe it.

The same applied to a photo beside which Moina had written "I took it all, every last inch!" Looking at it (it was in black-and-white, as all the photos were, although that in no way made them any less graphic) sent Cale's mind into a spin and he had to sit down. He went on looking, though. His repulsion was no match, it seemed, for the compulsion that kept his eyes all but nailed to this little book of horrors.

There was no order to it, either. Photos and letters and newspaper clippings and even pieces of poetry had been stuck in here any old way, and so Cale might come across a photo of Moina getting acquainted with a horse in a way that required no saddle, and the next moment he'd be reading a clipping whose headline, for instance, might be: *TEACHER FOUND NOT GUILTY OF CHILD SEX CHARGES.* Then, underneath: *Maureen Devereaux cleared. Judge declares evidence flawed.*

Maureen Devereaux? Oh well, not much of a revelation there, was it? Not really. It made sense to Cale that a woman like Moina Furneaux would have changed her name at some point. Moina Furneaux or Maureen Devereaux, it didn't much matter. Both were the same woman who, it seemed, had gone from job to job, from place to place, making some kind of trouble or another.

Another clipping here, one that was faded to the delicacy of tissue paper and went all the way back to the mid-forties, when Maureen Devereaux had been nothing but a slip of a thing. Maureen Devereaux, found guilty of lewd behaviour, but her punishment, which had been a three month jail term, had been commuted, after an appeal, to a suspended sentence.

However, the fact that fate had been kind to her seemed not to have entered her mind. In bright-red pen, she had written BULLSHIT! across the clipping, triple underlined, and so hard that the pen had almost torn a gash in the paper. Typical Moina. Likely her warped, not-quite-right approach to life had been fashioned down on the farm with that brother of hers, Ernie. Ernie Devereaux, who had no doubt been every bit as intelligent as his sister, but like his sister, the constant side-track of evil had probably led him away from the road of achievement, and into short-term, humdrum jobs that would not have fit his brain power...but would at least have fit his sordid lifestyle.

For Moina, a job as a temporary headmistress had given her access, not just to children, but also to their parents. A quick peek at the school records, coupled with a bit of nosing around, and more often than not she would have found an opening into which she could jump, and with the greatest of ease. Those openings had likely been men, either divorced or widowed, and as such they would have been vulnerable to a woman's hand around the house...and to a woman's hand in the bed.

How many men over the years had Moina captured this way? Dozens, most likely, Cale thought. Men who would have opened their houses to her, given her just about anything she wanted, and by way of thanking them, Moina would have returned to her dingy bedsit at the weekends to be pleasured by the male teachers who had likely formed a queue all the way around the block, along with anyone else who had fancied a turn: the tinker, the tailor, the soldier, the sailor, and so forth.

And Ernie? Further into the book and Cale found a small newspaper clipping on which had been planted a lipstick kiss that just about blotted out all of the text. By carrying the album over to the window, however, he managed to read through the lipstick and learn about how Ernest Devereaux had fallen into a hay-shredder, and that, although he had still been alive when he'd been pulled out of there (minus his left arm and much of his right leg), he had died in hospital two hours later. Back in 1946, that had been, when Ernie had been just twenty-nine years of age.

Below the clipping was a card, white with one single red rose on it. Cale opened it up. There was a photograph in here, too. He looked at that first, before moving it aside to read the words that were written in the card in Moina's jagged, almost brutal hand. In the photo Ernie and Moina (or Maureen as she would have been known back then) were sitting on a fence, Moina roughly ten years old, Ernie perhaps two years her senior. Behind them was a ramshackle shed around which grew silver birch trees. A warm, autumn day, judging by the leaves that thickly littered the ground. A brother and his little sister grinning at the camera, all of it normal, all of it unremarkable, just another shot for the family album, no different to any other brother-and-sister photo you would find in many homes…apart from the fact that Moina's legs were open and Ernie's hand was someplace where only Moina's underwear should have been.

"Ernie finds a juicy peach!" was what Moina had scratched beside this picture, and because it was not held in place by the little triangular corner tabs which held most of the other pictures in place, Cale crumpled it up and tossed it away, revolted.

'Ernie finds a juicy peach,' he whispered. 'Blimey O'Riley.' His fingers shaking, he read the words right then that were written on the card: "Ernie, not just my brother but my soulmate."

The idea that a brother could be become his sister's soulmate by sticking his fingers up her was lost on Cale. Soulmates, he always believed, were bound by love, by devotion, and perhaps by some uncanny anticipation of each others' acts and thoughts. But of course it was also a requirement that you were similar, and if your similarity just happened to show itself in the kind of depravity that Cale saw here, then he conceded, if reluctantly, that yes, they had been soulmates, all right.

Soulmates from a soulless place.

And who had taken that photograph, anyhow? Their mother? Their father? As he continued to thumb through this jumbled and dreadful account of Moina Furneaux's life, Cale came to the conclusion that he had been right in the first place not to try and delve any deeper into the background, and into the mind, of a woman whose upbringing had clearly been less than traditional. He'd just be bashing his head against a brick wall.

Nevertheless, that did not stop him from turning the pages. And eagerly. Every bit as eagerly as he had cupped and sucked Moina's breasts out in the workshop, unaware that flabby old DI Roy Cutlass had been out the back, snooping around.

Here was another picture of Moina, in her late teens, by the look of it, and dressed in a short, fur-trimmed coat. Standing by a car that was parked in a densely-wooded area. It was cold. Cale could see frost on the ground, on the trees, on the car...but not on the woman who lay at Moina's feet. The naked woman. The naked and very much *dead* woman. And Cale crammed a couple of fingers into his mouth and bit down on them.

I've killed before, Moina had confessed around the back of the sheds, her face dripping with Roy Cutlass's blood. *I ran this guy through with a knife because he stole money out of my purse while I was sleeping. Killed him stone-dead. I put him in my car, drove him over to Blackthorn Wood, and buried him there.*

Not just him, but other people had suffered the same fate, as well, so it seemed. And what had this poor woman done to deserve her fate, exactly? Probably not much at all. Likely she had simply strayed into Moina and Ernie's twisted little world, as a daydreaming person might stray up a dark alley, and the next minute she was dead. Dumped in a car. Photographed. Before being planted in Blackthorn Wood, no doubt. Just the way that Roy Cutlass's bits and pieces would have been planted up there, this weekend, had Moina not been stopped. And in a way the police, or the law courts, had never been able to stop her.

Cale took his fingers out of his mouth, fingers that now bore teeth marks, deep and pink. He couldn't go on with this, gazing at all this terrible stuff. He had to get back to Tommy. Had to. Yet he went on turning the pages, helpless.

Here was a picture of a teenage boy tied to a chair, an apple shoved in his mouth, and beside that, a perfectly ordinary picture of an old woman wearing a fruit hat and clutching a handbag. A turn of the page, and here was a letter from a man declaring his everlasting love for Moina…and to prove it, he had cut off his little finger and taped it to the bottom of the letter, right next to his signature and the hundred X's he had scribbled there.

'Oh God,' Cale whispered. 'Oh dear *God.*'

Next up was a photo of Moina clutching a scroll with a red, silk ribbon around it. At the side of it she had written: "Me, a teacher!" Just a straightforward picture of a young woman proud of her academic triumph. Yet right next to that was a picture of a teenage girl hanging by the neck from a tree. Again naked. Only this time it was not Moina looking on but Ernie - Ernie with a look on his face no more expressive than if he'd been looking up at a cloud in the sky.

Another turn of the page disclosed a newspaper clipping that said Moina had been convicted of prostitution. Again no jail sentence. A fine, that was all. And once again something was written over the clipping in that same bright-red ink that might in fact not be ink, he realised, but lipstick, or even blood. Anything was possible. FUCK THE LOT OF YOU! she had slashed there.

'And fuck this, too,' Cale said, closing the book and putting it aside. He clapped his hands to his face and sighed, and so heavily, he sounded to himself like an old man weary of living. A strange time to be reflecting on his life, but after looking at that horrific book, he began to wonder if he would have amounted to much, anyhow. He could have been a draughtsman, designing racing cars, or perhaps supersonic aircraft, but his father had steered him away from that.

But had he? Had he really? For surely everyone, even those with monsters for fathers, had it in them to stand up for themselves and do what they wanted, not what their fathers wanted. They didn't *just* have to stand there and take it, did they? Yet Cale Redstone *had* taken it. The way his mother had taken it...until there had been nothing more to take but death.

What *was* it about the Redstones, anyhow, Cale and Tommy and their mother? All three of them never living a life but an existence controlled by someone else? And what about their mother? Had she *really* been the beloved, almost holy figure that every now and then swept through Cale's dreams, running her fingers all over his face and delicately planting sweet kisses on his lips, the way, perhaps, that she did that, too, in Tommy's dreams?

Cale and Tommy had loved their mother, no two ways about it, but had their love for her blinded them? After all, she could have packed her bags and taken her children with her, couldn't she? A room might be ablaze, or flooded, but if you looked hard enough, more often than not there was always a way out. Your options almost always added up to more than just standing there and watching the flames lick at your feet or the water creep up your chest. But Natalie Redstone had chosen to stay in that room and perish...and *chosen* was the operative word in all of this. Chosen. Natalie Redstone had chosen to stay even though she was suffering, and also she must have known, if her suffering ever ended, that it would simply be passed onto her sons. And what kind of a mother would let *that* happen? If she had loved Cale and Tommy, had *truly* loved them, then surely she would have gotten herself, and her two boys, out of that mess, someway, somehow? Nothing much to think about, either, was there? You just got out of there. Bye-bye.

'Perhaps,' Cale said...but he was wavering. Why? Because it was then that he realised, like it or not, that he was pretty much like his mother. For five years he had stood by while Tommy had come within an inch of losing his life, and many times over. And what had Cale done about that? Nothing, that's what. Shameful enough that he did nothing to stop the cruelty. He hadn't even offered the boy a crumb of comfort whenever their father wasn't around. He could have done that, too. Several nights of the week their father had been out of the house, drinking at the Red Lion Pub, and so Cale could have cooked the boy a dinner, and maybe even let him watch a little TV. But no. Just as Moina had said in the kitchen that night, *No one knows because no one cares. We all just look in the mirror and say,* I'm fine, fuck the rest.

'I did *something* in the end, though, didn't I?' Cale said, and yet deep down he knew the truth, as all people do when they understand they could have done better, so *much* better, but never did because it always came down to me, me, me, I, I, I.

Yes, he had done *something* in the end. He had finally stopped Ewan Redstone from stripping the belt off his jeans and thrashing Tommy with it, and thrashing him so hard that the boy's screams had been like a shrieking train whistle.

However, had it not been for that toppled stack of timber, then things around number 3 Samuel Lane would still be the same. Ewan Redstone would still be thrashing the hell out of Tommy, and Cale would still be turning a blind eye and cocking a deaf ear to it.

I'm fine, fuck the rest.

The fact was, that toppled stack of timber had done the main bulk of a job that Cale would never have been able to do on his own. As brave as he had been to bash his father's brains in that day, all he had really done was bring to a close a life that would have ended soon enough. Cale had simply switched off the lights and drawn the curtains a little ahead of time, that was all. And maybe that's just how it had been for those people in that book here of Moina's. Their lights had been switched off, their curtains had been closed, and in all probability that would have happened to them, anyway, one way or another. And Cale realised now that there would *always* be another Moina Furneaux just waiting around the corner, along with another Ewan Redstone. It was how you faced-up to these people that prevented you from slipping into their clutches and winding up dead. Natalie Redstone had not faced-up. Nor had the people in those pictures. Cale had. But right now he felt as if he had cast a demon out of one person, only to watch it fly into another.

He turned away from the window. Had he been in a better frame of mind, it might just have occurred to him that with Moina dead…with Roy Cutlass crammed into that wardrobe over there…with that book lying there for anyone to see, that his prayers had been answered. The police, when they came across all this, would almost certainly think that Moina had killed Roy Cutlass, perhaps even Don Willoughby, as well. And as for who had killed Moina? That could have been anyone, couldn't it? Because one thing was clear: Moina Furneaux must have made many enemies over the years. Therefore, Cale Redstone's name might not be so far up the wanted list as he at first imagined…although in all honesty, he didn't much care about that. The police might not be closing in on him.

But the world was.

All he wanted was to get back to Tommy. That was all he could think about - apart from the demon, that was. The one that he may have cast out of one person, and put straight into another.

He called out the boy's name, three times over, up the stairs. Got no response. Thought to begin with that Tommy must be sleeping, but he doubted that. Then discovered he was right to doubt that because he heard a noise right then. In the kitchen.

Cale went out there. Drenched from head to toe. Mud splashed up his jeans because he had tumbled into a ditch on the way back to this place that was nothing but Sad's Place because Little Miss Orange Dress, by simply removing those letters, I and E, from the stable door, had cursed this place, it seemed, and perhaps all those who lived in it. And many of those, too, who had simply come into contact with it.

He saw the cutlery drawer first. It was open. Just as it had been open that night when Tommy had taken a knife to break into the writing desk, but for some reason - guilt, perhaps - he had not persisted. Then finally Cale saw Tommy. Here he came, hobbling towards Cale on his walking-stick, coming from the direction of the office. Still spaced-out on the sugar, made clear by the mad, piercing look in his eyes, and by the way his head jerked here and there.

'Ah, there you are,' Cale said softly, making sure to keep his displeasure, and his disappointment, under wraps. Wanting only to show his love for Tommy, but at the same time understanding that this time around the boy *had* persisted. He had gotten the desk open, and now he was clutching the fruits of his labour: the necklace, the Coca Cola necklace, hanging there in the boy's free hand.

'Yes, here I am,' the boy said. 'And what do you think I found, eh? Why, it looks like a necklace to me. My *mother's* necklace.' He shook it at Cale, and so hard that the twinkling, brown garnets clinked against the gold chain links. 'Thought you could keep it from me, did you? Well, that *little* plan didn't quite work out, did it?'

To begin, however, it still seemed as if Tommy might be approachable, that with a little work, the boy could be persuaded to sit down so they could talk this over, nice and calm. And eventually Cale would break the news to the boy, the news that he would have broken to him at some point, anyhow...even though that point had always seemed to Cale to be over the horizon somewhere, in a faraway place. But then Tommy chased away any chance of that by suddenly laying into Cale.

'You bastard! What kind of a brother must you be, to keep *this* from me? This necklace that mum loved and would have taken with her, had she *really* left home? You rotten, stinking bastard!'

Cale tried to remain calm, this despite the fact that he was tired, he felt unwell, and he'd been through quite enough shit today, thank you very much. He said, 'Listen to me, Tommy. The truth is, I *couldn't* tell you about that necklace, I just couldn't. It was hard enough for me that day, having to tell you that I killed dad. You think I could have told you about mum, as well, on top of all that? You think you would have *handled* it okay?'

'Never mind about that!' the boy said. 'What's a little bad news about mum when, for most of my life, I've been beaten, starved, and tied to clotheslines?'

Cale bowed his head a little. 'I never looked at it that way, Tom. I just wanted to protect you.'

'Protect me?' Tommy said. 'It took you long enough, didn't it? For five years you stood about, twiddling your thumbs, while dad went on doing what he did! Protect me? Don't make me *laugh!*'

'Oh Tom, don't talk that way, please. I thought you forgave me for that.'

'I did, until I found this!' He shook the necklace again, and with a hostility that was close to hatred, Cale thought. Then all of a sudden the boy switched his grip on his walking stick, by tossing it up in the air. When it came back down, he caught it so that now it lay in his fist, forehand style. Then he swung it at the kitchen table. Swept almost everything off of there, and down on the floor it went: plates, cups, saucers, cutlery, the toast rack, a box of cereal, a jar of marmalade. And the air was all at once filled with the tangy whiff of preserved oranges. Among all of this was some of Moina's stuff, too, makeup, mainly. A couple of lipsticks, a powder compact, an eye pencil, and a small, adjustable mirror. All of that hit the floor, as well. At the back of Cale's mind, he had known all along that he would have dispose of this stuff in some way, along with Moina's clothes, her shoes, her fancy bedding. But right now, none of that seemed terribly important.

Tommy was shaking. Drool dripped off his chin, to go with the tears that ran down his face. 'Back in the summer,' he said, 'I sat right there at that table, looking at that photo I found of mum wearing this necklace…and you said nothing! Not a single word! Just let me go on believing she was still alive somewhere!'

'Tommy, please, just give me a chance - '

'You've *had* your chance!' Tommy blasted. 'Now it's my turn! And God, you let me go to the letterbox almost every morning, and stand there, waiting for the postman, knowing all the time he'd *never* have a letter from mum! Knowing there would be no telegram, either, much less a phone-call! Not a thing! I might as well have been waiting for a cheque from the pools!'

'Tommy - '

'Then there was that time in the workshop, when I said it might be a good idea to place an advert in the paper for mum, and you said no to that! Gave me all that rubbish about how the wrong people might see it and get to thinking that something was wrong up here! Christ, what an idiot I've been, haven't I?'

'Tom, for Christ's sake, let me get a word in edgeways, would you? A lot of stuff has been going on around here that you don't know about, and I couldn't tell you about it, either. It was all about trying to give you a normal life for a change, after all you'd been through. I wanted to take the brunt of all that, and mostly I did. Did that just so you could go to school, as well as play with your friends whenever you wanted to, just like any normal kid. I'm only a boy myself, Tom. Even you said that. Maybe I should have realised that at the start of all this, before I bashed dad's brains in with that mallet. But at the time I did what I thought was best. That's all we do, Tom, all of us, for the most part. We just try to do what we think is best and hope it turns out okay. But it *didn't* turn out okay, did it? Everything around here is just a mess now.'

'I don't *care* about any of that!' Tommy said. 'You're missing my point! All I wanted, all I've *ever* wanted, is my mother back! But that's not going to happen, is it? Where is she, Cale? What happened to her?'

Cale said nothing.

'What happened to her!' Tommy shrieked. 'Tell me!' He rose up on his toes, and his hands and arms that were already shaking, began to tremble crazily. His left eye started to bulge. The wrinkled flap of skin over his right eye seemed to sag all the way down so that Cale could see only a thin blue line of the boy's eyeball. His mouth became a twisted, agonised cavity filled with two rows of white, even teeth that glimmered in the lightning flashes. Shadows danced on the walls. Thunder tumbled out of the sky like a rock-fall. Rain flung itself against the window. 'Tell me!' the boy went on. 'Tell me what happened to my mummy! I want to know! Tell me, tell me, tell me!'

He was hyperventilating, on the point of busting a blood vessel, it seemed to Cale. He went to the boy, if a little hesitantly. He made it halfway across the floor, his boots sloshing with ditchwater, and it was then that Tommy's face turned white, and he passed out. He fell down on his knees, and then toppled back, until all at once he was sprawled there, the walking-stick in one hand, the necklace in the other. The necklace lying in his hand like some sort of beautiful but evil serpent.

'Oh Tom,' Cale said, kneeling beside him. He gently took hold of the boy's head and placed it in his lap. Pulled away a sweaty lock of hair that had drifted over his face. Tommy hadn't passed out like this for a while, and back then, on the previous two occasions, Cale hadn't even considered that maybe the beatings that Ewan Redstone had doled out might just have damaged the boy's brain.

Tommy's eyes had rolled up, just like before, and his lids were fluttering. Cale gave him a panicky little shake, and said, 'Tom, wake up, wake up, wake up! We can work this out, we can talk, we make things better. You don't think we're going to let people like dad and Moina Furneaux beat us, do you? No chance. It's you and me, Tommy. You and me together. Blood brothers, that's what we are, isn't it?'

But the boy didn't stir, not even when one of Cale's tears dripped down on the boy's face. He was just there, among the ruined crockery, and the broken biscuits, and the scattered cornflakes, and trembling all over.

'I'll get you a drink of water,' Cale whispered. 'That ought to bring you around.' He took off his coat, bundled it up, and carefully slipped it under the boy's head. Stood up, then. Grabbed a glass off the shelf above the stove and went to fill it. It must have taken him all of five seconds to fill that glass, but somehow, in that small space of time, Tommy had silently gotten up off the floor, and when Cale turned, there he was, all of a sudden in front of Cale.

Tommy hit Cale over the head with his walking-stick, and with a strength that Cale would have found hard to comprehend, had he been *capable* of comprehension. The glass fell out of his hand and crashed to the floor. And Cale soon followed it.

Chapter 19: The Coca Cola Necklace

It was still raining but the storm had passed. He was aware of that, aware of how the rain tinkled against the window, no longer lashed against it. However, he was more aware of the pain over his left eye, and the bump there from which the pain came. The blood, as well. He was aware of how that had dried on his cheek, tightening the skin there.

How long had he been here, on the floor, among the bits and pieces that Tommy had swept off the table? Bemused, his eyelids tacky, Cale raised his chin and looked up at the wall clock. He saw three hour hands, grouped together like the spines of a fan, and three minute hands, doing the same. There were three clock faces, as well, closely overlapping one another. However, by focusing on one clock face, on one hour hand, and on one minute hand, he managed to read the time: 6: 30. He must have gotten back to the house last night around one in the morning, perhaps two. No later than two. Allowing for the unpleasant conflict with Tommy, he concluded that he'd been out on this floor for around four hours. And in that time a kid as volatile as Tommy could have gotten up to all sorts of trouble, couldn't he?

Cale raised himself up on an elbow, and realised, as he did this, that something was missing from this movement, a sound he had become used to whenever he got out of bed, or up off a chair. He got himself up on his hands and knees…and then it came to him: the keys. They had not clinked together, as they usually did. He put a hand up to his throat, and found no string there, looped around his neck.

'He promised me he wouldn't go in there,' Cale said. 'He crossed his heart and hoped to die.' All at once he was up on his feet and stumbling around in the busted glass and all the other stuff on the floor.

Tommy's walking-stick, he saw, was lying on the table, so at least he wouldn't have to contend with that again when he caught up with the boy. Next to the stove, meanwhile, was the necklace. Had there been a bar of sunlight, then that necklace would have glittered as brightly as it must have done the day that Ewan Redstone put it around Cale's mother's neck, a neck around which he probably never dreamed of putting his hands back then. Only the necklace, the Coca Cola necklace. But love it seemed, like that necklace, could become a thing with no sparkle in it, the moment it fell into shadow.

Beside the necklace was Cale's coat. He grabbed it and put it on. Spun around then, opened the curtains, and looked out the window.

There was Tommy. Outside Sad's Place. With a shovel in his hands.

It was the shovel Moina had used that day to create those flowerbeds with, but alas the storm last night had now destroyed the flowers in them. Winter pansies had been wrenched out of the dirt and lay all over the lawn in a hotchpotch of wet, limp colour. The deckchairs had been flipped over, and their canvas seats flapped in a wind that was still strong but no longer gale-force. The low table upon which Moina had put the drinks yesterday, along with Cale's sandwich, had been dashed against the house and was smashed to bits. But that was hardly the all-important issue, was it? The all-important issue was that Cale had to get out there, and right this minute...although he wondered what he could stop, when the boy had had a whole four hours in which to discover the truth, first hand, rather than hear it out of Cale's mouth.

Still, he went out of the door and across the lawn, the rain making the bump over his left eye tingle. He zigzagged his way around old chunks of wood, broken roof slates, and wet, leafy branches. Halfway between the house and Sad's Place, and Tommy looked around, clutching the shovel in both hands.

'Stay away from me!' he said, brandishing the shovel. 'You come any nearer, and I'll whack you with this, and harder than I whacked you with that stick of mine!'

Cale gently touched the lump on his head, but he felt oddly calm, all the same, perhaps because Sad's Place was open, the long, rust-speckled key poking out of the upper door, while all around Sad's Place was the junk that Cale had put back in there that day, on top of his mother's grave: the old paraffin heaters, the broken lawn chair, the busted gardening tools, the not exactly impressive painting of the Collie Dog, the yellowy magazines-and-books, and Ewan Redstone's armchair, of course, the one with the beer glass rings on one arm and the cigarette burns on the other. All of that, and yet little Tommy had somehow lugged it out of there, despite his gammy leg and his arms that were pencil-thin. Still pencil-thin even though he ate like a horse these days.

Then there was the tea-chest full of their mother's belongings: dresses, blouses, headscarves, several pairs of Capri pants, underwear. When Cale saw all of that, he finally understood that all of this had gone too far, *way* too far, for him to wriggle out of. And the dirt on the shovel, edging the blade? When he saw that, he accepted that his secret was out, and that although he still retained many secrets, the one he had wanted to retain the longest was now out in the open.

'So now you know,' Cale said.

'Yes, now I know,' Tommy said.

'So how do you feel about that?'

'How do you *think* I feel?' the boy said, glancing into Sad's Place. Cale glanced in there, too, but from this angle, he couldn't see what Tommy could. Not that he needed to; he was already entirely acquainted with the skeleton that had once been he and Tommy's mother. 'Dad killed her, didn't he? He killed her and then buried her in that place like a dead dog! How do I *feel?* I feel like I've got nothing left to live for, that's how I feel!'

Cale said, 'That's pretty much how I felt, too, Tom, when I found mum in there that day. But I had *you* to think about, didn't I? I couldn't just give up on everything.'

'You may have had me, but I never had you,' Tommy said. 'For five years I learned to get along on my own. Had to. If I hadn't, I would have died a long time ago, at the hands of the monster that did this to mum. I would have gone the same way. But what kept me going was the hope that one day she'd write to me, and ask me to come and live with her. But now that hope is gone. It's over.'

'I know, and I'm sorry for that, Tom. But didn't I make amends for that in some small way? Didn't I try to give you the life that mum would have given you, had she been here?'

'It was too little too late,' Tommy said. 'The truth is, I gave up on you years ago, Cale. I tried my hardest to forget about how things used to be around here, with dad always beating me, and you just walking past me like I was nothing but a ghost. But I *can't* forget. I just can't.'

'Tom, I can't change the past, can I? I can't change how I was to you back then. But we're brothers, aren't we? Not just brothers, but *blood* brothers. Doesn't *that* mean anything to you?'

'Not anymore. If there's any blood between us, then it's the bad blood that dad passed down to us.' He reached into the weatherproof coat that he'd had the good sense to put on over his pyjamas. Pulled something out. Tossed it at Cale so hard that it hit him on the chest before falling to the ground.

Cale bent down with an unsteady hand and picked it up. It was the little sprig of flowers he had made up that day, the Lady's tresses, the buttercups, the corn cockle, all bound together with the length of string he had plucked from the low rafters in Sad's Place.

'*You* put that on her grave, did you?' the boy asked.

'I did. As a mark of respect.'

'Respect, eh? Shame you didn't have any of that for me. If you had, I wouldn't have had to play Sherlock Holmes to get to the bottom of all this.'

'Sherlock Holmes?' Cale said. 'You didn't need to play *him* to get to the bottom of this, did you? You must have known that I put those keys around my neck, not just to keep Moina out of there, but you, as well. After all, you've been snooping around the house pretty much since the day dad died. And when you've been eating sweets, and guzzling fizzy pop, you're like a damn bloodhound, sniffing about all over the place. You want to talk about respect, Tom. Where's yours?'

'Don't turn things back on me!' Tommy said. 'I was the one who had to put two and two together when I found that necklace! If it had been left up to you, I would *never* have known that mum was buried out here!'

Cale was finding it hard now to keep his temper in check. Somehow he did, though. He began to walk towards the boy, believing that what he could not soothe with words he perhaps could with actions. Just wanted to hold the boy and try to make it better that way. But in the meantime, he had a little more to say: 'Christ, but you're so *selfish*, do you know that, Tom? Did you ever stop to think it was all but *killing* me to keep this terrible news from you? The fact that mum didn't just walk out on us that day, but dad murdered her? You think I *wanted* to keep that from you? I didn't. But what could I do? You threw a fit that day when I told you I bashed dad's brains in. In fact, you're *always* throwing fits. Threw one in the kitchen last night, didn't you, before hitting me over the head and stealing those keys off me? What would have happened if I'd told you about mum? Likely you'd have blown a gasket!'

He tripped up right then on that picture of the Collie dog. The frame got tangled up between his legs, he took his eye off Tommy, just as he had last night in the kitchen, and whack, depressingly, the boy hit him once again! The shovel clanged against Cale's skull, he slipped up on the wet grass, and down he went on his backside, dropping the sprig of wild flowers in the process.

His ears rang. His world rippled like a stone had been flung into it and he had to wait for it to smooth back out again. Once it had, he sprang to his feet, and said, 'You know, I ought to knock your head off for that!'

Then suddenly his fists came up before he could stop them. 'Which one do you want, Tommy, Hospital or Death? What's up, the question too difficult?'

Tommy staggered back on his heels. His jaw dropped down like a flap. His body stiffened. His left eye became wet and round and staring. His right eye swam in its drooping pocket of skin. His mouth quivered, at first with distress, and then with a dawning, horrified

273

understanding. 'So this is the real...the real Cale Redstone...we're...we're seeing...you and dad like two peas in a pod...now...now I know how easy it must have been for you...for you... to kill Moina the way it must have been easy...easy for dad...dad...daddy...to kill mum...who's next on your list Cale?'

He wasn't gabbling at a hundred miles per hour, but nor was he talking in that slow, measured way that ordinarily he regulated using the clock, tick-tock. This was a disheartening combination of the two, as if Tommy's brain was stitching all this together like some sort of crazy, malfunctioning machine.

'Well...don't think I'm...I'm hanging around...around to be your next...next victim...I won't give...give you the chance.'

'I don't *want* the chance,' Cale said. 'Tom, I wouldn't even harm a hair on your head, never mind kill you. I don't know why I said that. It just came out of my mouth.' He looked into Sad's Place, saw that his father's grave had not been disturbed, but he wondered if he wasn't lying under the dirt in there, and grinning. *You've started a ball rolling that you won't be able to stop. Told you that, didn't I?*

'Yeah, you told me,' Cale said to himself. He saw his mother's skull in there, her eye sockets filled with dirt, and he looked away, both shocked and depressed that Tommy would have seen that, too. Would have seen how his mother really was, not how she must have appeared to him in his dreams: a woman who had probably whispered to him, and many times over: *I'll write, and one day, you and I, we'll be together again.*

Cale looked back at Tommy, only Tommy wasn't there anymore. Only the shovel that he must have dropped in a hurry. Cale turned all the way around and saw the boy running across the lawn, and fast, in spite of that clumpy built-up shoe of his. Saw him pick up his bike, which was still lying there on the grass, where he'd left it last night. Jumped on it, and off he pedalled down the drive.

'Tom, come back!' Cale shouted. 'I'm sorry!' Then, under his breath: 'Oh God, why did I have to *say* that, "Which one do you want, Hospital or Death?" That of all things? What the fuck is up with me?' But he *knew* what was up with him. He was his mother, yes - that already had been established - but he was also his father. That was simply a fact, he guessed, that he along with everyone else in the world could not get away from. You were one, and you were the other, a blend of the two. You couldn't select the best bits from both, you got what you were given, and you had to live with that. But right now he wished he hadn't gotten the bit that had made him duplicate, to a tee, that threat of his father's, which to Tommy had become a signal to either run or to stand there and be beaten.

Cale ran over to the truck, fumbling the keys out of his pocket as he went.

Everything after that became a blur.

He got the truck started, but it took a while, and when it did fire into life, it was almost impossible to drive, because the damp had gotten deep down into the truck's works. The heater was slow and clunky, too. Even with the window rolled down, the windscreen took an age to clear. Cale wiped at the mist with the back of a hand, but instead of clearing it, he just seemed to move it around, or place a greasy, whirled smear over the top of it.

When he got out onto the road, he found it wet, slippery, and littered with debris, unsurprisingly. At first Tommy had been a speck in the distance, a frantically pedalling dot, wedged between the low monochrome sky and the glistening road, like Jonah caught at the back of the whale's throat before it swallowed him altogether.

It may have been the tears that did not run down Cale's face, but rather, they simply pooled there, like droplets of cloudy milk. It may have been the bump over his left eye and the ringing that still clanged in his ears, after first being hit by Tommy's walking-stick and then by the shovel. It may have been the truck, the way the hulking, smoking heap seemed to jerk and sometimes *leap* up the road, not glide up it. It may have been the memory of that revolting photo album he had found at Moina's place and could not shift out of his mind. It may have been the possibility that in the end Moina would have killed Tommy by stringing him up from a tree in Blackthorn Wood, naked, and likely would then have photographed the grisly spectacle. It may even have been the sight of his mother's rotted face, the fact that even now it still shook him, just the way it had that day when he first came across her body in Sad's Place. And if it still had the power to do that to Cale, then what had it done to poor Tommy? What terrible window had it opened up in that boy's already damaged brain?

But mostly, Cale came to believe that the blame could be laid at the feet of a destiny he could not stop, or suspend, or even dilute a little, but whose deadly flow he could only go with. He would reason that if you took a life in anger, then another would be taken away from you, and likely it would be a life you loved and did not wish to see the end of. And hadn't that happened to his father? In anger he had taken Natalie Redstone's life, and consequently his life had been taken in an accident that really should not have occurred because Ewan Redstone had been the most safety-conscious man Cale had ever known. Yet that day he had tried to get a length of timber out from the bottom of that heavy stack, and *whomp*! it had come crashing down on him, and it just went to show that if you took a life in anger, then life took one back, because life owned life, and it did not bargain, and it did not make deals.

If you took a life, then life took your life. Or someone else's.

And there was Tommy Redstone's life, riding along on that bike Cale had bought for him back in the summer. Way in the distance, just a bobbing, racing fleck. And maybe there were a thousand reasons that post-storm morning why Cale hadn't been able to stop when he wanted to. For all he knew, he may have briefly fallen into a trance behind the wheel. That had been a possibility, too.

But of course reasons didn't add up to much at all when really they were nothing but excuses waiting to happen. The fact was, little Tommy had been nothing but a spot on the horizon one moment, and then, all at once, there he was, not just in front of Cale, but being chewed up by the truck's front end and then being spat out all over the road behind him.

It happened in a flash, as all things seemed to that had somehow been taken out of your control. They happened in a flash and were then remembered, over and over, in vivid, microscopic detail: the sound of tubular metal buckling and popping...the crackling and folding of tin mudguards…the snapping, twanging sound of spokes being torn from the wheels…the ting-a-ling of the bell that had not been rung by Tommy's thumb but by the sudden, cataclysmic shake of the accident itself…and then came one specific sound that Cale Redstone would never forget: the sound of his brother being bounced between the road and the underside of the truck like a rubber ball, *boof, boof, boof, boof, boof, boof!* And then it was gone - Cale Redstone's idea of a nightmare that he could as yet not see, only hear.

But soon enough he saw it, all right. He thrust his feet down into the footwell as a man might plunge his burning feet into a bucket of water. And the truck came to a screeching, sliding halt, the kind of halt that would have left interlaced tyre tracks on the road behind had the tarmac not been so wet. The truck juddered. An old newspaper, Cale's book of receipts, a couple of pencils, his vacuum-flask… all of that flew off the passenger seat and down into the footwell it went, after first slapping against the dashboard. The broom in the back, along with the shovel, smashed against the cab's rear window. As did the handsaw, the one Cale had used that afternoon to prune back the trees in the police station's car park.

He got out, jumped down on the road, and his legs went out from underneath him. A steel band went around his chest and clenched him there. His breath rasped in and out of him, dry as sandpaper. The bump on his forehead ached as if he'd grown a diseased third eye. He was down on all fours, panting there, and when he raised his right hand, flipped it over, he saw blood there. A spot roughly two inches across and perfectly round. And he screamed. Was still screaming even when he realised it was not a spot of blood but the bike's rear reflector, stuck to his palm.

Blood or not, though, it didn't much matter, did it? It was still a pretty good indication that little Tommy had been put through a mangle from which most things came out the other end rarely looking the way they had when they went in.

Cale flicked his wrist and the reflector became unstuck, and it hit the road, and it rolled under the truck. Caring not that his legs had yet to regain their steadiness, he took off up the road, at first on all fours, and then finally rising up and running in a more or less reasonably straight line. Hands chopping at his sides. His coat flapping. His shoulder blades bunching against the flaky, itching tree of eczema that now covered just about all of his back. He saw nuts and bolts and bent spokes and half a wheel and the bike's handlebars and shredded tyre rubber, and some of those shreds were actually smoking. All of it scattered up the road. No bike anymore as such. The bike had been reduced to bits and pieces that could only be reassembled with the mind, not with the hands.

Cale saw one of Tommy's shoes, as well. It lay on its side in a puddle of rainwater, and it was the left one. He knew that by the chunky, compensatory sole. And then here was Tommy himself. He was lying on his back in a bloody, twisted heap. His raincoat and pyjamas had been torn to pieces, like he'd been mauled by a wild animal. A hand lay limply across his face, and his wristwatch, the one Cale had given him that day, seemed to be plugged into his left eye.

Cale was still screaming, but now, as he knelt beside his brother, he introduced words into that scream: *'Tom, don't look at the watch, tick-tock, look at me, look at me, look at me!'*

But Tommy did not look at Cale. Didn't even look up at the sky as the sun began to part the clouds and send down golden shafts of sunlight. He was dead. And Cale realised right then, even in his sorrow, that back in the summer, he had never *really* saved Tommy's life. No, not really. He had only delayed the inevitable, that if Ewan Redstone hadn't gotten to him, then someone else, or *something* else, would have.

Tommy Redstone had been no cripple, no matter what others had said about him. If anything was the cripple then it was the world itself for turning out devils that were healthy, while the angels needed sticks and wheelchairs to get about. Cale supposed it was simply the case that sometimes bad was too evil to beat, and good was too perfect to save.

It was just life.

And death was always at the end of it.

Always.

He fell down in the road beside his brother and wished that he was dead, too. He wished that more than anything.

Chapter 20: Sad's Place

The tail of the storm still whipped about, but it had lost its strength, all but, so that mostly it just toyed with the landscape, no longer tore it apart. The tearing apart had been done and now it was time to clean up the mess.

WPC Charlotte Perkins got out of her car, a little light-green Austin of England. There was a tree across the road she needed to get down, so she left her car at the top of the road, parked up on a shallow bank out of the way, and went the rest of the way on foot. She had to climb over a gate in order to get into the field that ran beside the road, for this was the only way to get around the fallen tree, and then she walked for roughly a mile until she came to a low house with a peg-tiled roof and a porch out the front in which potted plants grew in a thick, colourful flourish. There was a tree down in the garden, she saw, which had been blocking the path to the door, and she could tell that it had been moved out of the way but not altogether. Still, there was enough room for her to get around it, around its thick, mud-caked roots, and then she went up to the porch and rang the bell. Constable Betts answered the door, and smartly enough, too, given that he had no idea that Charlotte Perkins would be calling, and furthermore, his walk was stiff and slow where he had hurt his back trying to move that tree off the path.

He pulled the door open, wincing. 'Charlotte!' he said, and he smiled, even though it was laced with pain. 'I didn't expect to see you here. Or anyone else for that matter. I called the station and left a message that I hurt my back...' But then he looked over her shoulder at the stricken tree. 'Bloody thing. I should have left it alone and waited for help. But no, not me. What was I thinking, for crying out loud, trying to move it on my own?'

'God knows,' WPC Jenkins said. 'Men, be they young or old, always think they can move the world. Anyhow, I can't stay long. It'll be dark in a couple of hours, and I've got to get back across that field over there.'

'Right you are,' Constable Betts said, nodding. 'Why not kick off your dirty shoes right here in the porch, and then I'll show you through. Is that all right?'

'Of course.' She kicked off her shoes, closed the porch door behind her, and went into Betts's house, moreover, into the kitchen out the back. She sat down at the kitchen table, but Betts did not, choosing instead to lean against one of the worktops in here. 'Have you heard anything on the wireless?' she asked.

'A little,' Betts said. 'The signal hasn't been good due to the storm. I gather there must be a mast down somewhere, or damaged, at least, but I did hear that it was all happening up at Samuel Lane.'

'Yes,' WPC Jenkins said, and heavily. 'It's been quite a day. Quite an *awful* day. Little Tommy Redstone was knocked down on his bike. Knocked down by his brother. The poor little mite is dead.'

'Dear God,' Constable Betts said, clearly shaken. 'How did that happen?'

'We don't know, not for sure, not yet, anyway. And maybe we never will. But it gets worse. It gets much worse. We found two bodies in the stable out the back of the Redstone place. One is Ewan Redstone, we're certain of that, even though there was a hood, a pillowcase, actually, over his head and his head had been smashed in. The second body is likely to be Natalie Redstone, who, as you know, disappeared some five years ago. Everyone thought she'd left home to live somewhere else, but apparently not.'

'My word,' Constable Betts said. 'So it's likely Ewan Redstone killed her back then, but why?' And then, with a dark light suddenly there in his eyes, he told WPC Jenkins: 'You know something? The year before Tommy Redstone was born, a gang of gypsies turned up in Unity Gate. Or maybe not gypsies, not *real* gypsies, but they were travelling people, all the same. Well, one of them developed a fascination for Natalie Redstone. A handsome fellow, he was, with dark, curly hair and those sparkling blue eyes that you can see nothing but mischief in. He chased her about all over the place, as I remember, would never leave her alone, even though she'd often have Cale with her, who must have been only six or seven at the time. This gypsy, this traveller, he had a father who used to get about on a stick. He had a deformed face, a hump on his back, and one leg shorter than the other.'

'Tommy, that's what you're saying, isn't it?' WPC Jenkins said. 'That genes often skip a generation?'

'Yes,' Constable Betts said. 'It became my belief, especially when Tommy got older and I could see the troubles he had, that his father, his *real* father, was that handsome gypsy fellow. Not that I said anything to anyone. Just kept it to myself. Always have. Didn't even tell my wife at the time. But I suspect, if she was still alive, that she'd agree with what I'm saying.'

'I'm sure,' WPC Jenkins said. She put a hand lightly on her chest and let out a long, weary breath. 'My God, he must have led a horrible life, that little boy, and such a *short*, horrible life, at that.' Tears began to gather in her eyes, pooling there. 'I sometimes wonder what's the point of life, and where we're all going to, when there doesn't seem much to sing about along the way. But I'm sorry. I've seen and heard too much today, and I just want to go to bed and not wake up again in the world I closed my eyes to.'

'I understand,' Constable Betts said gently. 'But tell me what you saw and heard, anyway, then that way, we'll have each other at least, won't we?'

'We will,' WPC Jenkins said, smiling palely. 'And I came here to tell you what I know, didn't I? And I will. I will because *everyone* needs to know about hell so that we can try to change it back into a heaven, although I must say that heaven seemed a long way off as the day went on. We found the mallet that Cale had killed his father with. It was in the house, upstairs in one of the bedrooms. It seemed that Cale must have used it on someone else, too, because the way the bedroom was, full of a woman's things, that it couldn't be any other way. And it wasn't. All the evidence led us to a flat in Twelve Trees Road, a flat that was lived in by a woman named Moina Furneaux, who took over as headmistress, as *temporary* headmistress, at Brougham Moor School after Elsa Lovell died.'

'And?' Constable Betts asked, trying to not look eager but unable to help himself.

'And there she was,' WPC Jenkins said. 'We found her, or rather, we found her dead body, sitting on a filthy sofa like she was simply watching the television. Cale must have taken her there after he killed her, taken her there in her own car. And we found Cutlass, too,' she added. 'Cutlass in five bags.'

'What?'

'Chopped up,' WPC Jenkins explained. 'It seems that whoever did it used the bandsaw in Ewan Redstone's joinery shop.'

Constable Betts clapped his hands to his face, his face that was already twisted in pain somewhat, and now there was sheer horror overlaying that pain. 'Goodness me, but Cale Redstone has some explaining to do, doesn't he? Where is he? Up at HQ being questioned? After all, it's likely that Sergeant Willoughby's death is tied up in all of this, as well, wouldn't you say?'

'I would,' WPC Jenkins said. 'But unfortunately I don't think we'll ever get to the bottom of it all. After knocking down and killing his little brother, Cale went into that stable at the back of the house and hanged himself from the rafters in there. You know what I noticed? I noticed that the letters on the stable door used to spell Sadie's Place, but the I and the E had either fallen off, or been taken off, and so it spelled Sad's Place. But it fits, doesn't it? It fits the *world*, the way I see it. A world that is nothing but a sad place, and all I want is to go home now, get into bed, and dream of a happy place. After all, there must be one, mustn't there, Constable Betts? Tell me there is. Please tell me there's a happy place somewhere.'

'There is,' Constable Betts said, and in spite of the pain he was in, he put his arms around her and he told her that the happy place was here, yes, it was right here, in his arms.

Printed in Great Britain
by Amazon